EXTINCTION CYCL

EXTINCTION ASHES

AN EXTINCTION CYCLE STORY

NEW YORK TIMES BESTSELLING AUTHOR
NICHOLAS SANSBURY SMITH
AND ANTHONY J. MELCHIORRI

Extinction Cycle: Dark Age
Book 3: Extinction Ashes
By Nicholas Sansbury Smith and Anthony J. Melchiorri

GREAT WAVE INK
PUBLISHING

Thank you for purchasing this book. Sign up for Nicholas's *spam-free* newsletter to learn more about future releases, how to claim a book patch, special offers, and bonus content. Subscribers will also receive access to exclusive giveaways.

eepurl.com/bggNg9

You can also sign up for Anthony's newsletter to receive info on his latest releases and free short stories exclusive to subscribers.

http://bit.ly/ajmlist

They sent forth men to battle,
But no such men return;
And home, to claim their welcome,
Come ashes in an urn.

AESCHYLUS, Agamemnon

To Colonel Olson (RET)
and
Master Sergeant Hendrickson (RET)

for serving our great nation and for providing
vital feedback that has immensely improved
the Extinction Cycle novels.

— 1 —

"What is that?" Javier Beckham asked. He pressed his face against a window of S.M. Fischer's private jet.

Captain Reed Beckham looked over his son's shoulder, watching in disbelief at something he never thought he would see.

A nuclear-tipped missile launched from a submarine roared through the night, leaving a billowing white vapor trail cutting through the sky. Even as the missile vanished, the shock made him grip the hand of his wife, Doctor Kate Lovato, even tighter.

She was just as awestruck, staring in disbelief.

"That's no tactical warhead," Beckham said through clenched teeth.

"I thought President Ringgold said…" Kate began to say.

"Something must have changed," Beckham replied softly.

"Was that a space rocket, Dad?" Javier asked.

"No, it's a missile," Tasha said, her face painted in fear. She and Jenny had clustered around Beckham's son.

Computer engineer Sammy Tibalt craned her neck from her lie-flat seat. Sweat dripped down her forehead, and she could barely open her eyes. The bandages covering the bullet wound in her abdomen had bled through.

"Stay still," Kate said.

The engineer was lucky the bullet seemed to have missed any vital organs. It had gone clean through, skimming her side and causing mostly superficial damage.

"You don't want to reopen that wound," Kate said.

"Ah, shit this hurts," Sammy said, grimacing.

"We'll get you more painkillers soon."

The other ten passengers watched out the starboard windows as a brilliant light bloomed somewhere on the east coast. They included Master Sergeant Parker Horn and his girls, S.M. Fischer, Fischer's men, and a few lab technicians, plus the two German Shepherds Ginger and Spark. A flash of white burned away the dark night, followed by a growing orange fireball.

How close was that to their plane's destination?

Truth was, he had no idea where they were going. They had spent the past few hours in the air, and now it was nearly midnight. Their first landing zone had changed last minute after the pilot received classified coordinates for a second location on an encrypted line. He had told them he'd been ordered not to share them with anyone.

Beckham wasn't bothered by exactly where they were headed. He only cared that his family was headed somewhere safe.

If a safe place even existed now.

"The EMP from the nuke won't affect us, right?" Kate asked, returning to her seat.

"Most aircraft are equipped to handle an EMP blast," Beckham said. "I'm assuming this one is, too. And even if it's not, we should be far enough to be safe."

He was more worried about the effects of radioactive fallout. The radiation around the impact site could poison everything for years or decades depending on the altitude of the burst.

"Let's get back to your seats," Kate said to the kids. Her voice was surprisingly calm, but Beckham knew she was concealing her fear.

Ginger and Spark swarmed around Javier and the girls. Horn stood and herded them behind a curtained partition near the tail of the plane.

As soon as they were gone, Kate nervously tapped her heel against the deck. Dried dark-red blood splatter painted the white shoe. None of them had had a chance to clean up since the disaster at Outpost Manchester. The blood on Kate's shoe was from Doctor Jeff Carr, who had been shot in the head by a traitorous collaborator in their laboratory.

"Kate," Beckham whispered.

She stopped tapping her foot. A tremor shuddered down her body.

"Are you..." he started.

"I'll be okay," she said. "We completed our mission, and I can still stop this."

Beckham had known her long enough to sense her uncertainty. She didn't quite believe the words she said, still trying to come to terms with their harsh reality. He felt the same, but sometimes a little bit of a white lie was good, if not necessary, for sustaining morale.

"We'll save the Allied States, and we'll rebuild again," he said, giving her hand a squeeze.

"Boss," Horn said, taking a seat next to him. "You got a minute?"

"I'll give you two a chance to talk." Kate got up. "I'll check on the kids."

She kissed Beckham on the cheek, then disappeared into the back of the plane. Horn waited a few seconds before speaking.

"I'm scared," he whispered.

There were a lot of words in Horn's vocabulary, many borderline obscene. But "scared" was one Beckham had never heard from his best friend.

"I'm scared that we can't protect our families once we land, that this is only going to get worse until it's so bad there will be nothing left," Horn said.

"Me too," Beckham admitted.

"We might think wherever we're landing is safe, but shit..." Horn took a deep breath, his barreled chest expanding. "The enemy is stronger than we ever imagined. I don't know if this is a fight we can win."

"We can. We have to. There's no other option."

They were both in shock. After eight years of peace, everything had come crumbling down like a house of cards in a tornado.

By the time the sun rose, Beckham wasn't sure what would even be left of the Allied States. What he did know was several of the great cities of what had been the United States would be smoldering radioactive craters.

"When are we going to tell the kids about Outpost Portland?" Horn asked, reminding Beckham of their home that had been devastated by their enemies.

"When we get settled, we'll break it to them."

"I'm not sure we'll ever be settled anywhere again," Horn said, looking through a window. "And what about Timothy?"

"Tasha should know the truth," Beckham said. "But I'll leave that to you."

Horn nodded.

"Nothing in our future will be easy," Beckham said. "Not for a long time. But we're the glue that holds everything together, and I need you to be the rock you've always been."

Horn met Beckham's gaze.

"You can count on me, boss." He puffed up his chest. "I ain't no rock… I'm a motherfucking mountain."

Beckham smirked and patted Horn's shoulder. The shared moment of jocularity passed when the pilot announced they were beginning their descent.

Fischer went to the cockpit but his guards, Tran and Chase, remained behind.

Ginger and Spark suddenly came bolting down the aisle to Beckham. He couldn't help but smile when they started licking him.

"Dammit." Kate marched toward them and grabbed the dogs by the collars.

"I'll help," Horn said. He took the dogs to the back, and Beckham joined him.

"Where are we landing?" Javier asked.

"Yeah, is someone going to tell us what's going on?" Jenny asked.

"That missile…" Tasha said quietly. "That means the war is getting worse, right?"

"Everything's going to be okay," Beckham said.

Kate and Horn exchanged a quick look before sitting down again.

Beckham snagged his seat and hoisted Spark onto his lap. Horn took Ginger.

Turbulence rattled the bulkheads, and Spark whined.

"It's okay, buddy," Beckham said.

Another pocket of turbulence shook the aircraft, resulting in cries of surprise from the kids. Sammy wailed in pain. Ron and Leslie, two of the technicians that had come with them, helped brace her.

The first sign of the ground came into focus out the

window. A single cluster of lights shone below. Beckham squinted, trying to make out anything that might give him an idea of where they were.

The rest of the terrain was so dark he couldn't tell if it was flat, hilly, or mountainous. Glowing lights flared below in what appeared to be explosions.

Then came the lancing pulse of tracer rounds.

"You got to be fucking kidding," Beckham whispered.

The plane turned away from the battle and curved through the sky.

He tried to calm himself, not wanting to scare the kids any more than they already were. He squinted, trying to make out the ground. It took him a moment to realize they weren't above solid ground after all.

It was water.

A single light sparked in his view, illuminating an arm connected to a statue. Not just any statue—the Statue of Liberty. An eternal flame the Allied States had installed burned on the torch.

Seeing the beacon of freedom filled Beckham with pride and hope.

The plane finally leveled out over what had to be Long Island judging by the proximity of the statue. That made sense to him now. The location would be one of the most fortified and relatively easy to defend.

The tracer rounds and explosions must have been coming from the small outpost in Lower Manhattan.

He prayed they would last the night.

The plane jolted down hard a moment later. With the thrust reversed and spoilers out to slow them down, the plane shuddered noisily. Sammy cried out again but the kids kept quiet.

As soon as the jet stopped, Fischer's guards palmed in

magazines and opened the door.

Fischer joined them and held up a hand to the rest of the passengers. "Everyone, stay put for a moment."

"Keep your belts on in case we've got to fly again," Beckham said to the kids. "Just precautionary. Nothing to worry about."

Beckham and Horn grabbed their rifles. The kids were smart enough to know that wasn't just precautionary.

"Is it not safe here?" Tasha asked.

"Of course it is," Horn said. "You're with your old man and Reed."

The door opened again, and Fischer stepped inside, waving. "All right, let's go."

Beckham herded the kids together, while Ron and Leslie helped carry Sammy. Tran and Chase stood guard on the tarmac below the short exit stairs.

A single M-ATV and a military cargo truck waited outside. Two soldiers wearing fatigues and helmets sporting "four-eye" night vision goggles stood beside them.

"Everyone this way," said one of the men. "We need to get off the tarmac ASAP."

Beckham helped the civilians and kids into the back of the truck. He scanned their surroundings while they were climbing inside. The tarmac was in the middle of an area with mostly warehouses and factory buildings. He didn't see any sign of military presence besides the truck and two soldiers.

"Where the hell is everyone?" Horn asked the men.

"You'll see soon enough," said one of the soldiers with NVGs.

Once everyone was loaded in the cargo truck, they followed the M-ATV toward the factories.

Jenny nudged her dad's arm. "I know we're not going home now, but do you know when we can?"

Horn drew in a deep breath and then shook his head. "I'm sorry, honey, but I've got to be honest. I don't think we're ever going back."

***

A dull ringing reverberated in Sergeant Yas Dohi's ears. Throbbing agony swam across his body like he'd been pummeled by an Alpha Variant and then thrown into a tree trunk. Everything hurt.

Trying to remember what happened, he blinked, hoping his surroundings would jog his memory. But shadows blotted his vision and he only saw vague skeletal shapes.

Most of his senses were dull, except for his sense of smell, which was overwhelmed by the odor of charred wood and burning plastic.

Those scents slowly got the gears in his head turning, and an image of an inferno exploded in his mind. The events since they had landed in the C-130 on the California beach replayed, all the way up to the choppers.

He flinched at the memory.

The birds had fired on him and Specialist Justin Mendez outside the warehouses that were supposed to hold the seismic detection system equipment for Project Rolling Stone.

"Mendez," Dohi mumbled. He couldn't remember if the operator had escaped the Humvee before the rockets hit.

"Fitz," Dohi whispered into his headset.

There was no response, and he remembered the damn

thing was broke-dick, jammed by the comms equipment.

A surge of fear masked his pain when he thought of his team.

Master Sergeant Joe "Fitz" Fitzpatrick, Sergeant First Class Jenny Rico, and Corporal Bobby Ace had been with the injured Wolfhounds when the choppers attacked.

His stomach lurched, and Dohi twisted his head to the side, the movement painful. The contents of his belly came spewing up. A sour taste filled his mouth.

Slowly the blackness in his vision dissipated. Orange tongues of flame illuminated the area. Blurred images coalesced enough for him to see why he had trouble moving and his body ached. He was trapped under the tangled, charred branches of a fallen tree, only able to move his head and neck.

He used all his strength to push the branch from his chest. His ribs burned with every breath, bruised no doubt, but he could move now. That was good. With a grunt, he squirmed out from under the heavy branch.

Smoke drifted over the burned terrain, casting everything in a ghoulish gray haze. The flicker of fire danced sporadically in the woods. Not more than a couple dozen yards to his right, he saw the decrepit remains of a warehouse smoldering in gobs of melted plastic and bent metal.

Somewhere along the way he had lost his rifle. He searched the rubble and trees, dropping to a crouch when he heard faint low growls and the popping of joints.

As his hearing returned, the noises grew louder, and he found the source among the broken trees. Three Variants scrabbled through the limbs. Their ribs protruded against their gray flesh, and their joints appeared swollen against their shrunken muscles and skin.

Eyes bulged from their misshapen heads, and their tongues lashed out around their wormy, cracked lips.

Starving Variants.

They had come here at the promise of food, probably attracted by the cacophony of the battle and the smell of burned flesh.

And if they had found food, Dohi worried he knew what they were digging at.

Mendez.

Stalking them at a hunch, Dohi navigated the jumble of trees and smoldering plants, pushing his way through the smoky fog. The snap of breaking branches and popping joints filled the night.

What he didn't hear gave him hope. No slurps of tearing meat, no human wails of agony.

Dohi grabbed his hatchet with his right hand and slipped out his KA-BAR in his left. Another two steps and he made it directly behind the first of the three Variants. He swung the hatchet into the back of the closest creature. An audible pop of tendons and bone sounded.

The other two turned.

Dohi threw his KA-BAR. It thudded into an eyeball with a sickening pop. The monster staggered forward, then collapsed.

Before he could pull the hatchet from the first Variant or retrieve his knife, the remaining Variant coiled to pounce. Normally he could take a starving creature like that with his fists, but his body had taken a beating.

The Variant launched itself at Dohi. He braced himself, still struggling to pull out the hatchet. He abandoned his attempt to recover the blade and ducked as the Variant's gnashing jaws snapped next to his face.

He stumbled backward and fell into more chunks of busted trees.

Bending, he picked up a broken branch nearly the size of his arm and held it up as the beast slashed at his face. The monster pressed against the branch, snapping.

Saliva sprayed his face.

Dohi's muscles strained as the monster slammed him against a tree trunk. He wasn't going to beat this creature through strength alone. Not with his body this battered.

He rolled away, and then made a play for the hatchet sticking out of the dead monster. Grabbing it, he used all of his strength to yank it free.

Then he turned and swung wildly. The blade found a home in the center of the final creature's face, splitting through a wart-covered nose.

Dohi ripped it away with a slurp. Then he retrieved his KA-BAR. He sheathed the knife and gazed blearily at his surroundings, chest heaving. No other diseased monsters careened out of the smoke, and he didn't hear their clicking joints.

Safe enough for now, he could finish the job the Variants had started: unburying whoever had been trapped by these trees. The Variants had already done most of the work, shredding the branches to splinters.

A surge of adrenaline flowed through Dohi when he saw Mendez's face reflecting the firelight, dark brown eyes blinking slowly under the stack of branches pinning him to the ground. He let out a few wheezing coughs as Dohi tried to pull the branches off. Unable to move them, he used one to lever them off, but it snapped.

"Son of a bitch," Dohi said.

He feared for a moment he couldn't free Mendez. That Mendez would die right in front of Dohi because he wasn't strong enough to help.

Hell, no. That's not *going to happen.*

Dohi got down and started tearing branches off one at a time. Mendez's wheezing got worse for a few minutes, but lessened as Dohi cleared the tree limbs.

"Hang in there, man, I'm getting you out," Dohi said.

Mendez moved his lips but Dohi didn't hear a response.

He dug and dug, sweat dripping off his face, ears still ringing. He never heard the person approach before a hand grabbed his shoulder.

Dohi spun, reaching for his weapons to face a figure covered in ash and soot.

"Easy, brother." It was Fitz. He waved to two more figures in the smoke.

Rico and Ace ran over, dodging past crackling fires. Ash and dirt smeared their faces and fatigues, too. Suppressed M4A1s hung over their chests, and all kinds of twisted metal junk protruded from their packs.

Dohi didn't ask any questions and went back to pulling branches and debris off Mendez. The group spread around the main trunk that had pinned him down. Together, they heaved it off, and Ace dragged it away.

Dohi bent beside Mendez, checking him over. "You okay?"

Mendez took in a few final gasps and managed a nod. "Think... I...cracked a rib."

"Can you move your toes and fingers?" Dohi asked.

Mendez did both.

Rico bent down to help Mendez look for more serious injuries.

"You have no idea how glad I am to see you both alive," Fitz said. "Are you hurt?"

"Just rattled," Dohi said.

Ace handed Dohi a rifle. "Found this a few yards back."

"Thanks."

Rico and Ace helped Mendez to a sitting position.

"Martin is with the other Wolfhounds, waiting in the office building," Fitz said. "Comms are still down, and with nothing other than our tactical radios, we can't contact command anyway."

"So what next?" Dohi asked, sticking a knuckle in his ear. Trying to equalize the pressure so he could hear better.

Fitz looked at the smoke and fires devouring the warehouses.

"When we were looking for you two, we grabbed a couple of computers and other things from the debris," he said. "I want to make one more pass, just in case some of that SDS tech is still intact, but we don't have a lot of time. Those hostiles could return."

"Then we head back to the C-130?" Dohi asked.

"Correct," Fitz said.

"Assuming it's even there," Rico said with a snort. "I got a bad feeling we're on our own for the long haul."

— 2 —

Timothy Temper ran from a muscular Rottweiler infected with VX-99. The snarling mutated beast chased him through a forest. It barked viciously as it gained ground. His lungs burned with every step, and his muscles felt heavier, slowing his gait.

He had no weapon to defend himself and nowhere to hide. There was only one option: keep running.

Skeletal branches reached down. He ducked underneath them, jumped over fallen logs, and burst through bushes that tore at his flesh.

A steep slope dropped away into a shallow valley on the other side of a tree line. He slid down the muddy embankment until his shoes hit the rocky ground.

Water snaked through the center of the valley, trickling over rocks. He crossed the creek, the cold water filling his shoes as he carefully navigated over the slick rocks.

At the other side, he stole a glance over his shoulder. The Rottweiler crested the hill he had just slid down, letting out a ferocious bark.

In the moonlight, the bulging muscles of a second Rottweiler emerged between a pair of oak trees on the other slope.

He was trapped.

The only way to escape was through the creek. But as soon as he turned to run, his foot snagged on something and he went down hard. His head slammed into a rock, and icy water splashed over his frozen body.

The first dog was on him in seconds. It sunk its teeth into one of his arms, ravaging his flesh.

He let out a howl of pain, twisting to break free. The bloodshot eyes of the dog drew closer. It let go of his arm and lunged toward his face.

Timothy woke to darkness.

Smoke filled his lungs.

This time, he wasn't dreaming. Lucidity burned through the haze of pain and exhaustion. Another odor drifted in the air, a smell he recognized.

Burned flesh.

He tried to stand, but he was too weak. He fell back to the cold concrete floor.

"Hello…" he tried.

The words came out in a croak.

He reached up to his throat, probing tender flesh from a burn.

It was then he remembered.

The collar. It was gone.

Memories of his captivity crashed over him like a tidal wave. He recalled the bombs that had fallen over Outpost Portland in a last-ditch effort to destroy the Variants and collaborators.

"Hello…" Timothy said again.

Moaning came from the shadows, but it was all muffled. Then he heard what sounded like someone crying across the room.

The darkness obscured almost everything, but a few weakening flames cast ghastly shadows over hunks of fallen concrete. Moonlight streamed into another corner where a wall had collapsed.

The images transported his mind back to the chamber

where the Variants had slung him up on a wall inside the hidden collaborator base. Pete, Nick, and Alfred had decided then to spare Timothy and induct him into their twisted army of the New Gods.

Most of the other people in that chamber had become Variant food or died when the roof partially collapsed.

As his eyes adjusted, Timothy saw people crushed under blocks of rubble. Beams had fallen over him, protecting him from the same fate.

He crawled out from under one, making his way into a space covered in jagged boards and broken bricks.

Navigating through the debris, he made it a few feet before hitting something wet and sticky. He felt around just to confirm it was a body.

The cold flesh told him the person was long-dead, which meant he had been unconscious for a while.

Putting his wrist over his nose, he continued toward the sound of sobbing and moans. The closer he got, the more bodies he hit, and the worse the stench of urine and feces became.

The center of the basement was a mass grave. Chunks of ceiling had rained down on the people that had hidden here for safety.

A beam of light suddenly burst from near the wall across the room. It shot across the rubble and raked over the dead.

Was it a collaborator?

Timothy ducked behind a body.

"Anyone alive?" came a voice.

"Help…" someone replied.

Timothy rose above the corpse. Two figures were standing behind the collapsed wall, peering into the basement.

"Over here," someone else called out.

The light turned on the first person, and then came a burst of gunfire. A second burst peppered the debris in the other direction, silencing the sobbing.

Timothy went back down, flattening his body, heart hammering.

More gunfire pinged into the space, a few stray rounds punching into the body Timothy hid behind. Bullets hit the walls and corpses around him.

Finally they stopped, and the two flashlight beams probed the basement again.

In the glow, he saw another person on their stomach about five feet away. They put a finger to their mouth.

It was Sergeant Ruckley.

She held a pistol in one hand that she aimed at the men. Another Army Ranger lay prone next to her with a shotgun pressed against his shoulder.

There was no more sobbing or moaning. The two collaborators whispered to each other, and Timothy held his breath, waiting to see what they would do.

After what seemed like an eternity, the flashlight beams pointed away, leaving the basement bathed in darkness again. The sound of scuffling boots faded as the men retreated.

Ruckley crawled over and handed something up to him. Timothy felt the metal grip of a knife handle.

"We have to get out of here," she whispered. "Follow us."

As soon as she started to get up, she froze.

Timothy didn't hear anything at first, but then came the snapping of joints. He lifted his head. Two new figures stood on the collapsed wall. This time, they weren't men.

Moonlight glowed over the charred gray flesh of Variants. They scuttled down the scree of bricks and wood into the basement.

Timothy tightened his grip on the knife.

Ruckley backed up next to him. "Can you fight?"

"Yes," Timothy replied.

"We need to kill them quietly so we don't attract attention from the collaborators," she said.

The other Ranger joined them. He was a young Asian man, probably not much older than Timothy.

"Neeland, you take the one on the right," Ruckley said. "I'll take the one on the left. Timothy, if we screw up, you help. Follow me."

Timothy and Neeland crawled after the sergeant. The Variants were feasting on one of the people the collaborators had just shot. Snapping gristle and the crack of a bone echoed in the room.

Ruckley was almost to her mark when Timothy hit a piece of loose debris. The concrete clunked on the floor, and the Variants spun. One jumped to a mountain of rubble on Ruckley's left.

She slashed with her knife while the second Variant scampered toward Neeland.

Timothy tackled the beast. It opened a needle-toothed mouth that reeked of dead fish. He raised the blade and brought it down through the monster's nasal cavity. It crunched through cartilage and bone before hitting the soft brain tissue.

The creature went limp, falling over Neeland.

Ruckley plunged her blade into another monster's flesh over and over. Timothy helped her, jabbing his knife into the Variant's side. The beast crumpled, but Timothy didn't stop until the Variant let out its last breath.

Ruckley twisted toward him, panting, her uniform covered in blood. Timothy was drenched, too. He wiped his forehead off with a sleeve.

"You okay, Neeland?" Ruckley asked.

"I think so," he said.

She put away her knife and pulled out her pistol. "Follow me."

"Did you reach Command and tell them about the collaborator base at Mount Katahdin?" Timothy asked.

"Not yet." Ruckley shook her head. "I didn't have time before the attack. We need to find a radio."

"Shit..." Timothy said. He wanted to scream, but he whispered instead. "They have a nuclear weapon and labs and..."

"I can't do anything without a radio. We'll find one and then get out of here."

Timothy pictured Nick and Pete, too. "Not before we kill the collaborators."

She looked at him with narrowed eyes. "What?"

"I have to find those collaborators," Timothy said. "I'm not leaving this place until they're all dead."

***

Despite all the warnings from her military advisers and staff, President Jan Ringgold had moved central command back to the mainland. This was where she wanted to be, with her people suffering the onslaught of the Variants and their collaborator allies.

She knew it was risky, but that's why she had ordered Vice President Lemke to stay on the USS *George Johnson*.

Her rise to the presidency had been utterly unexpected and sudden when the president and vice president had died along with most of their cabinet during the Great War of Extinction. Circumstance and fate had given her no choice but to rise to the occasion.

So when Lemke had told her he was going with her to Long Island, she had been blunt about him staying on the ship. If she died, they needed a clear line of succession to continue the fight.

Two guards escorted her down the hallway of the underground bunker where they had set up their temporary command. They took a right at an intersection and then stopped outside the blast door that led to the emergency operations center (EOC) and the living quarters. The guards stopped there.

This was the new White House.

Instead of hallowed halls filled with historical paintings and antique furniture, there were corridors ribbed with steel columns and girders rising from cracked concrete floors.

The bunker had served as a Cold War-era bomb shelter, its location stuffed away in government files to only recently be rediscovered. It was one of a handful of places she and General Souza had in their back pockets to serve as a safe house when things got grim.

Ringgold couldn't think of a time when things looked grimmer since the first war.

She walked to her temporary quarters, stopping first in a bathroom that wasn't much larger than a coffin. A showerhead on the ceiling sprayed directly onto a tiled floor with a drain in the center. Next to it was a toilet and a stainless-steel sink.

After splashing a little rust-colored water over her face, she took a deep breath.

This is it, Jan, she thought.

After she tied back her hair, she walked back to the EOC doors. The guards opened it, immediately letting out the chaotic noise.

Voices clamored across the open space as officers spoke with representatives from other outposts. People rushed back and forth carrying computers and satellite phones, radios and boxes of supplies. They needed to modernize this place in a matter of hours to continue their operations.

Ringgold could feel and see the tension in the raised voices and hurried movements. Everyone here knew how desperate the situation was.

She made her way through the sea of officers and staff gathering intel from the outposts across the Allied States.

Her briefings would come soon, but first she wanted to see the newcomers that had arrived an hour earlier.

She made her way into another narrow passage, the sound of dogs barking down the hall. The noise guided her to an open door in another claustrophobia-inducing room. Inside, Horn was telling the two German shepherds to sit, while his daughters stowed their meager belongings in a small closet.

Horn seemed to sense her presence and turned. "Madam President."

The dogs wagged their tails as he held them back.

"Good to see you all have settled in," she said. "Where are Kate and Reed?"

"Just down the hall," Horn said.

Ringgold stepped into the room and bent down to pet the dogs. She glanced up at the girls. "Tasha, Jenny, how are you two?"

Jenny looked down. "Dad said we won't be going back home."

"Is Outpost Portland really destroyed?" Tasha asked.

Ringgold stood and looked to Horn who gave her a subtle nod.

"I'm afraid so," Ringgold said. "I'm very sorry."

Tasha's bottom lip quivered, and she put a hand over her eyes as if to hold back the tears. She wiped them away as Jenny sat on a cot, nose sniffling, eyes watering. The dogs both looked at the girls, their tails going limp.

"Everything's going to be okay," Ringgold said. "We'll rebuild, and we'll make sure you get a new house."

"But you can't bring back Timothy or any of the others," Tasha said.

"No, we can't, and I can't tell you how sorry I am for that," Ringgold replied. "But Timothy and your friends would want you to keep moving forward with your lives."

"Girls, let's get unpacked and let the president get back to work," Horn said.

The young women turned away looking devastated. It added to the guilt already consuming Ringgold.

When she returned to the hall, Beckham was standing there.

"Madam President," he said.

Ringgold gave him a hug without saying a word.

"Are you okay?" he said quietly.

She pulled away and nodded. Seeing Captain Beckham always gave her strength. "Where's Kate?"

"In the EOC conference room."

"Let's go then."

She turned and they walked toward the conference room. Beckham opened the door when they got there.

At a round table in the center of the room sat General Souza, Lieutenant Festa, Dr. Lovato, and S.M. Fischer. They all stood to greet her.

These were her most trusted allies. People who had stood by her through the worst patches of the war. All were here because they believed in the Allied States—and because this was their only chance of survival.

Motioning for them to sit, she joined them at the table. The clamor in the hallways quieted with the closed door, and she steepled her fingers together on the table. Behind them was a wall of old CRT monitors that hadn't yet been replaced. Souza and Festa each had a bulky laptop, but that was all her team of advisors had for communications for now.

"Let's hear it," she said, bracing herself for the bad news.

General Souza cleared his throat, then spoke. "All our warheads have been deployed, and we launched selective airstrikes at suspected Variant and collaborator targets."

"How many outposts have we lost?" Ringgold asked, bracing herself for the answer.

"We've lost communication with seventeen," Souza replied coldly. He checked his notes on the table. "Another seven reported heavy casualties and persistent Variant activity as recently as fifteen minutes ago. That brings us to forty-one remaining outposts as of thirty minutes ago, but many are close to radiation zones."

The cold fingers of fear curled inside Ringgold's chest, squeezing her lungs as Festa listed off the cities hit by the nuclear warheads. "Philadelphia, Chicago, Minneapolis, Denver, Kansas City, Dallas, New Orleans, Pittsburgh."

Beckham's jaw gritted at the report, but he said nothing. Fischer nervously pulled on his mustache. Kate stared ahead blankly.

"We hit them hard," Souza said. "I've deployed a handful of recon teams in armored scout vehicles, but only time will tell if the brains of the operation are dead. I firmly believe destroying them is the only way to win this war."

"Fighting on the ground out there, I can tell you from battle experience that things aren't like they were eight years ago," Beckham said. "There's something more powerful controlling the masterminds."

"It could be a well-connected human collaborator," Fischer said. "Spies, military weaponry, newly developed weapons. It all smells like someone with firsthand knowledge of top-secret operations."

"Have we heard anything from Team Ghost?" Beckham asked.

"Negative," Festa said. "We lost contact."

Beckham wrinkled his brow but retained his composure.

"So the SDS equipment is a loss?" Fischer asked.

"Don't write them off yet," Beckham said firmly.

Ringgold turned to Kate. "Right now, we need to fight this unconventional war with unconventional means, and Dr. Lovato, you might hold the keys to that. Can we move forward with the communication software your team developed to tap into the Variant network?"

All eyes turned to Kate.

"Before the insurrection at Manchester, the communication software worked on the mastermind," she said. "However, that was a very controlled study. We didn't have much time to finish it before…" She paused. "We lost Dr. Carr and Sammy Tibalt is severely injured, which means any further testing will be difficult."

"I'm very sorry to hear about Dr. Carr," Ringgold said. "He was a talented scientist, and his sacrifice will not be in vain. How's Sammy doing?"

"She's stable," Kate said.

"I don't mean to be insensitive, but I have more questions," Ringgold said.

"By all means, go ahead."

"From your reports, I gather you can now listen in on the Variants organic network and potentially send messages through it, correct?"

"That's what our preliminary results demonstrate," Kate said. "Sammy is the genius behind the software portion."

"Can you do what she did?"

"No," Kate said. "Well…maybe."

Ringgold thought about her next order, but she knew Kate would be up for the task. "I realize you're all reeling from your losses, but I need you to test the technology you've developed."

Beckham furrowed his brow. "In the field?"

"Yes," Ringgold said.

Kate and Beckham exchanged a look.

"She's not going without me," he said.

"Of course not," Ringgold said. "If you want to bring Parker, he can go or he can stay here with your children. I'll leave it up to you. Either way, get some sleep. We move out when the sun is up."

"I'll go, too," said Fischer. "On our way here, Cornelius and I organized a shipment of the seismic detection equipment I used in El Paso. I just need to know where to send it."

"I know of just the place," Festa said. "The outpost in lower Manhattan has repelled the most recent attack. It's close to us, and they have access to tunnels with webbing you can tap into, Doctor Lovato."

Fischer gave a nod and picked up his cowboy hat. "I'll

have the equipment shipped there immediately."

"Good," Ringgold said.

"Guess I'm going back to New York," Beckham said. "Hopefully this time we'll have better luck than we did with Operation Liberty."

— 3 —

"We got contacts at our ten o'clock," boomed Pete, his dreadlocks bouncing over his shoulder. He raised his gun.

Nick "Whiskey" Wisniewski stopped and turned toward his comrade. The man pointed into the darkness but Nick saw nothing. After leaving the University of Southern Maine, he and his crew of seven had trudged through the early morning hours on their way to the rendezvous point. They had already racked up five outpost soldier kills and still had a ways to go.

Despite the intensity of the bombings, there was a fair number of people that had escaped the blasts. His men were rounding them up now.

"There!" said Pete.

Nick spotted a man and woman dart out of a building. They started running. He took no pleasure in shooting them, but it had to be done.

He raised his M4 and lined the man up in his sights, then squeezed off a burst. The man went down still holding the hand of the woman. She tumbled to the ground next to him.

Then she let out an agonizing wail that was silenced when Pete slammed the butt of his gun into her forehead. Another man jogged over to retrieve her. With Pete's help, they dragged her back to their gang of prisoners.

They already had ten rounded up and tied together in a line.

A man named Ray guarded them with a shotgun in one hand and a machete in the other. He had already hacked one man to death who tried to break free. The man's butchered body was still tied to the line with the others, a reminder of what would happen if the prisoners tried anything.

Nick jogged over, changing his spent magazine as he ran. "Pete, we need to move. No more stopping to find people. Let's get back to the vehicles before the military hits again."

They had wiped Outpost Portland off the map, but it had come at a great cost. Over half their own soldiers were dead, and most of their vehicles destroyed.

The military had unexpectedly sacrificed their own in order to kill as many Variants and collaborators as possible. A ruthless act, which surprised Nick. Normally President Ringgold avoided collateral damage, but then again, maybe she hadn't given the order.

Maybe there was someone else in charge of the war now.

Either way, this just proved what he already knew. The New Gods were winning, and soon the Allied States of America would no longer exist.

A Variant's high-pitched shriek shattered the stillness of the pre-dawn hours.

The human prisoners huddled closer together. The sound might have bothered Nick, too, if the beasts weren't still under the control of the Alpha in the area.

He wasn't sure where the huge monster was now, but he had his remote to shock it into submission if it went rogue.

"Let's grab Alfred and move out," Pete said.

Nick returned to the place they had left Alfred a few

minutes before. He had slumped against the car they had propped him against, unconscious from his burns.

The low rumble of a fighter jet forced Nick to scramble for cover next to his injured friend.

Scanning the sky, he waited for a glimpse of the jet, but the roar of the engines grew distant.

"Alfred," Nick whispered, trying to rouse the older man.

"He's in bad shape," said Ray.

Nick reached down to check the bandages wrapped around Alfred's right arm and his shoulder. Shrapnel had punched into his back. Those bandages were already soaked through with blood.

Pete pulled a dreadlock away from his face for a better look. Then he sighed. "He's not going to make it."

Alfred's eyelids suddenly flitted open.

"I'll make it," he grumbled. "Don't leave me behind."

Nick bent down and scooped an arm under Alfred. He helped him stand, but Alfred winced in pain. He was a big man, and there was no way Nick could carry him all the way to the rendezvous point.

They set off with the other soldiers and their prisoners, moving slowly.

The next few city blocks had been hit hard by bombs. Foundations were all that remained of obliterated houses and businesses. Abandoned vehicles lay in the road, warped and charcoaled.

A graveyard of twisted corpses littered the asphalt of the next street. Clawed hands reaching skyward confirmed they were a pack of Variant thralls that had been caught in the inferno. Seeing the mangled corpses filled Nick with almost as much rage as seeing his dead brothers and sisters.

These were the creatures that were supposed to help them take back their land from the traitors, and every day more lost their lives to the very government that created them.

"We got a live one," said Ray. He aimed his machete at a juvenile.

The armored shell had blackened, and its eyeballs had melted into gobs of mangled tissue. It growled and moaned, writhing in agony.

"Put it out of its misery," Pete said.

Ray raised his machete. A crack to the skull ended the suffering. Its inhuman voice was replaced by a mechanical noise.

The *thump, thump, thump* of chopper blades.

"Contacts!" Pete said. "Everyone, off the road!"

The seven soldiers pulled the group of civilians into a ditch behind the remains of a collapsed building. Seconds after taking cover, two Black Hawk helicopters plunged through the smokescreen. They flew toward the city, door gunners opening up on targets Nick couldn't see.

He started to raise his rifle but Pete held up an arm to stop him.

"Unless you've got an RPG I don't know about, we don't have the firepower to take those birds down," he said.

"We can still take out those gunners…"

"Not without drawing them straight to us, we can't," Pete said. "This is not the time to make a move, so stand the fuck down."

Alfred groaned in pain, and Nick crouched to check on him. Pete went around the side of the building with two other men for a better view.

A few of the prisoners mumbled to each other.

Another three sobbed.

Ray held up his machete, still wet with blood. "Quiet, you fucking dogs. Another word and it will be your last."

A woman sobbed, but Ray left her alone.

The choppers circled over the university campus for another five minutes before vanishing in the plumes of smoke. For another ten minutes, the bark of the machine guns and the howl of dying monsters filled the early morning.

Eventually the creatures quieted and so did the gunfire, leaving only the thump of the choppers. That too ended as the birds raced away from the campus.

A cool breeze rustled the leaves on the ground.

Pete returned and motioned for the group to keep moving. Nick helped Alfred up, but he was losing strength and blood. He leaned on Nick, heavier than before.

"Hang in there," Nick said. "We're almost back to the trucks."

"I'm…" Alfred groaned and slumped, pulling Nick to the ground. They crashed to the dirt in a tangle of limbs.

Pete grabbed Nick and yanked him up. Alfred was lying on his side, eyes closed.

A touch to his neck confirmed his pulse was weak, and Nick could tell his friend was running out of time. If they didn't get him medical attention soon, he would die.

"Leave him," Pete said. "He's not going to make it."

Nick glared at Pete. "I'll carry him."

"You'd be carrying a corpse. He'll only slow us down."

"He's still alive, man," Nick said, trying to keep his voice low.

Pete gave Alfred a pitiful look. "Alfred's service to the New Gods has come to an end."

31

"Come on," Ray said. "Those choppers might be back."

Nick looked at the smoke-filled sky. They were right, but leaving Alfred felt wrong. The guy had been with them for years, serving with fierce loyalty.

"I'm sorry, brother," Nick said. He patted Alfred on the shoulder and then stood. As he jogged away, he looked over his shoulder, watching Alfred's chest move up and down slowly.

"Come on," Pete said.

He led the group of prisoners and other soldiers through the burned streets.

Their trucks would hopefully be waiting at the rendezvous point about two miles away. For the next twenty minutes they jogged hard, stopping only once to help a female prisoner that had fallen.

Ray raised his machete to kill the woman but Pete stopped him.

"We're almost back," he said. "No more killing for now."

Nick felt some relief. Too much of their own blood had been spilled tonight, and they had lost far too many potential converts.

Down the street, he noticed movement. A Variant climbed the side of a stone church. It skittered up a broken steeple and perched at the top, looking out over the ruins like a gargoyle.

Rearing back its bald skull, it released an unholy shriek. Dozens of its comrades answered the call, a message that they now controlled Outpost Portland.

"The New Gods will be pleased about tonight," Pete said. "Very pleased, indeed."

***

Beckham was lying in the creaking bed of the quarters he'd been assigned in the Long Island bunker. A pane of light slipped in under the closed door. Exhaustion gripped his body, but he couldn't manage to stay asleep. By four in the morning, he had jerked awake multiple times from incessant nightmares.

At five, he gave up on even trying to close his eyes.

Kate rolled over on her back, staring at the cracked ceiling, unable to find sleep, too. Javier was the only one getting any shuteye in a cot across the room.

Beckham pushed his body up against Kate's.

"Everything's going to be okay," he whispered.

She turned to face him. "You really believe that?"

"Yes."

She stared at him in silence for a while before facing the ceiling again.

He wasn't sure if she believed him, and hell, he wasn't sure he believed himself. But he couldn't lose hope. Confidence and optimism was a soldier's surest path to victory, and as much as he had tried to retire, he was, and always would be, a warrior.

They finally got up an hour later, roused Javier, and told him they were being sent out again. He sat up in bed, rubbing his eyes, his hair ruffled.

"Am I going too?"

"I'm afraid not," Kate said.

"You're leaving me again?" he mumbled.

"We won't be gone long," Beckham said. "You're going to stay with Tasha, Jenny, Big Horn, and the dogs. It'll be fun."

"Fun?" Javier looked to his mom, completely alert

now. "You want to tell Dad what fun means?"

She forced a smile.

"It will be more fun than where we're going," she said.

"I want to go with you," Javier said. "I can help. I can fight."

"Honey, it won't be safe," Kate said.

"You can protect the others here," Beckham said. "Ginger and Spark need you, too. You can watch out for them, right?"

Javier shrugged, and Kate bent down to hug him.

"Where are you going?" he asked.

"New York City," Kate replied.

An hour later, he and Kate were on a Black Hawk flying toward the city with S.M. Fischer, his guards, and four soldiers. Beckham dreaded going back to where he had lost so many of his brothers and sisters eight years ago in Operation Liberty.

The apocalyptic landscape was worse than he remembered.

Entire city blocks had burned to piles of ashen debris and the crumbled remains of towers. Mountains of rubble were all that remained of some of the city's most iconic landmarks. The city's bridges were mostly non-existent, blown apart before Operation Liberty to keep the infected from spreading. All that had done was trap the living in the city.

He remembered stories of people trying to swim across the river only to drown. And then there were the people who had leapt off the rooftops to avoid the slashing talons of the beasts.

Pillars of smoke rose from lower Manhattan, evidence of the battle from the night before. The bird went higher, giving Beckham a fleeting view of what was left of the

New York Public Library. The stairs and the front columns remained, but most of the walls and roof had collapsed inward.

A memory surfaced in his mind of the Variant hordes that had turned the building into an extended stay hotel. But it wasn't the battle that had occurred here that filled him with despair—it was the police officer and the boy that Beckham and Horn had found inside the Bank of America tower during Operation Liberty.

This was where he had rescued Jake Temper and his son Timothy.

Now they were both gone.

Beckham lowered his head.

"Reed," Kate said. She squeezed his hand. Her strength helped him find the courage to face the future.

Two Apache helicopters suddenly flew on the flanks of the Black Hawk. They raced ahead, and the pilots of the Black Hawk turned to follow.

"Nice escorts," Fischer called out.

"Haven't seen one of them for a while," said Chase.

"Waste of fuel if you ask me," added Tran. "Unless the Variants can fly like those freaks in Europe."

"There could be bats out here," Kate reminded him.

"Well, look at that," said one of the pilots. "The Brooklyn Bridge is still intact."

They flew over it. The bridge had indeed survived the past decade, but it wasn't unscathed. A few of the vertical cables had snapped and pieces of the road had broken through, dropping into the water.

Multiple ships were docked along the piers to the bridge's south. One was an old destroyer turned into a museum. There was also a cruise ship that had slammed ashore, smashing its bow. Scattered across the deck were what looked like piles of bodies.

But it wasn't all death and destruction below.

The first signs of life came into view. Four Humvees escorted an old UPS truck through a street littered with broken vehicles and debris. Soldiers in turrets raked their weapons over the road. One man raised a hand to the chopper before Beckham lost sight of them.

The Apaches turned toward the city and flew over Wall Street and the New York Stock Exchange. Most of the massive towers here had sustained damage from rockets that had blown out the upper floors. The walls of the bottom floors were blackened from the firebombs that had almost killed Beckham in Operation Liberty.

"There it is," said a pilot over the headset. "The 9/11 memorial is our LZ."

The memorial was walled off along the streets from the debris of destroyed buildings.

As the chopper did a quick flyby, it became apparent the outpost survivors of the prior night's battle had retreated block by block to a smaller, more defensible area. The smoke drifted from the east, rising from holes in the ground.

The outpost must have detonated bombs in the sewers and subways.

The Black Hawk descended toward the memorial. Two M1 Abrams tanks and Bradley Fighting Vehicles, both rare sights, were positioned at gates in the walls surrounding the site. Soldiers patrolled the platforms built behind the razor wire.

When the Black Hawk touched down, a crew chief opened the door. Beckham helped Kate out and away from the bird. Fischer almost lost his cowboy hat, but Tran snatched it and handed it back.

Three soldiers flanking a middle-aged woman with gray-streaked red hair waited across the lawn, their clothes whipping in the rotor wash.

The Apaches set down on rooftops nearby. The pilots climbed down from the cockpits and vanished from view as soldiers on the roofs stood guard around the precious birds.

"This way!" shouted the woman ahead. She led them through a maze of trees and past the dry memorial pools where they stopped.

The woman held out a hand and smiled, wrinkles forming next to her mouth that evidenced a lifetime of smoking. "Welcome to Outpost Lower Manhattan. I'm Commander Amber Massey."

"Captain Reed Beckham."

He shook her hand. He wasn't surprised when he received a firm grip. Anyone who had held a place like this, in a city that had never been cleared of the monsters, was going to be strong.

"I'm Doctor Kate Lovato," Kate said, introducing herself next. "My team is still in a classified location, but we're here to do an advance inspection. We'll need access to the closest tunnel with Variant webbing."

Massey cracked a sly grin. "You're kidding, right?"

"No, Commander," Kate replied. "My team is working on—"

Massey's grin faded to a frown. "When I was told we were getting new people, I thought Command meant special forces and reinforcements, not a science team and..." Massey's eyes flitted to Beckham and his prosthetic leg and arm.

"Captain Reed Beckham *is* special forces," Kate said.

"I didn't mean to offend anyone, but we were hit hard

last night. Lost a lot of good men and women defending these walls."

"That's why I'm here," Fischer said, tipping his hat.

"Um, who are you?" Massey asked.

"S.M. Fischer with Fischer Fields," he said. "All due respect, but we're here on orders from the president, and we're one of the best things that could have happened for this outpost."

Before Massey could respond, voices called out.

"Open the gates!" yelled a guard on one of the walls.

A barred gate rose. The two Humvees and the UPS truck Beckham had seen from the sky drove in from Greenwich Street. The vehicles stopped in the parking lot nearby. Soldiers hopped out and went to the back of the UPS truck to open the door. Then they helped civilians down, one by one.

Kids, women, and a few men. All of them wearing the same expressions of terror. One of the men still had red webbing attached to his arms and legs.

"My God," Kate said. "They must have been pulled from the tunnels."

"Those are the last of the survivors from an area outside the outpost," Massey interrupted. "I thought there would be more…"

"This won't happen again, ma'am," Fischer said. "We're here to protect them now. My engineers are on their way with equipment that will identify the Variant tunnels before they attack."

"Well, that's good news," Massey said. "I'm sorry if I came off a little harsh before. My people are hurting and dying."

"How many people are here?" Beckham asked.

Massey looked over her shoulder at a few of the

buildings. "Five thousand. Maybe. We lost an entire building with five hundred people last night."

"Weren't there originally twenty thousand people here?" Kate asked.

"Yes," Massey said coldly. "Like I said, we've been hit hard. We had to pull nearly everyone back behind these walls."

"Sorry to hear about your losses," Beckham said. "It's been a tough few days for everyone."

"That's putting it lightly."

"Can you tell me what all the smoke was we saw on our way in?"

"My demolition teams blew up a few tunnels and collapsed a subway last night. We set mines around other areas we suspect the Variants might come through."

A pickup truck pulled in from another gate, this one had more wounded people in the back. Medics gently removed two soldiers with long crimson gashes splitting their skin and red webbing tied around their limbs.

"Jesus," Fischer said, taking off his cowboy hat again.

"Jesus has nothing to do with this place," Massey said. "Now follow me."

She led them through the park, navigating past more until they reached a construction site. Only this wasn't just an old site that was never finished before the war.

Massey put her hands in her hips and stood next to Kate. "So, you want access to the webbing?"

"Yes," Kate replied.

"This is the one tunnel we've kept open," Massey said. She pointed down metal stairs that led to a hole with twisted rebar. Tendrils of webbing hung off the concrete and metal.

"Where does it lead?" Beckham asked.

"To the sewers where many of our people were taken," Massey said. "It's secure right now, but we were setting charges to destroy it so the Variants can't use it again. How long do you need access to it?"

"Hard to say," Kate said.

"Guess."

"A few hours, maybe half a day."

"How about until dusk?" Massey asked.

Beckham stepped up to the fencing, his hand on his M4 strapped over his chest. In the depths of the darkness, he saw more webbing stretching out like hundreds of snake tongues.

If there was a gate to hell on Earth, this was it. And he and Kate were about to descend into its depths.

— 4 —

Dohi was on point, leading Team Ghost and the surviving Wolfhounds through the wreckage of the National Accelerator Laboratory Campus. Dark pillars of smoke rose from craters around the buildings, scars left by the attacks from those mysterious helicopters.

Anxiety ate at Fitz as he waited for those thumping rotors again. Any moment, those bastards might come sweeping down.

He carried a pack full of scrapped computers and other devices they had scavenged from the warehouses. As bad as this broken tech looked, Fitz hoped the engineers and scientists could still do something useful with them.

"That's what so many of my bros died for, huh?" said Martin. The sole Wolfhound who hadn't been injured was walking close by and helping one of his comrades, a blond-haired man named Lawrence. Blood-soaked bandages were wrapped around Lawrence's arm where the cannibals had sliced off a piece of muscle and skin, then singed the wound closed.

"It's going to work," Lawrence said, eyes bleary. He still seemed to be in shock. "These guys know what they're doing."

"That butchered arm of yours is screwing with your brain if you think they got a single damn idea of what's going on."

"Quiet," Fitz said. "We're going to get you guys out of here, but you have to cooperate."

Fitz took a moment to scan the rest of them.

A big dark-skinned man named Jackson was on Rico's back in a fireman's carry. Both his legs had been chopped off by the cannibals. The cauterized stumps leaked yellow fluids into sodden bandages. His face had grown a shade paler since they had begun their hike away from the warehouses, and Fitz wasn't sure if he was going to make it. He'd been unconscious nearly the entire time.

Ace had a man with a scraggly beard and olive-green eyes, Hopkins, in a similar carry. Every bump, every jostle sent the man groaning in pain. His right foot was missing below the ankle.

Mendez was at least walking on his own, watching their backs on rear guard.

"Put me down," Hopkins begged.

Fitz remembered the guy bravely working with them to infiltrate the cannibal's base before, but all sense of bravery was gone.

"Put me down and leave me," he mumbled.

For a second, Fitz thought that maybe they would be better off leaving the injured Wolfhounds behind and coming back for them. Team Ghost could make it to the C-130H faster without them. Secure it and then return...

He shook the thoughts from his head. That was just exhaustion speaking. The last dregs of adrenaline had burned off, and they were faced with a stark, demoralizing reality.

Leaving any Wolfhound behind was condemning them to death. Either to their own wounds, starving Variants, or to the unknown enemies that had tried to cut them down from the choppers. He already felt responsible for the extreme loss of life.

Fitz motioned for the group to gather around the charred husk of a delivery truck. He looked around at the weary, ash-covered faces.

"We're almost to the edge of the campus," Fitz said. "From there we hike straight back to the C-130. If the choppers come back, split and run. Rendezvous is the LZ. Clear?"

Several nods.

"Seriously, just leave me," Hopkins said, eyes bleary. "You guys would do better without us dragging you down. You still got a mission, and we're holding you back."

"We ain't leavin' nobody," Mendez grunted.

"Keep quiet," Fitz ordered. "There might still be cannibals or Variants out there."

Dohi led them down the street toward the freeway. The odor of cooked flesh drifted through the air. Rubble lay at the feet of the buildings. Flames still licked piles of debris.

The team passed melted vehicles scattered along the cracked parking lot. A cluster of corpses were just ahead, skeletal remains frozen in agony where they had fallen to gunfire or flames.

Fitz passed a truck with a missing windshield. A cannibal gunner had been posted inside. His rifle lay outside the driver's side window, and his skeletal hands were stretched out as if he had been trying to escape when the rockets hit.

Charred muscles had shrunken into ghastly cables over his long bones. Not much remained of his face except his open jaw from when the man had let out a permanent, silent scream.

Fitz felt a hint of sympathy. The cannibals had been cruel, twisted human beings, but seeing even them slaughtered like this was hard to stomach.

That feeling quickly evaporated when they passed over the highway. He took the team past the location where Lieutenant Singh and the other Wolfhounds had been positioned.

"Oh, God, no," Martin choked.

Lawrence leaned on him, face frozen in shock.

"You still think these assholes know what they're doing?" Martin asked.

Lawrence didn't answer this time.

At the edge of the woods, mangled body parts surrounded bloodied craters. Bullet holes perforated tree trunks. Other trunks had been turned into splinters by rockets.

"This is all your goddamn fault," Martin mumbled.

Fitz heard it but ignored the man. He went to Mendez and glassed the freeway to make sure they weren't being followed.

"We have to bury them," Martin said.

Fitz turned to see him picking up an arm and a leg. That's when he knew Martin had lost it.

"Come on, man," Lawrence said, holding his wounded arm. "You need to trust them. We got to keep going. Got to get to that C-130."

"He's right," Fitz said.

Martin glared at him, but then nodded, pulling himself together.

Rico lugged Jackson over.

"We got a problem," she said.

"What's up?"

"He's burning up from an infection, and it's bad. The

antibiotics we gave him from the field kit aren't doing anything."

"We've got more on the plane," Fitz said. "Come on, let's move out."

Rico took in a deep breath and then kept walking with Jackson on her back.

An hour of slow moving took them around the booby traps in the forest. When Fitz heard the popping of joints, he signaled the team to halt.

It sounded like it was coming from one of the pits.

He crept to the edge and peered over the side of it. A Variant writhed on a stake piercing its abdomen. Bloodshot, reptilian eyes locked onto his as its long tongue lashed the air.

He made sure the others saw it before moving on.

The message was clear: Variants were still prowling these woods to find scraps from the battle.

The team trudged onward as the early morning hours turned to noon. The sun hung high overhead. Eventually, they reached the beginning of the cliffside trail that would take them down to the beach-turned-landing strip. Fitz wanted to sprint ahead and search for the Wolfhounds defending the C-130.

"Hold up," Rico said.

She gently laid Jackson on the ground. Fitz joined her after signaling to Dohi, Ace, and Mendez to hold security.

Rico knelt beside Jackson, her fingers against his wrist. His dark skin was covered in beads of sweat, and his lips were dry and cracked.

Fitz bent down.

"Pulse is weak," Rico said. She tried to drip water from her hydration pack into his mouth. He choked on the dribble, erupting in a wracking cough.

"We're almost there," Fitz said. "Hang on, Jackson."

A rotten odor drifted away from the bandages around his legs. No doubt from the festering infections.

Rico tried to give Jackson more water. A low noise gurgled at the back of his throat, like he was trying to talk. But then he went quiet, and his head tilted to the side.

"Almost there," Fitz repeated to Rico, to reassure himself as much as her. "You need help?"

Rico shook her head, then loaded the man on her back again. "He's not that heavy, to be honest."

Dohi waited for Fitz's signal before taking them to the edge of an abrupt cliff. The blue waves of the Pacific gleamed in the sunlight, and Fitz walked up to the edge.

Beneath them stretched the long, sandy beach where the C-130 and the Wolfhounds were supposed to be waiting.

A breath caught in his chest when he saw half-buried corpses and weapons scattered along the coast. The C-130 looked like a spent firecracker, half its fuselage torn open and leaking charcoaled supplies.

"Keep them away," Fitz said to Ace. The Wolfhounds had been through enough, and he didn't want them to lose hope. But Fitz felt defeated, like the eroding beach in front of them. Slammed over and over by waves.

Ace moved in front of Martin and Lawrence to keep them from looking.

"What?" Martin said. He had set his pack down again and was holding his gold necklace like it was the only thing keeping his mind in control. "What is it?"

Ace put a big hand in front of Martin's chest. "Hold on, man. We've got to make sure things are clear."

Fitz crouched next to Rico. She pointed to movement inside the cockpit.

He shouldered his rifle and peered through its optics, zooming in on the fractured plexiglass around the cockpit. Through one missing panel, he saw what had caught her attention.

A starving Variant tore at the neck of a dead pilot. Needle-sharp teeth came away from the flesh with strings of bloody sinew.

Fitz cursed their luck.

Everything that could have gone wrong had.

That's not exactly true, he thought.

His team was still alive.

Bringing up his rifle, Fitz waited for a good shot, but Dohi grabbed him by the shoulder.

"Boss, you need to see this," he said quietly.

Fitz followed him to another vantage point.

"Ten o'clock," Dohi whispered.

Fitz used his scope again but all he saw were seagulls swooping in to feast on the dead. Then he saw a camouflaged Zodiac on the shore.

Using his scope, he followed footprints in the sand from the small boat to the plane.

Dohi held up a pair of binoculars, indicating a spot further out over the ocean. He handed over the binos, and Fitz zoomed in on a ship just barely visible on the horizon. When he squinted, he thought he saw the shape of two choppers resting on its deck.

Now he knew where the hostiles had refueled their birds. But how in the hell did they get a ship and equipment like this?

He handed the binos back and aimed his rifle on the C-130 when Rico stumbled over. She crouched down, shaking her head incredulously.

"Fitz, you're not going to believe this..." she said.

Dohi and Fitz both looked at her as they crouched.

"What?" Fitz said.

"It's a Variant...but it's also a man..." Rico shook her head again. "Just look at the damn plane again."

Fitz and Dohi both got back up behind the rock cover and used their rifles to view the figures that had emerged outside the destroyed aircraft. Not one, but three men walked out of the wreckage, blood dripping down their chins.

A deep pang of terror shot through him when he saw their yellow, reptilian eyes and maws filled with jagged teeth.

These weren't men.

At least, not entirely.

These were some sort of Variant-human crossbreeds. And they were carrying rifles.

"They're like... Chimeras," Rico said. "Half-Variant, half-human."

"Chimeras," Fitz repeated, thinking of the horrifying amalgam of creatures that comprised the legendary monster in Greek mythology.

He thought he had seen the worst combinations of nature and science in Europe. But now he realized those mutated creatures paled in comparison to the things standing on the beach. These crooked half-beasts were exactly what the VX-99 program had set out to create all those years ago in Vietnam.

The perfect soldier.

***

Kate waited at the top of the metal stairs that would take her and her team into the bowels of Variant hell. A warm wind blew out of the hole at the construction site.

If she stared too long into the abyss, she could almost hear the whispers and moans of all the people that the beasts had taken down here. The scratch and click of scuttling Variants. The shrieks of an Alpha commanding the beasts.

Beckham stepped beside her, and the fear slowly subsided.

"Nothing we haven't seen before, so try not to worry," he said. "We got plenty of security, and I'll be right here."

Her husband was half-right about the first part. Kate had seen the creatures both in her lab and out more times than she cared to count. She had also experimented with the webbing and worked on a mastermind.

But she had never been inside one of their tunnels or lairs.

"It's not just the beasts I'm worried about," she said. "It's what they brought down here."

The thrumming chop of an incoming helicopter commanded her attention. Outpost soldiers posted around the construction site retreated to the wide lawn that had been serving as the outpost's helipad. Fischer had been hanging out near them with his guards and walked over toward Beckham and Kate.

Kate shielded her eyes against the midday sun. The silhouette of a Black Hawk descended toward the memorial park.

"That must be my team," she said.

Fischer joined them, dipping his cowboy hat.

"Just got word that my vibroseis equipment will be here in a few hours," he said. "I'm going to take a ride outside the walls to scout locations for it."

"Good luck," Beckham said.

"You too," Fischer said, dipping his hat again.

Kate watched the chopper disappear behind a line of trees. Only thirty seconds passed before it lifted back into the sky. The soldiers that had departed at its arrival returned now, escorting the technicians that would assist Kate in hooking up their computers to tap into the organic Variant network.

She recognized Ron with his buzzed head and bandages covering wounds from Manchester. Leslie was here too, her long blond hair tied in a ponytail. Between them walked someone Kate hadn't expected.

"Sammy!" she yelled.

The computer engineer limped, one tattooed arm clamped over her abdomen. Kate ran to her.

"What are you doing here? You're supposed to be resting," Kate said.

"We tried to tell her that," Leslie said.

"She doesn't listen," Ron added.

Sammy cracked a pained smile. "You think I trust a bunch of biologists with *my* computer program?"

"Seriously though, are you sure you're up for this?" Kate asked.

"Look, we need to infiltrate the Variant network as fast as possible," Sammy said. "I developed the software, and I don't think anyone here understands communication networks as well as I do."

Kate sighed. She wasn't going to argue with Sammy, because as much as she hated to admit it, the engineer was right. They absolutely needed her.

"Can we get some help with this stuff?" Ron asked, pointing to a few crates that the soldiers had helped carry from their chopper.

"What is all this?" Beckham asked.

"Splash suits and masks," Leslie said. "We're going underground. There might be contaminants, airborne and otherwise. This will help protect us."

"Understood." Beckham directed a few soldiers to open the supply crates.

"Wait, we're going down *there*?" Ron asked, peering down into the pit.

Leslie stepped up for a look.

"We've got plenty of soldiers to protect us," Kate said. "And my husband is taking the lead."

"Good enough for me," Sammy said.

Beckham gave orders to the other guards. There were twelve in total, all armed with rifles and decked out in body armor.

Kate looked to Ron. "Do you have everything we need?"

He shrugged his backpack off his shoulder and opened it to reveal its contents. "Two laptops—one spare—and a handful of flexible microelectric arrays."

"Good," Kate said. "Let's suit up."

Ron and Leslie helped the soldiers into splash suit coveralls. They taped their boots and gloves and fitted each with a full facemask respirator. Sammy gave Beckham a wrist monitor that reported oxygen and temperature levels to help gauge the tunnel's environmental compatibility.

Once the soldiers were outfitted, the science team donned their protective gear, each strapping on wrist monitors of their own. Kate took in a breath, smelling the slight plastic odor of the rebreather system.

"After you, Captain," Kate said.

Beckham led the way down the metal stairs into the old sewer line. Hot air emanated from inside like they were entering the throat of a giant beast.

"What's with the heat?" Ron asked.

Kate threw up a finger at the technician. She wasn't a soldier, but she knew the value of quiet when infiltrating unknown territory, even if you had been told it was likely safe. From all her time with Beckham, she had soaked in a few lessons. It was the only way to survive as long as they had.

Once they hit the bottom of the stairs, the tunnel curved into a relatively flat floor. Their boots slurped over fragments of the red webbing that had been destroyed by the demolition team prior to Kate and her team's arrival.

A demolitions team had rigged C4 charges throughout the tunnels with lines snaking away to the detonators. Seeing the explosive charges didn't bother Kate, but the rising temperature did. It was a good fifteen degrees hotter already.

Beckham flipped on his tactical light as they left the reach of the sun. Beams of white light with target designators speared the darkness from a dozen rifles.

Leslie gasped.

"Holy shit," Ron said.

Hunks of Variant body parts littered the area beyond an iron gate that the outpost engineers had installed earlier that day.

Beckham and the other soldiers shone their lights through the bars. They raked the beams back and forth before unlocking the gate.

The passage was only about ten yards wide and another six tall, but it was one of the largest Kate had heard about. This old sewer line was a major artery of transport and communication for the Variants.

Exactly the kind of place they needed to tap into.

Much of the webbing on the walls had burned to a crisp. In other areas, crimson ropes hung loose as if they had been torn by claws and bullets. Tangles of the webbing farther down still pulsed on their own, tendrils squirming like worms cut in half.

While segmented chunks of webbing lined the walls and floor, Kate couldn't be sure that they were connected with the main network. With the damage in this part of the tunnel, she had a hard time figuring out if *any* piece of webbing connected to the masterminds and other Variants miles from their location.

For their efforts to succeed, they needed an intact section, untouched by the demolition team. One that led to the larger network of tunnels and webbing that connected the masterminds. That was the only way to truly tap into the Variant and collaborator communications.

And that meant they had to go deeper.

Kate explained and Beckham took in a deep breath.

"Okay, follow me," he said.

The further they traveled, the worse the stench grew. Somewhere in the distance water dripped from the ceiling.

Beckham stopped a handful of times, and Kate listened for the popping of joints or growls of the beasts. All she heard was the constant drip and trickle of water.

They pushed onward. Another gust of warm wind traveled through the passage a few minutes later. Kate shivered from a sound that came with that wind.

A slight rustling mixed with ghostly moans.

"I got movement," said one of the soldiers.

Beckham signaled for two soldiers to follow him and

investigate as the others held positions around the science team.

Kate froze and watched her husband move into the darkness.

The lights bobbed, chasing away the shadows as their guns swept across the tunnel. Beckham's light landed on a long crimson tendril that strained and quivered slightly.

"Just the webbing," said the other soldier. He pulled out a knife and touched it with the blade. As soon as he did, something dropped from the ceiling.

He nearly tripped, stumbling backward as he brought up his rifle.

"Hold your fire," Beckham said. He trained his light on a cocoon of red that had dropped from the snapped webbing.

Kate took a few steps forward.

"My God," Beckham said.

The soldier with the knife knelt next to the cocoon. Beckham bent down and took out his blade, too. They carefully cut at the fibers. The scarlet vines fell away to reveal a shriveled, skinny man with gaping wounds in his side. Teeth and claw marks covered his body, and he let out a long, agonized moan.

"Jesus," said the soldier with Beckham.

The other guards advanced around them to hold security, and Kate moved over to help. She looked down the tunnel as the beams penetrated the inky darkness.

All along the ceiling and walls were other cocoons strung up in the webbing. People squirmed in a few of them. Others were completely still, the occupants unconscious or long-since dead.

Beckham pulled out his radio. "Command, Alpha One. We found some of your missing people. Requesting additional support. Medical included."

The transmission didn't go through, and he turned, giving orders for one of the soldiers to go back and get help.

Then he sent two of the other guards to clear more of the tunnel and free as many survivors as they could while they waited for backup.

Kate steeled herself as she heard the slurp of prisoners being let loose from the webbing. Beckham walked back over to her.

"Is this place good enough to tap into the network?" he asked.

Kate looked to Sammy. "What do you think?"

"This is as good as it gets in terms of network density," Sammy said.

"Let's try it," Kate said, trying to keep it together. She tried to take her gaze from the human prisoners with their horrifying wounds, but it was almost impossible, and she pictured her friends and family strung up in tunnels just like this.

Of all the places she had worked in the past, this was the worst. But her team had no choice. If they wanted to ensure the future of the Allied States didn't end up like this, they had to tap into the Variant network.

— 5 —

Dohi perched amid the windswept trees and bushes on a cliff overlooking the wreckage of the C-130. Past it, waves crashed over the shore. He watched three Chimeras sift through the ruins of the plane.

Outside the wreckage, two of the half-breed beasts fed on the corpses of the Wolfhounds scattered across the sand and rocks.

Mendez lay prone beside Dohi, surveying the macabre scene with his binos. Deeper in the woods behind them, the rest of Team Ghost monitored Hopkins, Lawrence, and Jackson. The injured trio continued to decline. Jackson was still unconscious, both of his injured legs looking worse.

While Hopkins could manage to stand on one leg, there was no way he could walk unassisted with his missing foot. He continued to beg Team Ghost to go on without the three of them, insisting they were nothing but a burden.

Even Lawrence with only an injured arm now looked pale as a sheet. His eyes had turned glassy, and he seemed in a constant state of shock. The trio needed antibiotics and better medical attention than Ghost could provide with their already depleted field kits.

"Looks like those things might be packing up," Mendez said.

"Go tell Fitz," Dohi whispered back.

Mendez nodded, then disappeared into the shroud of leaves and branches behind them.

Dohi watched over the beach. He still struggled to understand how these half-man monsters were even possible. When the Variants bred, they spawned armored juveniles.

But he'd never seen a juvenile that looked so human. These were something else—something more intelligent that could use a rifle and operate vehicles.

A terrifying abomination that the VX-99 had been designed for back in Vietnam.

Fitz crawled up beside Dohi.

"Where the hell did they come from anyway with that kind of firepower?" he asked.

"I noticed their ACUs had the California National Guard emblem on them," Dohi replied.

Mendez got down next to them. "You think these things were guardsmen?"

Dohi shook his head. "No, but I think they ransacked the National Guard armories and bases around the bay."

"Makes sense," Fitz said. "We've neglected the West Coast for years. They must have been stockpiling supplies we abandoned out here."

"If they were out here so long, why did they leave the cannibals alone until now?" Mendez asked.

"Because the cannibals weren't the real threat," Dohi said. "We are."

Dohi brought his rifle up and peered through the scope. One of the Chimeras tied up a large canvas bag near the Zodiac, then heaved it on the boat.

"What did he take?" Fitz whispered.

"I don't know," Dohi said.

They watched for another few minutes until the

answer became clear. A second beast emerged from the wrecked plane with another large bag and dropped it into the boat.

The third was crouched near a crater in the sand. He clawed through the mangled body parts, then picked up a charred leg. After sniffing it, he stuffed it into his bag.

"Dinner," Mendez said. He crossed his chest.

Dohi felt a bout of nausea well up in his stomach.

"Act like soldiers, look like beasts, and eat like them," Mendez said. "Worse than Variants, because they seem as smart as humans."

"Someone must have still been developing VX-99," Fitz said. "We've got to tell Doctor Lovato. This is more important than the SDS tech."

Fitz was right. The creatures in front of them combined the worst of both nature and man in one biological package.

The beasts hoisted a couple more packs over their shoulders and then dragged their Zodiac back into the surf. Two hopped in while the third kept pushing the boat into the waves.

"Get ready to move," Fitz said. "Mendez, stay on watch. Signal us if something's wrong. Dohi, you and I will search the C-130 for a radio and medical supplies."

Dohi led at Fitz's command, and they crept down the trail until they reached the beach. Their boots crunched over the sand as they approached the aftermath of the carnage. Only a few Wolfhound bodies had been left behind, and they were already stripped of meat.

The wind had swept sand over a boot with half a leg sticking out. A helmet protruded out of a sand mound, the soldier's mangled face partially exposed.

Dohi crept up to the fuselage of the C-130. Metal

panels peeled off the side of the plane like a giant had slammed an axe into the hull.

Fitz gestured for Dohi to lead.

He entered the plane at a crouch, hit by the acrid scent of burned plastic that made his eyes water. The stench of carrion came next.

Dohi stepped over the melted jump seats and broken ammo crates. He kept his rifle shouldered, peering down the length of the C-130. When he was sure it was clear, he motioned to Fitz.

"See if you can find some antibiotics, I'll check the radio," Fitz said. He navigated the wreckage to reach the cockpit, pushing past a few tumbled crates.

Dohi stepped over a dead man lying in a puddle of dried blood. Chunks of flesh and muscle were missing from his neck, teeth marks scarring the bits of skin left under the shredded remains of his clothes.

The smell only grew worse as Dohi pushed aside a few half-eaten corpses in his way. He reached the tail of the plane. A metal crate was marked with a white cross over red paint. He unlatched the crate and opened the lid. There were a few rolls of gauze and bandages, but that was it.

No blister packs with pills. No antibiotic sprays.

"What the hell?" Dohi asked, examining the crate. Then he noticed the scratches in the paint. They looked like claw marks.

He started back up toward the cockpit, checking the ammo crates on the way.

They were empty, too.

The Chimeras had scavenged all these supplies. The only thing they seemed to have left were a couple self-inflating emergency life rafts. Probably had no use for them given they were motoring around in that Zodiac.

He reached the cockpit, where Fitz was trying the controls of the radio.

"Everything's broke-dick," Fitz said.

Dohi examined the radio. It was warped and melted. Bullet holes showed where the Variant soldiers had fired into it for good measure.

"No ride out of here, and no way to contact anybody back east," Fitz said. "Did you find anything useful back there?"

"They took everything. Ammunition, extra weapons, medical supplies."

Fitz cursed, hanging his head low. Then he glanced out the cracked window of the cockpit.

Dohi followed his gaze to the ship on the horizon.

"They may have taken everything, but they haven't left yet," Fitz said. "If we can find a way to get out there, then maybe we can steal what we need and get away without being noticed."

"Maybe."

Dohi knew it was a long shot, but they had no other choice.

"We have to warn Command about the Chimeras," Fitz said. "They have to know."

"It's going to be a huge risk, even if we do find a way to get out there before they sail away."

"We better get moving then," Fitz said. "We have no time to waste."

***

Fischer waited inside a large garage with Tran and Chase. Ten outpost soldiers milled around them, ready to head out with them into the city. The clank of tools and voices of mechanics working on two MATVs, a Humvee, and a pickup truck echoed throughout the cold space.

There were other vehicles, including a snowplow. The edges of the blade were covered in paint that looked like it had been scraped off other cars.

As soon as the vehicles were fueled and ready, they would head out to scout locations for the vibroseis trucks already en route from El Paso. The oil and gas exploration vehicles weren't the sophisticated seismic detection equipment from Project Rolling Stone that General Cornelius had wanted, but it would have to do for now.

While Fischer waited, he loaded shells into his new tactical shotgun. Then he counted the bullets for his .357 magnum. He had only twenty left. There were only a few surviving outposts that manufactured ammunition, including Outpost Galveston under the command of General Cornelius. Even so, bullets were becoming rarer every day, especially with the threat of those outposts being lost as the enemy advanced.

That's what scared him so much about the collaborators.

They seemed to have access to fuel, weapons, ammunition, and vehicles. There were rumors now they even had helicopters. If that were true, the traitorous bastards were in better shape than what was left of the Allied States.

Tran and Chase finished loading up extra magazines for their M4 rifles. There was still plenty of the 5.56 mm and 7.62 mm ammo left for now, but their stock would be gone in a few days if they didn't get a resupply and the Variants pressed their attack.

If the outpost survives that long…

That's exactly what Fischer and his men were here for—to make sure the outpost didn't fall while Kate and her team tapped into the Variant network. As soon as they figured out where the real mastermind was, it would be the beginning of the end for the monsters.

"Good to go!" shouted a husky man with a long brown beard. "Let's mount up!"

The vehicles growled to life inside the open garage, the noise rumbling like dragons waking from slumber.

"Wait up!" yelled a female voice.

Commander Amber Massey jogged over in fatigues. A duty belt holding a pistol, extra magazines, and a radio hung from her waist. She also carried an MP5 submachine gun.

As the other soldiers loaded up, the large man with the beard walked over to her.

"Commander," he said in a deep voice.

"Sergeant Bonner, I'll be driving them," she said, gesturing toward Fischer and his men. "And we're taking Black Betty."

"You got it, ma'am," said Bonner. He tossed her a set of keys. She caught them mid-air and jerked her chin for Fischer and his bodyguards.

They followed her to a black pickup truck on a lift with oversized tires. Bars covered the side windows, and a cow-guard with spikes masked the grill.

"Looks like something from Mad Max," Tran said quietly.

Fischer grinned but said nothing.

Commander Massey climbed up to the driver's side. The three men used the footholds to climb up into the dual cab.

Bonner drove the Humvee out first, and the MATVs followed with 'Black Betty' going last. The trucks slowly drove away from the building and down a street inside the perimeter of the outpost.

As they drove, Fischer spotted what looked like medical crews carrying stretchers away from the fenced off area around the construction site where Kate and Beckham were working.

"What's going on?" he asked.

Massey sighed. "The science team discovered survivors."

"Survivors?" Tran asked.

She glanced in the rearview mirror. "If you can call them that."

Her words were cold but he sensed the sorrow behind them.

"Some of our people have been taken underground over the past few weeks," she added, her tone gravely serious. "The few people we rescued might be here physically, but their minds sure aren't."

Fischer swallowed hard, thinking about the horror these people had experienced. He recalled the tunnels at his fields.

I could have been one of them.

It hadn't really sunk in until now how lucky he had been.

The clanking of a metal gate sounded over the rumble of engines. He turned to see the first gate in the outpost wall lifting. The convoy rolled forward, prompting the guards to open the second gate.

"You boys ready to see New York City?" Massey asked.

"Ready as I'll ever be," Fischer said.

Truth was, he had never really liked the city. Too loud, too dirty, and too muggy in the summer. But he would have taken it back then compared to what it looked like now.

Destruction surrounded them in all directions. Above, below, on the ground. And even with the windows up, they couldn't escape the odor. The city smelled like death.

Mangled vehicles flashed by, blackened and crushed from firebombs.

Massey sped ahead of the convoy, taking the lead.

"All right, you're the boss," she said. "Tell me where you think the best place is for your trucks."

She eased off the gas until they were cruising at about twenty-five miles per hour. The street was mostly cleared of debris and vehicles, probably from the plow he had seen back in the garage.

Plastic and broken glass carpeted the sidewalks outside storefronts where windows had been blown away. Most of the doors to buildings were gone.

Fischer pulled a map he had requested earlier from his vest pocket. On it, Massey's people had marked areas indicating the sites of previous Variant attacks.

He ignored the subways and tunnels Massey's people had already plugged and or demolished.

"Let's start around City Hall Park," he said.

She took a right and drove to the park. The few trees still alive had lost most of their leaves, giving him a view of City Hall.

The building had collapsed inward from an explosion, and the resulting mountain of debris blocked his view of the other side of the park. Still there was plenty of room for a truck in the closest section of the lawn.

"This spot is worth checking out," he said.

The convoy stopped, and he opened the door.

"Whoa, I don't think so, Mr. Fischer," Massey said, reaching toward him. "Not safe to wander around right now. There could be Variants prowling."

Fischer hesitated, one leg already out. "Well, how am I supposed to see if these locations are good if I can't get out and survey them?"

"You can't tell from the truck?"

"Not really," he said. "I need to walk the ground a bit."

She pulled out her radio.

"We're getting out here," she said. "Secure the area, then form a perimeter."

Fischer stepped down to the pavement, his shotgun in hand. The park was bordered by a few major streets. Tunnels from subways, sewers, and waterlines stretched underneath them. This would be a likely route to the outpost. Having a truck positioned here would ensure they knew right away if the creatures were traversing those underground pathways.

First they would have to clear the intersection of Park Row and Broadway.

"Commander Massey, can you get your plow out here to move those?" he asked, pointing to the vehicles clogging the streets.

"Sure, I'll call it in when we get back."

"Good," he said, marking his map. "This location is perfect."

After scoping out the rest of the park, he went back to the convoy.

"Where to now?" Massey asked.

"Bogardus Garden," Fischer replied.

They drove to a small park between Hudson and West

Broadway. The trees were gone, destroyed during the war, leaving a wide space for another vibroseis truck.

"Looks good." Fischer marked it. This time, his view was clear enough he didn't need to get out.

An hour later, his map had been marked with multiple locations surrounding the outpost, forming a rough square. There was one location left to examine, and that was Pumphouse Park near the shoreline of the Hudson River.

They parked in a circle drive at South End Avenue, right next to the park. The trees here were all alive, though their branches were mostly naked from the changing seasons.

Fischer got out of the truck for a better look, and the outpost soldiers followed his lead. Commander Massey and Sergeant Bonner trailed him down a sidewalk.

"You sure this is a good place?" Massey asked. "So close to the shore and all?"

"It's not ideal, but it's the last blind spot—"

A scream cut him off, followed by the pop of a gunshot.

The team whirled around with their weapons aimed at the circle drive and their vehicles. Four of the soldiers ran toward Liberty Street where the screaming continued.

"Come on!" Bonner yelled.

Fischer spotted the source of the screams. A man was being dragged by a hulking Variant down the road. Gunshots rang out, and bullets punched into the bulky monster as it pulled him toward an open manhole.

The creature vanished down the manhole with the soldier.

A long scream echoed out of the opening. Two soldiers rushed toward the open hole, rifles shouldered.

One flicked on a flashlight and shone the beam in. But instead of going down, the other guy pushed the cover back over the top.

"What are you doing?" Fischer asked.

"He's gone," Massey said. "Nothing we can do for him now."

The rest of the team retreated to the convoy and Bonner waved for Fischer and his men to get back into the trucks. He stood there a moment, just staring, before finally retreating to the truck with Massey.

No one said anything until they were back in the cab. She grabbed the radio off the dashboard and brought it up to give an order. "Get the demo team to collapse that tunnel."

"But that soldier might still be alive," Fischer protested.

"We're doing him a favor." She put the radio down and placed the vehicle in gear. "When we get back, I'll show you what's left of the people we find down there."

— 6 —

Timothy took a slug of water from a canteen they had scavenged. Every step he took, his body and legs felt weaker and heavier. Soon, he feared he would crash if they didn't rest.

For the past ten hours he had followed Sergeant Ruckley and Corporal Neeland away from the Variant infested area around Outpost Portland. They hadn't found a radio or any help.

The two Army Rangers were the only survivors from their platoon.

A few hours earlier, Ruckley had discovered soldiers that appeared to have survived the initial bombing, but bullet wounds in their temples indicated they had been executed in cold blood.

She was still reeling from the find, and Timothy had seen her shed a few tears.

The soldiers weren't the only people they had found with bullet holes in their heads. Civilians had been murdered and left as scraps for the scattered Variants.

Evil ran deep through collaborators like Nick and Pete.

Timothy wondered if they were still out there.

A Variant's long wail snapped him from his thoughts of revenge.

Ruckley waved for them to take cover. They took cover in the shade of a bridge extending over a creek.

Evading the random Variants during their escape wasn't easy. The beasts were actively hunting for new prey.

"Why don't we just kill them?" Neeland whispered.

"Because our gunfire will attract more," Ruckley said.

Shit, even Timothy knew that.

"We've got knives," Neeland said. "It would be quiet."

Timothy shrugged but Ruckley shook her head.

"We wait them out," she said. "We're not going to take more risks than we have to."

For the next fifteen minutes they remained under the bridge. Two of the creatures clattered over the pavement above. Timothy heard one pause and snort as it sniffed the air for human flesh.

He shouldered the M4 he had pulled off a dead soldier. There was a suppressor on the end, but he wasn't sure that would matter. The monsters could hear a needle drop.

Timothy tensed at a distant scream. It was faint, almost like a whisper on the wind.

The sound wasn't from a monster.

Ruckley perked up like she heard it too.

The frightened shriek came again. This time the two beasts on the bridge bounded away, claws scratching on the pavement.

Ruckley signaled for Neeland and Timothy to follow.

They climbed up the muddy bank back to the main road. The beasts, on all fours, took off onto a front lawn and into a backyard of a house along the street.

Ruckley started in the opposite direction.

"Wait, what about helping that person?" Timothy asked.

"We don't know who they are, and chances are they're

already dead," she said. "We got bigger problems."

Timothy didn't care who they were, friend or collaborator. If they were the latter, all the better.

Fuck it, he thought.

He took off running from Ruckley and Neeland. It took him a moment to realize they weren't following.

But he kept going.

Another scream exploded from somewhere ahead, and a second voice called out.

This one a male. "Shelly!"

It didn't sound like these were collaborators, but it could be a trap. If they were collaborators, he would try and take them alive. Maybe they could lead him to Nick and Pete.

He ran hard, his shoes pounding the pavement until he got to the front yard the Variants had cut through. The breeze rustled his sweaty clothing as he sprinted, but he had to slow down. All his muscles were locking up from dehydration.

A glance over his shoulder confirmed the two Army Rangers weren't following. That surprised him, but they had made their decision, and he wasn't bound by Ruckley's orders.

He was driven by only one directive—doing what his father would have.

Shouldering his rifle, he followed the path the beasts had taken through the backyard. Another creek bordered the dying brown grass, separating the yard from two more houses up a hill.

He jumped over the creek and sprinted up the slope.

By the time he reached the front of the first house, the voices had quieted. He dropped low near the driveway to search the street to the left, then the right. Nothing moved except for shreds of torn clothing blowing in the parking lot of a church at the far end of the road.

Timothy remembered this place now.

A small community of people had survived off the grid here. Living off the land and sea.

The windows of the church were boarded up, but the front door was wide open. A sign in the front yard said, *Sanctuary for those that trust in Him.*

Long red streaks stained the sidewalk leading to the open door.

Timothy was too late.

Halfway there, he paused at the familiar sound of popping joints.

Then he heard the rip and crackle of tearing flesh, followed by the crack of bones.

All the sounds came from inside the church. He searched outside for any beasts that might be watching before advancing toward the building.

As he walked, he aimed his rifle at the open door, then peeked inside. In the shadows of the nave, he spotted a crouched figure, bent over a body.

Timothy moved his finger to his trigger, then squeezed off a burst of rounds into the Variant's back. The monster let out a gurgling moan and collapsed.

He lowered his rifle and stepped forward. Bodies were scattered inside the church, many already shredded into bloody ribbons.

No matter how much death he witnessed, it would never get easier.

Timothy considered whether he should go inside further to see if anyone was still alive. The chances were slim, but he had to check it out.

There was a sound coming from near the altar…a low

rasping, like someone having a hard time breathing. It grew louder as he approached between the pews. He aimed his rifle in the shadows until he saw red eyes glaring at him.

Oh, shit.

The rasping erupted into a vicious growl, then a guttural barking.

Timothy took a step back and tripped as a mutated dog barreled down the central aisle. He went down on his butt and fired a burst that went high, punching into a pew, splinters spraying from the impact.

Pushing himself up with one hand, he fired wildly with the other. Again, he missed the target. The creature followed him as he ran and leapt through the open door.

The beast launched itself into the air. He brought up his rifle to knock it away. It barreled into him, jaws snapping and saliva spraying across his face.

He hit the ground on his side, and the beast rolled onto the lawn. He managed to turn his rifle and fire. This time, the rounds blew off part of the hound's jaw.

But the creature *still* came at him, blood whipping from its broken face, until he sent a second burst into its ribs, taking it down.

More barking sounded in the distance.

A second dog charged from the backside of the church. With only a second to spare, Timothy swiveled his rifle and pulled the trigger. His bolt locked back. The magazine was empty.

The creature jumped into the air. He only had a moment to bring up an arm to brace himself for the impact.

A gunshot cracked in the distance.

The monster crashed into Timothy, knocking him to

the ground. He rolled away, ready to fight, but the abomination was already limp.

Timothy pushed himself up to see Neeland lowering his rifle. Ruckley ran toward the church. Her face burned red, and her nose twitched. She looked like she was biting back a mouthful of curses.

Neeland kept his rifle trained on the church door while she jabbed Timothy's chest with a finger.

"You ever do that again, and I'll leave you behind, you stupid shit," she said through a clenched jaw. "You got it?"

"I'm sorry, but there were people..."

"They were already dead, and you know it."

Timothy didn't exactly agree but nodded anyway.

"I want to hear you say, 'I will follow your orders, Sergeant,'" Ruckley said.

Timothy thought again about what his dad would have done.

"You listening to me?" Ruckley said.

"Yes."

"If you're with me, you follow my orders," she said. "Those gunshots probably attracted more of the beasts."

"Okay," Timothy said.

"Let's go," Neeland said.

Ruckley turned and started walking.

"Where are we going?" Timothy asked.

"Outpost Boston, unless we find a radio and or a ride before that," she said without turning.

Timothy followed her, relieved she hadn't made him promise to follow her orders. If she turned her back on defenseless people again or didn't go after the collaborators, then he would again do what he'd just done.

She had a mission and so did he. Hopefully they would both end with the same result—the annihilation of evil men like Nick and Pete.

***

The tunnels sweated with humidity. Water coursed over the webbing and the brick walls like tears. Beckham wished he could wipe the perspiration rolling down his nose under his full-face respirator mask.

It was a good twenty degrees higher than topside, and the mugginess made it almost unbearable. The plastic splash suit he wore was like walking around in a portable sauna. At least the mask protected him from the odor of death, trash, and waste this place must be filled with.

Three outpost soldiers and two soldiers from Command stood guard with him in the tunnel. A heavy-set corporal named Cotter looked like he was about to pass out, his face under the mask blanched.

"I'm sweating like a pig's nutsack in the summer," Cotter had protested.

"Suck it up, man," Beckham had replied. "You're not the only one hurtin'."

He couldn't wait to peel off this mask and suit.

Horn would have hated it down here. The big guy could deal with pretty much anything, but he despised humidity.

Then again, the retired operator probably didn't like playing babysitter, either. He had been filling that role quite a bit lately. Beckham thought of Javier, Tasha, Jenny, and the dogs back in the command bunker. All cooped up with the president, her staff, military officers, and soldiers.

It beat being down here, but Beckham still worried about them. No place in the Allied States was safe now. At this point, he wasn't even reassured although Horn, Ringgold, and the kids had a veritable army protecting them.

The enemy had a bigger one.

"You hear that?" asked Cotter.

"What?" replied another corporal named Daniels.

Beckham held up a hand to silence them. He listened for whatever Cotter thought he had heard. But the only sound was a distant dripping.

Cotter shrugged. "Guess it was nothin'."

"Maybe it was your stomach growling," Daniels said.

"Shut up," Beckham said. He raised his rifle and directed his beam down the passage.

A faint moaning sounded.

The men backed up behind Beckham as he took a few steps ahead.

"Variant?" Cotter asked.

Beckham shook his head. "Sounds like another survivor."

"God," Daniels said. "Let me guess. We're going to go rescue them."

"Not yet. Stay here, and stay frosty," Beckham said. "I'll be right back."

"Where you going?" Cotter blurted.

"Before we do anything, I need to check on the science team," Beckham said.

Beckham set off for Kate and her staff. They were located in a tunnel around the next corner, about a quarter mile from the entrance to the construction site.

The glow from the construction floodlights guided him, and he shut off his tactical light. The generators powering those lights thrummed as he rounded the corner.

Kate, Sammy, Ron, and Leslie hunched behind the laptops they had set up on a folding table like those the military used in their mobile outposts. It wasn't an impressive mobile lab station, but it was all they had to work with.

"You guys making progress?" Beckham asked.

Sammy shrugged. "This isn't as easy as I'd hoped."

"I thought you had this all figured out."

"In the lab, we did," Kate said. "But this isn't the lab."

"We're having trouble integrating the signals over the longer networks," Sammy said. "The signal doesn't amplify like I'd predicted. Worse, the signals we're receiving are coming in at frequencies we didn't experience with the mastermind."

"What's that mean?" he asked.

"It means, if we don't get the frequencies just right and our first attempt to communicate with the Variant goes wrong, they'll be able to find us," Kate said.

That didn't exactly inspire confidence, but Beckham trusted his wife.

"I have faith you'll crack this," he said. "But in the meantime, I've got to take a few men farther down the tunnel. Might be more survivors."

She paused. "You…"

"I'll be careful, don't worry."

Kate shot him a worried look, and he gave her a reassuring nod.

He returned to the soldiers and motioned for Cotter and Daniels to follow.

"Rest of you stay here and hold sentry," Beckham instructed.

Their three beams penetrated the steamy darkness as they advanced into the subterranean labyrinth. Sweat bled down his forehead and stung one of his eyes. He blinked it away.

The moaning they had heard earlier seemed to have stopped. He kept walking, just in case they were still alive. His prosthetic blade clanked on the concrete floor as he scanned the tunnel with his light to make sure no threats hid in the shadows.

In the next passage, he cleared the way to another tunnel.

At the next intersection, he signaled for Cotter and Daniels to take the right side while he checked the left. When he looked back to the right, he found both soldiers angling their lights at the center of the floor where a volcano of webbing grew through the bricks.

"What in the hell," Beckham whispered.

The tunnel below the sewer must have been dug by the Variants, which meant there could be other passages right below his boots.

Another long moan sounded, this time much louder. It sounded more like the hiss of air escaping a leaking tire. Beckham walked past the other two soldiers.

He flicked his beam over the walls until he saw the source.

On the ceiling above the broken floor, his light captured a human face. Bloodshot eyeballs protruded from their sockets. He ran the light down the webbing, expecting to see the rest of the body covered in a cocoon of webbing.

But there was nothing under the neck.

No chest, torso, hips…

Not even any bones.

"Holy…" Beckham whispered.

"What is it?" Cotter muttered.

Daniels took another step forward, then started to wretch. He pulled up his mask and vomited.

Beckham froze, his brain unable to comprehend what his eyes were seeing.

Of all the horrors over the years, this took the prize.

He finally managed to break from the shock. The vines had somehow become part of the head, feeding it like blood vessels nourishing an organ.

How in the hell was this possible?

The eyes seemed to watch him, and the lips moved. Air pushed out of the mouth, making that horrible hissing sound. Beckham wondered if the person was asking to die.

Cotter raised his rifle, looking as if he would grant that wish.

The lips opened wider to reveal a jaw rimmed with jagged, broken teeth. The head pushed forward, propelled by some of the vines, almost as if it was lunging at the soldiers.

Before Beckham could say anything, Cotter squeezed his trigger. A suppressed gunshot rang out. The ravaged face burst. Flecks of gore and bone painting the soldiers.

"God dammit," Beckham grumbled.

Cotter lowered his rifle.

"You stupid asshole," Beckham said.

"Dude, that was—"

A vine suddenly wrapped around his ankle and pulled his leg out from under him. Cotter screamed and dropped his gun. Flailing his arms for help.

Beckham pulled out his blade to free him, but crimson tendrils wrapped around his limbs too, yanking him against the wall.

Daniels was suddenly lifted to the ceiling by a rope of webbing that curled around his neck and arms. He also dropped his rifle, kicking as the webbing choked him.

It happened so fast, Beckham didn't even have time to save himself. The vines wrapped around him, pressing him harder against the wall. Webbing around their necks tightened, silencing any calls for help.

Beckham wiggled a hand free and reached for his radio. The vine around his arm squeezed, and he dropped it.

A draft of warm wind burst through the tunnel as he fought to free himself.

As the webbing tightened over their bodies, the carpet of vines coursed over the tactical lights on their rifles.

Darkness flooded the tunnels.

Something rumbled beneath them.

Paralyzed by the strength of the webbing, Beckham could only think about Kate. He had no way of warning her… Something was coming.

Kate took a seat next to Sammy at one of the tables. Sweat trickled down the back of her neck. She suppressed the urge to scratch it. The combination of the splash suits, respirator masks, and intense humidity and heat of the old sewers made their work nearly unbearable.

Thoughts of her family helped her persevere. The future of this country relied on the scientific experiments they carried out down here. Temporary discomfort was nothing compared to what was at stake.

Even more distracting than the heat was knowing Beckham was somewhere deep in the tunnels searching for more survivors. He hadn't been gone long, but she had started to worry. And while she admired his bravery and would never fault his courage, sometimes she wished he would play it safer.

But without courage like his—or really anyone's who was in the tunnels today—the Allied States would have perished long ago. All it took was for brave men and women to falter in the face of fear, and evil would triumph.

And that means you, too, Kate, she thought.

She snapped out of her thoughts and focused on the lines of text scrolling across Sammy's computer screen. Ron and Leslie crouched nearby, monitoring the microelectric array connections between the laptop and an organic cable of webbing.

Kate wasn't a programmer like Sammy, but she was beginning to learn how to interpret the various signals they received from watching the laptop's screen.

"How's it coming?" Kate asked.

"I think I'm ready to interact locally with the webbing," Sammy said. "Ron, check that laptop over there."

Sammy pointed to a computer on a different table thirty yards away.

"That means our signals are completely separate from the main network, right?" Kate asked. She worried an errant signal might put Beckham at risk.

"Whatever I send through this webbing won't pass beyond the network Ron and Leslie isolated," Sammy said. "We've got physical microelectric arrays that we can control in position to gate the communications."

Kate nodded.

"If we do our job right, no one but us will know we're interacting with the network," Leslie said.

Ron bent over the laptop. "My computer's ready."

"I'll send a test phrase," Sammy said. She typed the command.

"Got it, but…" He leaned closer to his screen. "I'm seeing something else, too."

"What?" Sammy asked.

Kate went for a look.

"I don't know…" Ron said. "External communications, I think."

"What are they saying?" Kate asked.

Leslie joined Ron, looking over his shoulder. "Looks like some of the signals are coming in clear," she said.

"I see one reporting ongoing Variant casualties," Ron said.

"That definitely isn't local," Kate said. "There haven't been any battles in Manhattan since last night. Can we determine where that signal originated?"

Sammy tapped on her keyboard and brought up the signals that Ron and Leslie were seeing. "You're right. This is coming from further north. Let's see if I can triangulate it."

A second later, a map appeared on her screen. Her software gave them a rough estimate where the signal had originated.

"That's near Outpost Manchester," Kate said.

The others paused. The terror they had experienced there was still fresh on their minds, and while they had escaped, thousands of innocents had perished.

"Can you confirm that's the right location?" Kate asked Sammy.

"Yes, the signal we're getting about the casualties from Manchester is from a mastermind."

"Then what are these other signals Ron and Leslie saw that we can't understand?"

Sammy shook her head. "If we were only interested in mastermind communications, we would be good. But this noise is indecipherable."

"Why?" Kate asked.

"We've tuned the software to listen into the voices of the masterminds, but not for other sources."

"But these other signals aren't directly from a mastermind?" Kate asked.

"No," Sammy said. "They're something else."

"Not sure I follow."

"The best way to describe this is that the masterminds' are one frequency on the radio. We have the software to listen to that frequency, I think. But the other signals we can't read are other radio channels. Maybe even AM instead of FM."

"So how do we tap into those?" Kate asked.

"That's the problem with working in the lab. We didn't get to see what this looks like in real life before deploying it."

Kate cursed. Not only could they not interpret all the signals, but her plan to send messages through the webbing and confuse the Variants had to be put on hold, too.

"How long before you can translate these other signals?" she asked.

"Hard to say," Sammy said, looking down. "We're starting at scratch for each unique messaging modality. I'll probably need the next couple days to interpret them."

"Massey won't be happy, but she'll have to understand," Kate said. "We need to do this right." She paused to think about something else bothering her. "Sammy, if the incoming messages we received aren't localized like we thought, does that mean the output from our computers…"

She let the words trail off.

Sammy clutched her side where she'd been shot. "Oh, my god. I… I…the meds must've gotten to me. I wasn't even thinking right…"

She sat straight again, her fingers working furiously across her keyboard.

"Sammy?" Kate said, fear rising in her own guts.

"Fuck." Sammy froze, staring.

"What?" Kate asked.

"All our test signals leaked from the webbing we tried to localize," Sammy said. "And every time we sent a signal, we got a bunch of responses. I missed them because we can't understand them."

"But that type of activity means they definitely received our test messages," Kate said.

Sammy nodded slowly. "They've probably been sending signals asking what the hell *our* messages meant."

"And when they couldn't understand them…" Leslie started.

"They would've reacted," Ron said. "Sensed danger."

Kate grabbed a radio from the table. "Reed, this is Kate. Do you copy?"

No response.

"Reed, are you there?!"

It hadn't been that long since he had departed. Maybe half an hour, but with the network activity and Beckham's silence, fear sent a chill through her body.

Something was wrong.

"I'll be back," she said to Sammy, starting to jog down the corridor.

"Wait!" Ron called out.

Kate ignored them and turned a corner, her boots slapping against a carpet of red webbing. The three soldiers guarding the area turned to her.

"Where's Captain Beckham?" she asked.

"He took Cotters and Daniels to check out some noises," one of the men said.

"And he hasn't returned?"

The man shook his head. He was an outpost soldier. One Kate had been introduced to before.

She tried to recall his name. "You're Parrish, right?"

The man nodded.

"Look, Parrish, Commander Massey told me I would have everything I needed for my mission here. That means you need to help me find Captain Beckham now!"

"He said to secure this area," a soldier said. "We're not—"

"I don't care! Come with me right now!"

The three soldiers stood there for a few seconds, staring at each other.

"Fine," Parrish finally said. "I'll go with you."

Kate looked at the other two men. "If you aren't coming, then give me a rifle."

"Hell no," replied one of the guys.

"You want to go then?" she said.

The man huffed and handed his rifle over. "If Commander Massey hears—"

"Tell her," Kate said. "I don't care. This is more important."

She set off, leading Parrish as fast as she could jog. Their flashlight beams guided them down the steamy tunnel.

They rounded a corner, and then another when she heard slurping and creaking. The sounds sent another chill through her limbs. Her grip tightened on the rifle as they advanced.

All the nightmarish things that could've happened to her husband flashed through her mind, and she struggled to dispel them.

Please be okay, Reed. Please.

They turned at another intersection, their meager lights piercing the dark. Rustling and snapping echoed down the passage. Then she heard something smack against the wall.

She sucked in a gasping breath when they neared the next corner, steeling herself for the sight of Variants tearing Beckham and the other men apart.

Parrish curled around another corner, and she

NICHOLAS SANSBURY SMITH & ANTHONY J. MELCHIORRI

followed, rifle raised.

Shapes squirmed in the darkness.

"Hold your fire," Kate whispered as her flashlight beam revealed the source of the ominous movement.

These weren't monsters. Vines covered the forms of the outpost soldiers and her husband, holding them against the wall.

"Reed!" Kate ran to him, pulling at the vines to free him. Parrish joined her, slashing at the webbing with his knife.

Beckham fought the rest of his way out of the prison. He almost fell on Kate and she helped him stand as his chest heaved for air.

"We have to go!" Beckham said between gasps.

Something rumbled in the distance. The webbing on the walls trembled.

Cotter threw a piece of webbing still stuck to his arm to the ground. "Now something worse is coming this way."

"We need to go, Kate!" Beckham said. "Run!"

***

The afternoon faded away. Soon the sun would retreat over the horizon, and the temperature would plummet as darkness covered the land.

Nick was prepared for the cold night, but most of the prisoners in the back of the pickup were not. A few wore only t-shirts, and even those with more substantial layers had rips in their clothing that exposed their flesh to the elements.

An icy wind battered them as Nick drove toward their checkpoint to refuel. Riding shotgun, Pete had dozed off, his head slumped against the window. His dreadlocks hung like beaded snakes over his face.

Nick looked in the rearview mirror at the SUV and pickup following them.

In the truck's bed, Ray gripped a mounted machine gun that he angled at the prisoners in Nick's truck. It was overkill really. The prisoners were tied to the same rope in the back. If someone jumped out, they would pull everyone with them.

Nick checked the sky for choppers. Since escaping Outpost Portland, they hadn't encountered any enemies, but he knew the military would be looking for them after their attack.

Thinking of the battle reminded him of how much taking Outpost Portland had cost them. Over half their soldiers had died, and the surviving thralls had mostly scattered. All the dogs he had spent months perfecting were missing or dead.

But their victory helped justify the losses. Soon he would be home with his wife and two daughters. If all went as planned, he would have a brief reprieve to spend time with them before they carried out the next orders from the New Gods.

An hour later, the fuel outpost appeared along the side of the road, providing a much-needed stop for Nick to stretch his legs and shake the fatigue from his head.

"Pete, wake up," he said. "We're here."

Pete sat up straighter and yawned as he looked out the window.

"Good. We'll stay here the night," Pete said.

"What?" Nick asked. "I thought we were heading straight back to Mount Katahdin after refueling."

"Too dangerous to keep driving. We hunker down

here. We'll hit the road again when we've got better cover."

The trucks following them pulled up. One of their comrades jumped out and opened the warehouse door. Nick parked his truck in the garage and killed the engine as the other vehicles slid in beside him.

By the time Nick got out, Ray had already jumped down and was waving his machete at the prisoners.

"Get your asses off and go to the back of the warehouse!" he yelled.

A frail bearded man was the first to step down. He turned to help the woman behind him. The Portland survivors kept their eyes down, avoiding contact with Ray and Nick.

"Set up a perimeter," Pete ordered the other men. "Get a drone in the air. I want eyes up ASAP."

One of the soldiers jogged over to a locked room where they had stored a basic drone and other tech gear. Equipped with infrared and night vision, the drone was their way of seeing any rogue Variants or hostile humans in the darkness.

"Fucking freezing in here." Ray rubbed his hands together. "I'll start a fire in the barrels out back."

"Hell no, you won't!" Pete yelled.

"But it's colder than Alfred's dead ass in here."

Nick glared at Ray.

"I don't give a shit," Pete said. "Get yourself a damn blanket or something, but don't be a dumb pussy."

Ray frowned and walked away, twirling his machete. The guy had an attitude and made Nick miss Alfred even more. He regretted leaving his old friend behind. He deserved a proper burial instead of rotting and decaying out in the cold.

Shouting suddenly came from the back of the warehouse where the prisoners were being rounded up. Ray swung his machete again. He hacked at the air in front of the only two male prisoners. The old guy with a long beard and a balding man missing his right eye both backed away.

The bearded guy was maybe in his seventies, and the one missing an eye looked to be in his fifties. Both had faces weathered by the outdoors. Their features were drawn tight, not from rage—but terror.

Nick felt the tickle of sympathy for these people, but he buried it almost as soon as it appeared. These heretics had made their choice. They had sworn fealty to an Allied outpost and support to the corrupt government, tying their lives to a traitorous lot.

If they were lucky, they would have an opportunity to atone for their sins and join the New Gods. And if they weren't lucky, their corpses would prove useful as Variant fodder.

The ten women and children behind them would have the same chance. The group sat on the floor, huddled together, shaking in the cold. Most had stopped crying, but one of the little girls sobbed into her mother's shoulder.

"Please," said the guy with the missing eye. "My wife needs water, and the kids do, too."

The old guy with the beard reached out with his bound hands. "We'll do whatever you want."

"Fucking right you will," Ray said. He eyed one of the women and licked his lips.

Pete walked over and gestured for Ray to back off. "Get them some water and food. Show them some New God hospitality."

Ray looked at him with a tilted head. "You serious, boss?"

"If you make me repeat myself, I'm going to hack off your dick and feed that to them," Pete said.

The other guys laughed, including Nick. Pete started to lead them away to the barracks and storage rooms.

"This is fucking bullshit," Ray mumbled as he cracked open a crate of supplies. "Neither of those guys can fight. They're deadweight. We should just kill 'em and toss 'em outside."

Nick was getting sick of hearing Ray talk.

"You don't get to decide who lives and dies," he said.

Ray looked up.

Pete stopped in front of the barrack door. His dreadlocks bounced when he turned. "Truth be told, that dumbass Ray is right. They're deadweight."

He sighed and walked over to the supply crate. Pete dug inside for something to eat while Nick sized the two male prisoners up.

Both were sitting on the floor now, looking at the ground. But not everyone appeared as defeated. A thirty-year-old woman with short hair glared at Nick with fiery rage—a look that told him she wouldn't hesitate to slit his throat if she had the chance.

That steely gaze reminded Nick of Timothy, the kid they had lost during the bombing. He was a firebrand. Nick had some grand plans for the young man, and it stung that they'd lost a potential warrior like that. But in the end, Timothy had played a useful role, providing the distractions that ensured the success of their attack.

Nick smirked at the woman still staring at him, and she raised her lip in a snarl.

"Man, I'm starving," Pete said. He pulled out some

food and scarfed a few bites down. Then he pried the cap off a bottle of beer they had brewed back at the base.

"I've got an idea," Nick said. He held a hand out to Ray who was stacking packaged food. "Give me your machete."

Ray tilted his head. "Why?"

"Just give it to me," Nick said.

"I ain't just giving you my damn machete."

Pete took a drink, watching curiously.

"Hand it over," Nick said, eyes narrowing.

"No, not until you tell me—"

"Motherfucker!" Nick screamed.

Anger from their losses and from Ray's constant bullshit boiled through his veins. He grabbed his comrade by the throat and started squeezing, then he balled his right fist and slammed it into Ray's nose.

The impact knocked Ray backwards, and he fell to the ground with Nick on top of him. The prisoners at the other end of the room cowered as he pounded Ray's face over and over.

The thud of the portly man's skull hitting the concrete echoed in the enclosed space.

A few shouts of encouragement joined the din, but there were also voices telling Nick to stop. He ignored them and crushed Ray's already bleeding nose with an elbow. The satisfying crunch eased some of the anger, but not enough.

Nick continued punching Ray until someone pulled him off. He didn't fight back when he realized it was Pete. There was one thing that could get you killed faster than a pack of wild Variants attacking you, and that was laying a hand on their leader.

"STOP!" Pete shouted.

Panting, Nick lowered his bloody fists. "Sorry, boss." The anger subsided and his vision cleared.

Pete let go, and Nick raised his hands in the air, palms up.

"I'm fine," he said.

Ray held his broken nose, still sitting on the ground.

"We've lost enough men," Pete said. "I don't need you dumb shits killing each other."

"That's why we need new recruits," Nick said. "And I know how we're going to get 'em, if Ray would just give me his fucking machete."

Nick picked up the weapon. Then he walked back to the prisoners, most of whom were gawking at him. He pulled his knife out with his other hand and then pointed at the woman with the short hair and the man with one eye.

"Stand," he ordered.

The other men huddled behind Nick. Pete stepped up, and Nick looked at him for approval. A shrug told Nick he was free to continue.

Ray stumbled over, blood trickling down his face, mumbling under his breath. A single blazing look from Pete got Ray to stiffen and shut his mouth.

Now that they had peace and quiet, Nick spoke.

"Get those two out of the rope," he said.

Two of his comrades untied the one-eyed man and the woman from the long rope. The man trembled with fear. The woman's fiery look had faded too as she shivered. Nick wasn't sure if it was because she was wearing just a t-shirt and jeans, or if it was from fear.

Probably both.

"You want to live?" Nick asked them.

Both managed nods.

He tossed the weapons on the ground between them.

"Everyone gets to eat," he said. "But only after one of you dies."

"But—" the man started.

"And the winner gets to join us."

Both prisoners looked back at the group. Almost all of them had stood to watch.

"Please," the man begged. "Don't make us do this."

"Don't hurt him," said a woman in the group. Maybe his wife.

The firebrand woman who had glared at Nick earlier studied the knife and machete. Her gaze flitted to the one-eyed man.

"No," he said. "I don't want to hurt you."

The woman took a step closer to the weapons, her hands shaking.

"No," he pleaded, but stepped forward anyway.

"One of you kills the other," Nick said. "Or I kill both of you. What's it going to be?"

A fleeting moment passed before they burst forward and scooped up the blades. The man got the machete, and the woman got the knife. She wasted no time thrusting it toward his chest.

He backed away, trying to parry her blows, but refrained from going on the offensive.

"Please," he begged again. "I don't want to hurt you! There has to be another way."

"There is no other way," Nick said.

The woman lunged and stabbed at his ribs. This time her blade sliced into his flesh, opening up a deep red gash in his side. He stumbled and gripped the wound.

Any semblance of pity the man had once exhibited disappeared. Now raw anger warmed his face, and his fear turned into desperation.

Nick grinned. These people had just learned what survival was. They no longer had the protection of the Allied States. They had only themselves to rely on.

The one-eyed man screamed and slashed out with the machete. She hopped back to avoid the blow. He swung again, too hard this time, stumbling.

The woman seized on his mistake, managing a clean slice across his neck.

Blood sprayed out, and he reached up to clamp his hand over the wound. She circled like a lioness over her injured prey.

In a swift movement that surprised even Nick, the one-eyed man swung the machete from the side, slicing a perfect cut across her neck.

She staggered backward, mouth gaping as blood sprayed from the injury.

"Oh shit," Pete said. He let out a soft chuckle.

The woman's fingers groped the wound.

Nick knew she was dead, but she fought for every last breath. She took another step forward, then dropped her knife, collapsing to a knee.

The man dropped his bloody machete, his own wounds weeping as his face turned pale from the blood loss. He reached out toward the woman with his free hand.

"I'm sorry," he mumbled, blood bubbling out of his mouth. "I'm…"

Both crashed to the ground.

Blood pooled out toward the other prisoners who stared in horror.

"Well, that didn't go as planned," Pete said with a frown. "But since they're both dead, I guess we'll keep our promise."

He glanced back at Ray. "Feed them and give them their water."

This time Ray didn't protest.

Nick watched him hurry back to the crates as Pete walked to the barracks door.

"Wake me up if the drone picks up anything," he said. "I'm going to bed."

— 8 —

Fischer shivered from a blast of cold wind. He couldn't do much but turn his back to the icy air. The collar of his jacket was already zipped up to his chin, just under three days-worth of facial hair that did little to shield his face from the frigid air.

The temperature wasn't the only thing causing him to shiver. He was scared and not too proud to admit it.

It wasn't just his life or the lives of his men that he worried about, but the five thousand lives sheltering around the World Trade Center memorial. The vibroseis trucks and the bravery of those defending them would determine whether they survived the next few nights.

That terrified Fischer. Terrified him to his very core.

He looked to Commander Massey who didn't seem to show a shred of fear. She was a leader, and a damn good one for keeping her people alive under such conditions.

They stood with Tran and Chase at the edge of City Hall Park. The vibroseis trucks had arrived. One was stationed on Park Row and another on Broadway. Fischer's engineers had worked all afternoon to set up the trucks with the help of the outpost mechanics.

They all knew it wasn't just a cold front blowing in tonight.

The Variants were already moving underground, according to the science team. Something had gone wrong down there. Fischer didn't know the entire story but had heard the webbing had attacked Captain Beckham and a pair of soldiers.

He wasn't sure how that was possible, but he didn't doubt it had happened.

Massey squinted at the sunset. "They usually attack a few hours after dark. Unless we get lucky tonight."

"I'd go for a little luck right now and a case of cold beer," Chase said. "Hell, I'd even settle for warm beer. I'm not picky."

"We're out of beer, but there's some champagne sitting in crates back around the memorial," Massey said over her shoulder. "If we survive tonight, I'd be happy to bust them out and—"

The rhythmic beat of a chopper's rotors cut her off. Everyone stopped what they were doing to watch a bird cutting through the sky.

"There they go," Massey said. "In and out faster than a bad one-night stand. I guess I should have expected that from Command."

Fischer studied the Black Hawk as it shrank in the distance. Beckham and the science team were on board. He didn't exactly blame the commander for feeling like that, but he didn't like her tone.

"Captain Beckham was nearly killed today," he said. "And the science team will be back to finish the job, but they can't risk staying here tonight."

"Instead of running, I thought you guys were going to shore up our defenses," Massey said.

"That's exactly what we're doing," Fischer said. "These trucks will help us identify the Variant tunnels so you can blow 'em to hell."

"We're very good at blowing 'em to hell, Mr. Fischer. You just keep your end of the bargain and let me know when and where to blow them to hell."

She walked back toward the lifted pickup truck, leading them toward their next destination, Zucotti Park. Fischer confirmed the trucks there were ready too, before they moved to the final spot, Bogardus Garden.

This was where Fischer planned on spending his night.

The green space was the smallest and only had one truck. But it was guarded by an M1 Abrams. If he had to fight tonight, he wanted to be with the tank.

Massey parked her truck on the sidewalk behind the M1 Abrams and climbed down. Fischer and his men met her around the front of the pickup, all pausing to admire the massive tan tank with its cannon pointing down Broadway.

Concrete barriers stretched across Reade Street. Two machine gun nests perched on the rooftops of adjacent buildings to fire on any collaborators that might drive in.

Screeching metal over concrete came from Chambers Street where a city truck plowed demolished cars into a wall to block off the intersection. A crew of soldiers with razor wire waited nearby to add it to the top of the improvised barricade.

Somewhere on the taller buildings, the Apaches were on standby.

Hunkered down behind the open windows of apartments and offices were teams of snipers. Massey had told Fischer there were over thirty posted throughout the sites to provide another layer of defense.

Overall, he felt damn good about the defensive forces assembled here, but urban combat was a world apart from the battle in El Paso. Concrete didn't react the same way to the vibroseis trucks as packed dirt and loose rock did. But at least it would be harder for the Variants to tunnel through, which would buy them more time to deal with any threat.

"Anyone hungry? We got sandwiches," said one of the outpost soldiers.

"Starving," Chase said.

Fischer walked over to the center of the park. Two of his engineers were already there grabbing food. A soldier passed Massey a sandwich and she took it to a bench to sit by herself.

Fischer walked over to see if she wanted company.

"You mind if I sit?" he asked.

She gave her answer by patting the empty spot beside her.

"I figured you'd be heading back to the outpost," he said.

"And I figured you'd be heading back with the science team."

Fischer took a bite of the sandwich. It was surprisingly better than he had expected. He chalked it up to the fresh tomatoes. There was never anything better than homegrown veggies from the farm or garden, and it made him miss Fischer Fields even more.

"You always been a city gal?" he asked her.

"I'm from Alabama, born and raised. Came here for a job. Fell in love…"

He shot her a look.

"With the city, not a guy," she clarified. "Never thought much about going back south."

"To be honest, I never did care for this city."

"It wasn't for everyone, but I do miss it. Not all of it, but the food, culture, and parks in the summer. God."

"How about Alabama? You miss it ever?"

"Not a lick."

Fischer figured there was a story there but didn't ask. Instead, he thought of Texas. He would have given up just about anything to be watching a Texas sunset right now, but like New York, his homestead was probably never going to return to what it had been to him— home.

"You really think these trucks will save us tonight? Or for that matter, tomorrow, or the night after that?" Massey asked. "And even if they do, when does this end? We can't keep fighting forever."

"The president and her people are working on something," Fischer said. "That's what Doctor Lovato was here for."

"I know, but science? Science got us into this mess in the first place."

Fischer understood the doubt, but he had learned to trust Kate and Beckham. It hadn't taken him long to see they were doing everything they could to save what was left of their country.

Darkness stretched over the cityscape. Generators rumbled to life, powering the industrial lights that clicked on across the site. In the past, he might have worried about attracting Variants with the rattle of the machines. The sound and vibrations through the ground would draw every damn Variant here like a moth to a flame.

But tonight, that was the idea.

Distract the beasts away from the outpost and destroy them before they could surface.

"Commander, I got some final checks to do," Fischer said, standing. "Pleasure talking with you."

Massey got up too. "If you and your men do what you have promised, I look forward to enjoying a glass of champagne with you later."

Fischer tucked the rest of his sandwich into his pocket

and dipped his cowboy hat at her. Then he went over to the vibroseis truck where one of his longtime engineers, Brian Meyer, sat drinking a coffee.

"Everything good to go?" Fischer asked.

"Yes, sir." Meyer adjusted the Fischer Fields baseball cap over his balding head.

Fischer did one last lap around the site, joining Massey. Tran and Chase trailed them. It was going on seven o'clock and darkness flooded the city. Guards and workers spoke in hushed voices as the temperature dropped.

Minutes ticked by, and Fischer grew more anxious. A glass of whiskey and a good cigar would go miles at cooling that anxiety right about now.

Fischer adjusted the sling holding his shotgun over the front of his jacket. Tran and Chase readied their M4A1s. All across the site the demo teams and soldiers prepared their weapons.

For a fleeting moment the wind ceased, and silence fell like a veil over the site.

The quiet lasted long enough for Fischer to think that maybe it would be like this all night—that maybe the monsters would rest instead of attack.

But the demons rarely slept. Especially at night.

The radio crackled on his belt, making him flinch.

"We got movement, sir," Meyer said over the channel.

"I'm on my way."

Fischer and his guards ran for the truck with Massey close behind. Her radio came alive with reports from other sites.

"Christ, they're advancing on all fronts," she said.

They reached the truck, and Fischer stepped up to the cab where his engineer was working. "What do you see?"

Meyer tapped on his screen for the geophone readings. Lines bounced up and down, spiking faster in coordinates where the tunnels were forming or filled with Variants. His engineer matched those readings with a map of the surrounding streets.

"They're right below West Broadway and Reade," Fischer said. "Move the Abrams and troops to Chambers. Judging by the direction of their tunneling, that's where I think they're going to break through."

The tracks on the M1 Abrams crunched over the concrete. The cannon roved toward Chambers.

Fischer watched the monitor. The geophone went wild, mountains of spikes crossing the screen. The Variants were nearly beneath them now.

"Get ready!" Fischer shouted.

Massey gave orders over the radio as the tank and soldiers moved into position. The tunneling suddenly slowed to stop, and the geophone's readings flatlined.

"What in the Sam Hill..." he said.

Fischer slowly got out of the truck and walked a few steps for a better view of Chambers Street. Floodlights illuminated the cracked concrete. The demolition team waited behind the soldiers and concrete barriers topped with razor wire.

Massey instructed everyone to get back now that the Variants had tunneled under their defenses. Silence once again reclaimed the night, but this time it was filled with palpable tension.

Fischer swallowed. Seconds later he heard the clunk of metal against pavement.

Something suddenly shot into the air from the street.

It was a manhole cover.

The metal disc crashed back to the asphalt. A moment

later, concrete and dirt bulged around the manhole opening. Fischer's pulse quickened as he waited for the first sign of a beast crawling from the earth.

The tank cannon lowered, centering on the undulating street.

"Everyone back!" Massey yelled.

Once the men retreated to a safe distance, she called into her radio. "Fire!"

Fischer clamped his hands over his ears. The high explosive round erupted from the barrel of the tank and exploded into the pavement. A deafening roar shook over the street, and the burst showered the area in fire and dust.

Everyone crouched to avoid the shrapnel. Part of the street collapsed. Fractures fissured through the broken asphalt, chunks falling into the abyss below. But the creatures didn't erupt from the hole like Fischer had expected.

Massey motioned for the soldiers to advance, their rifles at the ready. Fischer followed Tran and Chase toward the curtain of smoke and dust drifting across the road.

He moved his finger to the trigger of his shotgun. His ears still rang from the explosion. A faint screech broke through his muddled hearing.

Another beast answered the call.

"Get ready," Massey said into her radio, a hint of fear in her voice.

A single Variant rose from the gaping hole in the road using long, muscular arms to pull its bony body out. It let out a howl and all at once, a swarm of beasts scurried from the hole.

"Open fire!" Massey shouted.

Gunfire cracked from all directions, and a fierce volley cut down the vanguard of monsters. One of the beasts escaped the dying masses of its brethren. Fischer fired at the charging beast, sending the monster back to the hell from where it had come.

The other creatures scattered, dropping from the torrent of rounds. Sniper fire took down the beasts escaping the slaughter.

More starving creatures streamed out of the sunken street. Fischer let loose another round. The buckshot tore a Variant off its feet.

A loud clicking noise cut through the gunfire. Fischer knew the sound well. It was one he would never forget from the horrors at his ranch. He spotted the source—an Alpha emerging from the dust and smoke, its batlike ears twitching, huge shoulders coursing with muscle.

"Kill the Alpha!" he shouted.

Tran and Chase followed him for a better firing position. They stopped near a parked Humvee and opened fire at the monstrous creature as it advanced with a pack of sinewy Variants toward the tank.

Fischer squeezed the trigger again, sending a round into the Alpha's back. Blood sprayed from its devastated flesh, but it wasn't dead yet. It spun toward him, milky eyes seeming to stare right at him. He pumped in another shell and fired. The beast's ugly face disappeared in a spray of blood, bone, and brains.

"Demo team, now!" Massey yelled.

Two of the men threw grenades into the opening. Another threw what looked like a satchel charge. Fischer, Tran, and Chase dove to the ground and covered their ears.

Tremors rumbled through the ground as the

explosives detonated underground.

He uncovered his ears as the smoke dissipated, revealing a grotesque scene of dead and dying beasts. Bodies littered the street and pavement with body parts scattered in pools of blood.

Massey reached down to Fischer, and he took her hand, rising to his feet.

"They're done," she said. "Reload and get ready, because that was just the first wave."

***

The moon hung full in the sky, accompanied by a spray of white stars. Fitz and Rico hid behind the large rocks jutting up from the sandy beach. He pressed a pair of binoculars to his eyes.

He didn't need NVGs to scope the ocean. The moonlight was more than enough to reveal the silhouette of the ship still adrift. On board was everything Team Ghost needed, from medicine to a radio. And maybe even more importantly, answers about the frightening Chimeras.

Dohi prepared the life raft they had salvaged from the C-130. The raft itself didn't have a motor, but Mendez and Ace had spent the day fixing it with one. The duo had tracked down an old dockyard with a dozen broken boats, most in catastrophic disrepair. But they had managed to find a small rotted fishing boat inside a shed.

The hull was damaged which was likely why it had been in the middle of repair in the shed. Its attached outboard motor was in better shape and had appeared promising to Ace. He had employed his mechanical aptitude and restored the old motor just enough that it worked on their life raft.

Even better, it was a four-stroke outboard fishing motor compatible with kerosene fuels. Ace had explained they could use fuel still in the C-130.

The old motor wasn't silent, but quiet enough to get them close to the ship without being spotted. They had also scrounged up enough old netting and dark paint at the dockyard to conceal the bright-yellow of the rubber raft.

Rico reached over and squeezed his hand, an unusual display of affection in the field. They both knew how dangerous this mission was.

"You need me out there," she said.

"Dohi and I will be faster on our own. I'll spend too much time worrying about you if you're with us."

"And you think I won't worry here?"

Fitz sighed. "There's no one I trust more than you. I need you to keep the injured Wolfhounds safe and…"

"Don't even say it, Fitzie."

"If we don't make it back by morning, you have to go on without us. Get up to San Francisco or something," Fitz said. "Reaching command, even if that means leaving the Wolfhounds behind, is our mission now. They need to know about the Chimeras."

Rico gave him that look that told him she wanted to argue. To his relief, she said nothing.

One of the three helicopters suddenly lifted from the ship. Another followed, pulling into the star-filled sky and heading northeast.

Two less choppers also meant less troops aboard the ship.

"Shit, now might be our best chance," Fitz said. "I've got to go."

He pulled Rico close to him. He felt her warmth, the emotion flowing between them until he drew away.

"Come back to me safe, Fitzie," she said.

"I will."

Dohi pushed the camouflaged raft out into the surf. Fitz hopped in and Dohi followed. He started the small motor while Fitz prepared his gear.

The motor jostled around on the improvised attachment Ace had rigged up. But it worked, pushing them out to the ocean.

Fitz checked over his suppressed M4A1, then patted his tac vest. Only two magazines remained besides the one in his rifle. They were desperately low on ammunition. But if he could help it, he didn't plan on firing a single bullet.

Doing so was a last resort.

The craft advanced into the inky night as Fitz studied their target. The ship appeared to be an old freighter that had been retrofitted into a war vessel of sorts. Machine guns were posted along the gunwales. Most of the shipping containers had been cleared from the decks, making room for the helicopters.

He didn't see any patrolling guards, which was odd.

Normally Team Ghost didn't get this lucky. He pointed to a maintenance ladder rung. Dohi motored over to the hull. They quickly tied the craft to a rung.

Dohi scaled the ladder, and Fitz followed to the top deck. They climbed over the edge near the remaining chopper. The imposing superstructure loomed near the stern, opposite where they had boarded the vessel.

Fitz spotted two guards who patrolled near the structure with rifles. Neither seemed particularly anxious, strolling in an almost relaxed manner between the shipping containers.

If they were Chimeras, Fitz wondered if they had enhanced smell and hearing like a Variant. All the more reason to be cautious.

He signaled Dohi to start toward a hatch in the superstructure. They used the rows of shipping containers along the deck for cover. Fitz did his best to keep his prosthetics from tapping too loudly against the slick deck.

Both men crouched when footsteps sounded on the other side of the shipping containers. Dohi drew his blade and Fitz did the same.

His heartbeat pulsed loudly in his ears. He wondered if the hyper-predator soldiers could hear it.

The sound of the footsteps changed direction and Fitz gave Dohi the order to head for the hatch. Both got there without being spotted. But the hatch resisted, screeching slightly as Dohi opened it.

Fitz winced and shouldered his rifle, waiting to see if anyone outside had heard. When no one responded, Dohi pried the hatch open further, and they squeezed through.

The deck inside was illuminated in red lights, bathing the place in a hellish glow. Fitz took lead this time. He didn't know exactly where he was going and proceeded slowly.

He cleared two passages before the sound of boots came again. The noise echoed behind them.

Or was that in front of them?

Fitz continued down the passage that abruptly ended at a large hatch. A sign above read CARGO BAY in half-peeling big black letters. The sound of boot steps came again, louder now. Definitely coming from the corridor behind them.

They had no other choice but to go forward. Fitz

opened the hatch.

What they found inside was not a cargo bay. Clean white walls and benchtops furnished the space, looking eerily like a lab. Huge silver drums that looked like bioreactors stood in the middle of the room.

Equipment buzzed between banks of microscopes and computers.

Fitz heard voices at the end of the vast room along with the squawk of a radio. He and Dohi snuck that way using the shelter of the lab benches.

When they reached the other end, Fitz saw two men with surgical masks and scrubs covered in blood.

A man with gray skin lay sprawled across an operating table between them.

Not a man, Fitz realized.

Claws and bony features told him the patient was a Chimera. An endotracheal tube attached to a ventilator was jammed into its open mouth.

Fitz leaned in for a better look, seeing clamps inserted between the creature's broken ribs, holding the chest cavity open. One of the doctors reached through the opening.

The patient twitched slightly, and his eyes blinked.

Somehow, the patient was wide awake. He squirmed slightly each time the doctors prodded an organ. Metal restraints kept him in place and some sort of muzzle had his jaw locked around the endotracheal tube.

Reptilian eyes flitted toward Fitz, and before he could back away the Chimera started shaking. The surgeons turned toward Fitz.

He crouched back, but it was too late.

One surgeon started to run across the room toward an intraship telephone on the bulkhead.

"Stop him," Fitz said.

Dohi ran down the man and tackled him.

Fitz slammed into the other. The surgeon opened his mouth to scream, but Fitz yanked the scalpel from his grip and slid it across his neck. Blood bubbled from the fresh wound, and Fitz dropped the man to the deck.

The man writhed, grasping uselessly at the deep gash.

On the table, the patient fought the restraints.

Fitz hurried over, catching a drift of the terrible odor leaking from the beast's open chest. The half-man, or whatever he was, chewed through his endotracheal tube, then started to rip the tube out. Fitz brought his blade down hard into the skull.

Dohi wiped his hatchet on the scrubs of the other dead surgeon.

"What is this black magic?" he muttered.

"Don't know, but we need medicine, a radio, and then we need to leave," Fitz said.

After finding antibiotics, they moved to another hatch. It opened to a dark, narrow passage framed with clear acrylic walls. Fitz hit a switch, light blooming over the cells behind the translucent partitions.

He flinched when he saw the half-man creatures imprisoned in each. Two of the beasts slapped the clear plastic like primates. Other Chimeras mashed their sucker mouths against the partitions, leaving trails of saliva.

"These bastards must be testing VX-99 again, but how?" Dohi said.

Fitz didn't plan on sticking around to find out. Eventually someone would check on those surgeons. He left the lab and led the way to another corridor lined with hatches.

Dohi pointed at one that said ARMORY.

As soon as he opened it, both men stumbled back. A Chimera soldier stood guard inside. The monster looked equally as shocked.

Fitz put a suppressed burst into the chest, painting the bulkhead with blood. The beastly man slumped to the deck.

Dohi moved around the body and went to the weapon racks of rifles.

"Jackpot," he said.

"Holy shit," Fitz said.

Crates of supplies, grenades, and ammunition rested against the bulkhead. Stacks of body armor, MBITRs, and a few satellite phones were stored on shelves. For the first time since they had arrived in California, Fitz felt a glimmer of hope.

They scooped up the sat phones and batteries first, then shoveled magazines and grenades into their packs.

"Rig the C-4," Fitz said. "We'll need a distraction."

They set a few charges in the armory, then backtracked through the lab, placing explosives there, too. If this lab was vital to their enemies, it was even more vital that he and Dohi destroyed it.

Then they took off through the corridors the way they had come, quietly as possible. Boot steps and voices stopped them. Fitz listened, his heart racing until he realized they were talking casually, their voices coming out in growling rasps.

He continued, finding another intersection to take a new route back to the top deck. As he went to open the exit hatch, he heard the thump of chopper blades. It might be the last one finally leaving—or maybe the others had returned.

There was only one way to find out.

He yanked the lever handle and opened the hatch, his heart skipping a beat when he saw it was the latter. The side door opened, disgorging a half-dozen troops.

Fitz thought for a moment about finding a route below deck to the ship's aft, but Dohi tapped him on the shoulder. More soldiers were coming from behind them in the passage.

An alarm suddenly blared.

Everything seemed to go in slow motion after that.

There was only one way out of this mess—to fight.

Fitz nodded at Dohi who launched a grenade down the passage. Then he raised his rifle and followed Fitz onto the deck. The hatch clanked closed, commanding the attention of the six soldiers that had gotten out of the chopper.

Fitz open fired, and Dohi did the same. Three of their targets went down right away, and two more dove for cover. Only one brought up a weapon to fire, but Fitz put a bullet between the Chimera's reptilian eyes before the beast could squeeze off a shot.

An explosion boomed from the grenade.

Dohi tossed another grenade near the chopper as he ran with Fitz between the shipping containers. Bullets sparked over the deck.

The second grenade boomed, drowning the chatter of gunfire.

"Go, go, go!" Fitz yelled.

They sprinted the rest of the way over the deck until they reached the gunwale. He tossed the bags of supplies into the boat, but there was no time to climb down the maintenance ladder.

Instead, Fitz threw himself over the side. He fell, arms wheeling before splashing beneath the frigid water's surface. He kicked back up, gasping for air. Grasping the life raft, he pulled himself in. Dohi plunged into the water afterward, and Fitz helped yank him in.

Fitz untied the boat as Dohi tried to start the motor, but it wouldn't turn over.

Raising his weapon, Fitz prepared to fire.

They were sitting ducks now.

"Come on," Fitz said.

"I'm trying," Dohi grumbled.

Cursing, Fitz saw the glint of rifles as soldiers lined the gunwale taking aim. He fired a burst to keep them back. Then he pulled out the C4 detonator and squeezed the trigger.

The first series of explosions sounded like the clap of distant thunder. More explosions followed, a chain-reaction from the ordnance stored down there.

Fitz hit the next detonator. Another fiery blast tore up from the belly of the ship. Pieces of flaming debris were thrown into the sky as Dohi finally started the motor.

Shrapnel and flaming hunks of metal fell around them, sizzling when they hit the water. Fitz aimed his rifle again at the gunwale just in case any of the beasts reemerged.

As they motored away, a few of the beasts jumped, their bodies flaming.

Fitz finally started to relax as the boat sank.

When they finally made it back to shore, Rico ran to meet them. Fitz jumped out of the life raft and wrapped her into his arms. For the first time since they had landed in this God-forsaken place, he felt Team Ghost had finally pulled off a real victory.

And they finally had a chance to change the course of this war.

At midnight, President Ringgold sat alone in the EOC's briefing room in the Long Island bunker, waiting for her next SITREP. She longed to see her friends, Beckham and Kate, but after a rough day, the duo was resting with Javier. She had no desire to interrupt their hard-earned family time.

She sighed. The thought of coffee or some caffeine to keep her focused danced over her mind, but supplies here were meager. While she had avoided looking at mirrors too much, she'd stolen a glance at herself in her quarters before she had come up here.

The new wrinkles, bags under her eyes, and gray in her hair had made her wonder if she was becoming a different person.

Long before the war, she had seen how the stress of a presidency aged a person. With everything she had endured in her tenure as president, it was no surprise her body had suffered.

She quickly realized how selfish it was to worry about herself like that.

So what if she looked older?

You're alive. That's more than can be said for thousands and thousands of your people. People that you're responsible for.

She shook her head. The exhaustion and the fear of what her team was about to report had her on edge.

Someone rapped on her door.

"Come in."

Chief of Staff James Soprano entered. "Madam President, General Souza and Lieutenant Festa are here with a SITREP."

"Thank you."

The duo walked in, and Soprano closed the door, waiting outside.

"Madam President," they greeted her in turn.

"Gentlemen, please have a seat."

They took spots across from her at the table.

General Souza shuffled a few papers in his hands. "I'll begin with the most pressing. Minutes ago, we received word from Team Ghost in California."

Ringgold's heart nearly leapt from her chest. She had been all but certain they had been lost, but Beckham was right in not counting them out. Team Ghost always found a way to survive. "That's excellent news. Did they retrieve the SDS equipment?"

"We're not quite sure yet," Souza said.

Ringgold frowned. "Not sure?"

Festa took over. "The laboratory campus was taken over by what they believed were hostile independent colonists," he said. "Team Ghost also encountered a powerful paramilitary group which we believe are connected to the Variants and collaborators."

Ringgold rubbed her temples, trying to understand how these paramilitary groups had survived on the West Coast.

"Team Ghost was able to recover some equipment with the help of the Wolfhounds, who took heavy casualties, but it's unclear if the technology works," Festa said. "Most of it was damaged in an attack by this unknown paramilitary group."

He went on to brief her on all the events that had transpired from the moment Team Ghost had infiltrated the National Accelerator Laboratory to the mission to raid the freighter anchored off the coast.

"Team Ghost is with the surviving Wolfhounds now and waiting for evac," Festa said.

"There's something else," Souza said. "The paramilitary group consists of hybrid soldiers—half man, half Variant."

"Chimeras is what Master Sergeant Fitz called them," Festa said.

Souza nodded. "Whatever we end up calling them doesn't really matter. What matters is someone has continued the VX-99 program all this time, and for all we know these new soldiers will join the fight."

Ringgold wanted to slap the table out of anger. She simply couldn't understand the evil behind these masterminds who had reignited the nightmarish VX-99 program.

She let out a long sigh.

"I'm sorry, Madam President." Festa said.

"There's more?" she asked.

Festa swallowed.

"We have footage from the scouts I deployed after the nuclear attacks," Souza said. "Bring it up, Frank."

Festa set up his laptop so Ringgold could see the screen. "This is from a recon unit in Saint Louis."

With a click on the keypad, the video sprang to life. The feed seemed to be recorded on a camera from the front passenger seat of an armored scout vehicle.

"Holy shit," a recorded voice said.

The vehicle was driving over a highway, crossing the Mississippi River. Fires blazed across what had once been downtown, evident only by the skeletal scaffolding of towers that hadn't yet collapsed.

Ringgold noticed the famous Gateway Arch—or at least what was left of it. The middle of the arch had collapsed. All that remained were the hooked bottom halves of the landmark. Each looked like an enormous Variant fang jutting from the earth.

"Wait, wait!" one of the voices behind the camera said. "Zoom in!"

The camera's view of the arch magnified toward one of the remaining halves of the arch. Shapes scaled the structure, illuminated by the fires flickering over the park below.

"Variants," Ringgold whispered.

The camera finished zooming in. The monsters crawled over the remnants of the arch. Fresh red webbing covered the structures, too.

"How did the webbing survive the bombing and fires?" Ringgold asked.

"It didn't," Souza said. "The webbing you see is all new growth."

Ringgold's stomach churned. "So our sacrifices here were for nothing."

"The nukes killed countless Variants, but enough survived to start over," Souza said, massaging the bridge of his nose. "But there's more."

Festa clicked the keypad again. "This is Chicago."

Images of broken and smoldering skyscrapers flashed over the screen. Variants crawled over the massive Ferris wheel on Navy Pier. It was completely covered in new, throbbing red webbing.

"Kansas City," Festa said next.

The Heart of America Bridge had snapped and

collapsed into the Missouri River. But that didn't bother the Variants who had reconstructed their own rope bridge consisting of webbing between both sides of the ash-covered city.

"Dallas," Festa said.

Downtown was nothing but ruins. The videos showed a Texas thunderstorm squashing the scattered fires. Between flashes of lightning, Variants scrambled over the streets, unperturbed by the deadly radiation undoubtedly seeping into their flesh.

"The scenes are the same all over," Festa said. "Our smaller outposts haven't fared much better. Outpost Portland was completely leveled in the bombing run. We haven't found any survivors."

Ringgold's heart sank at the terrible news. She listened as he listed off other outposts they had lost, too. All of them wiped out.

"We hit them hard, but the Variants don't retreat and regroup like a normal enemy," Souza said. "They keep hitting us before we can recover."

"Our recon teams are working with whatever tech is still available in the field to track collaborator and Variant movements." Festa spread a map between them with arrows. "I haven't updated this map for a few hours. By morning, it'll likely change."

Ringgold was afraid to ask, but she had to know. "After the nukes, what kind of numbers are we facing?"

"Our analysts are having a difficult time getting an accurate count," Souza said coldly. "But if I had to estimate, I would put the collaborators at around a few thousand. The Variants could number twenty thousand. But with their offspring, it could be triple that."

"We want to be clear these numbers are not accurate," Festa said. "The only way to know for sure is if the science team can get us access to their communications."

Ringgold didn't want to bother Kate and Beckham after everything they had endured, but she needed them. She gave the order to retrieve them and Festa left her with Souza.

For a moment they sat in silence. She liked the general, but she couldn't help but feel like he and much of the leadership in Central Command had let her down. But then again, they probably blamed her for what was happening, too.

Right now, blaming others was not going to solve anything. Blame would be useless if they were all dead. Learning from their mistakes and moving forward was the only thing keeping them alive.

A couple minutes later, Kate, Beckham, and Horn entered and joined them at the table. Ringgold listened as Festa and Souza brought them up to speed on everything that had occurred over the past few hours.

Beckham was relieved to hear the team was alive, but after the relief, there was shock, and questions.

"I don't… I don't believe it. Or maybe I just don't want to," Kate said. "Variant hybrids—Chimeras—that can fire a gun and talk?"

"I'm afraid so," Souza said.

"Christ," Beckham said.

"You sure Fitz isn't seeing shit?" Horn asked.

"The whole team backed up his report," Souza said.

Horn shook his head. "I know, it's just…"

"If these Chimeras can fire weapons, then they are far more dangerous than any Variants we've fought," Beckham said.

119

Kate agreed with a nod. "First masterminds, bats, hounds, and the webbing network. Whoever's behind all this has been busy over the past decade. Creating Chimeras is perhaps the most logical next step—blending the best of humankind with the worst of the monsters."

"We have to find out who is behind this madness," Beckham said. "That's the only way to end this."

Ringgold looked to Kate. "I know your work was interrupted, but how close are we to locating the actual mastermind responsible for all of this Variant-collaborator organization?"

"I'm afraid we're much further from that than I initially thought."

A flush of frustration jolted Ringgold. "I thought everything we did with the mastermind in Manchester was supposed to be enough."

"It was enough for the mastermind in the lab, but the Variants and collaborators are passing all kinds of communications through the network we didn't anticipate. We can hardly listen and understand them, much less disrupt their messages."

"So how do we then?"

"It seems the masterminds transmit on one frequency, while the smaller Variants and collaborators use others. We were trying to translate them when we were extracted."

"So you need to go back to the tunnels."

Kate pursed her lips, looking at Beckham. "Yeah, that's the only way."

"Assuming the tunnels are even still there," Festa said. "Lower Manhattan is taking a beating tonight."

"When it's clear, we'll need all the time we can get," Kate said. "Sammy estimates another day or so at least. It could be more if we run into trouble like today. Whatever it takes, we have to get back there or somewhere with the webbing to do this."

"I'll support your mission with as many resources as we can spare," Ringgold said.

"Thank you," Kate replied. "I promise we'll do as much as we can here with the sample signaling data we recorded from the field."

"In the meantime, we've got another important matter." Ringgold turned to the retired operators who weren't so retired after all. "Captain Beckham, Master Sergeant Horn, Team Ghost is stranded with valuable intel and our SDS equipment. We need to evac them."

Kate looked at Beckham again. They exchanged a quick nod.

"When do we leave?" he asked.

***

Beckham sat in the troop hold of a Black Hawk, ready to go back to war.

Across from him, a strike team of six Army Rangers slept. Horn had dozed off too, his head bumping up and down slightly from the unsteady ride. His snores sounded like a chainsaw.

It was two in the morning, and the pilots were flying dark to avoid detection by collaborators. With talk of super-soldier Chimeras and the advanced weaponry they had at their disposal, it was the safest way to cross enemy territory.

Enemy territory, Beckham thought.

He looked out the cockpit, seeing nothing but darkness. They had truly entered the dark ages broaching extinction now, and humanity was to blame—not the monsters.

Men *were* the monsters. It was men who had developed VX-99 in the first place, and it was men now aiding in the resurgence of the beasts.

He closed his eyes, but he was too angry to sleep.

They were somewhere over Pennsylvania, heading toward Outpost Cleveland. The outpost was on the frontlines. From what Beckham had heard, it was hanging on by a thread. The LZ would be dangerous, especially with the reports of ongoing attacks. They had no choice but to land there to transfer to an available C-130 that would take them the rest of the way to California.

Most other aircraft were being used to evacuate civilians to safer outposts on the Eastern seaboard. This particular plane had taken damage the night before and had subsequently been stranded in Cleveland. Mechanics were supposed to be finishing up repairs now. Beckham hoped it would be ready when they landed.

Any delay in getting to Team Ghost could cost them their lives.

Lights on the horizon caught Beckham's attention. He leaned closer to the window. His vision blurred in his injured eye again, partially due to exhaustion.

But he didn't need perfect vision to make out the inferno in the distance. The blaze stretched across miles of terrain.

He put on a headset, got up from his seat, and made his way to the cockpit. "What's burning?"

Both pilots had pushed up their night vision optics as they looked at the glare to their south.

"That was Pittsburgh," said a pilot. "Hasn't stopped burning since the nuke hit."

A lump formed in Beckham's throat. Hearing that Pittsburgh was hit by a nuclear strike had been disheartening enough. Seeing it in reality after it had become hell on earth was worse.

He stayed in the cockpit, watching as they flew closer.

A crater in the middle of the city showed where buildings had been swept away in the tidal wave of fire. Flames consumed the land around the impact zone, chewing through old neighborhoods in another of America's most iconic cities.

Having seen enough of the horrific sight, Beckham returned to his seat. Most of the Rangers were still sleeping but Horn was awake now.

"'Sup, boss?" he asked, stretching his big arms.

"We're passing Pittsburgh."

Horn looked toward the cockpit.

Big white flakes now plastered the plexiglass.

"That snow?" Horn asked. "Bit early, isn't it?"

"Too big to be snow," Beckham said.

He checked the window behind them. The flakes left a black powder.

"That's ash," came a voice across the troop hold.

It was Sergeant Gray, a hulking dark-skinned man who reminded Beckham of a long-deceased Ranger that had fought with Team Ghost during the first war—a man named Tank because of his size and strength.

Horn sat up straighter, fully alert. He drew in a deep breath and shook his head. "Jesus."

"People and monsters," said another Ranger wearing eyeglasses named Nathan Brooks.

"Huh?" Gray said.

"The ash," said Brooks. "It's not just the buildings and trees. It's the remains of humans and Variants, too."

Horn ignored the Rangers and nudged Beckham's arm. "You get any shuteye?"

"Not really."

"You'll need it for Cali."

"I know."

Horn was right, but closing his eyes felt like a betrayal to the people who had died from the nuclear blast and the all-consuming flames. The military hadn't been able to evacuate everyone here in time when the bomb dropped.

"Seriously, boss, get some sleep," Horn entreated. "You used to nap in the shittiest conditions."

"That was before I had a family and the entire world was teetering on extinction."

"Yeah...and that's why you need your sleep."

Beckham nodded. "You win."

Sleep would help him save people.

All it takes is all you got, he thought.

The Marine Corps quote helped ease that burden slightly. He repeated those words in his head like a mantra until his mind cleared. Fatigue sucked him in, and he drifted off.

A voice jerked him awake sometime later.

"We got a hot LZ!" shouted one of the pilots.

Adrenaline cut through Beckham's groggy mind.

The Rangers were already slamming magazines into their rifles as the bird began its descent. Brooks, the corporal with the glasses, pumped shells into a shotgun.

Beckham glanced out the window behind him. He couldn't see much, but the apocalyptic urban landscape unfolding before him must have been Cleveland—or at least what was left of it.

"Captain Beckham, I'm not sure putting down is a good idea," said the primary pilot.

Beckham stood and went back to the cockpit. Flames scraped toward the sky from piles of rubble and toppled buildings.

Tracer rounds split the darkness.

Scanning the ground, Beckham saw the freeway that had been cleared of vehicles. The C-130 sat there, waiting.

"Our ride's still there," Beckham said. "Did they finish the repairs?"

"Yes, but I really don't want to drop you boys off in that shit show," the primary pilot said. "Some of the guards are already retreating with the mechanics."

He could have been pissed at them for running from the fight, but looking at the destruction surrounding them, it was hard to blame them.

A handful of military vehicles on the makeshift runway fled the defensive perimeter set up around the LZ. In the glow of industrial lights, Beckham spotted two small single-prop planes waiting to take off.

Muzzle flashes sparkled across the road as shadowy figures advanced on the vehicles.

"We have to get on the C-130," Beckham said. "We'll clear a path so you can take us down."

"Captain…" said the pilot.

"That's an order," Beckham said.

He returned to the troop hold and directed the other soldiers to put on their night vision goggles.

"Change of plans," Beckham said, shouting to be heard over the blast of the bird's rotors. "We're going to clear the LZ so the pilots can touch down."

The Rangers all nodded, and Horn stepped up to the crew chief who was preparing the M240 in the open door.

"Step aside, buttercup," he said.

The crew chief backed away, and Beckham handed

him a spare rifle to use instead. They opened the opposite door, and the Rangers moved into firing positions.

Even in the past few minutes, monsters had streamed toward the airfield. On both sides, they slammed into the fences. One section had already come down.

Creatures trampled over it, bolting toward the meager defenses. It was hard to see much, despite the optics. But Beckham spotted a few brave remaining soldiers, three armored vehicles, and two mobile trailers set up on the shoulder of the freeway.

Half the convoy had already fled. Those vehicles had pulled some of the Variants away from the C-130, but more monsters descended from the surrounding neighborhoods toward the broken fence.

The chopper circled, giving Beckham a better view from another angle. He flipped up his NVGs. The generator-run floodlights on the ground illuminated a group of at least ten soldiers fighting back the beasts approaching the tail of the C-130.

A massive fire ball suddenly blasted out of a building in the center of the outpost, distracting Beckham for a moment.

Maybe the collaborators had hit the outpost from the inside too, but he couldn't worry about that now. Their job was to clear this area, get on the plane, and retrieve Team Ghost.

The chopper lowered and Beckham gave the order to open fire.

The bark of the M240 rang out as Horn went to work, raking the barrel like an artist. He painted a group of Variants that were still climbing a fence, then turned his aim on a group that had already climbed over and were making a dash for the armored vehicles.

Everyone in the Black Hawk who had a firing zone squeezed off calculated shots, picking off the Variants. The dying creatures flopped over the highway, but more surged over the collapsed fence, rushing in from the ruined city surrounding the interstate.

"Keep them away from the plane!" Beckham shouted.

The chopper lowered as the Rangers fired. Targeting the moving beasts from above wasn't easy, especially in the dark. But the men had experience, and with Horn's help, they cleared a wide enough swathe to ensure a landing site.

In the distance, Beckham noticed a swarming cloud against the moon and starlight. Distant fires bloomed on the top of buildings where this erratic cloud touched.

Bats.

"Incoming!" Beckham shouted. "Bats headed our way!"

He retreated into the troop hold and grabbed Horn. A wave of explosive-laden, VX-99 modified creatures slammed into the cockpit, splattering blood on the plexiglass. The pilots screamed in shock and pushed the chopper down toward the ground to avoid the cloud.

"Bail, bail!" someone shouted.

Alarms blared throughout the bird. The voices of the pilots and panicked Rangers were silenced in a sudden eruption of fire. An explosion ripped through the plexiglass and metal.

Adrenaline churned through Beckham, making the world seem to slow around him.

He was still holding onto Horn, and together they jumped, plummeting toward the concrete. They fell nearly six feet before slamming against the pavement.

The impact knocked the wind from Beckham's lungs.

Pain shot through his joints. He rolled, stopping on his back.

Fighting through the agony, Beckham pushed himself to his knees, keeping low. Horn lay prone, blood running down his nostrils.

They watched as the burning chopper spun out of control, the cockpit completely enveloped by flames.

Two Rangers jumped out before the bird slammed into the shoulder of the road, exploding in a fireball. Shrapnel seared through the air.

Beckham turned from the catastrophe when he heard the fearsome growls of Variants. Gunfire lanced into the charging monsters.

A hand grabbed Beckham, pulling him up. The group of soldiers defending the C-130 had come to help, laying down covering fire.

Muddled voices came from all directions, but Beckham couldn't make them out due to the ringing in his ears.

In partial shock, he stumbled forward like a drunk, trying to follow the soldiers up the ramp and into the belly of the aircraft. Horn turned and helped Beckham inside.

Brooks and one other Ranger had already made it into the troop hold.

The outpost soldiers standing guard all piled in, shouting things that Beckham still couldn't hear. He felt the rumble of the engines as the plane pulled forward.

Variants flooded the freeway. They raced after the plane on all fours. Their sucker lips tore back into snarls as they dashed after the plane, only to be blocked out with the rear ramp clicking shut.

Panting, Horn collapsed on the deck.

"Jesus," he groaned.

Beckham could hear that. He rolled over to Horn. "You okay, Big Horn?"

"Yeah, I think so. You?"

"I'm alive," Beckham replied.

The outpost soldiers dropped into jump seats as the plane climbed from its improvised runway. Many of their faces were painted in horror. Horror that Beckham knew all too well. Escaping death wasn't new to him or these men, but losing brothers never got easier.

He pulled himself into a seat, and Horn followed suit. The engines roared as the plane pulled away from the carnage.

It was a while before anyone spoke.

"I... I lost my glasses," came a voice.

Beckham looked over to see Brooks.

"Least you made it out," said the other surviving Ranger. "What the fuck were those things?"

"Bats," Horn said. "Rigged with explosives."

"They didn't look like bats," the man replied. "They were huge!"

"The monsters are mutated by VX-99," Beckham said. "They're larger and far more aggressive than normal bats."

A few curses and angry voices followed. Beckham rested his head against the bulkhead. Something told him this was the easy part of what lay ahead.

He closed his eyes, and this time, he fell right asleep.

— 10 —

The roar of fighter jets woke Timothy violently. He shot out of his sleeping bag. Ruckley was already at the window with her rifle, peering at the sky through the cracked glass of the abandoned farmhouse they had found.

Moonlight glowed on her face as she looked out over a field overgrown with weeds. He searched the stars for the fighters but didn't see them. The growl slowly faded, until it was nothing but a low rumble.

"At least we're still in the fight," Timothy said.

"Of course, we are," Ruckley said.

She sounded confident, but after Outpost Portland, she had to know the Variants and the collaborators were winning this war.

Timothy sat back on his sleeping bag and took a sip of water from his bottle. They had been lucky to find a few camping supplies and other necessities stocked in this house. It had offered a refuge for the night, giving them the time to plan their next steps.

Ruckley looked at her watch. "I better relieve Neeland."

The young Ranger was holding watch in the living room downstairs. Timothy had already served his rotation. He had spent most of the time staring out the windows at the field, picturing Variants prowling through the tall weeds.

He had imagined every rustling stalk of grass might be a monster. It had been unnerving waiting for an attack.

He was glad his shift was over.

"See you in a few hours," Ruckley whispered.

Timothy rested on the sleeping bag and a pillow he had found. His body was dog-tired, but the sound of fighter jets meant he wasn't falling back asleep any time soon.

He found himself thinking of how nice it would be to sleep on a real mattress again. Every bed in this house was covered in dark stains and mold from water leaking through the ceiling.

He propped the pillow under his head and tried to think of happy memories, goading his mind to relax. Times when he and his father had spent their nights on Peaks Island fishing or those hot summer days diving for lobsters with spearguns.

He missed those moments of peace so much. More than anything, he just missed being with his father. Feeling his presence, knowing he was always there with words of reassurance or a long conversation when Timothy needed it.

Darker images flooded his mind.

That last night on the island, running through the woods. The gunshots. Returning to the bunker to see his father cold, lifeless. Pain turned to fear, forcing his eyelids open.

He should have stayed in that bunker with his dad. He would have rather died then by his father's side. Fighting instead of running with only decaying memories to hold onto.

Anger and guilt tore at his insides, a monster more powerful than a Variant. Sleep would be impossible now.

He sat up and rubbed his eyes, then heard a creak in the stairwell outside the bedroom.

Must be Neeland, he thought.

Timothy watched the open door, waiting for the young Army Ranger to appear.

But it wasn't Neeland who entered.

Ruckley stepped into the room, a mask of worry on her face.

Timothy instinctively grabbed his gun. "What is it?"

"Neeland's gone," she said. "Something might be wrong. Grab your things."

"Are we leaving?" Timothy asked, confused. "Maybe he's taking a shit."

None of the toilets in the house had been working, and they'd been forced to use a spot in the backyard.

"Maybe, but we can't risk it. Let's go."

Timothy stuffed his meager belongings into his backpack and heaved it over his back. He left the sleeping bag and pillow. Then he followed her down the stairs.

At the ground floor, she raised her rifle and strode out, clearing the room.

Timothy followed, bringing his gun up.

Two couches and a broken coffee table furnished the living room. There was no sign of Neeland. The weak moonlight streaming through the windows didn't reveal much. He didn't see any broken glass, blood, or trampled carpet to indicate a struggle or forced entry.

If there had been, Timothy would have heard it.

Ruckley led them through the living room into the kitchen. The curtains around an open sliding door blew in the breeze. That door led to the deck and Timothy joined her out there in the cool night.

The backyard was an acre of trees and grass that

bordered an old farm field filled with weeds almost as tall as Timothy.

Branches from the trees groaned and snapped in the breeze, masking any popping joints of prowling Variants.

Ruckley took the stairs down to the grass, using her night vision optics to check the area. Clouds passed over the moon, leaving Timothy nearly blind. He waited for it to pass, squinting to make out the shadowy shapes around him.

He briefly considered calling out for Neeland. But if the Ranger was taking a shit, he would return. If he wasn't, then yelling for the man was tantamount to calling all the Variants lurking in the area to dinner.

The clouds rolled away, and the moon again spread a carpet of white over the terrain. Timothy caught up to Ruckley and walked beside her. She suddenly stopped before a line of trees fencing off the property from the fields.

The tall weeds swayed in the wind like waves, back and forth. Almost hypnotic.

Timothy aimed his rifle over the field, waiting for Variants to come bounding out. His finger went to the trigger, and he steadied his breathing.

Ears strained, he listened for the noises of the beasts. Instead of snapping jaws and nightmarish screeches, all he heard were the rustling branches and the whistle of the wind.

"Where the hell did he go?" Ruckley whispered.

She turned, then froze, staring at the house through her NVGs.

Timothy didn't see anything. "What?"

Ruckley took a step forward and aimed her rifle at the barns on the eastern side of the property about twenty yards from the main house.

"Someone's watching us," she said. "Get ready to run."

Timothy felt a ball forming in his throat. It wasn't just Variants out there. As the implications crossed his mind, he found himself almost hoping it was collaborators.

No, not if they have the drop, he thought.

He would get his revenge, but not tonight—tonight he had to survive.

Something whizzed past his head as he took a step toward Ruckley.

"Go," she said firmly.

He turned and ran, seeing an arrow sticking out of a tree. It was still quivering from when it had stabbed into the bark. Another whistle of an arrow cut through the air. It lanced into Ruckley's arm, and she cried out in pain.

Timothy stopped to fire a burst, but his shots were wild. Without any night vision, he couldn't see the shooters wherever they were. He turned and ran for the fields, not slowing even when he pushed through the tall weeds.

The rough blades scratched at his bare face, but he kept going. He couldn't see Ruckley, but he heard her breaking through the plants behind him.

Voices yelled in the distance.

One was familiar.

It was Neeland. "Help me!" he shouted. "Please, help me!"

Had these people kidnapped the poor bastard?

The end of the field came into focus. A dense forest covered a hill not too far away but Timothy decided to crouch instead of making a run for the cover.

"Ruckley," he said quietly.

No response.

He waited a few moments, listening for her movements.

Only the wind swayed the grass. The distant shouts had stopped too, and he didn't hear Neeland anymore.

A chill of fear shivered through him. What if he was all alone now?

He refused to believe it. Ruckley was still out there, and he couldn't just sit here and wait for her. Cautiously, he advanced with his rifle ready to fire at anyone on the other side of the weeds.

A moment later he reached the edge of the field and scanned for contacts through the shifting blades. He didn't see anyone out there. Darkness had swallowed much of the landscape, and these people seemed to be expert hunters.

Suppressing his fear, he strode out of the foliage, staying low. The forest growing along the hilly terrain stretched before him. He ran low for cover.

"Timothy," came a voice.

He froze.

"It's me, Ruckley."

She was crouched behind a tree, waving with her good arm. The arrow jutting out of her other arm was broken.

Timothy joined her and hunched down.

She winced as she aimed her rifle at the farmhouse and the two barns. A fire had started in a pit on the gravel drive, the glow flickering on the faded paint of the bigger barn.

Timothy zoomed in on a pole sticking out of the firepit, flames licking the sides.

He spotted movement in the glare and moved his scope to the right. A figure dressed in camo was strung up on a cross. It had to be Neeland. His legs and arms were bound, and his mouth was now taped shut.

A group of four... no... five people circled around, all holding crossbows.

"Collaborators?" he whispered.

"I don't think so," Ruckley said. "I've never seen collaborators use crossbows. These freaks must be some sort of cult."

"We got to do something. All they got are bows. We can take them."

He pictured how she had let that couple back in the church get slaughtered, how she was ready to give them up so they could continue their mission. Would she do the same to Neeland?

"There could be more," Ruckley said. "They're crazy, but they don't seem dumb. This is probably another trap. We go down there, thinking it's an easy shot, then they jump us from the weeds and fields."

"We're talking about Neeland, though," Timothy said. "We can't let them roast the guy."

"I know," she replied.

Timothy scanned for more targets but saw none. The farmland was simply too dark.

"We have to be careful," Ruckley said, grimacing through her pain. "If we're doing this, you take the ones on the left, I'll take the right. Then if there are more in the fields, we'll flush them out. Conserve your ammo, and make each shot—"

Before she finished her sentence one of the figures ripped the tape off Neeland's mouth, then plucked a flaming stick from the firepit and tossed it into the wood under Neeland's boots. The flames leapt up Neeland's body.

"HELP ME!" Neeland wailed. "Oh, God! Ruckley! Help me!"

Flames devoured his clothing and flesh. An agonizing wail filled the night. Neeland shrieked the entire time, his voice erupting in an animalistic cry of agony.

"Go," Ruckley snapped.

"What?"

"Go, I'll catch up."

Timothy hesitated, then started walking away.

A single gunshot rang out, and then faded.

He didn't need to turn to know the target had been Neeland. To put him out of his misery.

Ruckley caught up a few seconds later. She breathed heavy, like she was trying to hold back tears from putting her friend and brother out of his misery.

Timothy didn't even try to hold back his own tears. He had hardly known Neeland, but the man had deserved better. And so had his dad.

Tears ran from his eyes.

Timothy wanted to think there would be justice for Neeland and his father, but he knew in this new world filled with monsters and war, nothing was fair. Justice was nearly as extinct as good people.

***

Dohi crouched at the edge of a hiking trail covered in long weeds, sweeping the path ahead with his night vision goggles. Behind him, he heard the crunch of Team Ghost and the Wolfhounds' boots over twigs and dry grass. After escaping the enemy vessel, their advance to the evac site ten miles from the C-130 was painfully slow, in part due to the Wolfhounds.

The damaged freighter had sunk, but one of the birds had escaped. Dohi knew it was searching for them.

That's why he had selected a straightaway section of I-280 outside Redwood City for their evac.

They were only a few miles away now, just north of what had once been El Corte de Madera Creek Reserve, surrounded by massive trees.

Almost there, Dohi thought. *Keep pushing.*

They had given Jackson, Hopkins, and Lawrence their first round of antibiotics. But the medicine didn't work instantaneously, and they needed real medical professionals.

Lawrence managed a steady gait, cradling his wounded arm. Dohi admired his fortitude. Martin was the only Wolfhound who had survived both the cannibals' and Chimera attack unscathed. Now he helped Hopkins, who was missing one foot below the ankle.

Despite Hopkins protests, Rico carried the man, occasionally letting him lean on her shoulder as he walked with his remaining leg.

Jackson remained unconscious, the stumps at both ankles still smelling slightly with necrosis. He was now on Ace's back, who walked with sweat trickling down his head.

The occasional distant screeches of Variants haunted them with every step. Somewhere amid the hilly, forested landscape, the beasts lurked. It wasn't just the monsters Dohi was worried about. There was no guarantee more Chimeras from the freighter weren't trawling the woods. And for that matter, the settlement of cannibals they had discovered in the National Accelerator Laboratory might not have been the only one.

Another howl pierced the night. This one was closer.

Dohi signaled for everyone to get down. Fitz came over to him and took a knee while Rico and Mendez held security.

"How many do you think are out there?" he whispered.

"Sounds like a pack," Dohi replied. "Judging by the frequency of their calls, they're hunting us."

He studied the trees and the undergrowth of the forest. He didn't see any trampled vegetation. No claw marks. Nothing to indicate any Variants had been here recently, which meant to him these beasts hadn't randomly showed up to this park.

They had Team Ghost's scent.

He took a deep breath, peering through his NVGs at the green and black landscape. The team was relying on him to guide them safely through this unknown land to the rendezvous point. He couldn't mess up like he had at the National Accelerator Lab.

Dohi gave the advance signal into the dark woods, cautiously approaching every gurgling stream and patch of bushes under the redwoods. Jackson's groaning got worse, and his breathing was ragged.

"He ain't going to make it much further," Ace whispered, his voice strained. "We need to put him down and change these bandages."

Ace was right. Dohi could smell Jackson's festering wounds. If he could smell it, that meant the Variants could, too.

Dohi checked his watch. They still had a couple hours before evac. More than enough time to change Jackson's bandages, but they couldn't do it here.

He surveyed the road ahead. Abandoned cars littered the cracked asphalt. A couple were nothing but charred husks, but it gave him idea. This place had once been a campground, too.

"Look," Dohi said, pointing up the road. "This place has an RV park. We might find some shelter there."

Fitz gave a nod.

The group marched along the road. Another Variant shrieked, and a second beast answered the call. Dohi thought they sounded closer, but maybe it was just the acoustics of the open road now.

The faster they took care of Jackson, the sooner they could get out of here. And if all went well, changing Jackson's bandages would cover the scent better, but they had to be fast.

He increased his pace, seeing a sign with paint peeling away in big flakes.

A short driveway led to an open space filled with wild grass. Nearly a dozen hookup spots for power, water, and sewer lines sprouted from the field. Of course none would work, but Dohi had hoped to see a few RVs and trailers here, abandoned during the first war.

All that was left was a single camper-trailer with broken windows. The door was crumpled on the ground. Silver scars marred the paint, showing where Variants had clawed their way inside.

Fitz gestured for Dohi and Mendez to clear it while the others waited at the entrance to the RV park. The two operators flitted through the grass, then paused in front of the open door.

Dohi listened for breathing or the snap of Variant joints.

With a nod, he entered. Mendez fell in behind him. Broken glass covered a built-in table and bench. Mold had crept over the kitchenette, and ragged curtains flapped at the back of the trailer where the bed was. Atop that bed was a skeleton, leathery flesh hanging off in ribbons, bite marks covering the bone.

"I'll take care of Jackson," Dohi said.

"I can help," Hopkins said.

"Yeah, put us to work," Lawrence added, gesturing with his good arm. "We're happy to do something."

"Right now, just focus on getting those bandages changed," Dohi said. "The smell of those things are going to attract every damn Variant around."

"Ace, Rico, you're on security," Fitz said. "Mendez, get Hopkins and Lawrence comfortable on that bench."

Fitz dug into his pack and tossed them a first aid kit. "Replace their bandages. Martin, take Jackson to that bed with me and Dohi. We need to clean him up fast before the Variants are drawn to the scent."

Ace carried Jackson to the back and waited to unload him onto the bed.

"Hurry," he grumbled.

Dohi removed the skeleton and took the bony remains outside, but he didn't have time to worry about honoring the dead with a burial when it was the living that he needed to take care of.

He went back inside, and Fitz took out more of the medical supplies they'd scavenged from the freighter to help Jackson.

Dohi examined the soiled bandages. Martin looked over his shoulder, muttering a prayer that was cut short by a Variant howl in the distance.

Dohi tried to ignore the sounds, but having Martin hovering over him and muttering in his ear wasn't helping matters.

"Be careful," Martin said.

"I know what I'm doing," Dohi said.

Jackson was unconscious, but his face contorted in pain when Dohi began unwrapping the bandages. They pulled away with a slurp from the bloodied stumps, tearing some of the diseased tissue.

Dohi unraveled the last bandage. The odor of death filled the trailer. Pus and blood leaked out of cracked, blackened flesh.

Martin retched and bolted outside to vomit.

Fighting his own instinct to recoil, Dohi examined the wound. The cannibals had screwed up when they had tried to cauterize the flesh.

Between the survival techniques his grandfather had taught him and the first aid skills he'd honed as an operator, Dohi knew this wasn't going to be an easy fix.

"I need to debride this wound, clean it, then reapply the bandage," he said quietly. "This necrotic tissue is going to get worse if we leave it, and the smell is going to keep those Variants on us until we take care of it."

"Do what you have to," Fitz said.

Martin walked back inside, wiping off his mouth.

"You good?" Dohi said.

A nod from Martin.

"Good, because I need your help. Put a cloth between Jackson's teeth. This is going to be painful, and he needs something to bite down on."

"And try to keep him quiet," Fitz said.

Martin tore a piece of old sheet from the bed and stuffed it between Jackson's teeth.

"Here we go," Dohi said.

He took out his utility knife and scraped at the dead tissue, periodically washing it with fresh water. The dead flaking skin peeled away to reveal raw, red infected tissue.

Jackson groaned louder.

"Oh, shit, what's going on?" Martin asked.

Blood started to spray from the wound, soaking into the bed like a dark shadow.

"Shit," Dohi said. "I think he had a nicked artery or something. The cauterized tissue was helping block it, but…"

Fitz dug through the first-aid kit for clotting gel, a hemostat, and sutures, handing the supplies over.

Dohi cleaned away as much of the blood and dead tissue blocking their access to the artery, then tried dousing the wound with the clotting gel. The bleeding didn't stop, and the artery had retracted deeper into Jackson's leg.

"This is going to hurt bad," Dohi said, pausing. "A lot. Martin, hold him down. Fitz, I need your help."

Martin's dark skin seemed a shade lighter, a quiet terror evident in his face. Fitz came over with Martin to hold Jackson down.

There was no way around this. Blood pumped from the wound. Jackson would be dead in minutes, and the smell of this blood would be worse than Jackson's wounds at attracting the monsters.

Dohi quickly probed through the infected tissue, pushing past the fat and skin.

Jackson snapped awake, eyes bulging from their sockets. He was fully conscious now. He screamed into the cloth, and Martin held the guy's head, trying to reassure him.

But even with the cloth between his teeth, Jackson's scream was loud.

"Hurry, Dohi," Fitz said.

"I'm working as fast as I can."

Dohi's heart thundered in his ears. He tried to ignore Jackson's screams and Martin's reassurances, the din filling the trailer. They might as well hang a flashing sign outside that advertised Variant food here.

"I got it!" he said, catching the artery with two fingers and snapping the hemostat on it. "Sutures, now!"

He tied off the vessel, blood pouring over his hand. Jackson still screamed in pain, writhing. Fitz and Martin struggled to hold him in place.

And then it was finished.

Dohi poured more clean water over the wound. No more blood gushed out.

Jackson sobbed, muscular chest heaving in gasps, before passing out again.

The bed and floor were soaked with blood. The guy had lost so much.

Dohi started wrapping Jackson's legs with fresh bandages.

A chorus of Variant shrieks came from outside. This time there was no mistaking their proximity. They knew Team Ghost and the Wolfhounds were here.

Rico came into the bedroom and said in a low voice, "We got multiple contacts."

"We're almost finished," Fitz said.

Jackson's unconscious moaning faded into a rattling sigh as Dohi finished the last bandage. The man was quiet now. Too quiet.

Dohi checked his wrist. His stomach plummeted through the floor. "He doesn't have a pulse."

"What? No, come on, Jackson," Martin said. He bent down to pump on the soldier's chest with his skinny arms.

Another howl screamed outside. This one sounded

closer. Two more inhuman voices answered it.

"Movement at our six, and ten, and…" Ace said. "Shit, they're coming from all directions."

The shrieks grew louder even though Jackson had gone silent. The blood-soaked room had brought all the ravenous monsters to their position.

Dohi looked at the lifeless man.

All this effort, all this risk for nothing. Jackson was dead, and now they were trapped in a trailer, surrounded by beasts being drawn to his corpse like hyenas around a wounded gazelle.

— 11 —

The wails of the injured and dying punctured the crackle of the flames dancing over City Hall Park. A tree buckled as flames devoured it. Ash and embers swirled in a harsh wind coursing down Broadway, carrying the stink of charred flesh and the rotten odor of dead Variants.

Fischer stood in the vibroseis truck near the courthouse with his engineer, Brian Meyer.

The engineer touched the blood-soaked bandage on his cheek. He needed stitches, but for now the bandage would have to suffice.

Frankly, he was lucky to be alive. So was Fischer. Tran and Chase had saved them from a pair of Variants that had managed to break through the other defenses and get to the truck.

After the first wave of beasts, they had lost too many men in Bogardus Garden to hold the position. They had been forced to move and consolidate their defenses around City Hall.

"How's it looking?" Fischer asked Meyer.

The engineer studied the geophone readings across his monitor. "So far, no activity to indicate new tunnels."

"Let's pray it stays that way. Shout if you see anything, even if it's so much as an earthworm coughing down there."

Fischer got down from the truck and joined Massey. Chase and Tran shadowed him, each looking nervously around the carnage.

"The vibroseis truck is ready for the next wave," Fischer said.

Massey nodded and let out a long exhale. "We lost nearly a third of our men in that last attack. Even if the Variants are weaker, it's going to be hell."

"We'll keep a close eye on those tunnels to ensure they don't catch us with our pants down."

"The M1 is ready to go again as soon as you spot something. It might be our saving grace."

"What about the other M1 I saw back at the outpost?"

"It stays there, to protect the civilians as a last resort."

Fischer looked up at the tall buildings around them for the helicopters.

"And the Apaches?"

"Running low on fuel," Massey said. "Trying to keep them as a last resort as well."

Fischer hated seeing them hold back on their most powerful weapons, but he decided it was a good plan.

Last resort, he thought.

"Radio if you need me," Massey said. "I'm going to check the defensive barricades again."

Fischer took a long swig of water, then looked between Tran and Chase. "You boys doing all right?"

"Remember how you promised a drink on the beach when this is all over?" Tran asked.

"Of course."

"I'm thinking a luxury cruise now."

"You both deserve it," Fischer said. "I know you didn't sign up for this when you joined Fischer Fields, but I have to commend you for stepping up when the country called for us."

"We go where you go, sir," Tran added.

Meyer called from the truck. "Mr. Fischer! I've got activity!"

Adrenaline flooded Fischer. He ran as fast as his old bones would take him back to the engineer.

Spikes of activity bloomed across the monitor. Seismic waves bounced around the neighborhoods surrounding City Hall Park.

Fischer grabbed his radio. "Commander Massey, they're on their way. I've got confirmed activity about six blocks north. Looks like they'll be inbound at Centre and Chambers."

"Copy, we're moving the M1 now," she replied.

The tank's diesel engines growled to life and the treads crunched over the disheveled street. Men followed behind it as they found new positions, aiming toward the intersection at the corner of City Hall Park.

"Four blocks now," Meyer reported.

Fischer gripped the barrel of his shotgun.

"Three blocks now!"

Ten minutes passed before the ground started to crater around a manhole on Centre. Fischer watched through the windshield of the truck. Tran and Chase got beside the vehicle, aiming at the shifting and cracking pavement.

For a moment, only the crackle of fires in the park and abandoned buildings nearby could be heard. Then the asphalt fell away in a loud crash.

A Variant climbed from the freshly formed pit, rearing back on its legs, muscles pulsing under sickly gray flesh. It opened its mouth, saliva spraying from its teeth as it screamed. A pack of monsters erupted from the tunnel behind it, a mix of armored juveniles and the sinewy adults.

"Open fire!" Massey yelled.

The concerted boom of rifle and machine gunfire exploded across the block. Tracer rounds cut from the machine gun nests in the neighboring buildings. Even as the first wave of monsters perished under the onslaught, others squirmed between the dead bodies of their brethren, climbing onto the street.

Grenades sailed toward them. Blasts sent chunks of singed meat smacking against asphalt and clouds of smoke blooming from new fires.

The M1 fired with a deafening boom. A geyser of asphalt and dirt burst from the hole with a resonating boom. The beasts' bodies were thrown into the air, then came down in a gruesome rain of mangled body parts. A wave of dust billowed from the impact site.

"They're still coming!" Chase said.

Fischer moved past Meyer and aimed out the open window of the truck. He sighted up one Variant galloping out of the rolling cloud of dust and debris.

With the butt of his shotgun tight against his shoulder, he squeezed his trigger. The blast tore through the monster's chest, sending it tumbling over itself.

"Shit, sir. Shit!" Meyer said. "We've got more activity under the park."

Fischer turned back to the screen. "Under us?"

"Yes! The beasts are digging a new tunnel."

Screams echoed outside as a Variant lunged at a soldier, tearing into him with claws and teeth. Another man went down as juveniles piled on top of him, ripping him apart like a pack of dogs.

Fischer held up his radio. "Commander, the Variants are attacking from Elk and Chambers!"

"That's near the M1," she replied.

The tank fired another round that decimated the

entrance of the tunnel. A group of beasts disappeared in a violent inferno.

Fischer expected that to be the end of them, but more monsters squeezed out from the cracked slabs of asphalt and rubble, bloody and burned.

Sniper rifles cracked from above, like angels of war, protecting the men on the ground from the creatures getting too close.

"They have stopped right below us," Meyer said.

"Get out of here," Fischer said. "Retreat to the main defenses and stay there."

"But sir…"

"Do it," Fischer said. "We can't hold this position."

Another pair of Variants made a break from the broken entrance of the tunnel. They rushed at the vibroseis truck. Fischer hopped beside Tran and Chase while Meyer ran.

They brought down the first monster, but the second ran low, ducking behind the bodies of its comrades. It coiled and jumped, soaring toward Fischer. He clenched up, watching in what seemed like slow motion as the beast descended on him, claws extended.

Suddenly the beast's mouth disappeared in a blast of pink tissue and bone spreading. Tran kept his rifle aimed at the creature when it crashed to the ground, finishing it with a shot to the back of the head. Blood pooled away from the beast to Fischer's boots.

He tried to control his breathing.

"Fischer, where are those monsters on Elk?" Massey called over the radio. "I can't spare my men there if they aren't actually coming."

"They're beneath the street," Fischer replied.

Suddenly part of Chambers street cracked. The

monsters had stopped climbing out of the hole on Centre. A loud roar carried up out of the fissures across Chambers.

But this was not the cry of a monster. It sounded like rushing water.

The heavy weight of horror plunged through his insides at the implications.

"Massey, pull your men off the streets!" Fischer yelled over the radio. "Get them away from the buildings and move that tank back to the park! NOW!"

Dirty brown water exploded out of the cracks in Chambers, pouring through the streets. Soldiers backed away from it like it was poison. It wasn't the water itself Fischer was afraid of. It was what that rushing water meant.

The tank growled as it rotated and then powered down Chambers toward the park. The asphalt buckled under its tracks, crumbling away in an instant. A massive hole ripped down the road, swallowing men and vehicles.

The tank crashed through the collapsing earth, followed by the second vibroseis truck. It took Fischer a second to realize what had happened. New York City's famous water system was fed by gravity, meaning the huge tunnels that had once transported tap water to buildings throughout the city were still filled with stagnant water.

"The Variants burst a water main!" Fischer shouted. "We all have to fall back!"

Variant shrieks echoed up from the splashing untreated water filling the tunnel they had dug. Human screams followed, giving Fischer no illusion of what was happening in this freshly formed canyon. He looked back into his vibroseis truck and saw more seismic activity on the screen.

Another sinkhole formed under a building where machine gunners and snipers were roosted. One of the Apaches was stationed atop it. The building started to quiver, cracks tracing up its side. The Apaches blades started spinning, but it was too late. The building collapsed inward, and a huge cloud of dust rolled over the park.

Panicked voices exploded over the radio.

"We're pulling back from Pumphouse Park!" someone yelled over the radio.

So it's not just here, Fischer thought.

His mind thundered with questions on how this could be happening. The Variants had pulled a tactical maneuver, distracting the defensive forces and striking in a way no one could've predicted.

A second building collapsed into the growing sinkhole. Water flooded the streets, and a debris cloud rolled over the defensive forces. Soon the gray and brown haze was too much. Fischer could only see shadows moving in the dust.

Screams and the sound of gunfire split the air.

Tran and Chase pressed up against the back of the truck, fighting off monsters emerging out of the haze. The truck's geophone monitor burst with more activity as sinkholes sucked in men and spat out more Variants.

There was no way he could hold the truck with just Tran and Chase. This station was already lost. There was nothing they could do but retreat.

Cracks formed in the ground around them, the earth trembling.

"Massey!" Fischer yelled into his radio. "We're

abandoning the vibroseis truck and headed your way!"

"Alpha!" Tran yelled.

His rifle burst to life as a creature barreled through the fog toward them. The monster let out an ear-splitting shriek, muscles rippling under its fur.

Bullets plunged into its flesh, blood spraying from the wounds. But the monster kept coming with a tide of Variants following in its wake.

"Move!" Fischer yelled.

Tran and Chase led the way, stopping every few strides to lay down covering fire.

The Alpha slammed into the vibroseis truck behind them, pushing it over. Variants scaled the toppled vehicle, jumping over it and chasing after Fischer and his men.

Fischer slowed when he saw a monster feasting on a body ahead. He fired a buckshot into the ugly creature, knocking it off the victim. A second passed before he realized the shredded body was Meyer.

Most of the engineer's face had been mauled off, and Fischer only recognized him by the Fischer Fields logo emblazoned on his coveralls.

"Goddammit!" Fischer shouted.

Gunfire cracked behind him as Tran and Chase back peddled while firing at the Alpha still hunting them.

"Run!" Chase yelled.

Fischer pumped another shell into his shotgun and brought the weapon up to blast a Variant in their path. Tran and Chase took measured shots at the other creatures, cutting down the Alpha's forces. They hit the bigger beast with periodic bursts and it finally started to slow.

"Reloading!" Fischer said as he plucked new cartridges from his vest.

Tran's rifle bolt clicked back. "Me too!"

The Alpha seemed to sense their momentary weakness and barreled forward, knocking aside smaller Variants. Chase fired, but the beast was too fast. It grabbed Tran, then yanked him backward, disappearing back into the dust cloud.

"Tran!" Fischer shouted. He pumped his shotgun and ran after the beast.

"Wait!" Chase yelled.

Fischer strode out into the dust cloud with Chase by his side.

"Tran!" they both yelled.

More explosions burst behind them, screams piercing the crack of increasingly sporadic gunfire. Fischer saw almost nothing through the rising dust cloud as other buildings collapsed.

He continued yelling for Tran, but the man was gone, taken underground where he would suffer a worse fate than being torn apart up here.

"Sir, we have to go," Chase said.

The roar of a diesel engine sounded in the distance, and Fischer followed Chase toward the noise. They broke through the dust to find a black four-by-four pickup with a group of soldiers in the bed, and another climbing up.

"Get in!" Massey yelled from the driver's window.

Fischer looked back toward the dust cloud one last time, praying Tran wouldn't suffer long.

A hand grabbed Fischer by the arm. Chase helped him up into the bed of the truck as they abandoned their friend to the monsters.

***

In the troop hold of the C-130, Beckham stared out one of the small windows. The first molten rays of the sun climbed above California. The pilots had said they were only about ten minutes out from Team Ghost's evac site. The morning light washed through the aircraft as the crew and a handful of soldiers in the jump seats made their final preparations for landing.

None knew what to expect.

This was enemy territory.

Horn clicked a drum into his M249 SAW. Then he reached inside his vest and pulled out a black bandana emblazoned with a skull, an old memento of his time on Team Ghost. He tied it around his neck.

Nathan Brooks, the Army Ranger who had lost his glasses, had offered to help, but like the other injured Ranger who had survived the crash in Cleveland, he couldn't do much. The kid was practically blind without his glasses, and the other Ranger had broken an ankle after jumping out of the Black Hawk.

"Once we land, everyone who can will hold security," he said. "This area is going to be hot, and we know there are hostiles, both human and Variant. But we want to go in and out quick and quiet. Do not shoot unless you're given the order. Got it?"

Nods all around.

The plane dipped lower and Beckham started toward the rear door when a message hissed in his earpiece.

"Captain Beckham, we just got a message about Ghost," said the primary pilot. "We need you up here."

Beckham hurried to the cockpit.

One of the pilots turned to him. "Command just pinged us. Ghost called them on the sat phone a while ago. They're surrounded by Variants about a mile from the rendezvous coordinates."

Beckham clenched his jaw.

"How do you want us to proceed?" asked the pilot.

With only moments to decide, Beckham scanned the sky for aircraft and the freeway below for contacts.

He didn't see any hostiles yet. "Take us down. Horn and I will go in on foot to clear their escape."

Beckham made his way back to Horn.

"Trouble?" Horn asked.

"Plenty."

"You know I'm always ready for trouble, but what does plenty mean?"

"Ghost is pinned down by Variants. We'll need to extract them."

Horn pulled his skull mask up. "Then that's just what we'll do."

"Prepare for landing," said the primary pilot.

A few moments later the plane touched down on the interstate, wind rushing over the spoilers as the engines applied reverse thrust, and they decelerated hard into a stop.

A crew chief pushed a button on the bulkhead, opening the rear ramp.

"Back into the fray," Horn grumbled.

He strode down the ramp with his SAW shouldered. Beckham raised his M4 and loaded a grenade into the barrel-mounted M203 launcher. He followed Big Horn into the morning sunshine.

"Good luck," came a voice.

Beckham glanced over his shoulder. Brooks raised a hand from the troop hold.

All but two of the thirteen soldiers and the crew streamed down the ramp past Brooks to hold security.

Beckham jogged toward the coordinates where Ghost was supposed to be waiting. Maybe after their sat phone batteries had drained, they had actually made it there on their own, escaping the monsters.

But Ghost and the injured Wolfhounds were nowhere between the trees and grass where they were supposed to be. They might not have escaped the position where the Variants had first surrounded them.

The team's last known location was only a mile away. Beckham started running, Horn following. They could make it in under eight minutes if they ran hard with their gear. Maybe less, but they weren't the same men they were back when they had been on Ghost.

They got through an open field in a few minutes but slowed on approach to the tree-covered hills. The terrain provided cover, which also meant shelter for a hostile ambush.

Horn held up a fist.

The chatter of small arms fire echoed over the hills.

"Sounds like one, maybe two guns at most," he said.

Beckham didn't like what that might mean and started running again. He didn't stop until he got to the crest of a hill. Navigating through the trees, he took a knee on an overlook of an RV park.

These were the coordinates where Ghost had reported they were being surrounded.

Corpses lay scattered across the grass. The ground was so soaked with blood that the dirt had turned to mud in some spots. But the bodies weren't human—they were naked beasts, flesh riddled with bullet holes, spread around a camper trailer.

Beckham zoomed in on the open door. The echoing pop of a gunshot pulled his gaze away from the scope.

Horn pointed to the edge of the forest.

Beckham led the way cautiously down the hill and across the corpse-strewn park.

One Variant was still alive. Partially buried in a crater of dirt from a grenade. The upper torso was still connected to the bottom by thick strings of gristle, somehow keeping it alive.

It reached up and took weak passes at them with a claw.

Beckham didn't waste a bullet or slow to pull his knife.

The beast wasn't going anywhere and wasn't long for this world anyway.

Shrieks sounded from the forest as they approached, and another gunshot answered. Then three more pops.

Beckham and Horn bolted toward the sounds. A trail of corpses took them through the forest and along a road.

Streaks of blood painted the asphalt. Empty bullet casings and shotgun shells lay scattered across the cracked street that traced up another hill.

Horn caught up to Beckham, breathing heavily, and they approached the top side by side.

They heard snarling and cracking, then a sickening crunch followed by a shout.

"You want more, *puta?*"

The familiar voice had to be Mendez.

Another voice, this one female, came next.

"Keep them back!" yelled Rico.

Beckham and Horn neared the top of the hill. Sweat drenched their fatigues.

About two hundred feet away, a group of ten Variants prowled around Team Ghost, circling and waiting to pounce.

Ace had a metal garbage lid that must've been from

the RV park with claw marks across it in one hand, and the butt of his shotgun in the other. Dohi tossed his hatchet at the closest Variant, scoring a hit to the neck, then he jabbed another creature with his knife.

Rico and Fitz used their blades to parry and strike a beast lunging at them.

Mendez slammed the butt of his rifle against a Variant's face. Cartilage and bone cracked at the impact, blood sloshing out of its slitted nostrils.

Team Ghost had formed a ring around two injured soldiers wrapped in bandages. They must be the surviving Wolfhounds. A third Wolfhound stood beside Ghost, fighting alongside them.

Beckham raised his rifle, centering it on the first target. "Ghost!"

Fitz glanced his way, then signaled for the team to close in around the injured as Beckham and Horn fired on the surrounding creatures. Blood gushed from monsters' new wounds, and wails of pain filled the morning. Three beasts made it out of the gunfire and started up the hill toward Beckham.

"I got this!" he yelled as he palmed in a new magazine.

Beckham cut the three creatures down with calculated bursts. Their bodies rolled back down the hill. Before anyone could celebrate the narrow victory, shrieks of more creatures rose in the distance.

Covered in dirt and blood, Team Ghost and the Wolfhounds looked like they had been through hell and back.

The group of battle-fatigued soldiers marched up the hill with Rico at the lead. She reached out like she was going to give Horn a hug, but then fingered at his vest.

"We need magazines," she said. "For the way back."

Horn and Beckham distributed ammo.

"Damn good to see you, Captain," Fitz said as he graciously accepted a magazine. "Wasn't sure we were going to make it out of here."

"We're not out yet, brother," Beckham said.

"What the fuck took you guys so long?" said one of the Wolfhound soldiers, a guy with a bloody nametape that read Martin.

"Give it a fucking rest," Mendez said.

"They're here, aren't they?" said another Wolfhound. The guy's nametape said Lawrence. He helped another injured Wolfhound who only had one foot.

"We need to move," Beckham said. "Keep close, and tight."

He took point through the forest, scanning for any camouflaged Variants lying in wait.

The pace back to the C-130 was agonizingly slow because of the wounded Wolfhounds that needed help walking. Dohi came up next to Beckham and they exchange a nod.

Shrieks of hunting Variants followed the group. Beckham checked their six. Horn signaled to him he'd spotted three hostiles. Variant scouts shadowing their retreat.

The beasts were like wolves, waiting for the rest of their pack before they would move in for the kill.

Beckham spotted salvation ahead. The big body of the C-130 on the freeway was surrounded by a dozen soldiers that had spread out to provide cover.

The sight gave the exhausted team the energy they needed to make the final stretch. As the Variants closed in, Beckham led them straight up onto the freeway toward the C-130's open troop hold.

Soldiers holding security jogged over to help take the wounded.

"Hell yeah," Mendez said. He turned to look at the road behind them. Taking a hand off his rifle, he crossed his chest and kissed his fingers, head angled toward the sky. "Thank you, thank you, thank you, Lord Jesus." Then he paused, tilting his head. "Aw, shit, not now."

Beckham followed his gaze.

A transmission crackled in his earpiece just as he saw the black aircraft against the blue.

"We got incoming, Captain, get your people inside, now!" said one of the pilots.

Beckham swallowed hard when he saw that contact was a Black Hawk.

"Go, go, go!" Horn shouted, waving for everyone to run.

They were sitting ducks on the interstate, and they had very few weapons capable of taking down that helicopter barring an extremely lucky shot.

As the team raced for the open hold, Beckham raised his rifle with its barrel-mounted M203 grenade launcher and Horn aimed his SAW, covering the others.

The engines on the C-130 thrummed to life, drowning out the panicked voices of the retreating soldiers.

Ace carried the Wolfhound with only one foot, and Rico helped the one with bandages across his arms into the plane. Mendez and Fitz stayed outside with Beckham as the chopper closed in.

"Fire!" Beckham shouted.

Rounds lanced into the bird. A door gunner on the Black Hawk opened fire with a mounted machine gun. Rounds tore into the belly of the C-130 and raked over the asphalt, sweeping toward Team Ghost.

Beckham launched a grenade, hoping for a lucky shot. But the grenade sailed wide, landing amid the trees and kicking up a fiery cloud of dirt.

Another soldier from the Black Hawk knelt at the open side door. He leveled an M72 LAW at them. All it took was one good hit, and their plane would be grounded, just like the C-130 that had initially taken Ghost here.

"Take him down!" Beckham shouted.

Bullets slammed into the side of the chopper. Horn unleashed his SAW at the man with the rocket launcher, and Beckham launched another grenade.

This one slammed into the troop hold as the LAW rocket streaked away. It missed the plane and exploded somewhere behind Beckham. The resulting wave of heat threw him off balance.

The chopper came screaming down toward them.

Beckham ran out of its path as it slammed down sideways on the right side of the road, skidding across the grass. Fire spewed from its engine as its blades split and flew off its rotor.

He stopped running, chest heaving as he scanned the road to make sure everyone was okay. Fitz, Dohi, and Horn were aiming their rifles at the downed bird in case anyone had survived.

Ace was screaming from the troop hold, and Rico came running out. She stopped near a smoking crater, hand covering her mouth.

When Beckham saw the twisted remains of a rifle, blood-soaked asphalt, and chunks of a torn boot he realized why he hadn't seen Mendez yet.

There wasn't anything left of him to see.

— 12 —

Kate sat at the edge of the cot after a night of tossing and turning. Thoughts of Beckham braving newfound dangers on the West Coast had kept her up despite being exhausted.

Carefully as she could, she maneuvered through the cramped room, careful not to wake Javier yet. He had been excited to see her again, not quite grasping that she hadn't meant to return to the Long Island bunker so soon.

The last report she had heard before retiring to her quarters was that Lower Manhattan had been hit hard. It pained her to think of the lives lost, and she couldn't help thinking this was even more devastating than one night of casualties.

She and Sammy needed to work in those tunnels again. If they couldn't, that meant extended delays in their efforts to decode the new signals from the Variant network and locating the hub responsible for the attacks. That also meant it would take even longer for them to observe how the Variants communicated so they could replicate their signals and disrupt their communications, hopefully fighting back with information warfare.

She splashed some cold water on her face from the stainless-steel sink in the bathroom, then got changed. When she was ready for work, she went to Javier's cot where she tousled his hair.

"Javier," she whispered. "I've got to do some work, okay?"

He rolled on his back, peering at her through half-opened eyes. "Is Dad back?"

"Not yet."

"Is he okay?"

"Yes, I'm sure he's fine."

Javier sat up. "Will Connor be watching us again today?"

"Yes."

Ringgold had assigned the kids a Secret Service agent named Connor to watch over them since Beckham and Horn were in the field.

Kate appreciated the gesture. It gave her the ability to perform her work knowing someone was keeping Javier, Jenny, Tasha, and the dogs safe.

That fact also made her feel guilty. Their children were being protected by the president's own people, snug and safe in a bunker, while so many other parents were literally dying to save their children outside these walls.

"I'll be in the lab," she said to Javier, then stood. "You can always call if you need me."

"I know."

"I love you."

"Love you too, Mom."

She left her quarters as quietly as possible while Javier fell back to sleep. Connor sat on a chair outside, dozing. As soon as she closed the door to her room, he woke and stood. Long scars crossed his face, evidence of a Variant attack.

"Good morning, Dr. Lovato," he said.

"Thank you again for watching Javier and the girls. I truly appreciate it."

"Doctor, it's my pleasure." Connor said. "Children are our future."

He locked his gaze with hers. She sensed pain behind those brown eyes. Maybe a lost child in his past.

She nodded and then started the lonely march toward the lab setup in the bunker. The halls were mostly quiet. A few hushed voices leaked from offices and rooms as leaders worked around the clock.

She caught only snippets of conversations, listening for any word about Team Ghost or Beckham and Horn.

President Ringgold came around the intersection, then offered a sorrowful smile when she saw Kate. "Dr. Lovato, just the person I wanted to see."

"Madam President, what is it?" Kate asked, her heart thumping.

Ringgold took Kate's hand, clutching it. "Your husband and Parker found Team Ghost. They're on their way out of California now."

"Oh, thank God!" Kate felt like a pressure valve had been released on her heart. "So they're all right?"

Ringgold bit the inside of her lip. "There were casualties, and I don't know all the details. But I do know Reed and Parker are okay."

She was relieved, but Kate's chest still tightened again. "Where are they going?"

"They're headed to Canada to refuel, and we're working with our counterparts north of the border," Ringgold said. "They'll also look at the damaged SDS equipment that Team Ghost and the Wolfhounds retrieved."

Kate only managed to nod as Ringgold continued.

"In Lower Manhattan, the Variants surged through the vibroseis locations and our forces retreated into the 9/11 memorial outpost," she said. "Between the Variants, bats, hounds and collaborators, we've lost communications with four more outposts, including Cleveland where Beckham and Horn boarded their C-130."

The president paused and put a hand on Kate's arm, gently. "How are you?"

Kate took a moment to compose herself. "I'll be fine. Are you okay?"

"I have to be," Ringgold replied. "They have us beat in numbers, but even the biggest snake can't bite if you cut off its head. Once we find it, that's exactly what I plan on doing."

"And I'm going to help you find it."

They parted ways, and Kate continued to the laboratory. She dreamed about a cup of coffee right now but realized she didn't really need the caffeine. Ringgold had given her all she needed to fuel herself through today's experiments.

Inside the lab, Sammy was already hunched over a laptop, the blue screen glowing on her face. Kate flicked on the lights, bathing the place in a yellow glow.

"Jeez, Sammy, have you slept at all?" she asked.

Sammy clutched her injured side and looked up from the laptop. "Did *you* sleep at all?"

"Not really." Kate pulled up a seat next to Sammy.

"I made a mistake in those tunnels," Sammy said. "And it almost got your husband and those soldiers killed. I won't fail again."

"Failure is an unfortunate part of science. We have to face the risk of failure before we stand a chance of succeeding. No one knew what we were dealing with."

Sammy nodded.

"So what are you working on?"

"I'm running a few scripts to parse the signals we recorded from the webbing. My natural language processing algorithms should translate some of it for us."

A few progress bars slowly climbed across the monitor, pixel-by-pixel.

"That's going to take a while," Kate said. "I've got a way to keep us busy in the meantime."

"What's that?" Sammy asked.

"We never had a chance to examine those VX-99 infected bats used at Outpost Portland," Kate said. "We received a couple of specimens here. Maybe we can find a clue in them that might help."

"I'm no biologist, but I'm happy to assist."

Kate led the computer engineer to a freezer where they had stored their samples. She took out a small object wrapped in plastic and foil.

Once she placed it on a stainless-steel table, she pried the wrapping off to reveal a mutated, large brown bat with a body slightly larger than her fist. Protruding vessels crisscrossed its wings. Patches of fur clung to nearly translucent flesh. Even in death, the little monster's overgrown muscles bulged under its thin skin.

Sammy placed a tray of dissection tools next to the bat. "What next?"

"It's easy enough to verify these bats were modified by VX-99, but that doesn't tell us anything we don't already know."

"Okay, so what do we do?"

"A full autopsy," Kate said. "I want to know how these things were controlled."

She used a biopsy punch to extract small chunks of skin, muscle, and organ tissue, depositing each into separate vials. At Kate's direction, Sammy froze them down for Leslie and Ron to analyze later.

Moving the bat onto its stomach, Kate noticed a bulge on its neck. She cut through its leathery flesh with a scalpel.

A glint of metal shone under yellow tissue and red blood. She pulled out what looked like a computer chip with a pair of forceps. With it came a pair of tiny silver wires.

After Kate cleaned the small rectangular object off with saline, Sammy deposited it under a dissecting scope.

"Holy shit," Sammy said. "I can tell you exactly what this is."

"What?"

Sammy turned away from the scope. "It's a microelectric array like the devices the collaborators were using to communicate through the webbing network."

"All of these technologies, from the bats to the webbing, and the masterminds, share common connections," Kate said. "They must come from the same source. A source that knows how to engineer electronics and computers."

"Yeah." Sammy swallowed. "Someone who knows this science inside and out. Biology, electrical engineering, all of it."

Kate thought of the similarities to the Department of Defense projects they'd discovered and the military tactics that their enemy had employed recently. "And someone with a military background."

"Jesus," Sammy said.

"We need to figure out the final pieces of this puzzle quickly."

"We will, and I won't mess up again. I swear to you."

Kate wanted to feel a sense of satisfaction at these new

revelations, but finding the missing links meant more men like her husband and Team Ghost would need to return to hell to destroy the demon behind it all.

A demon with unmatched resources and intelligence, weapons that were as powerful, if not more, than any army of monsters.

And Kate had a feeling it wasn't a Variant Alpha or an abomination like a mastermind—it was a human. Someone like Colonel Gibson who had started the VX-99 program back during the Vietnam War.

President Ringgold had been right. The science team's work might be the key to any chance of victory. And judging by what they had just uncovered, the chance of victory was growing smaller by the hour.

She examined the microelectric array. An idea struck her.

"Sammy, the tech for these arrays came from that scientist investigating neural-digital networks back at the University of Florida. Do you remember his name?"

"No, but I'm sure we have that somewhere."

Kate joined her at the computer. "Please look it up. I want to know exactly what DOD programs the guy was involved in."

"You think he's the real mastermind?"

"I don't know," Kate said. "It's a longshot."

Sammy went to work.

"Dr. Simon Wong," she said a few minutes later. "He was recruited by the DOD in 2006 after his work using microelectric arrays to connect rodent brains to various software."

"Can you find out where in the DOD?"

Sammy's fingers worked across the keyboard. "Says here he joined the Defense Advanced Research Projects

Agency. He was a project manager, overseeing the funding and execution of nearly a dozen separate projects."

"How long?"

"Until about 2013. Then…he died."

Kate felt the ribbons of her conspiracy theory start to float away. "If that's true, then he's not our guy."

"Then again, those secret government types have a habit of disappearing and reappearing all over."

"Can you find which projects he administered? Maybe there's a link there."

Sammy nodded, scanning through the various projects. "Woah, look at this. It's Project Rolling Stone. The seismic detection systems that Team Ghost went after."

"Dr. Wong specialized in digital and biological networks, so that makes sense," Kate said. "Did he manage any projects related to bioweapons or medicine? Anything involving cell culture or bioengineering?"

It took Sammy only seconds to skim through the list. "I found a few potential matches. There's the Center for Engineering Complex Organs, or CECO. It was funded by a few pharmaceutical companies, too, up in the Seattle area."

She looked at the list again. "There's also HumoSource, which developed medical products from donated tissues derived from cadavers. A third one is Memnet in San Francisco, a company that DARPA was interested in for neural networks."

"If we use these three locations to narrow down where those communications from the tunnel originated, would that help?"

Sammy thought on it before nodding. "That'll reduce the time it takes to confirm if these signals are coming from those locations rather than me trying to probe every single spot in North America."

"Then let's do it."

Only a few seconds passed as Kate watched Sammy work her magic.

"Boom, done," Sammy said.

On the screen, a heat map of the former United States revealed two locations glowing red.

"With about a ninety-five percent probability, these signals seem to be coming from near CECO in Seattle and HumoSource just outside Denver," Sammy said.

Kate sucked in a breath. "Time to tell President Ringgold. It looks like we just figured out where we send…"

She almost didn't want to say it, but she knew the team headed out there would be Team Ghost—or whatever was left of them.

***

Fitz sat between Rico and Beckham in the C-130. It felt good to be back with his friend and the former leader of Team Ghost, but the pain of losing another member of Team Ghost plagued Fitz.

They had lost so many friends over the years. But it wasn't just their friends. They had also lost parts of themselves.

He looked down at his prosthetic legs, and then over at Beckham's prosthetic limbs.

They had given so much to these two wars. Fitz wasn't sure how much either had left to give.

Closer to the cockpit, a pair of medics sat next to two stretchers bolted to the deck. Hopkins and Lawrence lay on them with IV tubes stretching from their arms. They were finally getting the medical attention they needed, and Martin was there watching over them, fingering his necklace, his lips moving in prayer.

Knowing they had saved three of the Wolfhounds helped ease some of the loss Fitz felt, but what about all the other lives? Their absence gnawed at his conscience.

The two Army Rangers who had come with Beckham and Horn sat next to the rest of the plane's crew closer to the tail, yet another team that had suffered heavy casualties.

"I'm sorry," Beckham said, seeming to sense Fitz's hurt. "It never gets easier, but this wasn't your fault."

Fitz looked at Dohi who had his head down. It wasn't just Fitz feeling guilty for losing Mendez. The rest of the team felt it, too.

He shifted his gaze to a small window. A snow-covered mountain range snaked over the earth. Ice across the rocky landscape reflected the glint of the morning sun. They were headed to Banff National Park to refuel and find out where they were headed next.

"I know Mendez and Lincoln didn't die in vain," Fitz said. "Their sacrifices will help us win this war."

"That's right," Beckham said, then sighed.

Fitz turned back to him. "So, tell me everything I've missed."

Beckham summarized the events over the past few days. The longer Fitz listened, the more he wondered what a path to victory even looked like.

Nuclear bombs had decimated cities. More outposts and bases had fallen. Each night was a battle to survive. The war had cost the Allied States territory, resources, and most importantly, tens of thousands of lives.

"Kate and her team have been trying to use the webbing network to track down where all the messages to coordinate the attacks are coming from," Beckham said. "There's someone, or something pulling the strings."

Fitz wasn't sure what to say. He wasn't sure if science could save them this time, if he was being honest, but he kept that to himself.

The news was far worse than he had thought. For the next few hours he sat next to Beckham in silence. Rico put her head against his shoulder. He tried to sleep but couldn't keep his eyes closed.

Every time he shut them, he kept replaying everything that had happened out there. All of his moves, all of his mistakes, and all of the soldiers who hadn't come home.

Turbulence snapped him from his thoughts. The plane shuddered, and the pilot's voice came over the intercom.

"We're beginning our descent," he said. "The winds are a little choppy, so hold on."

The medics each grabbed the handholds on Hopkins' and Lawrence's stretchers, bracing them when another patch of turbulence rattled the C-130.

Rico leaned against Fitz as they dropped past the mountain tops, snow and ice blowing over the plane. Through the gray and white shroud, Fitz spotted the aquamarine glimmer of the national park's famous lakes and rivers. Between the mountains, he saw the town itself, surrounded by walls made of timber.

At the center of the outpost stood a tall building that looked like a castle. All the vehicles traveling around the outpost seemed to be going to and from that building.

"I've always wanted to visit Banff," Rico said. "It's beautiful."

This place was once a symbol of humanity's close

connection to nature. Now it was a handhold for mankind's survival against the worst Mother Nature had to offer.

"Brace for landing," the pilot said.

A moment later the plane landed hard on a strip of the Trans-Canada Highway. The engines roared as they applied reverse thrust, slowing them to a stop outside Banff.

"Get ready to move out!" a crew chief said. He stood at the control panel near the plane's tail and started lowering the ramp.

Blustering cold wind whipped inside, blasting Fitz. He grabbed Rico's hand as they stood against the fierce, freezing gusts. The team gathered their weapons and packs full of scavenged equipment from the National Accelerator Laboratory.

"This way!" the crew chief yelled.

Snow swirled past as Beckham led the group to the asphalt. Already more white snow encroached on the cleared improvised runway.

Four armored personnel carriers waited with the rear passenger doors open. Canadian soldiers waved at them to hop inside. Team Ghost piled into the first APC with Beckham and Horn. The Rangers and Wolfhounds were loaded into another.

A Canadian soldier with a mottled gray uniform and the red-and-white Canadian flag on his shoulder closed the door, shutting out the snowstorm.

"Welcome to Canada," he said, reaching out to shake their hands. "I'm Sergeant Carter Prince."

"Thanks for hosting us," Beckham said.

Fitz also gave his thanks. He had worked with foreign soldiers before over the years. More often than not, non-

Americans showed resentment for the monsters the United States military had created almost a decade earlier.

Not this guy. Prince seemed sincere.

"Bet you're not used to the cold," he said.

"No, Sergeant," Rico said. "Not like this."

"Mendez never did like the cold," Ace murmured. He wiped at his eyes. It wasn't the first time Fitz had seen the big guy cry, and it wouldn't be the last.

"Eh, it'll get colder," Prince said. "But don't worry. Where you're going, you'll have a chance to get some warm drinks and chow."

The APC's tires crunched over piles of snow as they entered Banff. Fitz looked out one of the ballistic glass windows. Besides the natural protection the rugged mountains provided, the Canadians had constructed walls around the town topped with barbed wire and guard towers. Men in white parkas guarded each station.

Prince saw Fitz surveying the defenses. "The cold season slows the Variants down. The ones that aren't adapted, that is. It also means there isn't a lot of food out there, so a lot of them have starved off, but there are still creatures that show up from time to time."

"The cold might slow the Variants down, but the beasts hitting us to the south will come this way eventually," Fitz said. "And I promise you, the cold isn't going to stop them."

The APC skidded to a stop outside the front of a towering castle-like hotel. An old sign read, *Fairmont Banff Springs*.

Spotlights shone from various locations in the parking lot, illuminating machine gun nests poking out of the balconies, and snipers on the rooftops. The former luxury hotel had been turned into a modern-day fortress.

"Welcome to Western Canada Defensive Forces' HQ," Prince said. "Or what they used to call, 'The Castle in the Rockies'."

He opened the back door and led the others through the biting cold. While they unloaded their equipment, a group of four medics ran to another APC and took the Wolfhounds with them.

"Where are they going?" Fitz asked.

"We've set up another building as our infirmary," Prince said. "I can guarantee you those men will be well taken care of."

Fitz watched them race away, hoping Prince was right as the sergeant led Ghost and the others into a lobby with crackling fireplaces. Tables and chairs furnished the timber plank floors carpeted partially with furs.

Canadian soldiers and civilians were stationed at computers or circled around maps, immersed in conversation.

"Those are the engineers we scrambled to examine that equipment you brought from California," Prince said. "They'll start working immediately."

"Thank you," Fitz said.

Prince gestured toward a hall and opened a door to a conference room.

"This is where I leave you," he said. "Nice to meet all of you."

"Appreciated," Horn said.

The rest of the team gave their thanks and filed into a room.

Long tables had already been set out with food and hot cups of tea. A bald man with a tawny face, chiseled and sharp, stood at the end of the table.

"I'm General Kamer," he said. "Please, have a seat and

start eating. We've got a lot to go over, and I'm sure you're all hungry."

Fitz was happy to accept the invitation after making their own introductions. He found a seat next to Rico and dug into the still-steaming mashed potatoes and roast beef. Eating the warm food filled him with more than much needed nutrition. It also filled him with the guilt for those who weren't here to enjoy the meal, and his appetite started to wane.

"We don't get a lot of visitors during the winter," Kamer said. "I've gathered a few officers to listen in. I want to make sure we're all on the same page."

"That sounds good, sir," Beckham said. "I'm not sure how much the president already told you, but I can bring you up to speed."

Kamer took a sip of tea. "I think I know everything that's happened up until right before you landed. The most important matter at hand isn't what we've done, but what we'll be doing to move forward."

"You spoke to President Ringgold?" Beckham asked.

"Yes," Kamer said. He put his cup down. "I was moved by her resolve to fight back, and the Western Canadian Prime Minister feels similarly. We've also been in contact with the Mexican president to discuss the events plaguing the Allied States."

Fitz was thrilled to hear the other countries were finally talking, but he hoped it meant action and not just words.

"We're all in agreement," Kamer said. "This is not just a domestic matter for the Allied States. This a conflict with the potential to devastate North America, and the rest of the world for that matter."

"I wish Europe felt the same way," Beckham said.

"They should, but they were more devastated than we were here in Canada," Kamer said. "My impression is their struggle was worse than ours."

Flashbacks of the war in Europe surfaced in his mind, but Fitz suppressed them.

"Canada and the Federation of Mexican States, stand with you... We're in this fight together now," Kamer said.

"Thank you, sir, it's great to hear you say that," Beckham said. "How exactly will you be helping us?"

Kamer broke out a business smile. To Fitz, it looked almost like the patronizing grin of a politician. He didn't like that.

"Supporting your next mission and repairing that SDS technology to start," Kamer said. "We're also shipping ammunition and medical supplies to the Allied States."

"We're going to need more than that," Fitz said, unable to contain himself. "We're talking about threats unlike any the world has seen. We need men, aircraft, and weapons."

Beckham's face was red with frustration too. "Please, sir, as you said, we're in this tragedy together. But the only way we win together is if we actually *fight* together.

Kamer held up a hand to stay their protests. "At this point we are not able to commit soldiers. We've lost too many of our own."

Fitz and Beckham exchanged a glance.

"You hear about them Chimeras yet, General?" Horn asked.

Kamer looked uncertain. "I have a hard time believing such beasts exist. Variants with the brains of soldiers?" He shook his head. "I'm afraid I can't take your word about this without more concrete proof. As you know, the stress of battle can cause some intense visual phenomena that aren't necessarily real."

Horn clenched his jaw, which Fitz knew meant he was about to blow a gasket. Beckham noticed too and put a hand on the big man's shoulder.

"I know what I saw," Rico said. "And I saw monsters carrying rifles."

Kamer looked at her but didn't reply.

"You're making a big mistake," Beckham said. "All due respect, sir."

"I'd suggest you focus on your next mission, *Captain*," Kamer said. "Since you only have the one plane, we'll be lending support for these missions."

Fitz perked up, anxious to hear what came next, despite his frustration with Kamer.

"Team Ghost will be headed to Seattle to investigate a research site formerly known as the Center for Engineering Complex Organs, or CECO," said the general. "Captain Beckham, Master Sergeant Horn, you will be leading another team to investigate a site in Denver called HumoSource. I am told that Sergeant First Class Jenny Rico will be joining you."

Rico grabbed Fitz's hand under the table and squeezed. It was tough enough going into the field with her, knowing she was in danger. And now, she would be out of sight, far from him, venturing straight back into enemy territory.

"We will provide aircraft for both missions, but due to a shortage and ability of able planes, I'm afraid we can only take Captain Beckham and his team as far as Wyoming," Kamer said. "There you'll be met by another Allied States team and will board a helicopter better fitted for the conditions in Denver."

"Understood," Beckham said.

"Before we go anywhere, I want to make sure the injured Wolfhounds are taken care of," Fitz said.

"Rest assured, they will be," Kamer replied.

"I'd like to see to that personally," Fitz said. "I was responsible for getting them back here, and I want to make sure they make it home safe."

"Not a problem." Kamer passed out briefing folders so they could study their upcoming mission. "In regard to the business at hand, I was also informed a science team tracked down the Variant-based communication signals originating to these points. Your teams are to infiltrate both locations and identify any potential targets. The objective is to find this Master the Variants and their collaborators are taking their orders from."

Fitz looked over at Beckham and Horn. They didn't seem shocked by the mission, but they did seem surprised to be joining it. While he was glad to have them back with Team Ghost, Fitz knew this was bad news.

It meant the Allied States was running out of soldiers. And with every passing hour, they were losing more. Men like Mendez and Lincoln. Canada didn't seem willing to step up as much as Fitz had hoped.

Before the war was over, there would be more devastating losses.

Fitz just hoped it would all be worth it—that they would be victorious. But from the sounds of it, he wasn't sure victory was possible.

Timothy was out of water and food. The only thing he had left was ammunition, but there wasn't much of that left between him and Ruckley.

For the past day, they had trekked across southern Maine into New Hampshire, trying to find refuge. Ruckley had pushed on all the way to Newburyport. They had hoped to find an old military depot the Allied States had used to store ammunition and equipment outside the city, but they never made it. Her injuries and their exhaustion had gotten the better of them. They were so close, but Ruckley simply couldn't take another step.

Timothy had discovered an abandoned United States Postal Service building to serve as their temporary refuge. The windows and doors were still barricaded by plywood from the first war, but he found a way in through the service garage with two mail trucks.

Evidence of the last war still remained in the dusty space. Broken ventilation vents showed where Variants had dropped inside. The twisted skeleton of a Variant and scattered bones from a human lay strewn across the floor.

Timothy stood outside the open doors of one of the mail trucks. Ruckley slept inside the vehicle on a sleeping bag Timothy had found deeper in the facility.

Removing the arrow had damaged her muscle, and she had lost a lot of blood. Timothy had cleaned it up the best he could to keep the scent from the Variants.

Still, he knew they were out there. He kept his rifle close, and his eyes on the bay windows of the garage.

It wasn't just the beasts he had to watch out for now. Collaborators and other dangerous groups like the cult that had burned Neeland alive would kill Ruckley and Timothy without a moment's hesitation.

He checked on her again. This time she was shaking, pallor in her face. He examined her bandage. The skin around it was tender and red, definitely inflamed and probably infected.

That wasn't a surprise. They had lost their field kit when they fled the farmhouse. That would've made stitching her up and cleaning the injury easier, but they had to rely on cloths and sewing needles he had scavenged.

None of that would save her. They needed real medicine, water, and a radio.

"Sergeant," Timothy said, nudging her gently.

She groaned, then swung the pistol still gripped in her hand at his face.

"Easy, easy!" Timothy said.

Realization passed over her eyes, and she lowered the gun.

"What?" she muttered, sweat dripping over her forehead. "Someone coming?"

"No, no, I just… You've got a fever. Seems like it's getting worse."

She sat up and drew her back against the inner wall of the truck. She started unwrapping her bandage.

"Christ," she grumbled. "Of all the injuries, I never thought a stupid arrow would be the one to take me down."

"You're not down yet."

Timothy leaned closer for a better look. The flesh around the wound had festered fast.

"We need to get you antibiotics," he said.

"And where do you think you'll find those?"

"Maybe they have some at the depot. I can go look while you rest."

"You're not going alone." She swung her legs out of the back of the truck. "I'll go with you."

She stepped out, wobbled, and then reached out for Timothy. He helped her sit back down.

"You were saying…" he said quietly.

Ruckley put a hand on her head. "I… I'm dizzy." She sighed. "You're right."

"You're not going anywhere. I'll do a supply run. It's our only shot of getting to Boston alive."

She reached for her water bottle, and he helped her drink what was left. Then he helped her lay down in the truck and then closed one of the doors.

"I'll be back as soon as I can," he said.

"Be careful."

"I will."

Timothy grabbed a map they had found and his gear. Rifle in hand, he crossed through the garage and then peered out the window of a side door to check the parking lot for hostiles. Finding it clear, he went outside, the cold afternoon wind numbing his exposed face.

He scanned the buildings and houses down the street, but nothing in the ghost town stirred.

According to the map, the depot was three miles away. Three miles wasn't a terribly long distance, but Timothy's feet were already swollen and sore. He was exhausted from the hours they had already been hiking.

Plenty of large million-dollar houses lined the streets

but searching them would be futile. All the broken windows and busted doors told him any useful supplies were already long gone.

Rifle at the ready, he started down a road toward a bridge over the Merrimack River. Moving during daylight was risky if there were collaborators out here, but night wasn't that much better with Variants hunting in the dark.

Besides, Ruckley might not have until nightfall.

He spotted a bicycle on the side of the road, but the tires were flat.

So much for luck today.

When he reached the bridge, he scoped the other side. Seeing nothing, he ran across as fast as he could. A few damaged boats were still in slips at the harbor, and there was a sailboat that looked in pretty good shape.

At one mile under his belt, he stopped to catch his breath and check his map. The depot was two miles to the west on a peninsula.

He crossed a street and headed into another neighborhood rife with more abandoned mansions. Trash and abandoned cars littered the road ahead.

Empty suitcases were open on the front stoop and driveway of one house. Evidence of a failed exodus from the first war.

With a sigh, he continued. The wind died down, and he suddenly felt an odd sensation. As he neared the depot, he stopped, listening.

There didn't seem to be anyone or anything out here. Not even Variants.

An overwhelming sense of loneliness gripped him. Like he was the last man on Earth.

He pressed on until he saw the depot. Using a car for cover, he crouched and pressed the scope to his eye.

There were two connected buildings at the depot. One was an older structure made of brick. The other was a longer warehouse. Both were enclosed by a razor wire-topped fence that had crashed down in a twenty-foot section.

A bulldozer and a Jeep Wrangler with flat tires were parked outside the closed warehouse garage doors. At the front entrance of the brick building, he saw a dirt bike on its side.

Timothy set off for a better view of the back, only stopping when he saw bodies across the corpse-covered asphalt. The back loading bay into the building was open. There were more bodies inside, some wearing fatigues.

Whatever had happened here hadn't been too recent, judging by the smell of rot wafting in the cool air.

He headed over the toppled fence, careful not to snag his clothing on the razor wire. After hopping over the wire, his boots hit the pavement with a thud.

The sound sent a chill through his body.

He froze, waiting for the shriek of a beast to answer. When it didn't come, he crept toward the loading bay, passing the bodies. The recent rains had mostly washed the blood away in the parking lot, but the inside of the garage was speckled with dried pools around the corpses of both men and monsters.

Timothy navigated the graveyard and looked for a door into the offices and supply rooms. There were two. One was open, and the other closed.

He tried the closed one first. It clicked, locked.

Then he entered the opened door and followed a carpeted hallway, boots crunching over spent casings. Light streaming through open doors guided him, revealing a blood trail across blue carpet.

It streaked off into the second open doorway leading from the hall.

Timothy checked the first room, an office furnished with a handful of metal desks, a few chairs, and rows of file cabinets. But no medicine or water.

He continued to the next doorway. It led to a supply closet where the blood streaks pointed to the body of a Variant. He nudged it with a boot, finding it was as stiff as a board.

The closet contained only cleaning and office supplies.

His thoughts turned back to Ruckley, wondering how long she would make it by herself. Would it be the Variants or infection that got her first? Either way, he needed to hurry.

Timothy continued down the hallway, clearing each room. Blood spatters marred the interior all the way toward the doorway connecting the brick building to the warehouse.

He opened it and aimed his rifle into the heart of the depot. The windows were all covered by boards or metal plates, blocking out the sunlight. He turned on his tactical light and swept it over the space, revealing a large room with shelves of supplies and closed doors with signs showing they led to the barracks.

This place was a treasure trove.

He set off into the rows of shelves to search for medicine, sifting over the shelves with his light, examining the crates and boxes.

Nothing in the first aisle grabbed his attention. But a rustling noise stopped him mid-stride. Then silence. He waited for the sound again.

He heard it again, this time more clearly.

Just the wind on the side of the building.

Timothy continued his search until he found a shelf of medicine. Someone had already raided it, leaving bloody handprints on the boxes.

But there was still plenty left. He scrounged through the cardboard boxes until he found a handful of packets filled with antibiotics. He stuffed them into his pack. Then he grabbed a field kit that had everything he needed to clean Ruckley's wound.

Hell yes, finally some decent luck, he thought.

When he turned to leave, a figure stood in the open doorway of a side room. They were shadowed but it looked like they had a gun pointed at him.

"Don't shoot," Timothy said. "I'm just here for medicine to help an injured Army Ranger."

The figure kept the gun on him for a moment.

Was this a collaborator? Maybe another cultist?

The guy had the drop on him, and Timothy knew he couldn't bring his rifle up in time to fire.

Running wasn't an option either.

He had been caught dead-to-rights.

"Please, I don't want trouble," Timothy said. "I just need medicine and water and I'll leave."

The figure lowered the gun and leaned against the wall. Timothy raised his rifle just enough to let his tac light illuminate the figure.

It was a soldier.

The bearded man slumped against a wall, gripping a blood-soaked bandage wrapped around his gut.

Timothy rushed over and set his rifle down. He caught a whiff of something putrid as he leaned down.

"Sir," he said.

The man grunted and pushed at the ground to sit up. That's when Timothy saw everything from his ribs to his crotch were soaked with blood.

Jesus Christ, how is this guy still alive? Timothy thought.

"Who are you?" the man whispered.

"I'm from Outpost Portland," Timothy replied. "I escaped a few—"

"What happened to Portland?" the man interrupted. Desperation filled his eyes.

"It was destroyed, sir."

The man loosened his grip and let out a whimper.

"My family..." he said. "My family was there."

Timothy put a hand on the man's shoulders as tears streamed over the man's face.

"I'm sorry," he said. "I lost my dad and friends, too."

The guy looked up, blinking past the tears.

"I'm sorry, too," he said. "This wasn't supposed to happen...things were supposed to get better."

Timothy felt this man's raw pain. Reaching down, he grabbed his hand, connecting with a soldier he didn't even know.

"Let me help you," Timothy said. "I'll get those bandages changed."

"No... My family's gone. No point in fighting anymore."

He pulled his hand away from the bandage. Then he reached into his vest and fingered around before pulling out a key.

"There's a dirt bike outside," he said. "Got some juice left in it. Take it and get those meds back to your friend. There's water inside the room behind me and some ammo."

Timothy took the key. "I can't take your water and ammo."

"You need it more than me."

Timothy hesitated. He hated asking this man for anything else, but he had to. "What about a radio?"

The soldier shook his head. "Long story, but there was another survivor. He took it with him when he left."

Timothy wasn't sure what to say, so he gave the man's shoulder a gentle squeeze. "You're sure about all this?"

"Yes, kid. Now *go*."

He helped the soldier readjust his body so he was resting against the wall comfortably.

"Thank you, I won't forget this," Timothy said. He left the man and grabbed the water bottles from the room. Then he grabbed some ammo and made his way outside, not looking back.

He stood the bike up, then hopped on with his backpack full of gear. As it rumbled to life and he drove away, a gunshot cracked from inside the depot.

Timothy said a prayer for the man as he scanned the road for hostiles and twisted the throttle to go faster. The motor was loud, but he made it back to the bridge without being noticed.

Glancing down, he checked the gas gauge.

There wasn't enough to get to Boston, but there was another way...a dangerous way, but a way nonetheless. He eyed the boats in the harbor off the bridge.

Screw walking the rest of the way, once he got Ruckley cleaned up, they were going to sail to Boston.

***

Nick saw the mountains on the horizon under the gray sky. He could smell the rain in the air, though it hadn't hit them yet. After a long journey, they were almost back to base.

189

He couldn't help but feel like they were limping home, and after leaving the fuel outpost, things hadn't gotten any better. One of the female prisoners had escaped their ropes and jumped out of the pickup truck.

Nick had asked Pete if they should turn around to look for the prisoner, but Pete had shaken his head.

"If she survived, then she deserves to live," Pete had said. "Can't waste the time on one person."

Then, an hour from the base, the right front tire on the pickup went flat, forcing Nick to stop and change it for the final leg of the drive.

The convoy navigated through a hidden entryway to the forest skirting the mountain. Storm clouds rolled overhead. Lightning forked over the peaks, followed by the growling roll of thunder.

Nick eased off the gas and turned on the wipers as sheets of rain slammed into the windshield.

He knew some of the history behind the place that had become his home. This was one of the most pristine nature preserves in Maine, and the isolated mountain had become part of one of the United States government's most secretive projects. Only the top officials had even known of the bunker and the single missile silo built during the Cold War.

There was only one missile here for a reason. The nuclear warhead was a prototype that rivaled the Tsar Bomb, arguably one of the most powerful weapons ever created. This was a deterrent the government had created and hidden away, almost lost to time.

And now it was a secret weapon of the New Gods.

For Nick, this place had protected his family since the end of the Great War of Extinction, when he had first joined the army of the New Gods after hearing a radio message broadcasting the existence of a safe and powerful community.

He had been hiding in a cabin about fifty miles from here with his wife and two daughters. They had been running out of food and were slowly wasting away. They had had no choice but to risk the long journey through Variant-filled territory to get here. Coming to Katahdin was the best decision he had ever made.

The bunker was more than a refuge. It had symbolized the start of a new way of life.

And Pete was the reason for it all.

Nick looked over at the man with dreadlocks. The former defense contractor had known about this base because of his classified work keeping it updated at the turn of the century before it was almost all decommissioned. There were multiple former military officers who had worked here, defected from the military, and now called this place home. They had handed over the authenticator codes for the silo to Pete years ago.

Pete had then introduced this base to the human allies of the Variants, long after those in the government who had known about it died during the war.

Now it was one of a handful of forward operating bases they were using to support their offensive to secure the Land of the New Gods.

"Can't wait for a shower," Pete said.

"And a warm meal," Nick said. But what he really looked forward to was seeing his family.

He pulled onto a steep dirt road leading to the bunker's entrance. The tires thumped over the rocky ground now wet with rain-soaked mud.

The prisoners in the back of the truck ahead huddled together, enduring the full brunt of the cold rainfall like livestock might. But Nick didn't feel any sympathy for them.

These people were still the enemy. He wouldn't worry about their comfort until they swore allegiance to the New Gods like he had.

He slowed the truck as they came around another muddy bend. A figure emerged from behind a cluster of rocks on the side of the road carrying a sniper rifle. The man raised a hand as they passed. He was one of many lookouts around the bunker.

Nick probably passed a half-dozen more snipers without even knowing it. Even he didn't know exactly where all their scouts were positioned.

The road twisted through a thick slope filled with pine trees. It ended as the canopy thinned out at the base of the mountain. Wooden beams blocked off an old mining shaft that dated back to the Prohibition era.

All sorts of tunnels snaked through the mountain that had once been used to store and brew bootleg booze during the early nineteen-hundreds.

The trucks stopped and two more guards showed up to move the beams, allowing them to pass into a narrow corridor. Headlights from the trucks washed over the thick concrete walls of the tunnel.

This was the side entrance to the base, but there were other exits and entrances across the mountain, including those that housed the ballistic missile.

Nick parked in a bay where other vehicles like Jeeps and pickups were lined up in neat rows. Four guards stood sentry outside a steel door.

"Welcome back," said one of the men.

"Get these prisoners inside," Pete said. "Rest of you, unload the trucks. Nick, meet me in the command room in thirty minutes."

The men did as ordered. Nick used the brief break to find his family. He took a stairwell down twenty stories, stopping once to catch his breath. Normally he could handle the stairs, but now he was completely drained.

This attack had rattled him to the core, and after losing Alfred, he was feeling slightly defeated and hadn't caught a wink of sleep, even when they'd stopped at the fuel depot.

When he saw his wife and daughters eating at a picnic table in the massive living space the families all shared, his fatigue vanished.

"Diana," he called out.

His wife stood and turned. When she saw Nick, she smiled the same smile he had fallen in love with twenty years ago. Their younger ten-year-old daughter Lily had just shoveled a spoonful of beans in her mouth.

She jumped up, grinning and rushing to hug him.

Freya, their thirteen-year-old, didn't seem as excited. She swept her frizzled brown hair away from her face and smiled, but it seemed forced.

Nick gave Diana a hug and then pulled Lily in tight. Freya joined them but kept her distance.

"Hey, Dad," she said coolly.

"How's everyone?" he asked.

"Good now that you're home," Diana said. "Are you hungry?"

"Starving, but I got a meeting in a few minutes. I just dropped down to say hello."

"You aren't going to stay?" Lily asked.

Freya looked away, clearly agitated. She had an acidic teenage attitude, and she frequently let out spiteful diatribes about how she hated it here.

Nick could handle her bullheadedness, but it was her questioning the New Gods that had caused the most tension.

The last time she had done that was a month ago.

He still felt bad about slapping her across the face during that outburst, but it had been for her own good. Her protection, in fact. At least she hadn't spoken out again. That single slap was nothing compared to what the other men would do if they heard her.

Pete would have no problem punishing a teenager by death, even if it was Nick's own daughter, for the words of a heretic.

"Dad, are you going to be home for a while?" Lily asked.

"Hopefully for at least a few days," he said.

Lily looked down in despair.

It took him a few seconds to realize she was staring at the bloodstains on his pants and boots. Her gaze flitted to the blood on his chest.

"Are you hurt?" she asked.

Nick sighed. His daughters and wife knew he was a soldier. They understood what he did, but it didn't make what he had to say any better.

"I'm okay," he said. "But Alfred didn't make it home this time."

Diana gasped. "What?"

"I tried to save him, but…" Nick said. "He was too hurt. There wasn't anything we could do."

Or was there? Nick wondered.

The memory of leaving Alfred on the road replayed in his mind.

He checked his watch. "I'm sorry, we'll talk more later. I've got to go now."

Nick hugged his wife and told his daughters he would be back soon. Then he headed for the command room. Pete was already there with a few other staff members in charge of the comms and security.

"Got some good news," Pete said. A shit-eating grin formed on his face. The biggest grin Nick had seen in all the years he had been here.

"A New God general is coming *here*," Pete said. "Together, we'll prepare for the final stage of the war."

— 14 —

The afternoon sun glinted off the names inscribed on the bronze parapets surrounding the deep pools of the 9/11 memorial. Standing around the memorial were some of the veteran outpost soldiers and about one thousand of the civilians they were trying to protect. The other four thousand had remained in their buildings and underground.

Everyone outside hung their heads for a moment of silence and prayer at Commander Amber Massey's request.

She stood in the bed of her black pickup truck. Her red hair danced in the cool wind blowing over the crowd.

Fischer and Chase were among the mourners. The irony that they were around this hallowed memorial to honor the dead of last night's battle was not lost on them.

So many had given their lives in such a short amount of time. The Allied States was like a puddle in the Texas desert. It grew smaller and smaller with each passing second, and there was no rain or respite on the horizon.

Massey scanned the tear-streaked, exhausted faces. "I know you're all tired, and I know some of you want to abandon the outpost and try your chances out there."

Fischer saw some people nod.

"You are free to leave if you'd like," Massey said. "This is still the Allied States, a place built on the very Constitution and Bill of Rights that gave us the United

States of America. That makes you free men and women."

Chase shot Fischer a glance, perhaps wondering if Fischer wanted to try their luck leaving.

"I, for one, haven't fought and bled for this outpost to give up," Massey said. Her voice boomed with the self-assuredness of a seasoned military commander. "I plan on staying, to the end, whatever that may be, fighting for the sacred ground we stand on today."

"New Yorkers don't run!" one man shouted.

A few heads bobbed in agreement.

"That's right," Massey said. "New Yorkers are some of the toughest people on the planet! When the terrorists hit the towers at whose bases we stand at now, what did people do? They ran back in to help the trapped and the injured!"

"We always help our neighbors, even if we don't like them!" a woman yelled.

A few people laughed.

Massey smiled at the woman. Then her expression grew serious. "Make no mistake. The enemy will return and they will hit us hard, but we will beat them back again and we *will* find a way to win this war."

Fischer thought of Tran and Meyer as the crowd held up their weapons into the air. The guard and engineer joined a long list of men in Fischer's employment who had given their lives.

But Tran was more than just an employee.

He was a friend and confidante. Someone who had stood by his side since the death of his wife, serving him in his greatest time of need.

"Stand with me and fight!" Massey yelled.

The cheering grew louder. Outpost officers dispersed

through the crowd, organizing teams to bolster the razor wire-topped walls and move weapons to new positions. Snipers marched off to the skyscrapers surrounding the outpost where they would find perches to give them a bird's eye view of the apocalyptic urban ruin.

"Do you think Tran's still alive?" Chase asked.

"I sure to God hope not," Fischer said.

"If he is, should we…" Chase spat on the ground. "I know finding him would be nearly impossible, but I would feel like a coward if we didn't try."

"Me too, but we have no idea where to even start looking. The best thing we can do to honor Tran is keep fighting."

Chase dipped his head.

Fischer put on his cowboy hat. "Let's go see where we can help."

Massey had dismounted from the truck and stood at the end of a row of white oak trees with her back turned, looking out over the skyrises.

"Commander," Fischer said.

She turned to face him and wiped at a tear rolling down her face.

"We're with you, Commander," Fischer said.

"I knew that already," she said with a smile. "You're a Texan. Texans don't back down from a fight either. Remember the Alamo?"

"Once again, our backs are up against the wall, but we either hold what we have left of this country or else we run across the Atlantic," Fischer said. "This country, no matter what it's been through, is my home and we're happy to help where you need us."

Massey looked over her shoulder. "My people retrieved one surviving vibroseis truck, but we don't know how to use it."

"What about the SDS equipment? Do you know if Team Ghost ever located it?"

"I'm not sure."

The words filled Fischer with worry. Not only were they down to one truck, he wasn't sure of the status of the SDS equipment that General Cornelius believed could change the war.

"So just one truck left?" he asked.

She nodded.

Chase looked at the ground. He was the only man from Fischer's company still with him. All his engineers had died in last night's attack. His stomach felt weak when he thought about what he was agreeing to do. His engineers were far better at operating the trucks, but they now had no choice.

"I'll operate the truck myself," Fischer said.

"Thank you." Massey put a hand on his shoulder. "I'm glad we have you with us."

Fischer heard his wife's voice in the back of his mind, telling him they should leave Lower Manhattan. Even in death, she was looking out for him. Every time he had heard her voice, he had almost died.

"I'll show you to the truck," Massey said.

She started walking, leading Fischer and Chase toward the northern wall.

The outpost around them was alive with workers. Men and women sat at tables cleaning weapons. Others loaded magazines, and an assembly line hoisted crates of ammunition to machine gun nests.

Fischer wondered how many bullets they actually had left.

At least they still had the Bradley Fighting Vehicles

positioned at the corners of the outposts. He saw an Apache, too, roosted atop a building just outside the memorial. They might have lost one of the M1 Abrams and an Apache last night, but they still had one left of both.

She stopped when they reached the vibroseis truck. Fischer stepped into the filthy open cab of the truck, still stained with blood. It was a shitty place to die, but if this was his destiny, so be it.

Better than being taken to the webbing-covered tunnels.

And at least if there was anything left of him, they could always bury him in Texas.

Massey stepped away to listen to a call on her radio while Fischer prepared the electronics in the truck. Chase leaned in.

"Anything else I can do to help?" Chase asked.

Fischer shook his head. There wasn't anything more Chase could do.

This was on Fischer.

A few minutes later Massey returned.

"Got some interesting news," she said.

Fischer looked up from the controls. Maybe the SDS equipment was on its way here.

"We're going to have some company," Massey said with a sly grin. "Might actually get some reinforcements after all."

***

"I knew when we found those locations, there would be a chance you would be investigating one." Kate's voice crackled over the satellite phone. "My work is putting your life at risk again."

Beckham stood in the lobby of the Fairmont Banff Springs hotel, thinking of what to say. Team Ghost was packing up their gear around him and making final preparations for their missions to search for the Master behind the monsters' resurgence.

"Reed?" Kate said. "Are you still there?"

"Yes, I'm sorry, it's just… I don't know any other way. Team Ghost needs help. We lost Mendez, Kate." He paused, watching the disastrous chopper attack in his mind. "He was there one second, and then…gone."

A moment of silence passed between them.

"I'm so sorry, Reed," she said.

"It's time for Horn and me to really step up and fight in the stead of those who have fallen. Meg, Riley, Davis…now Mendez, Lincoln, Jake, Timothy, Bo, Donna…and so many others who have given their lives."

The list went on and on, dragging all the way to the first war, and Beckham let his words trail off. "If we don't step up now, there won't—"

"I know," Kate said, cutting him off. "The only way we can live together like a normal family again is to win this war. We all have to be willing to make the ultimate sacrifice."

Beckham knew this wasn't going to just be him at risk, but hearing Kate acknowledge that made his heart flip. For that matter, she had put herself in harm's way to complete her scientific work.

"Are the kids okay?" Beckham asked. "And the dogs?"

"They're fine. They just miss you and Parker."

Beckham choked up a bit. God, he just wanted to hug Javier and Kate and Horn's girls, who might as well be his adopted daughters. He wanted to toss a ball for Spark and Ginger to chase, and sit out on their deck at Peak's Island to watch the sunrise while enjoying a coffee.

But the only way to realize that kind of future was to face the evil lurking out there.

"Trucks are coming," called a Canadian soldier from the lobby entrance.

A convoy of vehicles drove toward the circle driveway outside the hotel.

"I got to go, Kate," he said. "Be safe. I love you."

"I love you, too."

He almost hung up, but then heard her speak again.

"Wait, Reed, are you there?"

"Yeah, I'm still here."

"When this is over... I was thinking... Javier could use a brother or a sister."

Beckham smiled. "Yeah, he'd like that. So would I."

"Then make sure you come home in one piece. That's an order, Captain."

He smiled wider. "I'll see you soon, my love."

She hung up and Beckham handed the phone back to the Canadian officer who had lent it to him. Then he walked back to Team Ghost.

"How is everyone?" Horn asked.

"Good. The kids are doing just fine."

"And Kate?"

"Okay."

"She doesn't want us to go, does she?"

Beckham shook his head.

"I don't blame her," Rico said. "You guys already put your time in."

"Yeah, well, things have changed," Beckham said. "You guys can't get rid of us that easily. You're stuck with me and Big Horn now."

Fitz glanced over as he packed his ruck, but he didn't say anything.

The team strapped on their packs and then huddled behind the big glass front door to the hotel. Snow fell in a blizzard-like torrent outside. Already a foot of it had accumulated on the hotel grounds.

"God, I hate the cold." Horn shoved his hands in his parka's pockets.

Beckham wrapped a scarf around his face, then zipped his parka up to his chin.

For the past few hours they had rested and filled their stomachs, but there was one last thing to do before they once again parted ways: honor Specialists Lincoln and Mendez.

"Everyone ready?" asked Prince. He had been on the radio making sure security was tight for the ride that would take them to their planned stop before heading to the aircraft that would take them back to the States.

"Let's go," Fitz said. He opened the doors and stepped outside, a gust of wind slamming into the team.

Beckham tried to keep his scarf up but the wind blew it loose, frigid air slicing through his beard. He pulled the scarf back up and followed Fitz down the stone steps to a convoy of three armored trucks and a white SUV with a brush guard. All the vehicles had chains over their tires.

Team Ghost piled into the white SUV with Prince.

The Canadian soldier behind the wheel drove down a road curving through the snow. With the sun hidden behind dark clouds and the relentless snowstorm, visibility was limited.

Dohi had insisted they go somewhere where they had an expansive view of the mountains, lake, and forest surrounding them to say some final words for their fallen comrades.

Prince said he knew just the place for a short ceremony, and it wasn't far from the runway. They might not be able to find a view because of the snowfall, but all the same, Beckham thought it was important they found a decent spot to pay their respects.

Lincoln and Mendez deserved a proper burial, but like so many others who had died in the line of duty, that just wasn't possible.

The Canadians were providing extra security for the ceremony and the takeoff, hence the three APCs driving along with them.

The convoy drove over a road framed by six-foot-high snowdrifts.

"Going to be twice as high by the time winter ends," Prince said.

A thick forest of pines appeared in the distance through the haze of snow. The mountains behind them cast a foreboding skyline. Jagged peaks lined the horizon like the teeth of a gigantic prehistoric animal.

"This is the turn off," Prince said.

The driver followed the APCs. Through the screen of snow, Beckham could make out a lookout over a frozen lake. Picnic tables covered in snow protruded out of the drifts.

Beckham imagined what this place was like in the past, when families came to enjoy a weekend or day in nature. But like most places in the world, this was now enemy territory. No one would eat a sandwich enjoying the view anytime soon, and that wasn't just because of the snow.

"Dohi, let's make this quick, okay?" Beckham said. He didn't want to be insensitive, but he had to say what needed to be said. They couldn't afford to delay the mission or expose themselves to undue threats out here.

"Understood," Dohi said.

The team stepped out into the howling wind. Canadian forces formed a perimeter around the picnic area with their rifles cradled. Prince remained close, but kept enough distance to give them some privacy.

Dohi went to the edge of the lookout and bent down. He cleared a spot in the snow with a glove and then picked up some dirt.

Beckham and Horn stood between Rico, Fitz, and Ace. They formed a half circle around Dohi. He rose to his feet and looked at the lake, then the mountains.

"Before we part ways again, I wanted to spend a minute to honor the lives of Lincoln and Mendez," he said. "My people are of a different faith, but we all share one very special thing—we come from the same place, and we return to the same place—ashes to ashes, dust to dust, as my Christian brothers might say."

He crumbled the frozen chunks of dirt in his hands and let them fall to the ground.

"Amen," Ace said.

"Today I pray that the souls of our brothers reach whatever afterlife they believed in, far from the demons that ail Mother Earth," Dohi said. "And with the aid of Mother Earth and Father Sky and all of the Holy People, I pray they find peace and sanctuary."

Dohi said something in Navajo, then fell into silence. When he finished, he performed a traditional ritual, pounding his chest, gesturing to the sky. Almost all of it was done in silence.

Beckham bowed his head and prayed.

A few minutes later, after dead silence, Dohi turned

away from the mountains.

"Thank you, Dohi," Beckham said. "Anyone else want to say anything?"

Fitz took a step out from the half circle. "Losing a brother or sister is what every leader fears. Mendez and Lincoln weren't just brave warriors. They were loyal friends who sacrificed their lives so we could keep fighting."

Beckham knew exactly how Fitz felt, having experienced it countless times.

"And that's exactly what we're going to do," Fitz said, then looked to the sky, snow piling at his blades. "Until the end, and until we meet again."

"Damn right," Rico said.

"Mendez and Lincoln were just kids," Ace said. "I'll miss them breaking my balls and their jokes."

"I got this gut feeling they're looking over us right now," Rico said.

Beckham brightened at the thought. He often felt his friends and loved ones were doing just that. Knowing they might still be watching out for him had gotten him through some very lonely, dark times.

Prince walked over, his radio crackling.

"Hate to interrupt, but...we got an issue near the highway," he said. "Two bears have been spotted."

"You talking polar bears or some shit?" Ace asked.

Prince shook his head. "Polar bears would be less of a threat. These bears are just the names we gave the Alphas. These beasts have adapted to the snow and cold. They're as big as grizzlies, hairier, smarter, and a hell of a lot meaner."

"Damn," Ace said.

"Best to beat them to the aircraft," Prince said. "You

guys ready?"

"Yeah," Fitz said.

Beckham gave a nod. He looked at the mountains again, taking solace in the pristine view for one last moment. The snow, as bad as it was, gave it a decidedly peaceful look.

He turned away and returned to the vehicles with the other soldiers. Once back in their seats, Dohi kept his head bowed and Ace wiped at his eyes.

The drive to the highway only took ten minutes. Three APCs were parked around the fuel tanker and two aircraft, soldiers encircling them for added protection. The C-130 was being de-iced, and a small single-prop plane was facing the opposite direction.

"That's our ride?" Horn asked.

"What do you want, a luxury jet?" Rico asked.

"That looks like a bush plane for a hunting trip," Horn said.

"This *is* a hunting trip," Beckham said.

Horn shook his head. "As long as it doesn't crash before it gets us out of this cold."

The whine of other, smaller motors growled over the highway. A group of Canadian soldiers on snowmobiles drove toward them. The soldiers on the snowmobiles had what looked like harpoon guns.

"Okay, let's go!" Prince yelled over the chorus of different engines.

Team Ghost got out of the SUV and huddled together, waiting to board. Fitz faced Beckham and held out a hand.

"I guess this is goodbye again," said the younger soldier.

"It's more like see you soon," Beckham replied. He

shook Fitz's hand and then pulled the man into a hug. As they embraced, Beckham said, "Honor the ones we've lost by fighting for the ones we can still save."

"I will, Captain."

Fitz moved on to Horn, who picked the smaller man up in a bear hug.

"Good luck, Big Horn," Fitz wheezed.

"You too, brother."

Rico went up to Fitz next.

Beckham turned to give them some privacy. He adjusted the straps of his pack and rifle as he watched the snowmobiles at the edge of the road. There were two more in the distance, the engines rumbling faintly.

Prince and Horn stepped up next to Beckham.

A guttural growling came from the direction of the distant snowmobilers. The riders shot toward a beast barreling through the snow. Beckham had to use binoculars to see the creature.

Already two long harpoons stuck out of the furry bear-sized monster with a humanoid face. The snowmobilers chased it with a mesh net they held between each other.

The creature flailed as the men trapped it. Several of the riders fired with rifles into the monster's flanks. But it still slashed at the net, forcing the snowmobilers to stop.

One of the men hopped off and aimed his harpoon gun. He fired straight into its neck. The creature let out a monstrous roar damn near loud enough to cause an avalanche.

"Ugly bastard was trying to sneak up on us," Prince said.

"Man, I really, really do not like it here...no offense," Horn said, shivering.

"None taken."

"Didn't you say there were two?" Ace asked.

"Yeah, so that's another reason to get moving, eh?" Prince said.

Fitz and Rico had parted, and she walked over to Beckham and Horn.

"Ready to board?" she asked.

Beckham finally said goodbye to Dohi and Ace before they departed. Fitz followed the two larger men to the C-130, looking back over his shoulder, his eyes glued on Rico.

"See ya' soon," Fitz called out.

Beckham watched what was left of Team Ghost split to take separate paths. For the second time that day, he prayed they would all see each other again.

— 15 —

The roar of the engines rumbled through Dohi.

Once again, Ghost was about to be dropped into enemy territory. The team was smaller than ever with the devastating loss of Mendez, and Rico taking off on another leg of the mission with Beckham and Horn.

Dohi felt an overwhelming sense of loneliness, especially poignant in the huge empty belly of the C-130 even with Fitz and Ace nearby.

Fitz rested his chin against his chest as he tried to grab a few moments of sleep. Ace had his arms folded, head back against the bulkhead. His eyes were closed, and Dohi could hear him snoring over the engines.

Besides the crew chiefs, it was just the three operators. The huge airplane seemed like overkill for the small group, when so many people were still needing evac back at the outposts.

In the center of the plane was a rigid-hulled inflatable buoyancy (RIB) boat that the Canadian forces had lent them for their incursion into Seattle. Kamer had seemed proud to offer it to them, but to Dohi, it was just another reminder of the minimal support their neighbors in the north were offering.

This was supposed to be a stealth mission, perfectly suited for Dohi's unique abilities. He was anxious to find the Center for Engineering Complex Organs, assuming it still existed.

If it did, then their mission would morph into one of intel grabbing. They would scout out the premises and identify any leaders involved with the attacks on the Allied States, determining if the enigmatic Master called this place home.

To Dohi, the plan was like shooting an arrow in the dark and hoping it hit something. But with no other leads, this was the only shot they could take.

Fitz looked up, blinking away his sleep.

Dohi saw the worry in his eyes now that Rico had gone off with Beckham and Horn. He tried to think of something to say, but he couldn't come up with any reassuring words that seemed appropriate.

All he could manage was, "How are you doing, brother?"

"I'm okay," Fitz said. "You?"

"Ready for whatever comes next. You think this could really lead to something, though?"

"If we can find evidence of CECO's involvement with the Chimeras and all these recent attacks, yeah, I do," Fitz said. "We bring that kind of intel back, and I have a feeling the Canadians will join this fight."

"Kamer already knows about the collaborators and the losses we've taken. Why would this mission change his mind?"

"All they've seen are the normal hordes of Variants and those 'bears'. This war must seem like another world to them, and they probably don't believe it's as bad or organized as we say it is."

"They'll think differently when the Chimeras are in their backyard with an army of Variants, too."

"By then, it'll be too late." Fitz paused. "For all of us."

One of the crew chiefs near the rear ramp spoke over the open comms.

"We're approaching the drop zone!" he said. "Get ready!"

Ace woke with a start, grumbling and checking over his suppressed M4A1. He stood and checked the straps on his chute. Dohi and Fitz made their final preparations.

"Five minutes," said the crew chief. He hit a button, activating a sling that dragged the RIB on its drop platform toward the rear ramp.

Dohi slipped on his chute. Using the handholds hanging overhead, he waddled toward the rear of the plane with Fitz and Ace, each holding their gear.

"Back into the belly of the beast," Ace said.

The crew chief hit the lever to lower the rear ramp. Howling wind filled the fuselage. Cold air tugged at Dohi despite the thermal underwear and ACUs he wore under his dry suit.

Leaning forward slightly, he peered over the open ramp.

Beneath them lay a thick carpet of gray. By now, they should be somewhere over the Puget Sound, but he couldn't see the water nor the islands dotting the vast body of water through the fog. Their ultimate destination was Seattle. Toward the southeast, it was also concealed by haze.

"We're almost over Marrowstone Island," said the crew chief. "That's going to be your drop zone and your rendezvous point. Remember, this is low-altitude, so pull those chutes right away!"

Fitz dipped his helmet.

A few pangs of sunlight shone behind the fog, making it grow a slightly lighter shade. Team Ghost didn't usually execute missions in the daylight, but this fog provided better cover than even the dark of night.

The normally nocturnal Variants would be lying low, and any Chimeras, collaborators, or other hostile contacts would suffer from the low visibility that even NVGs or thermal imaging couldn't pierce.

"Deploy the drogue!" shouted the crew chief at the rear ramp.

Two other crew chiefs pushed the RIB and its platform onto the rear ramp. The olive-green drogue parachute burst from the back of the platform and caught in the wind. It dragged behind the plane, pulling the RIB to the end of the rear ramp.

"As soon as the boat drops, you boys are next!" the crew chief said. "Wait for my signal!"

Dohi felt the tingle of electricity coursing through his nerves. With all the fog, he could barely see thirty feet around the plane, much less the ground and water below. He had to trust the pilots, their instruments, and his own wrist-mounted altimeter that they were being dropped at the right place.

Father Sky, look out for us, he prayed. *And Mendez, if you're watching, this one's for you, brother.*

"RIB, out!" the crew chief said, hitting another button.

The drogue chute yanked the RIB and platform out into the fog. A second later, the set of five parachutes secured on the RIB exploded outward, big canvas domes catching in the wind. The launching platform separated from the boat and plummeted, its drogue parachute twirling away into the fog.

"Go, go, go!" the crew chief shouted.

Ace hurtled out of the plane, followed by Fitz. The gray fog swallowed them and the RIB. Dohi flipped down his night vision goggles and leapt into the abyss. He spread his arms and legs out to control his descent, letting the air batter his body for a few seconds while he maintained an arch position.

Twisting his wrist, he checked his altimeter, then he pulled the strap on his chute. It burst open, his body whipped forward by momentum.

As the canopy lowered him, he tracked his descent with the altimeter. The NVGs couldn't see through the fog at what awaited him below, but they did let him see the white glowing blink of the infrared tags on Fitz and Ace's NVGs refracting through the mist.

It took him a few seconds to locate them drifting beneath his location. Another couple hundred feet beneath the operators was the RIB with its own IR tags flashing around its gunwale.

Dohi toggled over, following the others, just a few dozen feet above them. A loud splash sounded over his rippling chute. He presumed it belonged to the boat hitting the water.

Another few seconds later and he hit the cold water.

Dohi cut off his chute and paddled toward the IR signature from the RIB.

Silver waves crashed over him as he swam, finding the gaps around his neck in the dry suit. By the time he drew close enough to see the RIB, Ace and Fitz were already aboard and had the motor started.

Fitz reached down to help Dohi climb into the craft. Ace cruised away, plowing through the fog at half-throttle to reduce their noise.

The nearly two-hour long trip was spent in relative silence. Ace occasionally glanced at a handheld GPS to navigate.

As they continued their journey, the fog lifted enough that they no longer relied purely on the device. Dohi flipped up his NVGs to the gray-green of the rising bulk of islands. To the southeast, the looming shapes of Seattle started to coalesce.

"Almost there," Fitz said. "Dohi, keep an eye out for a good place to pull in."

"I think—"

He never completed the sentence.

A monstrous creature burst from the stormy water's surface and landed in the boat. Water sluiced off a Variant with webbed feet and hands. The beast roared and slashed at Ace. The big operator fell back against the gunwale.

Dohi reached for his hatchet, ready to cleave off the creature's grotesque face. But it lunged first, slamming into his chest. He tumbled over the gunwale and into the water.

The freezing cold stung his face as he tried to see through the murk, panic swelling through his chest. He clawed his way back up to the surface, but before he could gasp for breath, something sharp tightened on his ankle, yanking his foot down.

He twisted his neck enough to see a sinewy arm stretch from the darkness. The Variant's claws had wrapped around his boot.

Dohi struggled, the weight of his gear and the monster's strength pulling him deeper. With gills, it didn't need to kill him with claws. All it had to do was hold him under until he stopped breathing. Then it would tear him apart and feed.

But the beast didn't seem patient enough for that.

Instead, it maneuvered around him using its webbed

hands to shoot through the water. Even with the silt obscuring his vision, Dohi saw a mouthful of jagged teeth.

His muscles started to burn, desperate for oxygen.

The monster bit at his face, and Dohi did all he could to try and keep away from the maw. Over and over it snapped as it pulled him down.

Through his panicked brain, he tried to free himself from the strong grip. He and the monster became a tangled mess of limbs and claws.

He reached for his knife, finally slipping the blade out of its sheath. With the weapon in hand, he stabbed at the ribs of the monster. Dark clouds of blood punched out of the wounds.

But the lack of oxygen had taken its toll. Dohi's muscles began to lock.

Another stab, and the creature pulled back, bubbles streaming from its mouth as it let out a muffled roar. More blood mixed with the silt as the Variant thrashed.

The glint of metal flashed through the water, cutting across the beast's gills. Letting out a gurgle, the creature went listless, sinking.

Dohi's consciousness started to fade just as hands grabbed him, pulling him again. This time, toward the surface.

He broke through a moment later, sucking in the frigid air. Fitz surfaced next to him, also gasping.

Ace reached over the gunwale of the RIB and dragged them both on board.

Then he returned to the motor and sped away. Faster this time in case more Variants were skimming underwater after them.

Dohi lay on his back, still heaving. His muscles were

tingling, but his head no longer pulsed from oxygen deprivation.

"Thank you," he managed to say. "Thank you for saving me."

Fitz patted him on the shoulder and turned as Ace took them closer to shore. They would have more cover there and could find somewhere to stash the boat while they continued on foot.

Ace finally found shelter for the boat near Smith Cove Park, just north of downtown Seattle. As they pulled in, the sun emerged, providing a clear view of the city.

"Ho*ly* shit," Ace bellowed.

Dohi lifted his binos to his eyes, taking a minute to soak it all in.

Piles of rubble along the harbor where abandoned ships and boats had rammed together formed a monstrous island of flotsam.

Farther inland, half the skyscrapers were nothing but blackened husks, burned out from past fires. The iconic Space Needle reached like a finger toward the gray sky, half its saucer-shaped observation deck gone.

But it wasn't the destruction of the city's skyline that had caused Ace's reaction.

Vines hung from the tip of the Space Needle down to the park around it and other neighboring buildings. Dohi saw specks moving on those vines, which he assumed were Variants.

Dohi passed the binoculars off to Fitz.

"If we don't find the real Master here, then God help us," he said.

Dohi recalled his original fear going on this mission. They might have shot an arrow in the dark, but the arrow had hit a target. The question now was whether they could handle what they discovered in this new hell.

***

President Ringgold entered the lab at the Long Island bunker with a backpack over her shoulder. The four Secret Service agents shadowing her waited outside with her chief of staff, James Soprano. None of them were happy with her decision, but she wasn't out to make them happy.

Inside the laboratory, she found Kate and Sammy helping their assistants, Ron and Leslie, load the rest of their gear.

"Are you all ready to head out?" Ringgold asked.

Sammy turned in her direction, wincing in pain.

"Are you good?" Ringgold said.

"Yes, we've integrated all of the unprocessed natural language signals we derived from the Variants' communications and—" Sammy started to explain.

"I mean, do *you* feel okay?" Ringgold asked.

"Oh," Sammy said, embarrassed.

"Yes, I'm okay."

Kate smiled. "We're ready, Madam President."

The doctor's tone was confident and helped reassure Ringgold.

"Good, the helicopter is waiting for us," she said.

"What do you mean 'us'?" Kate asked, confused.

"I'm coming with."

"Is it safe?" Ron asked, timidly.

"If it's safe enough for all of you, it's safe enough for me," Ringgold said.

"Ma'am, the people there are going to go nuts when they see you," Sammy said.

"She means that in a good way," Leslie clarified.

"I guess we'll find out soon," Ringgold said.

As they exited the lab together, the agents and Soprano surrounded their small group and escorted them outside the bunker. The cold afternoon wind greeted them on the walk to the helipad. Marine One waited, engines already fired up, and Marines had already formed a perimeter around the bird.

Ringgold saluted the Marine guarding the chopper. She climbed into the cabin with Soprano taking a seat next to her. The science team and her four Secret Service agents all piled in next.

The crew chief closed the door to seal out the cold, and Ringgold relaxed in the leather seat as the cabin filled with warm air. The pilots wasted no time getting them airborne.

Ringgold spent the ride to Lower Manhattan discussing Kate and Sammy's plans for the tunnels, along with the unfolding implications of the sites in Seattle and Denver that Team Ghost was investigating.

She knew the country's situation was dire, but now they had a real lead on who their enemy was and where that enemy was likely hiding. Before it seemed like they had been shipwrecked, flailing to stay afloat in rough seas, but now she saw the shoreline on the horizon.

A pilot's voice interrupted their conversations. "We're approaching Lower Manhattan, prepare for landing."

Long columns of dark smoke snaked up across the city from the battle that had gone through the night. Embers smoldered where towers had collapsed, and dark, oily water flooded the streets around the crumbling remains of City Hall.

Never in her long tenure of public service had she

expected the horror that had gripped her people like it had over these past few weeks.

The only sight that gave her hope was the Statue of Liberty, still intact, the eternal flame burning on her torch. She took a mental photograph of that image, stashing it into her memory. The statue represented the ideals they were fighting for—the ideals she knew they would realize again.

"Beginning our descent now," the pilot said over the intercom.

The chopper swooped between the skyscrapers, avoiding the remnants of scaffolding and frames that stuck out like busted bones breaking through flesh. They lowered to the LZ and hit the ground with a soft thud.

A cold breeze swam through the cabin after the crew chief opened the door. The four Secret Service agents hopped out first. One ducked and beckoned for Ringgold and Soprano.

"It's clear!" he said.

Ringgold let the science team exit first, then followed behind them, Soprano following her. She took the first steps out of the chopper, the rotor wash from the winding down blades kicking up her hair. With one hand, she shielded her eyes from the midday sun as her pupils adjusted.

After she brought her hand back down, she was greeted with a welcoming party led by a woman with red hair. She had the straight poise of a seasoned commanding officer. A handful of other military officers in uniform stood alongside her.

The female commander snapped into a brisk salute. "Madam President, welcome to Outpost Lower Manhattan."

Ringgold saluted back. "Thank you," she said. "Good to be with you."

"I'm Commander Amber Massey, and...well, it's an honor to meet you." She broke from formalities and extended her hand.

Ringgold exchanged greetings with Massey and the other military officers, and the civilians who had come to introduce themselves to her as well. She was prepared to be bombarded with demanding questions and perhaps angry words, but the faces around her seemed grateful.

"Thank you all for the warm welcome," Ringgold said. "I want to talk more with each of you to see how we can help, but first Dr. Lovato and her team need to get to the tunnels to begin their work."

"Of course, we're finishing our final security sweeps," Massey said. "In the meantime, we can help you prepare your equipment and suit up."

She turned to a thin man in olive fatigues. "Daudelin, can you show them the new staging tent?"

"Yes, ma'am," he replied. "Dr. Lovato, please follow me."

Kate and her team followed the soldier toward a tent set among the white oak trees lined in rows around the outpost.

Ringgold and Soprano stayed with Massey as the crowd dispersed.

"James, I want you to start meeting with officers in the command center," Ringgold said. "We should go over aid shipment logistics and evacuation rates."

"Yes, ma'am," Soprano said.

Another soldier stepped up to guide the chief of staff into the outpost.

"Where would you like to go first, ma'am?" Massey asked Ringgold.

"I'd like to visit your medical facility."

Massey's brow furrowed at that request, and she paused.

"That bad?" Ringgold asked.

"There are some horrific injuries, Madam President."

These were the people who had been willing to sacrifice their lives to protect this country. As their leader, she figured she ought to understand what she had asked of them in defending outposts like this.

"I'm prepared," she said.

Massey led Ringgold toward the museum at the 9/11 memorial.

Ringgold noticed people around the base pause their work, looking toward her as they passed. She saw a few whisper to each other, as if they didn't quite believe the president was on the ground in their midst.

The Secret Service agents followed closely, scanning the civilians and soldiers. She couldn't help but wonder if any were collaborators.

A soldier held open the door to the museum. Immediately the smell of antiseptics hit her. The moans and whimpers of the injured filled the first room she entered. Medics, doctors, and nurses treated patients wrapped in bandages laying on cots set up in rows along the museum floor.

Ringgold went to the first cot she saw. A Hispanic woman in her thirties lay on the cot. Bandages covered her chest and left arm.

"Is it really you..." the woman started to ask, squinting.

Ringgold offered a warm smile and knelt by the

woman, placing a hand on her uninjured shoulder. "I'm with you," she said. "And it's an honor to be next to someone as brave as you."

The woman's eyes focused. "My brother died to help save this place from the monsters we were told were gone."

Ringgold had prepared for this.

"I'm so sorry," she said. "We're doing everything we can—"

The woman turned away, and Ringgold stepped back, sighing.

Determined to continue, she went between the cots, shaking hands and listening to the stories of the injured. Some doled out criticism; others, praise.

Regardless of what they said to her, she thanked each and every one of them. She made no excuses for underestimating the power of the Variants and didn't make empty promises to them.

Soprano would have cautioned her about what she should say to these people. Sure, this might be political suicide to confront the truth like this, but politics didn't matter anymore.

Her goal was to simply show her people she was there for them. That she would always be there for them, and that she was one of them.

"We have more people waiting outside," Massey said after Ringgold had visited nearly everyone in the museum.

They went back to the memorials. The sun had since vanished behind dark, rolling storm clouds. A cold sprinkle fell over them as she greeted more outpost civilians.

"Ma'am, we better find shelter," said one of her agents. "The storm looks like it's getting worse."

Massey directed Ringgold to a wide canvas tent. Inside were a few tables that were laid out with maps and computers. Nearly twenty soldiers and officers were hard at work, Soprano among them.

Thunder boomed outside, making most of the people look up.

"It looks like I brought the bad weather with me today," Ringgold said.

"At least you're here," Massey said. "Your presence is going to help motivate people and reassure them we can get through another attack." She paused, looking concerned. "But I've got to be honest…"

Ringgold steeled herself.

"We can't take much more," Massey said coldly. "What you saw today is all we have left."

16

"You sure you can sail?" Ruckley asked.

She sat in the back of the mail truck parked in the post office garage. The color had returned to her face, and her fever had broken.

In just half a day, she had perked up. The antibiotics had worked. Now that her wound dressings were clean again, they were ready to continue toward Boston.

"My dad taught me how to sail," Timothy said. "Our biggest problem today is going to be whether the boat is in good shape. Sailboats don't do well if they're neglected. If we can find a good boat, then we'll just have to hope we're not spotted on the way to Boston."

"Variants can swim, you know."

"Yeah, and they run, too. Fast. Wherever we go, they're out there. But how many are really going to be out in the ocean, when there's plenty of available food on land right now?"

She shrugged. "I guess it depends on if they want surf or turf for dinner."

Timothy smiled. "All I know is I don't plan on sticking around here until they make *us* dinner. I just want to get to Boston, radio command, and blow Mount Katahdin sky high before the collaborators do anymore damage."

"Sounds like a plan, kid."

He finished packing the rest of their gear. They had discarded some things they didn't need so they could move faster, keeping just the necessities like medicine, food, water, extra ammo, and warm clothing. He had also cleaned their rifles.

"The river is only about a mile away," he said. "You ready?"

She jammed a magazine into her rifle and chambered the first round. "Lead the way."

Timothy opened the garage's back door, did a scan of the parking lot, and then walked out into the cold evening. With only a few hours of light left, he wanted to move fast and launch the sailboat as quickly as possible.

If all went to plan, they would be in Boston by morning.

But it looked like that would have to happen in the rain.

Ominous storm clouds loomed from the east, rolling in their direction and releasing the first sprinkles that splattered on Timothy's coat.

By the time they had made it just a block, the sky opened up, dropping water on them by the bucketful.

Just our luck, he thought.

He could endure the cold rain, but Ruckley wasn't in the clear yet. Her immune system was probably still weak from the infection, and coming down with pneumonia wouldn't do her any favors.

If Ruckley was uncomfortable, she didn't show it. She walked fast, not far behind him, eyes ahead, and scanning for hostiles.

They pushed on for a good fifteen minutes, clearing street after street in the rain. Eventually, he spotted the bridge over the river.

But this time it wasn't empty.

A black SUV was parked in the middle. He didn't

remember it being there before.

He motioned to stop. Then he snuck behind the cover of a wide tree trunk in a front lawn. Ruckley took shelter behind an adjacent tree.

"What's wrong?" she whispered.

"I didn't see that SUV on the bridge earlier," he said quietly.

He went prone and pressed the scope of his rifle to his eye. Rain pattered his body as he lay under the leafless branches and zoomed in on the bridge.

Rust covered the SUV's wheel wells, but otherwise it looked to be in good condition. The tires were aired, and the windshield and windows were all intact. They were tinted, preventing him from seeing inside.

He glassed the rest of the bridge and its vicinity but saw nothing to indicate suspicious activity besides the new vehicle.

"Screw the boat," he whispered to Ruckley. "Maybe we can get a good car."

She put a finger to her mouth, and Timothy soon heard why.

A second vehicle rumbled toward the bridge, this one a pickup. Unlike the black SUV, he saw men in the front cab and more in the bed.

Way too many to risk opening fire.

But if they were collaborators…

Timothy zoomed in to see if he recognized them, but none looked familiar.

"Maybe they're friendlies," he said.

"Or maybe they heard your motorcycle earlier. They could be looking for us."

A deep chill ran through Timothy. He centered his crosshairs on a figure in camo.

"Wait until they leave," Ruckley said.

Timothy nodded.

Twenty minutes passed. The men stood on the bridge as puddles formed around them. Timothy wondered if they were waiting there to stop someone or something.

Another forty minutes went by, cold water puddling around Timothy. It soaked his clothes and turned the overgrown lawn into a muddy mess. His feet went numb, and he wiggled his toes to keep the blood flowing.

Ruckley had hardly moved, but her face had drained of color. She was shivering.

He prayed she wasn't getting sick again. He doubted her body could take another viral thrashing.

They had to get out of the rain.

"Maybe we should go back…" he started to say.

She shook her head.

Another ten minutes ticked by until they heard the thump of a helicopter. Timothy tilted his head to the gray sky. The noise came from the northeast. He spotted the chopper that seemed to be headed southwest toward Boston.

An engine roared to life on the bridge. Loud voices called to one another as the men pointed at the incoming bird. Timothy could now see it was a Chinook. The man in camo climbed back into the pickup's bed.

"Now's our chance," Ruckley said. "Get ready to move."

Timothy pushed at the ground, his freezing muscles numb.

As he stood, the men still on the bridge spread out, crouching, rifles aimed at the sky. The man wearing camo pulled a LAW rocket from the truck bed. He too directed the weapon toward the clouds.

"Shit," Ruckley said.

Shit was right, Timothy thought.

These guys were trying to take out the chopper. They must be collaborators after all.

The black SUV peeled away, and suddenly came tearing down the road as the Chinook grew closer. Maybe the bird was carrying evacuees to safety or hauling reinforcements to bolster an outpost's defenses.

A rocket streaked away from the LAW launcher. The pilots didn't even have a chance to maneuver. The rocket slammed into the Chinook's belly, exploding on impact. Fire and smoke bloomed around the bottom of the big bird.

Gunfire erupted from the Chinook, tearing into pickup truck.

While he and Ruckley had refrained from blowing their position before, now the stakes had just gotten higher.

She gave the order to fire.

Timothy aimed at the guy with the rocket and pulled the trigger. The top of the man's skull exploded in a spray of red. The other three men looked around, confused.

Ruckley squeezed off a burst into the mid-section of one man. Timothy took out another with two bullets to the stomach. The third man ran but didn't make it far.

The pickup suddenly exploded, and the resulting inferno swallowed the running man.

That left only the SUV.

The driver did a U-turn and sped away. Timothy fired a few shots but then decided to conserve his precious ammunition. He turned to watch the distressed Chinook.

The pilots somehow had managed to stay in the air so far. Smoke billowed away from the fuselage. But a second fire erupted from its engines, and the tail rotor stopped working, putting the bird into a tailspin.

Timothy and Ruckley watched it pass overhead as it spun wildly.

"Down!" she shouted.

They both ducked down as it rammed into a riverside mansion, exploding into a blinding burst. Timothy shielded his face with a hand, and a wave of heat rolled over him as he hugged the mud.

For a moment he just stared in shock until Ruckley grabbed his shoulder.

"Get to that boat before the SUV comes back," she said.

Timothy jogged down the riverbank as flames licked the sky. Dark oily smoke drifted away from the crash site. No one could've survived that crash, and Timothy felt a pang of regret that they hadn't acted sooner to stop that man with the rocket launcher.

But all he could do now was focus on getting out of here.

As soon as they got to the sailboat, he untethered it and then started raising the sails. Ruckley followed his instructions, and in a few minutes the sails filled with wind from the dissipating storm, carrying them down the river.

The small white craft sailed past the burning wreckage on the shoreline. The charcoaled cockpit of the Chinook was visible, sticking out of a collapsed brick wall of the house it had slammed into.

Once they hit the ocean, Timothy never looked back, focused only on steering the boat. If the brief battle was any indication of what this night had in store for them, he wondered what Boston would be like when they pulled into port.

Assuming they even made it.

**

The pilot of the single-prop plane was a Canadian man named Liam Tremblay. He had spent most of the long flight asking Beckham what was happening in the Allied States and telling him a bit about the cancer that was slowly killing him.

Before they even took off, he had warned them he was sick, which explained why he was so thin and gaunt. While Liam hadn't said how advanced it was, he assured the team he could pilot the plane.

Flying into enemy territory while suffering from tragic disease told Beckham all he needed to know about Liam's character. The man wasn't just brave. He was a determined and caring soul despite the dire circumstances.

In the back seats, Horn and Rico were sleeping hard. Beckham had stayed awake to keep Liam company. He had always wondered what their northern neighbors thought of the Allied States. After all, the United States military had created the monsters now plaguing the world.

Surprisingly, Liam didn't hold a grudge.

"If it wasn't Variants, it would have been another virus or something that nature cooked up," he said. "Maybe even an asteroid, or super volcano, or aliens, eh?"

"Not sure about the aliens, but I get your point," Beckham said.

"To be honest, most Canadians don't feel the same. They blame your government and are skeptical about helping your new government. Took a while to even find someone willing to take you guys back to the States, but I volunteered when I heard about the mission."

Beckham realized now why they were flying in a bush-plane with a guy dying of cancer. The Canadians must have thought this was a suicide mission. They didn't mind sending a guy who was not only willing to take on this assignment, but also might not have much time left on this earth.

He had hoped General Kamer would reconsider how much he was willing to help the Allied States, but this confirmed the reality of the situation. Kamer had a long road ahead of him before he would be convinced.

"Looks like we just cleared Montana," Liam said. "We're in Wyoming now."

Beckham leaned to see out the side window, but there was too much thick cloud cover to make out anything below.

Their destination was an abandoned Air Force base in Cheyenne. Once they landed, they would switch to a helicopter that Command had sent along with a team of recon Marines. Their next destination would be Denver.

"I still don't understand how the Variants could have gone undetected for so long," Liam said. "I thought you all were watching the border."

"We were, but the beasts were mostly underground. North America is a big continent, especially when your military is a fraction of the size it used to be and you don't have all the resources you used to. Even more importantly, the Variants had human help. Collaborators were planning this attack for eight years."

"*Human* collaborators?"

"Yes."

Liam sighed and shook his head, but his focus seemed to drift from the conversation. He grimaced and then took a drink from his thermos.

The plane shook and raindrops pattered the windshield.

"Going to try and take us under this," Liam said. "Hold on."

Beckham watched as Liam punched a few controls. Then the pilot maneuvered to start a descent that lasted a few minutes. The plane shuddered the entire way before evening out.

Liam started their conversation off from where he'd left it. "But you can stop them, right? The Variants and their human allies? There's no way they can take over the Allied States, destroy all your outposts, and then march north, eh?"

It was amazing to Beckham that their neighbors didn't realize the full brunt of what was happening to the south. Then again, it had happened so fast sometimes even people in the States had trouble wrapping their minds around it.

"We'll stop them," Rico said from the back seat.

She was sitting up now. Horn was awake too, scratching his unkempt, long red beard.

The plane trembled again from another pocket of turbulence.

"Are we almost there?" Horn asked, looking out the window with wild eyes. "I can't stand much more of this shit…"

"About forty-five minutes to go," Liam replied. "The Marines should already be on the ground, unless they're late, too."

"Nah, the Devil Dogs are never late," Horn said.

Beckham was glad to be linking up with the Marines. He was always honored to fight with the warriors.

"Beginning our descent," Liam said.

The plane vibrated violently as he flew lower through the thick clouds. A few agonizing minutes later, the nose broke through the gray screen.

Beckham got his first look of the Wyoming city where they were headed.

Empty roads wound between buildings, not a moving vehicle in sight.

"Prepare for landing," Liam said.

The plane dropped lower to the brown terrain, and now Beckham saw a more detailed picture of this city. Nature had regained control. Weeds and overgrown prairie grass sprouted over lawns and covered parks.

To the east, a few blocks of houses and buildings were burned to their foundations. It took him a moment to realize their LZ was in the middle of the charred wreckage.

The wheels lowered toward an air strip at the Air Force base, now nothing but a few buildings standing amid a sea of rubble and flattened hangars.

"Touching down," Liam said.

The plane bounced slightly when it hit the airstrip as Liam fought against a choppy side wind. As they slowed, Beckham searched for the Marine recon team and their chopper.

"Anyone see 'em?" he asked.

"There they are," Rico said, pointing.

Beckham twisted and followed her finger toward a mountain of rubble. A stealth Black Hawk sat nearby. Liam directed the small plane toward the bird. When they reached it, he killed the engine, and leaned over.

"Best of luck on your mission," the grizzled pilot said.

"Thanks for the lift," Beckham said, reaching over to shake Liam's hand. "It was great to meet you, my friend."

"Yeah, it wasn't as bad as I thought," Horn said. "I didn't throw up."

Liam chuckled. "Good because then I'd have to charge you for cleanup."

The team and Liam hopped out into the cloudy, cold afternoon.

Beckham cradled his rifle, looking around the base. A breeze rippled his fatigues. He started toward the Black Hawk.

Rico picked up her bag and started off for the bird, but Beckham held out his prosthetic hand.

"Hold on," he said. "Where the hell is everyone?"

Something was off.

The Marines and pilots were nowhere in sight. While Beckham wasn't expecting a welcome party, he thought they would be greeted with more than stone cold silence.

"Get down!" an unfamiliar voice shouted.

Rifle fire cracked through the air, and Beckham's prosthetic leg kicked out from under him. He hit the pavement hard, on his side. At that angle, he spotted a Marine in a prone position on the other side of the Black Hawk. The man was gesturing for Beckham to take cover.

Horn pulled Beckham back behind the plane where Rico and Liam had already taken cover.

Another round split the air, and a bullet lanced into the engine, oil spilling out.

"Son of a bitch," Liam said. "Where the hell is that coming from?"

Beckham looked down at his shattered prosthetic. The bullet had blown off the bottom half. It definitely had to be a high-caliber rifle.

Another one punched into the plane with a crack.

Liam cursed. "Where is he?"

"Twelve o'clock, on the roof of that radio building," Horn said. "Cover me, and I'll distract him."

"I'm faster," Rico said. "Let me do this."

Beckham pushed his rifle scope up and zoomed in on the building. He couldn't see the sniper, but he could see the rooftop.

"Okay," he said. "Rico, you go."

"You head left, and I'll blow this fucker's head off," Horn said.

"I've got you too, Rico," Beckham said.

She crept toward the tail of the plane as Horn counted. On three, she took off running. A shape pushed up over the lip of the roof, and Beckham fired a concerted burst.

Horn let loose a spray of bullets from his SAW. A cloud of red mist exploded upward.

Beckham lowered his rifle and searched for Rico. She had made it behind a concrete barrier. Relieved, he looked back through the scope and waited for another shot.

"Contact!" Horn shouted.

"Friendly!" someone yelled back.

Horn aimed at a Marine gripping his shoulder, blood soaking through his fatigues. Beckham hopped and Liam reached out to help him amble over to the Marine. He was short with a five o'clock shadow, brown eyes, and a cleft chin. Maybe twenty-five or thirty years old.

"Damn good to see you," he said, his voice wheezing. "I'm Sergeant A.G. Parnell."

"Any more snipers out there?" Horn asked.

Parnell shook his head. "That was the last one."

"Where's the rest of your team?" Beckham asked.

The young man looked down. "I'm it."

"I'm sorry," Beckham said.

Liam helped Beckham sit on a pile of rubble. As soon as he did, Beckham felt the deep dread of the pointless losses. The men who had been willing to risk their lives, hardened warriors, had been cut down before the mission even got off the ground.

"About an hour after we landed, three snipers opened fire. Must've seen us or heard us when we flew in," Parnell explained. "We took cover behind that rubble. We got two, but they flanked us and took out everyone but me. That guy had me pinned. Couldn't even stick out my head without him cracking shots."

"Rico, Horn, go make sure the snipers are actually dead," Beckham said.

"You got it," Horn said, already running off with his SAW. Rico stayed close behind him.

"I'm going to check the plane," Liam said. "One of those shots hit the engine."

"Bring us a field kit, please," Beckham said.

Liam left Beckham seated on the rubble and returned with the kit before heading back to check the plane.

Beckham looked at Parnell's wound. The top of his shoulder was a bloody mess. The Marine was definitely not in fighting condition.

"Have a seat so I can help," Beckham said.

"I'm fine," Parnell said.

"Bullshit, Sergeant. Sit down."

Parnell finally complied, and Beckham went to work.

"Honestly, I'm surprised you can still stand," Beckham said. "How bad's the pain? Do you need anything for it?"

Parnell shook his head. "I already took what we had in our field kits. The pain's barely a dull throbbing."

"You're going to want more when that wears off."

He applied antibiotic gel and wrapped the wound in quick-clotting combat gauze. By the time he finished, Horn and Rico had jogged over.

"Dead?" Beckham asked.

"Dead as rocks," Horn said.

"Were they collaborators?" Rico asked.

"Not sure," Horn said. "They didn't have radios, and I didn't see evidence of Variant activity nearby like that nasty red webbing stuff. These guys might've just been some desperate bandits."

"Bandits who knew how to shoot," Parnell said, grimacing. "I still can't…"

His words trailed as he looked out over the airstrip where his brothers were dead.

"Can you bring them here?" Parnell asked. "I don't want them out there, just rotting."

"Yeah, man," Horn said ruefully. He walked off to retrieve the bodies with Rico.

Liam returned from examining his plane and let out a long sigh. "The plane is done. I had a feeling this was a one-way ticket."

"Not necessarily."

"Oh?"

"Can you fly a chopper?" Beckham asked.

Liam shrugged. "I haven't for years."

"Well, you're gonna have to try."

Rico helped Horn finish dragging over the bodies of the Marines. Together, they laid the men beside the chopper and covered them with jackets.

Parnell went over and knelt, whispering prayers under his breath.

On both flanks, Beckham was joined by Rico and Horn.

"We got to get going," Rico said quietly. "No time to bury them."

"Bring them with," Beckham said.

They started to load the bodies while Beckham searched the troop hold, trying to figure out how he would carry out this mission with his busted prosthetic leg.

There were crates of gear, including CBRN suits and masks to protect against the radiation in Denver, but he didn't see anything to fix his busted prosthetic. Nothing in there could help him walk, let alone run if he had to.

Parnell watched Horn and Rico carry the last of the bodies into the troop hold.

"I'm sorry, brother," Beckham said.

Parnell nodded and wiped at his face with his bandaged shoulder.

Beckham looked to the cockpit where Liam was still going over the controls while stroking his bony chin.

"We good?" Beckham asked.

"I think so, but you better all hold onto something," Liam replied. "This is going to be a rocky ride."

"Before we get into the air, put one of these on," Rico said. She held up a CBRN suit to Liam. "You won't have a chance if you're flying."

Liam waved the suit away. "I'm not going to live long enough for it to matter anyways. And if we're going in dark, I can't wear night vision goggles with that."

Rico held the suit back.

"Seriously, I've got death inside me," Liam said. "This is my last hurrah."

Beckham felt his heart crumble. This man was the best of humanity, in a time where the best were needed more than ever.

It was a rough lift off, but Liam got them in the air. Beckham looked over at something else humanity desperately needed. Marines. The five brave warriors were no longer in the fight.

17

Dripping water echoed throughout the webbing-covered tunnel. Kate listened for the telltale scrapes of claws against walls or the rasping growls of a stalking Variant under the hum of the generator.

Floodlights illuminated their rudimentary workspace, casting the tunnel in a brackish glow. The light reflected off the thin layer of water rising just under their ankles. Water from a broken main.

Her team was spread between heavy black folding tables like those Command used in their forward operating bases. Ron, Leslie, and Sammy each wore splash suits and respirators to protect themselves from any potential contaminants, which was even more important with the dirty water.

The more she listened to the creaks and groans of the tunnel, the more every creeping sound reminded her of clicking Variant joints. Every shadow seemed to move, like a monster preparing to strike. Even with the four outpost soldiers holding security, she couldn't shake the uneasy feeling.

This place was frightening enough on its own to inspire nightmares.

She shook away her fear and pictured the hope she'd witnessed with President Ringgold's arrival. Sure there were people who didn't want her here—people who blamed her for the new war. But most were just glad to have their president with them.

"Sammy, get the computers set up," Kate said. "Ron, Leslie, hook up the microelectric arrays to the webbing. This time, we won't be gating them."

The lab techs started opening the packs and boxes they'd brought. Sammy slipped a pair of laptops from her pack and placed them on a table.

Sweat trickled down Kate's nose as she worked. She resisted the urge to lift her mask and wipe it away. Instead she checked her wrist-monitor. The temperature was nearly ninety-degrees.

Sergeant Nguyen, the outpost soldier leading the escort team, saw her glancing at her monitor. "Why's it so damn hot?"

"The webbing," Kate said. "It has a very high metabolism. It's kind of like a warm-blooded animal producing body heat."

"So this shit is living?"

"Absolutely. It burns through a ton of calories to produce that kind of heat and keep itself nourished."

Nguyen tilted his mask at the wall to examine the webbing. "That means the damn stuff needs a lot of *us* to keep it fed."

Kate nodded. "Aside from us, they eat every animal the Variants can find. Even bugs are absorbed."

"Connections are ready," Leslie said.

Ron traced a network cable over the tables. The cable connected to a microelectric array clamped to a segment of webbing. He handed the end of the cable to Sammy, and she plugged it into her computer.

"I think we're ready to go." Sammy stood at a table as Kate joined her. "Just give me the word and I'll tap us in."

"We can decode everything, right?" Kate asked.

"The code worked on all the signals we recorded before. So unless the Variants and collaborators are using new modes of communications, we should be good, but…"

"It's okay," Kate said. "You can do this. Decode the signals, and if it actually works, we can move on to trying to communicate with them."

Sammy had promised Kate she wouldn't make a mistake again, and now Kate could tell she was nervous.

"I need to sit," Sammy said, gripping her side.

Ron set up a folding chair for Sammy, plopping it into the water. Sammy clutched her injury as Ron helped lower her into the chair. The way Sammy worked, Kate sometimes forgot it hadn't been that long since the engineer had taken a bullet to her abdomen.

She was extremely lucky it hadn't caused any significant organ damage.

In fact, they were all lucky.

Without Sammy, Kate had no idea where they would be with this research.

"Okay, I got this," Sammy said with an exhale. She tapped at the laptop. "I'm engaging the connection."

Nguyen shifted nervously. "Anything we need to prepare for?"

"Not if we've done our job right," Kate said.

"And if you didn't?"

"Then get ready to run."

Nguyen turned slightly to look down the corridor.

"All systems are booting," Sammy said. "The processing algorithm is reading incoming signals."

A flurry of text scrolled across the computer screens, each color-coded to represent different signals.

Hundreds of messages scrolled before the team.

"Prisoners incoming," one said.

"Squads requesting access to transport tunnels."

"Supplies requested for forward operating units."

Everything was in decipherable words, although the meanings weren't perfectly clear. Kate assumed squads referred to human collaborators, and supplies meant weapons or food. Finding the information they were looking for was like trying to keep her eye on a single rock in an avalanche.

"Sammy, is it possible to isolate signals with keywords?" Kate asked. "We need the most important details first."

"Just give me a few words. I can narrow it down right now."

Kate thought about their most pressing concerns. "See if you can narrow down the next outposts they're attacking."

Sammy typed a couple commands into her program. Seconds later the clutter on the screens cleared to reveal a few select communication intercepts.

A stab of fear coursed through Kate when she saw the messages isolated by Sammy's filtering. One stood out to her.

It was their location.

They all knew that another attack was inevitable but seeing the outpost in Lower Manhattan as an immediate target chilled her to the core.

"Sergeant Nguyen, radio Commander Massey," Kate said.

"And say what?"

"That it's time to leave," Kate said. "We're a target and there's no telling when this attack will happen."

"Shit…" Nguyen hesitated.

"Go," Kate said.

He nodded and went topside to deliver the news. Kate continued to work with the team.

"We could try sending out a message to stop the attack," Leslie offered.

Sammy shook her head. "We're still trying to make sure we understand all the signals. If we try communicating back now, it'll be a red flag to them. I need more time."

Nguyen returned twenty minutes later.

"Uh, Doctor Lovato," he said, sounding nervous. "The president said she isn't leaving without you."

"I'm not going anywhere," Kate said.

"She said she knew you would say that."

Kate looked over her shoulder. "What else did the president say?"

"That she won't evacuate until she's sure there's an imminent threat. And if you think it's safe enough for your team, it's safe enough for her."

Ron, Leslie, and Sammy all looked at Kate for orders.

"Keep working," Kate said. "Sammy, any evidence of when this attack is expected?"

"I can scan for more info, but it might take a bit."

For the next fifteen minutes they collected more data, but some of it was difficult to decode. Just when Kate felt they were about to get a real answer, a loud thump resonated through the tunnel.

Dust and dirt fell from the ceiling plopping into the water. Strands of webbing broke free, hanging like dead snakes.

"What the hell was that?" Nguyen said.

More loud thumps shook the tunnel. These were more

powerful. It sounded like boulders slamming on the surface above.

"I don't..." Kate was interrupted by a cacophony of explosions above ground. Cracks formed in the ceiling. Dumping dirt in torrential columns.

"Move!" Nguyen grabbed Kate.

The rest of the soldiers backed away, their rifles aimed at the dark passage.

Sammy grabbed a computer, then hobbled to scoop up the microelectric arrays.

"Sammy, leave them!" Kate yelled.

Ron and Leslie helped the injured engineer and together, the team hurried the best they could through the shallow water. But their speed was hampered by Sammy's wounded gait.

Explosions boomed above the tunnel as they moved. The webbing recoiled, as if the throbbing tissue itself was trying to retreat.

Kate reached the entrance of the cavern just as the thuds tapered off. Shaking, she looked back into the tunnel. Piles of dirt and rock protruded from the shallow water, but it hadn't collapsed.

Nguyen aimed his rifle at the steps leading out of the hole. "Clear."

The science team and soldiers made their way up the stairs to the sight of fires raging across the former construction site.

Screams sounded in the distance, and Kate spotted figures running from the flames. Black smoke plumed away from tents and buildings.

Nguyen guided them forward cautiously, around blackened craters pocking the memorial site. Trees burned, their branches raining embers.

Kate's respirator started to fog up. She took it off. The odor of charred flesh and smoke stung her nostrils. She coughed as she followed Nguyen.

"We've got to find the president," Kate said.

Nguyen pulled out his handgun. "You know how to use this?"

"Of course."

He handed the sidearm to her. "Just in case. Follow me and stay close."

"Sammy, Ron, Leslie, stay here with the other guards," Kate said.

Nguyen led Kate around the fires sizzling across the memorial. Several trucks and cars were destroyed. Twisted, simmering metal was all that remained of the vehicles. She paused when she saw the mangled rotors of a helicopter.

Not just any helicopter.

Marine One was a flaming heap of debris.

"There!" Nguyen shouted.

He sprinted toward the command tent where Commander Massey stood outside, trying to organize the emergency response on a radio. Flames danced on top of the tent as four Secret Service agents pushed open the flaps to escape. Two aimed at Nguyen and Kate as they approached.

"Easy!" Nguyen said. "I've got Dr. Kate Lovato with me."

"Kate!" a voice cried.

President Ringgold pushed out from behind the agents. Part of her suit coat was torn, and ash covered the side of her face. S.M. Fischer and a few other familiar faces streamed out of the tent.

"Are you okay?" Ringgold asked Kate.

"I'm fine," Kate said. "Are you?"

Ringgold nodded. "Scared, but not hurt."

"What happened?" Kate said, looking around in shock.

"Bats," said one of the agents. "They came out of nowhere, an entire swarm packed with explosives."

Kate raised a hand to shield her eyes from the glare of the late afternoon sun. She slowly turned to look at the rooftops around the memorial, most of them burning or destroyed. Her heart sank when she saw the last Apache helicopter. Smoke drifted away from the destroyed machine.

It wouldn't be long before night set in.

And now they were stranded.

***

By the time Nick returned to his two-bedroom apartment, his wife and two daughters were asleep. Only a meager yellow glow bled under the door to the apartment from the outer corridor. He used that weak light to cross the otherwise dark living room and nudge open the door to his bedroom.

"Nick," Diana said groggily. "Is that you?"

"Yes, I'm sorry to wake you."

He slid into bed and kissed her cheek.

"You were gone longer than you said."

"We had to run some new security ops," he replied.

"Everything okay?"

"Yes."

She turned slightly. "We're safe?"

"Yes."

It was the same thing she always asked when they

went to bed, and his response was no different than before. After so much time living in the wild, on the run and trying to survive, she still hadn't grown accustomed to the safety this base provided.

He hadn't either.

This base was one of the most protected and largest in the Allied States territory. His side was also winning the war. But he never forgot they were still located in *enemy* territory.

Living here had perks, though. Their own apartment for one. Almost every other family lived in tents in the open hangar-style chamber a few floors above. Many of the rank-and-file soldiers did too, including Ray.

Diana took a deep breath, and Nick drew closer to her.

He hadn't slept for a full night in days. Feeling the warmth of his wife and the comfort of a mattress and blankets made sleep come quickly.

He slept until the sound of voices jerked him awake. Reaching out for Diana, he found her side of the bed empty.

Blinking, he shot up, trying to see in the dark, windowless room. Light filtered in under the closed door. He put on his pants and scooped up his pistol. Then he opened the door.

His family was seated at the kitchen table. They weren't alone. An ugly grin from Ray's battered face greeted him. The man was standing in the living room with his characteristic unsheathed machete hooked to his belt.

Not exactly the face he wanted to see first thing in the morning.

Nick looked to his daughters and forced a smile. "Good morning, girls."

Both Lily and Freya were drinking fresh-pressed apple juice and eating breakfast. Diana drank a mug of coffee.

All benefits from his job as the second in command.

Diana handed him a thermos of coffee.

"Good morning, Dad," Lily said with a wide smile.

Freya avoided his gaze.

Nick was tired, but he wasn't too tired to see Ray stare lustfully at his wife for more than a beat.

"What are you doing here?" Nick growled at Ray.

Ray flitted his gaze to Nick and smirked. "I came to get you."

"Why?"

"You're late."

Nick looked at his watch, cursing under his breath. He was already half an hour late to the command center. Pete would chew his ass out if he didn't hurry.

Rushing back into his bedroom, Nick changed into his fatigues. He brushed his teeth at the sink. Then he took a swig of water, grabbed his duty belt and went back to the living room.

"Leaving again?" Freya asked, rolling her eyes.

Lily frowned when Nick nodded.

"Got work to do, but I'll be home for dinner," he said. "Be good for your mom, and study hard."

Diana slipped a homemade granola bar in Nick's vest and gave him a peck on the cheek.

"See you tonight," Nick said.

As he embraced his wife, he saw Ray looking at Diana again.

Son of a bitch!

Nick let go of Diana and followed Ray out of the

room into the empty concrete hallway, his heart racing with anger. He knew the guy was trying to piss him off, but Nick was having a hard time not taking the bait.

It didn't help that Ray immediately started running his mouth. "Hope you enjoyed your beauty sleep. 'Cause Pete's pissed."

Ray was *definitely* baiting him, obviously still mad about when Nick had used his face as a punching bag.

"Guess that's what happens when people sleep—" Ray started to say.

Nick halted in the hallway. "You don't learn, do you? It's almost like you want to get your ass kicked again."

Ray raised his cut chin in anger.

"We're down on men," Nick said. "That's the only reason you're still alive. And while Pete might not let me kill you, that doesn't mean he won't let me take your tongue."

"You—"

Nick stepped up to him. "Look at my wife again like that, and I'll cut your eyes out, too."

He kept walking, leaving Ray to think about the threats. The click of boots sounded as Ray finally started to follow Nick to the stairwell.

They took the ten flights up to the command center. By the time Nick reached the top he was only slightly winded. He took a sip of his coffee as he waited for Ray. The guy was in worse shape and still a full two flights below.

His machete clanked on the railing repeatedly. The dipshit must have thought it was extra badass to have it hanging from his belt without a sheath, but now he sounded like a dinner bell.

Nick ate his granola bar as he waited.

They didn't *really* need this guy. He was a piece of shit, and not much of a soldier. They were probably just wasting resources keeping his fat ass fed.

Would anyone really miss Ray if the guy tripped and took a tumble?

Nick tucked his granola bar away and took another drink of coffee. Ray finally emerged on the landing below. Sweat beaded across his forehead.

Halfway up, he stopped to catch his breath.

"I wish the fucking elevators worked in this shit hole," Ray said.

"Hurry," Nick said, cracking a smirk. "Don't want to piss Pete off more, right?"

Nick watched Ray climb the steps.

With his head down, Ray sort of reminded Nick of his old deceased friend Alfred. But then Ray looked up with that crooked gaze he had directed at Diana.

"Want some coffee?" Nick asked.

"From an asshole like you?" Ray replied, his face drawn in disgust.

Nick dangled the thermos in front of Ray's face. Ray swatted at it, then took a step back at the edge of the landing.

"At least I have a reason for being late now," Nick said.

"What?" Ray tilted his head.

Nick kicked him square in the chest as hard as he could.

Ray grunted and flew backward, arms flailing. He hit the stairs on his back and then rolled down them on his side. A sickening slurp sounded as his machete cut into his body.

He tumbled down the rest of the stairs, smearing a

trail of blood until he had come to a stop on the landing.

Nick watched with grim satisfaction as Ray squirmed in a pool of blood.

"That was an unlucky tumble," Nick said, taking the stairs down.

Ray lay there, gripping his side, staring at the wound in horror.

Nick crouched next to him and smiled.

"You're...you're..." Ray stammered.

"You should have kept your mouth shut and your eyes to yourself, you piece of shit."

Ray gurgled, trying to speak again.

"What's that?" Nick asked.

He leaned closer and cupped an ear to try and make out the words.

Despite the horrendous injuries, Ray managed to speak clearly one last time.

"I fucked your wife," he said.

18

The streets of Seattle stank of rotting fruit. Fitz crouched next to a counter at an old food stall in Pike Place Market. Rays of waning sunlight fell through holes in the roof, illuminating long green vines.

Mold and mildew grew up the walls of the abandoned market, plants reclaiming the food stands and souvenir shops. Ace and Dohi moved with Fitz between the plants sprouting from cracked floorboards.

For the better part of the day, the trio had crept through the city toward their destination. Nature had almost completely reclaimed Seattle. And so had the Variants, in parts like the Space Needle.

But so far, the three-man team had only encountered a few starving monsters daring to prowl in daylight, desperately searching for food.

The soldiers had dispatched them quickly with hatchets and blades, but as they drew closer to CECO, Fitz didn't expect things to continue this easily.

The center was located a block north of Seattle University on East Pike Street. If all went well, they could simply take East Pike from their current location straight to the laboratory facility.

Fitz walked through the dense plant matter, leaves and stems squishing under his blades with each step. Ahead he saw an old bakery. The shelves inside had collapsed in a jumbled mess. A scratched and broken sign advertised fresh cupcakes.

He thought of Rico, as he often did in places like this, wondering what it would have been like to visit this marketplace sampling foods with her. They would only worry about what they were going to eat next, rather than what was trying to eat them.

He prayed she was safe with Beckham and Horn. The fact she was with them helped put his mind at ease.

A distant howl wailed over the ruined city.

He held up a fist, and the other two froze.

Another Variant shriek echoed through the empty streets outside the market.

Had they been detected?

Fitz counted the seconds, waiting for a third cry.

It didn't come.

After another minute, Fitz signaled for Dohi to take point. They exited back outside, staying behind abandoned cars lining the curbs. Shattered glass from the vehicles and storefronts sparkled on the concrete between the plants growing out of the street and sidewalk.

Dohi advanced under the crumbling buildings. Scattered bones from animals and humans lay in clumps. Marred by teeth marks and sun-bleached. Almost all of them appeared to be old skeletons that spoke to the slaughter that had taken place years ago during the first war.

The team was halfway to the CECO building when another chorus of Variant cries exploded somewhere to their east. Fitz shrank into the shadows of a storefront with Dohi and Ace.

Clouds drifted across the sky, blotting the sun as they waited. The scratch of claws bounced against the walls of the neighboring buildings. Soon the scraping faded, and silence reigned again.

Fitz waited another ten minutes just to be sure. Again the team advanced in combat intervals, moving slow and low.

The closer they got to the CECO, the more often they heard the shrieks of Variants and the popping of their joints. Fitz guessed they were drawing close to a pack.

Dohi paused behind a moving truck with flat tires. Fitz lifted his rifle and zoomed in on a building three blocks away at the corner of Pike and 11th Avenue. All the black windows of the modern structure appeared intact, but red vines roped over the sides of it and out of its open doors.

This was the CECO facility.

Cocoons of red tissue covered what looked to be prey, humans and animals, suspended off the side of the building. A few Variants crawled along the webbing, sniffing at their prey.

But it was the five Chimeras standing at the front entrance of the office that gave Fitz pause. They had a variety of weapons that included AK-47s, M-16s, and shotguns.

The monstrosities gazed about the street with their reptilian eyes.

Fitz lowered his rifle and shared a knowing look with Dohi. This certainly confirmed *something* important was going on in CECO. But before they could figure out whatever it was, they had to get past the guards or find an alternative entry point.

At their current location, he didn't see any.

"Got any ideas on entries?" Fitz whispered.

"Go in through the back?" Ace said quietly. "Might be a loading dock we can use. More cover there."

"Not a bad idea, but we're going to want cover to get there."

Across the street from CECO was a six-story apartment building. It wasn't covered in webbing and looked like it had a great vantage.

Fitz thought about their options. He didn't like what he had come up with, but it might be their only choice to proceed.

"Dohi, take position on the top floor of that apartment complex," Fitz whispered. He hated sending the man up alone, but someone was going to have to go solo so they could split up. "Cover Ace and me. We'll search for another entrance."

"Copy that," Dohi said.

He took off into an alley, then disappeared into the apartment building. Fitz waited nearly ten minutes.

"I see him," Ace said, pointing up to a balcony.

Dohi was flat on his stomach, just barely visible over the edge. He flashed them a hand signal, indicating they were clear to move.

Fitz took Ace across the street and headed north. They took a right when they reached a park overgrown with swaying wild grass. Then Fitz led him toward the back of the CECO building.

Another Variant howled from somewhere to their north, maybe inside the park.

Ace and Fitz took shelter behind a burned-out vehicle halfway down the block. Rustling sounded somewhere on the street. Ace moved over to a van to cover them from the other direction.

Birds suddenly exploded from nearby trees, tearing into the sky.

Fitz saw the tall grass in the park shift as something

moved through it. He prepared his rifle as a muscular Variant burst out of the weeds, stopping to sniff the air and search the block with narrow yellow eyes.

Ace peered out, rifle at the ready.

Fitz waved him off.

Not yet, he thought. No need to blow their cover.

The creature caught a scent and dropped to all fours, skittering toward them. It paused halfway there, twisting to look over its spiny back.

The grass shook, disgorging two more Variants. They too dropped to all fours, spreading out over the street.

Fitz's brain raced, trying to figure out what they had done wrong. Had the rub they had used to mask their scent worn off already, weakened by their boat trip through the Puget Sound?

The beasts drew closer, no more than twenty yards away, their eyes raking across the trash strewn over the street. Fitz leveled his rifle, ready to fire if the beasts got too close. His heart pounded so hard he wondered if the creatures could hear it.

Ace kept his rifle trained on the filthy monstrosities. If it came to a gun battle, at least they had the drop.

Claws scraped over asphalt. The pack slowly made their way toward Fitz, now only ten or so yards away. They were so close he smelled their sour flesh.

Ace shuffled at the side of his moving van, crouching for a better vantage. The closest beast approached Fitz, lashing a long tongue over sucker lips.

It reared up on its legs, then let out a long howl.

Fitz sighted the monster's head, sucking in a breath, ready to squeeze the trigger.

A whistle came from the front of the CECO building. The small pack of beasts tilted in that direction, and then like dogs, took off together. They disappeared down 11th, toward the CECO entrance.

Fitz waited for their howling to abate, and Ace signaled it was clear.

The duo followed the street to the corner of 11th, giving them a good view of the back side of the building. The monsters that had run down the street were gone, leaving the doors along the back unguarded.

Ace had been right—there was a loading dock, but the large garage door was shut. Trying to gain entry would almost certainly attract the monsters they'd just seen.

Fitz pointed to a fire escape tracing up the side of the structure. It led to several more doors and the flat roof. That might give them a way in.

Fitz started to sneak toward the fire escape. Another whistle sounded from the front of the building. His earpiece burst to life, forcing him to stop and listen.

"Ghost One, contacts headed your way from the park and from the CECO entrance," Dohi said.

Ace ducked behind a dumpster, and Fitz dove next to him.

Variants exploded from the park, their voices raised in a demonic chorus. The tap of claws against asphalt clattered down the street.

Fitz and Ace pressed their backs against the dumpster, trying to remain hidden. They heard the clatter of galloping monsters careening toward their position, joints clicking.

Then another pack flanked them from the south of the street, forcing the men around the side of the dumpster to hide.

Soon the meager shelter they had found would be worthless when the monsters stormed over their position.

"We got to move," Fitz whispered to Ace.

He ran to the fire escape and scaled the ladder, his prosthetics clanging on the iron rungs. Ace followed him up.

The monsters barreled down the street beneath them, heading in the direction of the whistling. Fitz couldn't tell who was calling the Variants, but they had the monsters trained like disciplined hunting hounds.

A loud shriek burst from the street. One of the Variants froze amid the flow of the others. The diseased face turned up toward Fitz, and it wasted no time letting out an ear-shattering screech.

The rest of the pack paused.

The first time they had managed to evade the beasts, but not now.

"Faster," Fitz said.

He kept climbing as the Variants jumped to the side of the building, ascending like spiders on the brick and using the webbing as a ladder. Dozens of jaws snapped and lips popped.

One of the beasts jumped to the fire escape and leapt at Ace. He kicked its snarling face with a crack that knocked the beast backward.

Fitz looked back up. They were almost to the top, but if there wasn't an escape door on the roof, they would be forced to engage the monsters.

Maybe it didn't matter. By now, whoever controlled the beasts would have noticed them chasing after fresh prey.

A chilling message hissed into his ear.

"Ghost One, hostiles on the roof," Dohi said over the comms.

Fitz got to the top of the roof to find four Variants

lingering between the thick vines of red webbing. He slid over the lip of the roof and fired a suppressed burst into the closest creature, then a second, and third. Another shot, and the fourth was dead.

He turned back to the stairs as Ace reached up. The sight below filled Fitz with cold terror.

The entire side of the building was covered in crawling monsters. Fitz helped pull Ace over the side and then started to back up looking for an escape. He saw a rooftop door, but another pack of Variants had emerged behind it.

Heads exploded in sprays of mist as Dohi picked them off.

Fitz turned back to Ace and gave the order to open fire.

The Variants poured up around all sides of the roof, surrounding them. They fired calculated burst after burst, knocking the creatures backward.

But they kept coming, like always, they surged forward. Driven by hunger and the desire to kill.

The bolt on Fitz's rifle locked back. He ejected the magazine, grabbed a new one, and jammed it into place.

Before he fired again, another shrill whistle sounded.

The Variants froze, nearly two dozen of them forming a circle around Fitz and Ace. The rooftop door burst open, and a Chimera strode out, leading a squadron of ugly half-beast soldiers with faces covered in crooked scars. Evidence of brutal surgeries to construct their frightening visages.

Their reptilian eyes radiated a cold hatred, and their thin, gray lips peeled back to reveal teeth that looked eerily similar to a normal Variant's. Most had stubby claws at the end of their fingers, and their noses were squashed, nothing more than a pair of snake-like slits.

They growled and spoke in gravelly voices commanding Fitz and Ace to get down.

The two operators came back to back.

"Boss, what do we do?" Ace asked.

Fitz's heart sank, fear wrapping its chilling fingers around his insides.

Fighting would get them killed. Surrendering might, too. It was either die now, or take their chances, and hope Dohi got away.

"Drop your weapon," Fitz said.

He lowered his rifle, and Ace did too.

As soon as they did, the Chimeras descended on them.

***

The air reeked of melted plastic and burning oak. Ash fell over the outpost like snow as the last remnants of daylight faded over Lower Manhattan. The few surviving firemen struggled to put out the flames smoldering on what was left of the canvas tents and buildings.

Fischer waited outside the 9/11 museum that served as the infirmary. With the command tent burned down, it now housed the temporary CIC. He took a deep breath, then removed his cowboy hat and shook some of the ash off the brim.

He had stepped out of the museum for a breath of fresh air before his next strategy meeting. But like one of those brutal dog days of Texas summer, there was no cool fresh air to be had.

A glass of whiskey to take the edge off sounded like heaven right now. His old body wasn't used to the sheer volume of adrenaline that had been rushing through his blood vessels this past week.

He checked his watch. It was time for his next meeting.

Carrying his hat, he walked back into the museum toward the offices that had become the center of defensive operations.

The groans of the injured filled the long makeshift hospital. Precious little medicine remained for those people. Fischer had heard that they would run out of the antibiotics and painkillers before the next morning.

Seeing the suffering and knowing another Variant attack would come sooner than later hit him harder than an angry bronc. But like trying to tame a wild stallion, the only way to beat past those thoughts was jumping back in the saddle.

He stepped aside to let a pair of medics past. They hurried down the rows of patients suffering gruesome burns.

God help their souls, Fischer prayed.

Seeing the injured reminded him of his wife's worst days when she'd been ill. How she had moaned and writhed, and how he had desperately wished he could change places with her to ease her suffering.

There was nothing he could do for her then and nothing he could do for these people now besides prepare to defend them from the next attack.

The sound of raised voices echoed out of the offices. Fischer left the medical ward and went to the temporary CIC for the imminent meeting. Officers sat around communications gear and computers.

At one conference table, President Ringgold sat with Commander Massey. Chase and Chief of Staff James

Soprano were busy helping a few officers set up new equipment.

Fischer sat, placing his hat in his lap.

"Madam President," he said politely.

A deep sadness filled her eyes, but it passed and she turned to Commander Massey.

"Let's get started," Ringgold said.

"I'll start with some good news," Massey said. "Thanks to the president, we have a resupply coming."

"Resupply?" Fischer asked.

"General Cornelius is sending air support and vehicles to assist with evac," Ringgold said. "It'll take some time to organize but should be here tomorrow."

"Good," Fischer said. "That means he can get the president to safety, too, right? Or do we have another chopper on its way from command?"

"I'm not going anywhere," Ringgold said.

"Pardon me?" Fischer said, trying to conceal his shock.

"I'm not abandoning the outpost," Ringgold said. "Even if I wanted to, it's too dangerous. There might still be bats out there to take out air support."

"Cornelius is sending advanced thermal detection systems complete with automated turrets, kind of like what the Navy uses in their automated Phalanx CIWIZ systems," Massey said. "With a little work, we can modify them to fire shotgun shells. Might be our only chance at preventing those suckers from tearing us apart again."

"That takes care of our threat in the air, but we still have to worry about those on the ground," Soprano said. He looked to Ringgold. "Souza and Festa said they could send a boat, but…"

"No choppers, no boats," Ringgold said.

Massey took a deep breath. "Now for the bad news. After last night, we only have about two-thirds of our remaining forces in combat ready condition."

Fischer had thought it was worse than that.

"That's where you come in," Massey said, turning to Fischer.

"We need that early warning system back in place. I've got to organize the defenses here, but I trust you to find a good spot for the vibroseis truck. I'll send out a group of my best with you, and we'll reinforce whatever position you choose with everything we can spare."

Fischer stood. "You can count on me, ma'am."

Massey waved over a group of soldiers led by a stocky, bearded man who had a thick head of dark black hair. "Sergeant Dwyer, Fischer's ready."

"Yes, ma'am," Dwyer said. "Follow me, sir."

"Good luck," Ringgold said.

He tipped his hat at her, then waved at Chase. They tailed Dwyer out of the museum. A concrete pathway covered in ash led them between blackened trees.

The vibroseis truck waited for them in the next street behind a Humvee and a repurposed Marine MRTV. The big Marine transport truck was already loaded with crates of weapons and materials for barricades to reinforce defensive positions.

Two Bradleys idled behind the other three vehicles, and twenty soldiers stood around them carrying weapons. Some wore military ACUs, but others looked like civilians. Some of those civilians appeared too old or too young to fight.

Dwyer gestured to the forces. "We're ready to defend that truck with our lives."

"Me too," Fischer said.

The sky had turned a shade of purple, darkness on the horizon. Deep in his mind, Fischer heard his wife's voice telling him to leave, to escape while he still could.

It's too late for that, he thought.

He wasn't going to cut and run now. Tran had given his life for this place, and Fischer planned on doing the same if it meant saving the people hunkered down here.

Chase split off and hopped into the cab of the vibroseis truck. Fischer followed Dwyer to the lead Humvee and stepped into the front passenger seat.

"Where to?" Dwyer asked.

"Start driving north."

Fischer pulled a map from his vest. He tugged his overgrown mustache as he studied candidate locations he had considered earlier.

Guards opened the gate ahead. The convoy drove out, once again, into enemy territory. Now getting closer and closer to the memorial.

Fischer studied the past locations he had used. Bogardus Garden and City Hall Park were perfect locations, but the sinkholes and rubble of the previous attacks had ruined them.

"We should pick a spot close to the outpost in case they need our help or we need to retreat," Fischer said. "A relatively open space would be best. Somewhere that doesn't have a jungle of waterlines running under it if we want to prevent another sinkhole disaster."

"How about Battery Park?" Dwyer asked. "Specifically, the ballfields."

Fischer looked at the map, pressing his finger on the spot. "Not a bad idea."

The caravan navigated between the burned-out vehicles and debris littering the streets. Heading farther away from the memorial.

"Always liked baseball," Dwyer said. "How about you, sir?"

Fischer smiled. He appreciated the sergeant shooting the shit with him.

"Good American sport," he replied. "I loved the Astros."

"I worked out of Quantico for a long time before the Great War. Loved my Nats."

"Maybe someday we'll see a game again," Fischer said.

"Never count us New Yorkers out."

Fischer had been so focused on getting through the next couple of hours and mourning the death of Tran, he hadn't considered what might happen after the war.

Hope was important. Even if it was just a couple of men making idle chatter.

As dusk settled over the city, any hope of a bright future seemed less and less likely.

They arrived at the fields as the sun dipped behind the skyrises. The last rays of light cut between the buildings and retreated over the muddy, overgrown fields that had once been two baseball diamonds.

The land was flat enough for the vibroseis truck, and the towers around it would be perfect for sniper positions. And with the open ballfields, there was plenty of room for evacuation routes and space for all their other vehicles.

"Good suggestion, Sergeant," Fischer said. "This will do."

"I'll start the barricades."

Dwyer relayed orders on the radio.

The vibroseis truck was parked between the two unkempt baseball diamonds, and the other vehicles circled around it for protection.

Soldiers piled out and started setting up defensive positions. Others set off into the neighboring buildings to help the snipers find the best vantages.

Fischer walked over to the vibroseis truck as Chase stepped out.

"You ready for this, son?" he asked.

Chase sighed. "There are a lot worse places to die than on a baseball field, sir."

— 19 —

Dohi perched at the edge of an apartment balcony. The sun was hidden behind dark clouds, and shadows cloaked Seattle.

He peered through his binos at the Variants crawling over CECO like ants, using the webbing covering the building as scaffolding.

On the ground, a group of Chimeras held a tight perimeter.

An hour had passed since the bastards captured Ace and Fitz. Dohi's pulse still hadn't returned to normal. He couldn't have saved them without being made.

Right? he thought.

He had constantly second-guessed himself, wondering if there was something he could have done differently. A shot he could've taken or an opportunity he had missed to distract the Chimeras and their monsters.

You can still save them.

Dohi retreated into the rooms covered in dust and mold. He considered his options again in the apartment. Trying to gun down the guards to get into CECO wouldn't work.

He did not even have the ammunition to wage a one-man war against the forces he'd seen. Sneaking in through the roof would be a terrible decision too, given that's where the enemy had captured Fitz and Ace.

269

If going above ground wouldn't work, that left one option.

Dohi gathered his pack along with a few useful items he'd scavenged from the apartment building, stuffing them into his pack. He thought about the surrounding city block as he crept down the stairwell, boots smashing the layers of dust and mildew as he made his way to street-level.

The webbing draping off the CECO building didn't spread past the surrounding block. For the facility to connect with the Variant's communication network, the webbing had to go somewhere.

The obvious answer was underground.

Dohi navigated around the human bones and skulls littering the lobby. He stopped when an idea formed in his mind.

Bending down, he carefully grabbed a few long bones and a couple smaller ones, stuffing them into his pack before pushing open the back door to the alley.

From the alley, he couldn't see the CECO building, but he listened for the calls of the Chimeras and the Variant packs.

When it was all clear, he maneuvered past a dumpster. Then he set out along the cracked asphalt until he reached a manhole. He pried it open as quietly as possible.

The sour scent of rotting fruit escaped the tunnel.

He flipped his NVGs down, then slowly lowered himself inside.

The dark subterranean world came alive in a flood of green, white, and black. A current of fetid water flowed a couple inches deep in the middle of the tunnel.

Webbing stretched over the concrete walls of the

tunnel. A net of vines bridged over the surface of the water.

Memories of being trapped in a tunnel like this surfaced in his mind.

The webbing crawling over him, probing at him, worming its way around him as if it were trying to pierce his flesh.

With a deep breath, he descended into the darkness, counting the steps and intersections to estimate his position under the apartment building. He headed toward where he presumed the CECO building would be.

The echoing chatter of a pair of Chimeras in the tunnel told him he was on the right path.

He stopped as the webbing suddenly pulsed, throbbing as if it was pumping blood through a giant creature. If he made a misstep now, it wouldn't just be him strung up in this webbing. Fitz and Ace would share a fate worse than death as permanent captives of these Chimeras.

The chatter grew louder. It seemed to be coming from a lit up T-intersection.

Next to the corner of the intersection, Dohi flipped up his NVGs. He snuck a glance around the corner. Two Chimeras stood at the end of a twenty-yard stretch of tunnel in front of a steel door. Their reptilian eyes shimmered in the glow of lights hanging from the cracked ceiling.

Webbing protruded through ports in the wall around the door. The door appeared to be secured by a keycard slot next to the handle.

Dohi knew he couldn't sneak up on the two guards.

Shooting them was an option, but even a suppressed shot would resound noisily in this enclosed space.

Whoever was on the other side of that door might hear and lockdown the facility, spoiling his plans.

The only easy way in, Dohi figured, was drawing them away from their position and into his clutches.

He had come prepared and retreated deeper into the dark corridor off the T-intersection. From his pack, he drew a small penlight and a length of long black ethernet cable. He recalled the words of his grandfather as he set up the trap.

Distraction is your enemy on the hunt. But it is also your best tool. If you cannot catch your quarry unaware, catch them confused.

He used the ethernet cable to create a snare, placing the loop under the slow-moving water. Then he stuck the longer bones from the building into the netting.

Next to them, he flicked on the penlight and directed the small light over the bones.

The Chimeras' eyes would be drawn to the penlight when they rounded the intersection, blinding them. Then he could take them out silently.

But before that, he had to draw them away. He wasn't sure if he could get both to move, but he was certain he could draw at least one away.

He snuck to the other darkened side of the T-intersection. There he positioned himself in the shadows so that the corridor with the soldiers ran off to his left and the penlight was in view in front of him, just past where the Chimeras' corridor intersected.

Shedding his pack, he took out a smaller bone, holding it between his hands.

The two beasts finally stopped talking, and he bent the small bone. The snap echoed down the corridor. He pulled out his knife and hatchet and crouched in the darkness.

For a moment, he heard nothing. Then, a few trenchant whispers. A knock on the steel door, and it creaked open.

Dohi's heart hammered. He heard the voice of a third Chimera joining the other two.

That hadn't been part of the plan.

Footsteps splashed through the water toward his trap.

The soldiers were close enough Dohi could hear them more clearly.

"Probably just a rat," one said in a gravelly voice.

"I'll split it with you," said the other.

Dohi listened for the third soldier. He only had one chance, and this last-minute variable added to his plan might screw it up.

The splashing footsteps grew louder as Dohi waited. The first Chimera finally rounded the corner, leading with his rifle. His eyes immediately shot to the penlight and the bones.

The second Chimera appeared, eyes drawn to the light, too.

Keep going, Dohi thought. The first was almost to the snare, just another—

When he hit it, the Chimera didn't notice. He started to move his foot until the snare tightened around his boot. He fell forward onto the walkway.

Dohi didn't know where the third Chimera was, but he had no choice but to act now. He lunged from the shadows on the walkway. He wrapped a hand around the standing beast's mouth and sliced through the mutant's throat, letting him down slowly.

As the fallen Chimera pushed himself to his feet, Dohi jabbed his knife through its neck. Blood sloshed out of the beast's mouth.

Footsteps splashed down the corridor as he twisted the blade.

Dohi turned with his hatchet in hand to face the final monster. He swooped around the corner and launched the weapon.

The blade hummed through the air and cracked into the forehead of the monstrous beast. It sprawled backward into the murky water with a splash.

Dohi hurried over, patted the beast down, and found a keycard.

For good measure, he dragged the body around the intersection with the other two, then stripped one of the creatures.

The filthy fatigues fit Dohi better than he expected. He pulled a mask off another dead guard and then set off for the door with the keycard.

The disguise wouldn't pass muster if anyone actually got close and caught him, but he hoped it would be just enough to cause confusion or doubt, giving him the extra second he might need in any future encounters.

He reached the steel door and slid the card over the slot. A green light appeared, and the lock clicked back. Dohi slowly pushed open the door to the CECO facility.

He was in.

Now he had to find Fitz and Ace.

***

Timothy watched the water from behind the wheel of the sailboat, searching for the gray flesh of Variants cutting beneath the waves. The trip had gotten off to a rocky start. After seeing a pack of the beasts on the shore, they had been forced to slip into a cove where they had waited for two hours in dense cover before the monsters moved on.

Then the rain had picked up, soaking Timothy and Ruckley again as they struggled to relaunch the sailboat. Normally Timothy wouldn't even consider sailing in a storm, but they hadn't really had much of a choice—not with the thought of Mount Katahdin weighing heavily on his mind.

Eventually the storm had finally settled, and the waves had calmed. Their journey had gone more smoothly for the past hour.

Now Timothy kept the sailboat close enough to shore to keep an eye on the land, but far enough to be out of the immediate grasp of any threats.

Their luck, like the weather, could change at any moment, and he stayed vigilant, scanning for enemies.

Ruckley was doing the same. The infection from her wound didn't seem to bother her now that the medicine had kicked in full-force, but the damage to her muscle made it hard for her to hold a rifle.

"Any idea how long until Boston?" she asked.

Timothy looked at a map he had in a clear plastic Ziploc bag, then searched the distant shore for landmarks that might line up with it.

"Maybe another few hours at this speed," he said. They were hardly moving now that the wind had died and the gray clouds from the storm were finally parting.

Ruckley switched positions to the portside gunwale to look out to sea. He figured she was searching for swimming Variants. She raised a pair of binos to her eyes.

"I think I see something," she said.

"What is it?"

"A ship. Looks like an old cruise liner…" she paused,

not taking a breath. "Oh, shit…"

"What?"

She hurried over and handed him the binos.

When he took them, he saw what had her disturbed.

Smoke billowed off the starboard side of the ship. The storm had concealed it before, but now he could clearly see it.

He could even make out the small shapes of people on the top deck. Hundreds, maybe even thousands of them. These were some of the ships the government had used to help evacuate people from other outposts.

And they were in major trouble.

Life rafts were being lowered into the water, but there didn't seem to be enough to hold everyone.

"That's not the only ship," she said, pointing.

Timothy scanned the water. Sure enough, there were two more farther away, both burning. He handed the binos back and started to turn the wheel to the port.

"What are you doing?" Ruckley asked.

"We have to help."

"Help? How are *we* going to help?"

"We can take a few people on board. Surely they have a radio, too."

"There's nothing we can do for them," Ruckley said. "And our mission hasn't changed. We go to Boston, and we find a radio there, without risking our boat and our lives."

Timothy stared at the ships, conflicted. There were thousands of innocent people out there and, if he was estimating generously, maybe enough life rafts for a quarter of them.

"If we go, we risk being overwhelmed," Ruckley said. "And how will you pick the few people from the thousands to save?"

She looked at him, waiting for an answer.

He gave it by twisting the wheel back toward the shore.

She was right.

While thousands of refugees burned and drowned behind them, he stayed the course for Boston. This was war, and they were losing. Every choice from here on out would be difficult.

Anger replaced the hollow sense of horror at the senseless act that had led to all those deaths. This had to be the work of the collaborators. There was no doubt in his mind.

"Here," Timothy said, handing Ruckley the map. "Maybe you'll have better luck than me figuring out exactly where we are."

She looked out at the shore as the sun dropped toward it.

In the final hour of sunlight, Ruckley figured out their location.

"If that's what I think it is, we're about five miles from Boston," she said, pointing to a peninsula. "Better start taking us closer to shore."

Timothy nodded. A cool sense of relief filled him as he guided the small boat back toward land. By the time they got within view of the houses along the shore, darkness was setting in, making it impossible to see.

Waves lapped at the hull as they bobbed blindly in the ocean.

There wasn't a single light in the distance where Outpost Boston should be.

The moon emerged from behind the clouds, its reflections sparkling on the choppy water.

"Do you see anything?" Timothy said.

"Negative," Ruckley replied.

His stomach started to twist. "We should see the lights from Outpost Boston by now."

A cold wind blasted over them, and he shuddered.

He was starting to worry the outpost had been destroyed, but as they sailed closer, a faint glow sparked in the distance.

"There," he said.

Ruckley stood, using her binoculars again.

"Is it Boston?" he asked.

She stared through the lenses, saying nothing.

"Sergeant," he entreated, feeling afraid. "Is it Boston?"

Lowering the binos, she walked back to the wheel and grabbed it.

"Have a look yourself," she said, handing him the binos.

He aimed them at the glow on the horizon. It flickered, orange and red. The light was definitely from Outpost Boston, but the glow wasn't from electricity—it was from fires.

It was destroyed. They were too late.

Timothy didn't want to believe it. He kept his eyes pressed to the lenses, hoping to see tracer rounds or hear the crack of gunfire. Anything to let him know the outpost soldiers were fighting back. That someone out there was still alive.

But as they closed in, he only saw flames and sporadic explosions.

Then he saw something swarming in the air, silhouetted by the bright tongues of fire.

"Bats," he said.

It was then he realized what had happened to the

ships. The collaborators had used their VX-99 infected bats to attack them.

Ruckley steered them toward the burning outpost.

"You up for this?" she asked.

"I'm not running."

"Good, because there isn't anywhere else to go."

Timothy took the wheel on the final stretch. Ruckley stood at the bow, helping guide them into the harbor. Other boats in the docks burned. Flames danced over debris and floating patches of oil.

He navigated past the wreckage, careful to avoid embers swimming on updrafts of the air so they didn't catch the sails. An empty pier ahead seemed like the ideal place to dock, and Timothy pointed to it.

"Take in the sails, then grab some rope," he said.

Ruckley followed his instructions, grunting as she strained her damaged arm to lower the sails. She went to the bow as he turned them. They gently hit the side of the pier. She jumped out and tied them to the cleats on the dock.

After grabbing the meager amount of gear they had left, Timothy dismounted and followed her down the dock. An explosion boomed into the air a few blocks from the harbor, the fireball rolling upward into the sky.

Embers rained down as Timothy ran with Ruckley through the devastation. He inhaled smoke, then began coughing. Ruckley was coughing too as she looked for another route.

Finally, she pointed toward a yard filled with shipping containers. The smoke wafted overhead from the buildings on the other side.

Timothy ran through the maze of containers using the glow of the fires.

A howl sounded somewhere above the crackle of fire.

The shrill shriek didn't stop them from pushing onward.

Ruckley led them around the containers until they reached a parking lot with a view of the razor wire-topped fences surrounding the outpost.

On the other side, cars burned on the streets and bodies lay sprawled in torn heaps. A group of three Variants hunched around a burned corpse, tearing pieces off like they were a pack of wolves.

One looked in Timothy's direction, ropy meat hanging from between its teeth.

Ruckley pulled on his vest, and Timothy shrank back into the shadows.

"Can't go that way," came a low voice thick with an Irish accent behind them.

They both turned and Timothy leveled his rifle at a man with a mutton-chop beard. A baseball cap was pulled low over his face, shadowing his eyes.

He held a submachine gun hanging from a strap over his chest.

"You're pointing those cannons in the wrong direction, friends," he said.

Timothy kept his gun up, but Ruckley lowered her rifle.

Behind the man was a group of children and a few women peeking out of an open shipping container. The soldier waved them back inside.

A loud cracking sounded in the distance.

Timothy turned back to the outpost. A building nearly ten stories tall began to collapse. As it fell, a furious cloud of dust and embers erupted from its base. The resulting shockwave sent a wave of smoke rolling over the feasting beasts.

The creatures scattered, squawking as their popping joints carried them away.

Timothy and Ruckley dodged around the shipping container. The man with the submachine gun jumped inside with them, closing the door to seal out the rolling cloud of debris pounding against the container.

The metal sides trembled as Timothy scanned the inside of the long container. There were ten people in here, huddled together, shaking with fear.

The Irish guy was the only soldier.

"We need a radio," Ruckley said. "You got one?"

"Afraid not…" he leaned down to look at her name tape. "Sergeant Ruckley."

"Why are you still here?" Ruckley asked.

"The last ship pulled away before we could get aboard," the man replied.

"He came back for us," said a woman.

Timothy pictured the ships burning out at sea. "It's probably better you didn't make the ships."

"What do you mean?" the soldier asked.

"They didn't make it very far," Timothy replied.

The Irish man hung his head. "Goddamn bastard collaborators."

"So what's your plan now?" Ruckley asked.

"We hide. You?"

"We need a radio," Timothy said. "Which means we've got to search the outpost."

"You'll die," said the man. "Variants are everywhere. Only way to escape them is by sea. Getting into Boston on foot would be hell, unless you've got a set of wheels."

"Did any survive the attack?" Timothy asked.

The Irishman stroked his whiskers, thinking. "I have a truck."

"Where?" Timothy asked.

"Where's your boat?"

"Not far," Ruckley said. "But it's just a small sailboat."

The man seemed to brighten. "Why don't you give up on that radio and take us all out of here on that boat?"

"No way," Timothy said. "I'm not leaving until we get a radio."

"Look, I need to get these people out of here. We can't hide forever." The guy reached into his vest pocket and pulled out a set of keys. "So how about this? I've got a truck. Might've survived, but I can't guarantee it. I'll trade it for the sailboat, if you want to take the chance."

Timothy reached for the keys but the man held them back.

"I'm telling you that you're going the wrong way," the man said. "It's suicide."

"I've been told that before," Timothy said, taking the keys.

"Holy fucking hell," Parnell said.

He was jacked up on morphine by the time they saw Denver from the stealth Black Hawk. Liam piloted the craft with the night vision optics from one of the former pilots. They were flying dark toward their target outside the city, hoping to avoid anyone or anything that might still be alive.

As they drew closer to their LZ, Beckham had a hard time believing anything could have survived down there.

Moonlight illuminated enough of the city that the sight was breathtaking. But not in a good way.

Command had fired one of the most advanced nuclear weapons left in their arsenal on Denver.

A crater had swallowed the center of the city, demolishing the buildings and streets that had once crisscrossed the terrain. Instead of the normal airburst detonation, this nuke had targeted the Variant hives and tunnel networks beneath the city. That had required subsurface targeting, resulting in the terrifyingly large crater.

"You sure anything is going to be left of this site?" Rico asked. "Maybe it's not even worth the risk of investigating."

"Good question," Beckham said.

He tapped the deck of the helicopter with his new leg, a contraption made of a metal rod, duct tape, and plastic debris that Horn and Rico had secured to his busted prosthetic. The result resembled a peg-leg that a pirate might have sported centuries earlier.

But as long as he could walk, Beckham didn't give a shit. Walking meant he could fight. Although hostile forces weren't the only threat here.

The entire city was radioactive from fallout.

To protect his body, he wore one of the CBRN suits like the rest of the team. But Liam had refused to put one on.

"You really don't want a suit?" Beckham asked the pilot.

"No, I can't use the night vision with the suit and visor on."

"Radiation is still going to be at lethal levels."

"I understand the risk, but if I can't fly with NVGs and we all crash, then none of us survive."

"At least nothing's left to eat us down there, right?" Horn said, his voice slightly muffled behind his mask and respirator. He checked the tape over his gloves and sleeves before opening the side door.

"I wouldn't be so sure about that." Rico said. She got up for a look outside.

"No, but it's better than Seattle," Horn said. "That place must be a nightmare."

He froze, probably realizing his insensitive remark.

"Fitzie can handle it," Rico said.

"I know. I didn't mean anything by that."

"It's all good, big guy," Rico said. She slapped Horn on the shoulder.

Beckham checked over his suit again as they prepared for landing.

"Hold on tight, okay, eh?" Liam said.

"Parnell," Beckham said. "You good?"

The injured recon Marine looked over from his seat.

"Yeah," he replied, giving a nod that rustled his suit.

Parnell had insisted on joining them, but the Marine was loopy from the meds. Even if Beckham trusted the guy to shoot straight on those painkillers, the injured Marine would slow them down more than Beckham with his peg leg. He had finally convinced Parnell to stay and guard the chopper with Liam.

The bird lowered over the destroyed city streets, flying over mounds of collapsed buildings and a disintegrated highway overpass where chunks of concrete had smashed a convoy of vehicles.

"Oh, my God," Rico said.

"What?" Beckham asked.

"That's the former outpost," she said.

Beckham didn't see what had caught her attention. The city looked the same here as it did everywhere.

"How do you know?" he asked.

"See all those cars and trucks around the interstate?" she asked. "Looks like a convoy, either trying to escape or looking for shelter."

In the pale moonlight, Beckham surveyed the remains of the caravan. Every car represented a family or group of neighbors who had been fleeing when the nuke had landed.

These refugees had died partly because of him. Because he had agreed with the order to drop the bombs and fire the missiles that had destroyed so much of their own country.

An overwhelming sense of regret washed through him.

"Lord have mercy on us," Beckham whispered.

Parnell made the sign of the cross with his good hand.

Another few minutes passed by in silence, everyone in the troop hold shocked by the destruction.

"Here we go," Liam said.

He prepared their final approach on the outskirts of the city. Beckham looked for their target—Golden, Colorado. The facility that had once developed medical therapeutics from donated human tissues.

Now Beckham feared it was being used to make monsters from those tissues instead.

"Looks clear," Liam said. He circled on the first pass. "I don't see any hostiles."

"Take us down," Beckham ordered.

"Copy. Everyone hold on to something."

Beckham grabbed a handhold as the chopper descended. They landed hard, slamming the wheels on the pavement, and Parnell whimpered in pain from the restraints pressing on his wound.

Rico and Horn hopped out to secure the area. Beckham stood next to Parnell. Snow fell around them, mixing with the carpet of ash on the ground.

"You sure you'll be okay?" Beckham asked the Marine.

"I'm good." Parnell grabbed an MP5 submachine with his good hand. "Long as I can reload."

Beckham held up his prosthetic hand. "Take good care of Liam and the chopper."

"You got it, Captain." Parnell stood and stepped outside. He wobbled slightly until he leaned against the hull of the bird.

Beckham hobbled over to the cockpit. "This could take a while. If we're not back in a few hours—"

"I'll wait as long as it takes. I don't have to be anywhere else."

"Thanks, Liam. You're a good man."

Beckham lowered himself carefully out of the chopper and joined Rico and Horn. The town of Golden had been far enough from the nuclear blast it had mostly survived. By the looks of it, their target, HumoSource, had too.

But the entire place looked like a ghost town.

The team advanced through the darkness, flakes of snow falling lifelessly from the sky. It was like entering a post-apocalyptic wintery wasteland.

Filthy snow covered the streets and rooftops. The rectangular HumoSource building wasn't far and Beckham saw it a moment later. He had expected it to be covered in red webbing, but it too was painted in the dirty snow.

"Rico, take point," Beckham said.

She took lead, her suit crinkling as she cleared the sidewalk in front of the building. Snow and ash fell around her, filling her footsteps nearly as soon as she left them. The doors to the lobby were open.

She peered inside using the light mounted on her rifle, then gestured it was clear.

They advanced inside. Shadows smothered the interior. Beckham and Horn flicked on their tactical lights.

Their beams revealed a lobby furnished with tables and chairs covered in dust. It appeared this place hadn't changed since before the Great War, and Beckham had a hard time believing the intel Kate and Sammy had provided.

The only evidence of life here were boot prints in the dirt covering the floor. Those could've been from bandits or civilians. He saw nothing that led him to believe there was a mastermind or even Variants around.

Beckham gave Rico an advance signal. Despite his

reservations, they had to make a comprehensive sweep to ensure they didn't miss anything.

Rico led them down a corridor framed with large-glass windows that revealed vast cleanrooms. Large stainless-steel tables were lined up in rows, and industrial refrigerators and cabinets full of glassware were pressed against the walls.

They passed a door that led to an anteroom into the cleanroom. Pegs on the wall inside held ragged-looking coverall suits and boxes of rotting latex gloves lay on a table beside them along with stacks of cleanroom booties to cover shoes.

The layers of dust were thick here too.

Rico took them past another set of glass doorways, each leading to a room filled with cubicles. Beckham limped up to one of the glass doors and shone his light through. It fell on desks filled with old computers and telephones, boxes of papers stacked next to them.

The thought that this was another dead-end was hard to swallow, especially with the sacrifices of the Marines who hadn't even made it here.

Rico took another corner, locating something Beckham hadn't expected—a blast door to an underground shelter. The wall that had blocked off the door was broken open, drywall and boards ripped apart.

Even more surprising, the blast door was open.

More footprints tracked through the dust. These went both in and out of the door.

Rico looked back for orders.

Beckham paused, then gave her the nod to continue. She went through the shelter door using the tac light to illuminate a pair of massive elevator doors with a mirrorlike finish.

Two buttons next to them operated it, but the power was out.

Beckham found the entrance to a stairwell. Horn went first with his SAW shouldered. Rico followed and Beckham went last. He took each step carefully, his damaged prosthetic ringing on each step, making his descent difficult.

By the time they hit the bottom of the five flights, he was sweating inside his CBRN suit, and pain throbbed up what remained of his leg.

Horn stopped at another steel door, and Rico joined him. It was slightly ajar, and Horn used his body to press it open, the sound echoing in a cavernous space.

The trio slipped inside, their flashlights piercing the overwhelming black.

An incessant buzz filled the long room, almost like they had entered a beehive. Beckham nearly took a step backward when his light hit a swarm of flies.

He kept walking, ignoring the insects that could only mean something dead was down here.

In the middle of the room were examination tables and rolling carts full of bone saws, dissection tools, and more. Against one wall were rows and rows of smaller doors that appeared to be part of a massive morgue cabinet.

Horn went to one and slid it open. Then he stepped away to flash his light over the remains of a corpse. There were so many squirming maggots inside that the rotting flesh looked like it was moving.

Beckham pulled open another to find the same morbid sight.

Each mortuary drawer was stuffed with decayed bodies.

The nuclear attack had cut the power. Without electricity, the morgue cabinet had stopped working, letting the corpses rot away. Judging by the maggots chewing through their flesh, the corpses hadn't been left alone all that long ago.

That meant someone had been storing these bodies, but the question was why?

The images of all those horrifically decayed people lingered on Beckham's mind as they entered another chamber in this subterranean hellhole.

This was worse than the first.

There were six surgical tables, each topped with a bloated corpse. Behind the tables were lab benches covered in microscopes and other equipment. Freezers and refrigerators stood next to them.

Beckham walked in slowly, stomach churning as his light fell on the decomposing cadavers. They were all in various stages of dissection. Cut open chests and stomachs revealed leathery organs twisted in rot. But these bodies weren't like the ones in the morgue cabinets.

Even with their putrefied flesh, Beckham noticed the claws at the end of their fingers. Their lips had dried out, peeling back to reveal pointed teeth.

Horn and Rico spread out to sweep the rest of this macabre lab.

"What is this place?" Horn asked.

"The morgue from hell," Rico said.

"Gather any intel you can find," Beckham instructed.

They scrounged through the plastic vials they found in the thawing freezers and the refrigerators. A pair of computers lay in another corner. These weren't covered in dust like the ones they'd seen upstairs. Beckham pried out the hard drives from each.

"Got everything?" Beckham asked.

Rico nodded.

"Let's go then."

"Good," Horn said. "I can't wait to get the fuck out of here."

The team made their way topside.

Beckham hobbled out of the open lobby doors with his rifle shouldered, scanning for targets. The chopper was still there, and two figures were standing in CBRN suits in front of it. Parnell must've finally convinced Liam to don a CBRN suit. Beckham was glad to see it.

"You changed your mind?" he asked, lowering his rifle as they approached.

Liam raised a pistol and pointed it at Beckham. Parnell raised his MP5.

Beckham froze.

"What are you doing?" he stammered.

Liam walked forward with the gun trained on Beckham. Three more figures in CBRN suits suddenly came from around the chopper. Two had hostages—Parnell and Liam, still not wearing a suit.

Realization set in. These people must have ambushed the pilot and Marine, then stolen those suits and weapons.

"Take it easy," Beckham said, his mind racing, trying to figure out if these were collaborators or someone else.

"Give me the word, boss, and I'll light these fucks up," Horn said.

Rico roved her gun from target to target. "I got a full magazine with hollow points for you assholes, just try me!"

"No," Beckham said, holding up his prosthetic. Even if they took out a couple, these people would take out at least one of his team members.

That was a risk he was unwilling to take.

"Everyone, put down your weapons," Beckham said. "Let's figure this out and talk. No one needs to die."

"We just want a ride out of here," said the person with the pistol pointed at Beckham. The voice was female and she sounded sick, her voice crackling.

If these people had just put on the suits, they were probably already suffering the first symptoms of radiation poisoning.

"We can help you," Beckham said. "Just put your guns down."

"Take us somewhere safe," said the woman. "Promise us that, and we'll put down our weapons. I swear that's all we want."

Rico let out a huff and lowered her rifle slightly.

"Ain't no place safe anymore, lady," she said.

***

Kate surveyed the networking station in the tunnels beneath Lower Manhattan. The temperature was high as usual, and sweat trickled down her neck under her splash suit. It was almost as bad as the stale filtered air in her mask.

Besides a few piles of loose rock and dirt in the ankle-deep water, nothing in the tunnel looked amiss. The equipment was still here, and aside from a knocked over floodlight, it was all unharmed.

The generator had still been running when they had returned, casting the space in a blinding yellow glow.

Nguyen and his three soldiers had taken their sentry positions. Ron and Leslie checked over the network cables connected with the webbing, monitoring the physical connections with the red growths covering the walls.

"How's everything look?" Kate asked.

Sammy sat in a chair behind a computer station and checked the monitor. "We're in better shape than I thought we would be."

"Good. Go ahead and open the signaling gates," Kate instructed.

Sammy's fingers worked across the keyboard. Then she sat back as her programs loaded.

"You okay?" Kate asked, noticing Sammy clutching her side again.

"Yeah. I don't think we'll have any major problems decoding the Variants' signals now. It won't be long before we know enough to send signals of our own."

"I'm not talking about the software. I'm talking about you."

Sammy paused. "I'm hurting, but I won't let that stop me."

Kate placed a hand on her shoulder. "That's admirable, but don't push yourself too hard. Ron and Leslie have been keeping pace with our technical work. They can step in if you need a break."

Sammy's programs reported the computer had a complete connection with the Variant network.

"You want me to search for keywords again?" Sammy asked.

Kate nodded. "See if there are any other attacks planned for our location."

They searched through the cascade of signals pulsing through the webbing into Sammy's computer. It took a few minutes for her natural language processing algorithms to decode the messages and provide them a report.

"That's strange," Sammy said.

"What?" Kate asked.

Sergeant Nguyen walked over, cradling his rifle. "Something wrong?"

"No, it's working," Sammy said. "We got hits for keywords like 'attack' and 'New York.' None of them mention another attack tonight in this vicinity, though."

"Well, that's good, right?" Leslie asked.

Nguyen adjusted the strap on his rifle, stepping closer. "Yeah, why do you think it's strange?"

"Because the monsters haven't given us a break since they started this war," Sammy said. "It's odd that they would send those bats and nothing else."

Kate worried they were missing something. A piece of the puzzle that wasn't obvious. "We're only looking at real-time messages, right?"

Sammy nodded. "That's correct. Everything we see is being intercepted right now."

"If the Variants already sent the orders to attack the base, then we may have already missed it," Kate said. "We need to monitor this station 24/7. We might've missed vital information since the last attack."

"Shit," Sammy said.

"So there might be another attack, after all?" Ron asked nervously.

"I don't know, but I want to download all incoming signals from here on out," Kate said. "We can't afford to miss a single second of Variant messages. That means we'll need a remote server and extra drives. The hard drives on these computers can't store everything."

Kate turned to Ron. "I need you to help set that up, okay?"

Ron nodded.

"I'm sure we can help find that for you in the CIC," Nguyen said. "I'll send one of my men back with Ron. Is there anything you else you need?"

"Not yet, but give us a second," Kate said. "Maybe we can send some useful intel back to the CIC with them. Sammy, see if there are reports of any attacks planned for other outposts."

Moments later Sammy had a list of outposts that had come up in her queries.

Kate thought of all the men, women, and children at those outposts. They had to warn them.

"Sammy, make sure this list of outposts is comprehensive," she said. "Sergeant Nguyen, Ron and your man can give President Ringgold this list when they go back to the CIC."

Nguyen sent Ron and a soldier off to the CIC.

At least now the people in those outposts would have a fighting chance at escaping, even though she wasn't sure if there was anywhere to escape to.

But Kate was no longer content with learning how to listen to the Variant communications. They had designed this software for another purpose, and now that Sammy had cracked the code on all the monsters' signals, they would put it to the real test.

"You designed this software for communicating with the masterminds, too," Kate said. "I don't want to just be passive observers. I want to be pro-active. We need to disrupt their communications. It's time to send some signals of our own."

Sammy took a deep breath and nodded. Her fingers

danced across the keyboard as she prepared to send out the signals.

"I've already identified the source nodes for the masterminds where most of these signals originated from. We now have a complete range of signals we can deliver thanks to our work in the bunker," Sammy said. "If we try to spoof them, we should be able to route a message through the masterminds that can be disseminated to the other nodes and the end-user Variants and collaborators."

"English?" Nguyen asked.

"We can tell the Variants what to do," Kate said.

"That means, if it works, we can call off the attack," Leslie said.

"Maybe," Kate replied. "Okay, Sammy, where do we begin?"

"We have comprehensive examples of the language the monsters use to give each other commands now. All I have to do is model our signal off that..." Sammy said. "And when you're ready, I'll send it."

Kate read over the command. It mirrored the cadence and manner of text-based messages they'd seen the masterminds send to each other.

Delay attack on Danbury until tomorrow night.

This is what they had been working for. Kate had hoped they would be able to test this in a laboratory setting, but as they had learned when they first tried observing the Variant signals out here, a laboratory setting just wasn't good enough.

She tried to take solace in the fact that they now had a full library of signals from Variants and sources of all sorts. Hopefully this time they would do better than when their failed experiments resulted in her husband and the other soldiers getting attacked by the red vines.

If this succeeded, they could change the face of this war. They could interfere with the commands between Variants, and even if they couldn't get the masterminds to do exactly what they wanted, they could sow confusion in their ranks.

But it could also backfire spectacularly, Kate realized.

She thought they had all the data they needed this time to make it work.

With no other choice, Kate gave the order.

"Send the message," she said.

Sammy pressed a single button that could change everything. The rest of the team gathered around. All of them no doubt feeling their kicking hearts as they waited to see if the Variants would acquiesce.

A computerized reply from a mastermind appeared on their screen a moment later.

Kate clenched her hands together and bent down to read it.

Message unclear. Biological signature indeterminate. Suspected error.

"What does that mean?" Leslie asked.

"I'm not sure," Sammy said.

She sent a few more inquiries, and the responses all came back the same.

"It's not working..." Sammy leaned away from the computer. "Why isn't it working?"

She sounded desperate.

"This biological signature thing doesn't make sense," Kate said. "What's it asking for?"

Sammy read the text again. "I think I know what's going on. We're sending messages through a computer. Everything we're reading is actually coming from masterminds, though, not computers."

"I thought the software was ready," Leslie said. "Did we do something wrong?"

"The truth is, my algorithms do a good job translating the signals into a language we can understand. Think of it like a computer dictation program. For instance, when you dictate something, your computer transcribes the words you say into text on your screen."

Nguyen sighed. "So? What's the problem with that?"

"When the computer transcribes all that, you lose things like tone and volume. All those subtle clues that tell you whether a person is sarcastic or angry or serious, for instance."

"Well, how do we do that?" Leslie asked.

Kate had kept quiet to consider the implications of what Sammy had said. She didn't like what she was about to say, but there was only one way Kate could think of to inject the biological signature their messages were missing.

"We need to connect with the webbing," Kate said.

"I thought we already were," Leslie said.

"No," Kate said. She put a hand over her chest. She recalled the story she heard of Dohi being captured. How the webbing had subverted his consciousness. And how the webbing had captured Beckham and those outpost soldiers elsewhere in this tunnel.

The webbing wasn't just capable of connecting to the network—it was designed to integrate with human and Variant bodies.

"We need a biological connection," Kate said.

"Jesus, are you saying what I think you're saying?" Leslie asked.

"She's right, we need a person instead of just a computer to connect to the network," Sammy said.

"That's insane," Nguyen said.

Once again Kate imagined the families like hers that were out there frightened in the face of unimaginable horrors.

"I'll do it," Kate said.

Sammy hesitated. "Are you sure?"

"There's no other way."

Nguyen looked between Kate and Sammy. "Use me. You're too important, Doctor Lovato."

"Which is why *I* need to do it," Kate replied. "I have the most experience interacting with the masterminds. Throwing you in there would be like dropping someone who can't speak Spanish into Mexico City and telling them to blend in. It simply wouldn't work."

Nguyen didn't argue with that logic.

"Leslie, cut off a piece of the webbing, and bring me one of the microarrays," Kate said.

Using a knife, Leslie cut off a foot-long length of red webbing from the wall. It pulsed in her hand like a worm as she brought it back to Sammy with the microarray.

The computer engineer clipped the microarray to the webbing and attached the microarray to her laptop.

"You're just going to use this to plug into the webbing?" Leslie asked.

"Yeah, basically," Sammy said. "We learned from the webbing when it attacked our people and from the mastermind when we had it in our custody back in Manchester that these red vines can pierce a person or Variant's skin. It can connect directly to their nervous system."

"My husband saw the head of a Variant in the tunnel when he was captured," Kate said. "It was still alive, even without a body."

"Because of the webbing?" Nguyen asked.

"I believe so. We accidentally activated the webbing before, and because of our mistakes, it tried to integrate him and a few other soldiers into the network."

"Shit, so you're going to try to do that again?" Nguyen said. "You're not going to test this out on mice or something first?"

Kate shook her head. "There's no animal model for this, and it's too late. We simply don't have the time."

"Leslie, hold the webbing at the base of Kate's neck," Sammy said. "We haven't run into any contaminants yet, but I want to minimize the amount of Kate's skin exposed to the air just in case."

"Understood," Leslie said.

Kate sat down on a chair and felt the wet warmth of the webbing against the base of her neck.

"I'm going to try the commands that triggered the webbing when it attacked your husband," Sammy said. "If it works, you'll be connected straight to the computer and the network almost immediately. The computer should still be able to translate the signals' words so you can understand them, but now we'll also have your additional tonal and contextual input."

Kate mentally steeled herself. She wasn't sure she ever could prepare for something like this, but she did her best to manage her breathing and heart rate.

"Do it," she said.

A click on the keyboard was the last thing Kate heard.

Electricity jolted through her nerves, and her vision darkened. Pain swam through her body, filling her vessels with fire. She vaguely recalled Beckham saying he had experienced a similar sensation.

Suddenly, she reached a strange clarity. The pain

dissolved, and she heard voices in her mind.

She was connected.

Kate focused on the words they'd sent before.

Delay attack on Danbury until tomorrow night.

Over and over, she repeated those words in a commanding tone as the darkness in her vision filled with wild sparks.

Countless voices chattered in her consciousness, some angry. Some in pain, others in shock.

Suddenly another voice boomed past them.

Confirm attack delay on Danbury?

It was directed at her.

Yes, confirm, she thought.

The pain started to overwhelm her again, distracting her. The fire in her veins was too much, and she let out a scream.

Her vision suddenly returned, and she opened her eyes to the web-covered tunnel. A masked face hovered in front of hers.

It was Sergeant Nguyen.

"Are you okay?" he asked.

Kate's head throbbed, but she nodded. "I think so. I heard the voices. Thousands of them, like a hive of trapped minds."

"You sounded like you were being tortured," Sammy said quietly.

Kate sat straighter. She had never felt so exhausted. "Did it work?"

"I…" Sammy turned to her computer to read the messages flickering over the screen.

Leslie and Nguyen helped Kate to stand. She leaned down to read the text.

Squinting, Kate read the last words that Sammy had

intercepted from a mastermind.

Attack on Danbury cancelled.

It had worked.

— 21 —

Nick followed Pete under a canopy of pine trees outside the mountain base to greet the general of the New Gods. Now that it was dark, they expected the convoy to arrive soon, but they hadn't heard anything from their contacts on precisely when they would arrive.

Using his flashlight, Nick carefully made his way down the steep trail. As much as he wanted to meet one of the leaders responsible for planning this war over the last eight years, he had been distracted by thoughts of Ray and his wife.

While his mind had drowned in those thoughts, Pete had hardly spoken about what happened in the stairwell. That changed now that they were alone outside.

"Ray didn't just trip down those stairs, did he?" Pete said. He brushed his dreadlocks over his shoulder and turned slightly for an answer.

Nick opened his mouth to speak, but Pete held up a hand.

"Don't lie to me, Nick," Pete said. "You know I hate liars."

Nick had seen Pete kill for less.

"Ray said he fucked Diana," Nick said. "I kicked his ass where he belonged, into a puddle of his own blood."

Pete reared back slightly.

"Well, did he?"

Nick swallowed hard. "I don't know… If he did, I'll…"

"What you'll *do*, is focus on our mission with the New Gods," Pete said. "That's an order."

"I know. I'm focused more than ever before."

"I told you I hate liars." Pete stared at him. "You don't seem focused. Ray didn't exactly die on the stairs. He's haunting your thoughts."

Nick held Pete's gaze.

"Fuck Ray," Pete finally said. "We won't need him for what's next, especially if I'm right about the last part of this war."

He patted Nick on the back.

But that didn't help him feel any better. He couldn't fathom Diana betraying him with Ray of all people. What could possibly be the reason?

Focus, Nick. Focus.

He pulled his coat hood up over his cap. As the minutes ticked by, the temperature continued to drop.

Pete led them between the dense trees over a hidden trail until they reached an overlook. There was a sniper there in a ghillie suit.

The sniper looked away from his scope, but remained in position.

"You see anything yet?" Pete asked.

"Nothing on the road, sir."

Nick stepped up to the edge of the rocky outcrop. A dirt road snaked through the valley below. That was where the general's convoy should be coming from.

They endured the cold in silence, waiting. Nick wiggled his toes and curled his fingers repeatedly to keep the blood flowing. A light drizzle made it worse. The cold rain stung his bearded face.

The more time that passed, the more his mind drifted back to his wife and Ray. Had she really touched that filthy piece of shit?

The thought broke his heart. Everything he had done was for her and their girls. Everything!

He had risked so much to give them a life better than wasting away in that cabin, fighting to build a life for them here.

A distant hum snapped him from his anger.

Pete heard it too. He shouldered his rifle and looked to the sky.

Had the military found them? They had been close before, bombing the exterior of the mountain where they kept some of their prisoners.

"Get down," Pete ordered.

Nick scanned the clouds for an incoming drone, but spotted a small black helicopter. He recognized it as it grew closer. It was a Little Bird that Special Operators had once used. Figures rode on the platforms.

"Oh fuck," Nick said.

He aimed his rifle, his heart pounding. If the military had brought one chopper, there would be more. While their small army here was well-armed, a Delta Force or Navy SEAL strike team landing in full force could be devastating.

Pete's radio buzzed.

"We just received a message that the general is landing," a voice said.

The report sent a wave of relief through Nick. He lowered his rifle and exhaled.

"Shit, let's go," Pete said. "We can't be late."

"Watch the road," Nick said to the sniper. "Make sure no one followed them."

The man nodded. Pete started back over the path, running fast. Nick followed, his flashlight bobbing. They took another rocky trail that was guarded by two sentries who saluted when they passed.

Pete ignored them and continued until they came to a clearing. Lungs burning from the cold, Nick tried to catch his breath at the edge of the forest.

The chopper had already landed, its rotors idle.

A group of people entered another hidden opening into the mountain, this one meant for vehicles. Pete and Nick ran to catch up before the blast doors closed. Sporadic banks of overhead lights cast the corridor in a dim glow.

Guards posted along the sides of the blast doors were on their knees, heads bowed at the envoy of five men dressed in black fatigues. It didn't take long for Nick to spot the leader.

The general was nearly a foot taller than his men and much wider.

"Welcome to Mount Katahdin," Pete said. "I'm Commander Pete…"

The general turned, his face no longer concealed by the shadows.

Nick risked a glance, expecting the man to be part Variant.

But this creature was *all* monster.

A black robe covered the beastly frame of an Alpha Variant that looked as if he had survived from the first war. Nick hadn't seen one for years.

Before he could get a good look, Nick went down on a knee next to Pete, both bowing.

"Show me…" said the general in a deep, crackly voice. It cleared its throat before continuing. "Show me the weapon."

"Yes, General," Pete said.

"Now," the general boomed.

Pete and Nick stood and hurried around the Alpha Variant and its entourage. The escorts walked like humans, but behind their masks Nick saw the golden eyes of the Scions. He had only seen a few of the biologically engineered super soldiers the New Gods had created, and being in their presence now was thrilling.

The beasts cradled automatic rifles and had saw-toothed cutlasses strapped over their backs. These biologically engineered Scions were the apostles of the New Gods and the secret weapon that was winning the war.

And the Allied States hadn't even seen their full potential yet.

VX-99 had indeed created the super soldiers it was designed to—and Nick was in their presence. He couldn't help but feel some pride. After all, it was partly thanks to his research that they had found a way to use VX-99 on other creatures, like bats and dogs.

But he couldn't take credit for these men. That was done out west.

Pete took them into the silo, passing down the corridors until they got to a blast door. He used a keycard to open it and then stepped onto a platform.

"This is it," he said.

Nick followed him over the metal catwalk, keeping his gaze down.

The general stepped onto the platform. His armored, reptilian feet and claws clicked on the metal. Pete turned on the lights, and Nick got his first good look at the creature examining the missile.

Standing seven feet tall, with shoulders as wide as two men, the size alone impressed him, but it was the horrific face that made this Alpha a truly remarkable beast.

His crocodile-like jaw cracked open as he breathed through long slitted nostrils and exhaled through thin sucker lips. Sunken eyes flitted up and down at the missile.

The general whirled toward Nick and Pete, robe whipping behind him as he strode over.

Nick lowered his eyes as it scrutinized him and Pete. Hot breath washed over them as the creature exhaled.

"Look... at... me..." it hissed in a scratchy voice.

Nick stared at the slotted yellow eyes that seemed to stare into his heart. Like all of the Alphas, this one could hardly speak without its voice crackling.

"Our enemies are infiltrating the network..." the general said. "We must find out where they are doing this."

It took a moment for Nick to grasp those implications. How in the hell had their enemies gotten into the network?

Pete nodded. "Yes, General, I'll radio my team right away."

He pulled out his radio, but the creature gestured to the nuclear missile.

"Prepare the weapon," he said. "We must proceed with the last stages of our plan. The infiltration of these heretics won't matter then."

Pete bowed. "It will be my honor, General."

The creature snorted at Nick. "You, take me to feed."

Pete exchanged a glance with Nick.

"Take them to the prisoners," Pete said. "I'll prepare the missile."

"Right away," Nick said. "Follow me."

He led them through the tunnels and toward the entrance to the chambers where they had fed their thrall armies in the past.

When Nick stepped into the first chamber, he recalled Timothy, the young man they had brought here. New fresh meat was pinned on the walls, strung up by the few remaining thrall Variants roaming the foothills.

"There," Nick said.

He pointed to three humans, their heads drooped, sleeping or unconscious.

The general ducked into the chamber, but his men stayed back, holding guard.

Nick felt the icy stab of fear as the Alpha descended toward the three prisoners. He wasn't sure why, but being so close to such a remarkable monster was both terrifying and humbling.

One of the prisoners, a female with long hair slick with blood, looked up and moaned. Her eyes cracked open in the moonlight.

The Alpha ripped her neck with a slash of his claws before she could scream. Blood sloshed out onto the ground.

It leaned down to feed, opening its long reptilian jaw. The lips bloomed open like flower petals, extending over her face and clamping down. The beast slurped and sucked off the flesh for a few long moments. When it was done, it pulled away, leaving glistening bone and muscle.

A long tongue whipped out of the sucker lips to lick the blood off its face.

Most people would have turned away in horror, but not Nick. He watched the beast that would help lead them to victory with a grim fascination.

***

A voice pierced Fitz's mind from a pool of blackness. It sounded like it was calling to end the attacks on all the outposts.

Was that… Kate? he wondered dreamily.

It couldn't be Kate. Even in his dream state, he knew that wasn't possible.

An agonized scream snapped him awake.

His eyelids flipped open, but the world around him was a crimson blur. A sickening odor of rotting fruit and putrid meat filled his raw nostrils.

He reached instinctively for his rifle, but his hands were stuck.

Memories crashed down around him like an avalanche.

He recalled the Chimeras swarming him and Ace. He remembered their hunger-filled eyes. He had expected claws and teeth to sink into his flesh, but the monsters had taken him and Ace prisoner.

The last thing he recalled was a Chimera slamming the butt of a rifle into his forehead in some sort of lab.

Now questions broke through the haze of pain.

Where was he?

What were they going to do to him?

And where was Ace?

He tried to twist his head to get a better look at his surroundings, but something tugged against it. His legs and arms, too, were completely secured.

He bent his head forward just enough to see he was cocooned in crimson webbing. That same webbing had punctured his fingers, squirming just beneath his skin.

The more he blinked, the clearer his vision became until he could see a wide room the size of a basketball court with a ceiling nearly twenty feet high. Thick red webbing, throbbing and writhing, covered every surface including him and other prisoners.

The scene reminded him of the cathedral in New Orleans and the theater in Minneapolis where they'd encountered the masterminds.

But there didn't seem to be a mastermind here. Just tables filled with laboratory equipment and a row of three huge silver cylinders. Fitz vaguely recalled Kate calling these machines bioreactors.

He struggled to get free, but the webbing tightened with each thrash until he could hardly breath.

Another yell wailed across the room.

It sounded terrifyingly familiar.

"Ace!" Fitz yelled.

"Don't...aaaargh!"

Fitz tried to push his head against the webbing to look for the man. "Ace! Where are you?"

"You want to see your friend?"

The voice came from below, but Fitz couldn't see the source.

Suddenly the webbing lifted him like an octopus grabbing prey. It deposited him into the center of the room. A few tendrils remained wrapped around his torso and limbs, probing painfully at his nerves.

Fitz saw the source of the voice—a bald man who looked to be in his sixties wearing a white lab coat. Acne scars pocked his upper cheeks, and a ragged beard hung under a pointed chin. He had one blue eye and one brown. Both were wild, like those of a crazy person.

The scientist or doctor, appeared human, but his skin was almost translucent. Blood vessels pulsed and protruded against his flesh. Fitz guessed the man hadn't seen daylight in years.

The man walked to a lab station where he stopped at a computer that was connected to the webbing. With each stroke of the keyboard, vines rustled above Fitz until a writhing mass of vines lowered next to the scientist.

"Ah, you're awake," the scientist said. "I'm Doctor Lloyd, welcome to my office…"

Fitz said nothing.

"Not quick to talk, are you?" Lloyd said. "Your friend hasn't been very talkative either."

He typed again, and a few vines of webbing recoiled in the wall, revealing Ace. Dark bruises covered his face and arms. Blood streamed from his nostrils, dripping into his beard. One of his eyes was swollen shut.

"Don't…" Ace mumbled, his cracked, bleeding lips barely moving.

"Let him go," Fitz said.

Lloyd glared at him with those wild eyes. Then he stepped over a vine of webbing on the floor. "You don't come to the Land of the New Gods and give me orders. You're weak, a slave."

"Weak?" Fitz asked. "Let me out of this webbing, and we'll see how weak I am, you fucking coward."

"If that's what you want…"

Lloyd tapped on the keyboard, and the webbing loosened, whipping from his fingers. Fitz fell a few feet, crashing to the floor. He immediately tried to stand, but instead fell forward.

He had no way to stand.

The Chimeras had taken his prosthetics.

All he could do was crawl toward the twisted scientist.

Before Fitz made it two feet, Lloyd tapped on the keyboard and the webbing wrapped around his thighs and chest, pulling him upright in their putrid grasp.

"Your friend Ace wouldn't answer my questions," Lloyd said. "If he won't, maybe you will."

Fitz said nothing.

"Let's start with how you found this place."

Ace grumbled, drooling blood.

Lloyd smiled a grin as yellow as a Variant's eyes. "Is it just you and this man that came to the Land of the New Gods? Or are there more out there?"

Fitz looked at the ground.

"Make this easy on yourself."

"We came alone," Fitz replied.

"I think you're lying." Lloyd raised a brow, his ugly face scrunching into a forest of wrinkles. "Are you?"

Fitz spat but the spit didn't make it far, and Lloyd simply grinned and retreated to the keyboard. "Have it your way, slave," he said.

"We ain't going to tell you shit," Ace mumbled.

"I wasn't asking you, old man," Lloyd said.

He tapped on the keyboard and the red vines around Ace twisted, pulling his arms behind his back. Ace clenched his jaw, trying to hold strong and fight, but eventually it was too much, and he let out a scream of agony.

Anger ripped through Fitz as he watched his brother-in-arms writhing in pain.

"Stop," he shouted. "STOP!"

Finally, at the tap of a key on the computer, the webbing loosened.

Ace spat out a mouth full of blood, then gasped for air.

"That... that... the best you got?" he grumbled.

Lloyd shook his head, then turned away from the

older operator.

"Even if I believe you were dropped here alone, the Allied States' military is much bigger than one old man and a crippled soldier. So tell me, how many soldiers does President Ringgold have?"

"Enough to fuck you up," Fitz said.

The vines around his chest tightened until he couldn't breathe. Seconds ticked by, his lungs burning worse. His vision swam with red as he neared unconsciousness.

His captor finally tapped the laptop again, and the webbing loosened.

Fitz sucked in a deep breath, his mind whirling.

How the hell was he going to get out of this?

All he could do was hope that Dohi was out there, planning, coordinating their rescue. If he could just buy more time...

"I'll ask you one more time, how many soldiers are left?" Lloyd asked.

"I don't know," Fitz stammered.

Lloyd hit the keyboard, and the vines squeezed again. Once more Fitz approached the edge of unconsciousness before the webbing released its hold.

He tried to breathe but his lungs and ribs ached.

"Last chance," Lloyd said.

Fitz tried to speak, but the words wouldn't come out. He was too weak. All he could do was shake his head.

For a third time, he suffocated under the strength of the vines.

The man walked over, focusing his blue and brown eyes as he hunched down. "You really won't like what happens next if you don't answer."

Fitz decided the only way to survive was to prolong the interrogation.

When the questions ran out, so would his usefulness. They would be discarded just like any other human. Probably strung up for the beasts to feed on.

"I'm getting bored with this game," Lloyd said. "But I've got other methods…"

All it takes is all you got, Fitz thought.

The motto helped ease some of the pain.

Lloyd grinned again, a crazed look passing over his blue and brown eyes.

He returned to his computer. Fitz stiffened, preparing for the vines to renew their assault. But this time they didn't tighten.

Ace wailed in agony. The webbing pulled at his arms and legs, stretching him like he was on a medieval rack torture device. Sweat coursed over his bruised face, and a sickening pop echoed from what was probably a dislocated shoulder.

"Fuck you!" Ace yelled.

Fitz tried to stay strong. He could take all the physical pain in the world, but watching his friend, his brother like this… A dislocated limb was painful, but not ultimately debilitating. But if the vines kept stretching, to the point of no return, it wouldn't just be Fitz missing limbs.

"Stop!" Fitz said. "I'll tell you! Just stop, and I'll tell you."

Lloyd tapped a button on the keyboard, and the vines let go of their iron grip.

Ace panted, wincing. "Don't tell him anything… brother… don't…"

Fitz ignored him. He had to prolong their lives.

"Ringgold has about thirty thousand troops left," Fitz lied. "All spread out between the Air Force, Navy, and Army."

Lloyd ran hand over his bald, pale head, seeming to mull the answer over.

Ace looked at Fitz but hopefully he understood what Fitz was doing.

Thirty-thousand was a gross overestimation. They had nowhere near those numbers, but if this man wanted answers, Fitz would provide them. They just wouldn't be the truth.

Lloyd didn't seem entirely satisfied, but he moved on to other questions.

The cycle repeated. Over and over. Fitz did his best to endure the interrogation. Ace was tortured, cursing and pleading with Fitz not to say another word.

And Fitz gave the crazy scientist some answers, almost all lies and exaggerations, sprinkling just enough truth to make it sound believable without compromising the country he had sworn an oath to protect.

He wasn't sure how long he could keep doing this. How long before this hell-on-earth ended.

Lloyd resumed torturing Fitz, the webbing yanking on his limbs, squeezing until he was certain he had a few cracked ribs.

Please, Dohi, help.

But nothing changed. No one broke in to stop the torture. No explosions brought down the facility, and Dohi didn't show up with guns blazing.

The pain finally stopped hours later when Lloyd yawned, cupping his mouth with a palm.

"I'm not stupid enough to believe everything—or most—of what you told me, but we'll have another chance to talk," Lloyd said. "And if I find out you're lying...well, I have plenty of mouths to feed around here."

Fitz said nothing, struggling merely to retain his consciousness.

"I'll get everything I want eventually," the scientist said with a yellow grin. "In the meantime, I need to rest."

Ace tried to spit, but the bloody spittle ended up mostly on his hairy chest.

That got a laugh out of Lloyd. "You've both seen the godly warriors we've created. Scions. Men with the power of the creatures you call Variants."

He strode toward Fitz, getting close enough that Fitz could smell his stinking breath.

"I personally helped perfect the process of turning men into monsters, and if you're lucky, you'll both join our ranks like the other slaves I've captured," Lloyd said. "If you're not lucky, you'll end up as food for my army."

He tapped Fitz on the chest. "Your choice, slave."

— 22 —

Timothy and Ruckley hid behind a pile of rubble outside of an abandoned two-story building. Embers drifted lazily around them, singeing against their fatigues.

They were crouched, waiting for a chance to get to the parking lot past the still-standing walls of a lobster shack with an interior that had been gutted by fire. At the parking lot was the truck the Irishman had traded for their sailboat.

A pack of Variants prowled the street, hunting for survivors. The popping of their joints grew distant and Ruckley got up.

"Okay," she quietly. "Let's go."

Timothy got up, but a high-pitched shriek forced him back down.

Ruckley turned and pointed her rifle at a filthy Variant cresting the mound of rubble, her aim shaky due to her injured arm. With no other option, Timothy fired into the beast's chest. It slumped, tumbling over its own limbs.

Two more Variants skittered down the rubble, pouncing at Timothy. He didn't have time to shoot and instead smashed one of the creatures in the sucker lips with the butt of the rifle, breaking out a mouthful of jagged teeth.

The monster recoiled, giving him just enough time to blast a shot through its broken jaw. Then he turned to help Ruckley.

The second ash-covered creature had wrestled her to the ground, making it difficult for Timothy to find a clear shot. It snapped at her face, and sunk claws into her already injured arm. She let out an ear-splitting scream.

Timothy let his rifle drop on its sling and pulled out his knife. He jammed the blade into its hairy flesh, tracing a deep crimson line over the black, diseased skin until it let Ruckley go.

The Variant flopped to the side, wailing until he silenced it by slitting its throat.

He reached down and helped Ruckley stand.

"We have to move," he said.

She stood there dazed, holding her injured arm. Blood soaked over her bandages.

"Come on," he said.

They staggered into the street, the shrieks of other Variants calling out.

The truck was only about three hundred feet away, but they had to pass through the smoke drifting across the road.

Timothy aimed his rifle at two more beasts that hung back in the cover.

He waited for a clear shot, unsure of how much ammo he had left. One of the beasts went down on all fours and started toward him in a gallop. He fired a shot that hit it in the neck. The other creature took off to flank, but he took it down with a shot to the knee and then another to the back.

Ruckley was struggling to walk and he went over to her to help.

"Almost there," he said.

She put her arm around his shoulder, and he guided her the rest of the way to the truck, scanning for more hostiles in the curtain of smoke. With her safely inside, he closed the passenger door and then went to the rear bumper.

Using his rifle butt, he smashed out the brake lights to better conceal their drive out of town. Another quick scan of the area was clear, and he got into the driver's side, inserting the key and praying it would work.

The truck fired right up.

Finally, some good luck.

He just hoped the rust-pocked Ford pickup was faster than it looked. The fabric seats were torn, and the dashboard was cracked. It had to be twenty years old.

A glance at the full fuel gauge at least confirmed the Irishman hadn't lied.

"Go," Ruckley groaned.

Timothy pulled out of the lot and sped away from the burning outpost. Variants gave chase on the sidewalks. One creature leapt from a building at the truck, but Timothy turned sharply. It crashed against the asphalt, rolling over and over.

Another creature barreled down the road beside them. It reached out to grab onto the vehicle and this time, Timothy slammed it with the side of the truck, sending it skidding into a light pole.

Ruckley winced as she gripped her arm. Blood poured out between her fingers.

"God," she said.

"You have to stop the bleeding," Timothy said. "The med pack is…"

His heart fluttered when he realized he had left it at the debris pile when they were attacked by the Variants.

"Shit!" Timothy said, pounding the wheel.

"I have some bandages in my pack."

Her voice sounded weak. He debated pulling off, but that would be suicide.

He had to keep going until they were clear of the city. Finally, he flipped on the headlights. He didn't like driving with the lights on, but he couldn't see shit out here. The cover of dark wouldn't matter if they ran into a tree or pile of rubble.

In the rear-view mirror, he saw the burning outpost, but looked away to focus on the road and the future. On people he *could* save.

And those that he was going to kill.

They had to get to a radio, and if he couldn't find one, then fuck it, he would just do what he should have done before—drive to Mount Katahdin. Even if it meant driving a hundred miles per hour all night to get to the base, he would gut Nick and Pete before they could launch that nuke.

Timothy pushed the pedal down. The engine rattled in response. The beams illuminated abandoned vehicles pushed up along the median and shoulder of the two-lane highway.

The headlights would make them a target to any waiting ambush, but it was impossible to maintain any speed without them. He just hoped the speed would make them *less* of a target if anyone, or anything did decide to try and stop them.

"Goddamn," Ruckley said as she cut away her shirt to reveal the wound.

The gashes were long and deep.

She grimaced and then closed her eyes, taking in deep breaths.

"I have some antibiotics in—" she stopped. "Timothy, watch out!"

He looked back at the road and swerved just in time to avoid a crashed motorcycle. The side of the truck ground against the median until he pulled them back into the left lane.

He eased off the gas to about sixty miles an hour, his heart rate returning to normal.

"Keep your eyes on the road," Ruckley said before returning to wrapping her arm, using her teeth to hold one end of the gauze.

By the time she finished, the glow of the fire behind them had vanished over the horizon.

From the corner of his eyes, Timothy saw Ruckley wincing. She was clearly in a lot of pain. There wasn't much he could without stopping, but at least she had slowed the bleeding.

The next hour passed by relatively quickly. It was almost nine o'clock, and Ruckley seemed to be doing better.

At this speed, he wouldn't get to the base until three in the morning. That was assuming they didn't run into any trouble, which seemed unlikely.

Especially when he spotted a roadblock formed by burning cars ahead.

"Shit," he said.

Ruckley pulled out her pistol.

Timothy turned off the headlights and pulled off to the side of the road.

"I'll check it out," Timothy said.

"I'm covering you," Ruckley said.

"No way. You're hurt."

"Don't argue with me."

Timothy relented, and got out. Together, they approached the wreckage from the right side of the road.

The heat of the fire rolled over the pair. The closer they got, the more flaming debris he noticed.

A tire burned in the middle of the two lanes.

He crouched when he saw a charred body.

"I'll check it out," he said. "Cover me."

Timothy ran toward it with Ruckley holding up her pistol.

As he moved, he caught the strong scent of charred flesh and burned hair. The glow of the burning vehicles revealed what remained of the clothes on the corpse. It looked like a standard-issue combat uniform.

This was a soldier.

He looked back up at the wrecked cars. This wasn't an intentional roadblock. This was the site of an ambush.

They advanced toward two pickup trucks.

The vehicles were torn open like they'd been caught in an explosion. More smoking bodies were scattered in the dirt on the side of the road and across the median.

They navigated past the two trucks to find a Humvee. Its back tires were flat, and the rear bumper was scorched, but it wasn't burning.

Timothy hurried to the front of the truck. The windshield was splintered from an onslaught of high caliber rounds. Blood had splattered the glass of the side window.

He opened the door to find the driver dead, punctured by multiple bullet holes. The passenger was slumped over against the door, his upper body covered in blood and riddled by gunshot wounds to his chest.

Timothy turned on his flashlight and directed it at the dashboard.

His heart kicked at the sight of the radio.

"Does it work?" Ruckley asked.

"Let's find out," he said.

Timothy gently pulled the dead driver out and put him on the ground next to Ruckley. She watched the road with her pistol in her good hand.

Sliding into the blood-stained seat, Timothy grabbed the receiver. With a twist of the channel-selection dial, it buzzed to life.

They had finally done it! They could warn command about Mount Katahdin!

A flood of relief poured over him until he heard another voice.

"Drop your weapons!"

The relief turned to shock.

There was a working radio right in front of him, something he had been fighting to find for days. And now, right after they had found it, the collaborators had spotted him.

He reached for his pistol, but the same voice came again. "Don't touch that."

"We're friendlies," Ruckley said.

Slowly, Timothy turned to see two soldiers wearing night vision goggles standing in front of the Humvee. They approached cautiously carrying suppressed M4 rifles.

Not collaborators after all.

Survivors of the convoy.

Timothy raised his hands and backed out.

"Easy," he said. "We have an important message to send to Command. We just need to use the radio."

Ruckley introduced herself and Timothy.

The two bearded soldiers, a Corporal Winslow and a Corporal Carey with the US Army, had been on their way to Outpost Boston to help when they were hit by an IED and then ambushed by collaborators who had taken off after the attack. Their fatigues were covered in dust, oil, and the blood of their brothers.

When the corporals finished explaining what had happened, Ruckley gave a rundown of their journey from Outpost Portland and the intel on Mount Katahdin.

"A nuke?" said Corporal Carey. "No way the collaborators have a nuke."

"I saw it with my own eyes," Timothy replied. "I was a prisoner at Mount Katahdin."

"Fuck," said Corporal Winslow.

"I have to radio this in," Ruckley said.

"Yeah," Winslow said.

She picked up the receiver and dialed the encrypted channel for Command. She got through to a comms officer and used her authentication codes to finally reach Lieutenant Festa. Once she had him on the line, she relayed the intel.

Finally, Timothy felt some real consolation that they might have actually succeeded.

But his mission wasn't over. Not until he was sure the collaborator base was destroyed.

"We need evac," Ruckley said to Festa.

His response wasn't surprising.

"I'm sorry," Festa said. "I'm not sure that will be possible right now."

There wasn't any to give. It was too dangerous with the bats and other anti-aircraft weapons the collaborators had, and the military was running low on aircraft. They couldn't even confirm if they were able to attack the collaborator base.

Ruckley stepped back out when the line went dead.

All the relief Timothy had felt melted away.

Had things gotten so bad that Command couldn't even authorize an attack on a damn nuclear silo?

Maybe they didn't believe his intel or maybe they really were worse off than he'd thought. Or maybe they were afraid to announce their plans over the open channel in case the collaborators overheard. He hoped it was the later.

Still, not knowing worried Timothy.

"The hell are we going to do?" Winslow asked.

"We ain't got nowhere to go," Carey said.

"We do have somewhere to go," Timothy said, "and we've got a truck to get us there."

Ruckley and the other two soldiers both looked at him.

"We have to make sure that base is destroyed," Timothy said. "Stock up on weapons and ammo, and give me some NVGs. We're going in dark and fast."

***

President Ringgold finished off another cup of coffee in the temporary CIC within the offices of the 9/11 Memorial Museum. The chatter of officers coordinating defensive operations, triage, and other outpost duties buzzed alongside computers and radios.

At nearly two in the morning, this was her fourth cup, and so far, the caffeine had done little to assuage the suffocating grasp of exhaustion. But at least she had some. Coffee, like bullets, and people, were in short supply.

Of the original five thousand people who had come to shelter in the walls around the memorial outpost, there were only four thousand left. All holed up in the buildings within the final defenses.

Their only saving grace was that they hadn't been hit by another attack after the bats. The streets around the outpost were silent, and their remaining brave warriors were watching the darkness for monsters.

It wasn't just trained professionals that had answered the call of duty.

Fischer was one of many civilian volunteers on guard tonight, sitting in his truck, watching for enemies underground.

And soon, Captain Reed Beckham, Master Sergeant Horn, and Sergeant Rico would arrive in the stealth helicopter from their mission in Denver.

She prayed the quiet lasted, but her gut told her the Variants were planning something for tonight.

Commander Amber Massey sat at the head of the table next to her communications team. She looked up when an officer came in with a SITREP.

"Fischer still hasn't detected any tunneling Variants or other subterranean Variant activity," said the officer.

Massey simply nodded.

Next came Dr. Lovato's assistant, Ron. A soldier assigned to Sergeant Nguyen's team accompanied him.

"How are things going down there?" Ringgold asked.

"A bit crazy," Ron said. "Kate connected to the Variant network using the webbing."

"Connected how?" Ringgold asked.

"With her body," Ron said.

"What?"

Ron nodded. "Good news is it worked. She stopped an attack on Danbury, and prevented others. Judging by the signal activity, we're optimistic that things are going in our favor."

Ringgold didn't exactly celebrate. She didn't like Kate playing with fire, especially when she was using her own body.

"Tell Kate to be careful," Ringgold said. "I don't want her taking any unnecessary risks by tapping into the network."

"Understood," Ron said. He slipped away with the soldier.

Soprano came in from the other room with a piece of paper. Ringgold prepared for more news but found herself thinking more about Kate and what she was doing down there. She prayed the doctor wasn't going to sacrifice herself.

"Just got this from Vice President Lemke," Soprano said. "It's a list of outposts reporting no contact with hostiles tonight."

"Danbury, Providence, Allentown, and Freehold," Ringgold said. "Ron's right. Their plan is really working. They are convincing the Variants to stop attacks."

"Let's hope it holds for us, too," Massey said.

Ringgold scanned another list of outposts being evacuated.

"Civilians are being flown out, driven out, or escaping in boats where they can," Soprano said. "Everything is going as planned. Most are on their way to Texas and Florida, but some are being taken to the classified location where Vice President Lemke and the fleet have been transferred."

Only a few people knew about the location Ringgold had chosen—Puerto Rico.

"Soprano, get me General Cornelius on an encrypted call," she said.

"Yes, Madam President," Soprano said. He pushed a conference phone into the middle of the table and dialed in the direct command number for General Cornelius.

One of his officers answered. Ringgold requested to speak to the general. She didn't wait long before his grizzled voice sounded over the phone.

"President Ringgold, good to talk to you," Cornelius said.

"And you, General. I'll get right to it—what's the status of the SDS equipment."

"I'm moving the functioning equipment from Canada. As soon as the sun rises it'll be on its way to the outposts you noted for protection."

Ringgold was relieved to hear that. She would have ordered the movement earlier, but the air threats made it too much of a risk. And with other outposts under attack there simply wasn't any way to get it installed.

"I have good news, too," Ringgold said. "Our science team's efforts to disrupt some of the Variant attacks seem to be working."

Ringgold continued the conversation to coordinate how they were going to share the strategies with Cornelius. The general was still holding onto Galveston with his forces, and they could use the break from attacks as much as the people Kate had helped.

But before they could settle on logistics, Soprano returned to the room with a satellite phone.

"President Ringgold, I'm very sorry to interrupt but I just got an urgent call," Soprano said. "It's from General Souza, and he says it's an emergency."

Her heart thudded. "General Cornelius, I have to go.

I'll contact you again as soon as I can," Ringgold said.

"Good luck," he said.

"You, too."

She ended the call and Soprano handed her the phone.

"Talk to me, General," she said.

"Madam President, I've got a credible report that the collaborators have a nuclear warhead mounted on a ballistic missile at Mount Katahdin in Maine," he said. "We have reason to believe they're planning to use this nuke in the near future."

Everything around Ringgold seemed to fade into the background when she heard those words. The urgent chatter, the noise of footsteps on the tiled floor, the odor of smoke still hanging in the air. None of it stood out to her now that the words 'nuclear weapons' resonated in her mind.

Souza went on to explain the history of the facility and the ominous threat they now faced.

"My God, we have to stop them," Ringgold said.

"You need to get out of here and take the science team with you," Massey said.

"What?" Ringgold asked, still partly in shock.

"The collaborators could erase an entire outpost at any given moment," Massey continued. "If they find out you and the science team are both here, where do you think they're going to launch that nuke?"

Ringgold stood, feeling light-headed.

Just when she thought the nightmare couldn't get worse, it did.

"As soon as Beckham arrives, we'll retrieve the science team and depart for Command," Ringgold said.

Massey nodded and Soprano assembled the Secret Service agents. By the time they were outside, a helicopter was already touching down.

"That must be Captain Beckham," Ringgold said.

She jogged away from the 9/11 Memorial Museum.

To help mask their position from threats, they had turned off all the floodlights and spotlights around the interior of the outpost. But with the still glowing embers of the burning oaks and the moonlight, they had enough light to guide them toward the open lawn where a helicopter sat on the charred grass, blades winding down.

From out of the side door, Captain Reed Beckham limped toward her with Master Sergeant Parker Horn beside him. A group piled out of the chopper next, none of whom Ringgold recognized. Several of them had their arms tied behind their backs.

"Madam President," Beckham said saluting.

She saluted back, looking at the improvised prosthetic he wore. "Are you okay?"

"I'm fine."

Commander Massey stepped up and Beckham gestured toward the group behind him. "We have people that need immediate medical attention. It's a long story, and we're not quite sure if they're friend or foes yet."

Beckham pointed toward a skinny older man and a Marine. "These two are definitely friends. They're the only reason we made it back here. They'll need all the medical attention you can spare."

Massey gave orders and a few of her people ran over to help.

"Where's Kate?" Beckham asked.

"In the tunnels, but before we get her, there's something you should know," Ringgold said.

As quickly as she could, Ringgold explained the report about Mount Katahdin.

"A nuke? How's that possible?" he stammered.

"How is any of this possible?" Horn said. "The collaborators have been planning for almost eight years."

"Jesus," Beckham said. "Once we get you and the science team out of here, we have to take out that base."

"Agreed," Ringgold said. "We don't have much time. Now come on."

In a matter of minutes, they were descending the stairs into the tunnel where the science team was working. Their escort soldiers and Secret Service agents guided their journey through the humid, webbing-covered tunnels.

Ringgold thought over every communication she'd had over the past several hours. They had been careful to encrypt every message, every call. But what if a prying collaborator had intercepted a single message and knew she was here?

For that matter, what if collaborator scouts had spotted Beckham arriving?

The nuke might take flight any second.

Once they rounded another turn in the tunnels, they saw the floodlights where Sergeant Nguyen and his men were guarding the science team.

The soldiers parted as the president's team approached. Behind them, Ron and Leslie worked beside Sammy and Kate at their computers, all wearing splash suits and respirators.

Kate stood at their arrival.

"Kate!" Beckham said, limping ahead.

She ran to embrace him. "Reed! What are you doing down here?"

"Evacuating you. We have to leave right now."

"What?" Kate looked to Ringgold. "You need to be in

splash suits."

"No time," Ringgold said. "The helicopter is waiting for us."

Kate looked back at her team. "We're actually *stopping* attacks. We can't leave now. We can still save more outposts."

"Kate, we have no choice," Beckham said. "Pack up your gear, and let's go."

"There isn't another incoming attack," Kate said. "Everything we've intercepted indicated the bats were it."

"Kate, the collaborators have a nuke. If they find out about your work or that the president is here, they will turn this place into what I saw in Denver."

Kate stood silently for a second.

"It's true," Ringgold said. "We can only save more lives if we survive."

Kate finally nodded. "Get everything packed up now."

Ringgold retreated from the tunnel to wait at the chopper as it was refueled. The shock of this new intel helped expel the exhaustion clouding her. Now a plan began to coalesce. No doubt the collaborators thought they were a step ahead of the Allied States.

She planned to prove them wrong.

From what Souza had told her of Mount Katahdin, it was a Cold War era nuclear weapons facility that was supposed to be top secret. Simply ordering an airborne attack would not guarantee they could stop the nuclear facility buried deep underground.

In fact, the base had been built to withstand a nuclear weapons attack, so there was very little they could do with the meager Air Force they had left.

A special forces team that could go in quiet to pull off a surgical strike and sabotage the facility from the inside was a much better option.

She turned as Beckham, Horn, and Rico helped Kate and the science team toward the chopper.

They were the perfect soldiers for the job.

The Battery Park ballfields were as quiet as a church during Sunday prayer. S.M. Fischer rested in the cabin of the vibroseis truck, praying that he would see another Sunday.

The seismic monitors glowed across the dashboard, silent.

A cold, dry wind curled through the open window and rustled the long dry grass around the vehicle. It reminded him of those chilly winter nights in the Texas panhandle. He longed to be back at his ranch, riding through his fields in his pickup or on a horse to check on his grazing cattle.

But those days were almost certainly over.

"It's quiet," Chase said just outside the door. He leaned against the truck, cradling his rifle. Moonlight glowed over the other soldiers guarding the truck.

"I've been praying for the quiet to last the night," Fischer replied to Chase.

"Me too."

A soldier jogged over and Fischer swung his legs out of the truck. It was Sergeant Dwyer stopping to do his rounds.

"See anything?" Dwyer asked.

"Nothing so far," Fischer said.

"Good," Dwyer said. "Only four more hours till sunrise, then I get to thaw my frozen balls."

Chase chuckled. "I never looked forward to being awake for a sunrise as much as I have over the past few days."

"Every day we're alive is another to thank God for," Fischer said.

"Yeah, well, tonight I'm thanking you for sticking with us, and watching over the outpost," said the sergeant. "We're more than grateful than you know."

"It's our privilege," Fischer said, downplaying the man's compliment. He wasn't one to readily accept high praise.

"This is our home, and these are our families, and neighbors," Dwyer continued. "You could've cut and run like the others, but you didn't."

"We're with you till the end," Fischer said. "I just wish I had cigars and whiskey to offer you and the rest of the brave souls out here tonight."

Dwyer smiled, but then his expression turned sour. "Morale was good until the president left, but we'll make do."

"She had no choice. If we lose her and that science team, the war is over."

"Yeah…"

"We just got to hold out a little while longer," Chase said.

Fischer didn't want to the conversation to sidetrack into something negative so he checked the vibroseis monitors for good news. The monitors revealed no sign of activity.

"Still nothing," he said. "The science team must have done something remarkable down there."

Dwyer shrugged. "I've heard too many promises of a cure or a new biological agent to stop the monsters. But every time we launch something like that at the enemy, they come back stronger than before."

His radio crackled, and a voice broke over it.

"Delta One, this is Echo One."

It was Sergeant Nguyen, who was now assigned to patrol outside the outpost.

"Go ahead Echo One, this is Delta One."

Nguyen sounded out of breath. "We spotted contacts. Potential hostiles, and they're headed—"

Static buzzed over the line.

"Echo One, do you read?" Dwyer asked.

Fischer's heart pounded.

Dwyer spoke again, his tone more urgent. "Echo One, do you read? What's going on?"

Still no response.

"So much for no activity," Dwyer said with a grunt. He depressed the call button on his radio. "All Delta units, make ready. Potential hostiles in the area."

Fischer scanned the monitors in the vibroseis truck. "I'm still not seeing anything."

"Maybe it's bats," Chase said, scanning the sky.

"I don't see shit," Dwyer said.

Fischer grabbed a pair of binoculars from his dash and searched their surroundings. He checked the sniper nests and then searched the starlit bowl of black above, but saw nothing.

"Anyone got eyes?" Dwyer asked over the radio.

The replies all came back negative.

Chase nervously aimed into the distance with his rifle. Men along the barricades stood up at the ready.

"Come on, Echo One," Dwyer tried again, pacing next to the truck. "Tell me—"

A crack split the air.

Dwyer's face disappeared in a spray of broken bone and blood. His body slumped to the ground, twitching.

Fischer stared for a moment, trying to process what had just happened. Everything around him seemed to slow. Adrenaline thundered through his vessels as flashes of gunfire exploded from the rooftops where the snipers were perched.

Soldiers on the ground scrambled to take cover from bullets lancing into their positions.

Rounds punched into the truck, forcing Fischer down.

For a moment, he lay crouched beneath the dash, trying to make sense of things.

Had their own snipers turned on them?

Were there collaborators in their midst all this time?

He snapped from the shock and grabbed his rifle. Carefully, he rose to scope the buildings. He quickly noticed the snipers firing on them were different than the ones he had seen earlier. And the positions where the outpost soldiers had been were dormant.

It was then he realized what was happening.

The collaborators had infiltrated the buildings, killed the outpost snipers, and were now raining hell down on the field.

More bullets slammed into the truck. Cracks spread through the windshield.

"Mr. Fischer!" Chase shouted.

"I'm okay, stay down." Fischer grabbed his radio. "Command, this is Delta Two. We've got hostile contacts hitting our position from…everywhere!"

Another volley of bullets hit the truck. Smoke hissed out the hood as rounds punched into the engine block. The smell of oil and burning plastic filled the air.

Get out of there! A voice called in his mind.

It was his wife.

The bright glare of rockets flared from a building. Fischer watched them smash into the Bradley Fighting Vehicles. Balls of fire erupted from the two vehicles, flames billowing from the gaping wounds in their sides.

The staccato bark of the machine guns sounded as the outpost soldiers fought back. Tracer rounds cut through the black of night.

"Sir, we need to move!" Chase said, yelling above the din.

Fischer checked the dashboard.

The seismic monitors were still calm, belying the attack outside. They had been so concerned with a Variant attack that they hadn't expected collaborators to infiltrate their defensive positions.

He considered abandoning the post, but his job was to watch for Variant attacks.

"Get in here," Fischer said to Chase.

The soldier climbed inside, keeping low. "Sir, all due respect, but what the *hell* are we doing?"

"We aren't running, that's for sure," Fischer said. "Now help me identify some of those targets."

Chase aimed his rifle at the buildings, looking for hostiles. He reported them as he saw the muzzles flashes.

Fischer, in turn, reported them over the radio. "Contacts on the sixth floor of the Grayson apartment building."

A wave of tracer rounds sprayed into the windows. The gunfire stopped, but the flash of another rocket flaring from an apartment pierced the dark above the sixth floor.

The rocket narrowly missed the vibroseis truck, bursting on the ground and sending up a geyser of dirt.

Then came the gunfire.

Rounds punched through the metal. The glass shattered, spraying over Fischer.

Chase cried out in pain, gripping his thigh as blood pumped between his fingers. Pieces of glass rained down on Fischer as he crawled over to his wounded friend.

Chase tried to scoot closer.

"Stay down!" Fischer yelled.

He reached into one of his vest's pockets, scrounging around for hemostatic bandages.

"Move your hand," Fischer said. "We got to stop the bleeding."

Fischer pushed down on the wound.

More bullets broke through the door, punching into Chase.

In the glow of the dashboard, Fischer saw the wild fear in his friend's eyes. He choked something out, then fell to his side and pinned Fischer down.

More rounds hit the truck. Chase's limp body jerked several times as bullets pierced his flesh.

"No," Fischer sobbed.

Fischer stayed there for a moment in shock, staring in horror at his dead friend covering him like a human shield.

Get out of there! RUN!

The voice of his wife didn't snap him from the shock.

It was a bullet to the arm. He used his shoulder to push Chase off and then scooted across the blood-soaked floor of the truck.

Fischer tried to push himself against the dashboard, but another round hit his back, slamming him down. Despite the two injuries he couldn't feel much pain. That was a bad sign.

When he tried to move his legs, he realized it was worse than he had thought. The round to his back had hit his spine.

This was the end of the road for him.

Alarms went off across the dashboard. He tried to crawl back toward it, realization hitting him as hard as those two bullets.

The collaborators had softened their defenses, and now the Variants were on their way. Tunneling underground to finish the outpost off.

Fischer struggled to breathe.

His mind swam, and he remembered that day before the war, back when he'd first visited President Ringgold to figure out if he would support her in the now-suspended elections.

He had been hesitant, seeing her as a leader who had ignored the Variants.

Now he realized he'd been wrong.

There was nothing they could have done to prevent this evil. What was happening wasn't her fault. It was the fault of the evil men who had created the monsters.

The country was lucky to have a leader like Ringgold to make the tough decisions, to know when to fight, when to retreat, and when to rethink their strategies. Hopefully, she would work with General Cornelius to find a way to beat back the monsters.

But the fight for Fischer was over.

"Godspeed, Madam President," he whispered. He crawled over and put a hand on his dead friend.

Using his other hand, he pulled out his revolver. His fingers brushed over the words engraved on the barrel, *Monster Killer*.

The alarms in the vibroseis truck blared again, and

somewhere in front of the truck, the ground gave way. Clods of dirt exploded upward, showering the cracked windshield.

A demonic shriek erupted from the hole.

Fischer repositioned his body just as the door to the truck was ripped off and tossed aside. An ape-like face with milky white eyes looked inside. Ropey muscles bulged across the body of an Alpha.

Fischer aimed his gun, his shoulder screaming in agony. He pulled the trigger, firing into the creature's chest. It staggered back with each shot, screaming in rage.

He fired again and again until the gun clicked, empty.

Blood poured from bullet holes in the barreled chest of the beast, but the abominable creature remained standing. It took a step forward, opening a mouthful of fangs.

Fischer reached for more bullets in his vest.

The Alpha took another step, reaching out for him when it was struck by a bright light. The beast looked to the left just before it vanished in a blur of metal.

Fischer lowered his gun and rested his head on the dashboard.

Voices called out among the gunfire.

One of them was familiar.

Commander Massey climbed inside the cab of the truck. Two men followed, and they carefully picked Fischer up. He was carried to the back of her pickup and gently put into the back of the bed.

He lay there, looking up at the dazzling sky, wondering if he had earned a spot up there, or if he would be going to hell.

No hell can be as bad as the one I've experienced here, he thought.

Fischer closed his eyes, and let the dark take him.

***

Making progress through the Center for Engineering Complex Organs facility was agonizingly slow for Dohi. Trying to watch his own back while sneaking through a building filled with enemy forces had required every ounce of focus and skill he had developed over the years.

So far, there were no clues leading to Fitz and Ace. And he knew he was running out of time—and so were they.

He *had* left a trail. Of bodies. They were scattered in the tunnel beneath the CECO and in the hallways where he had encountered more Chimeras.

Dohi increased his pace through a hall, keeping low, hatchet in one hand and suppressed pistol in the other.

The facility had once belonged to a normal medical therapeutics company. Filled with laboratories, offices, and manufacturing facilities. All lit in a sickly yellow glow from lights peeking out beneath crimson vines covering the walls and ceilings.

The pop of Variant joints clicked down a corridor, and Dohi shrank into a doorway. Using his shoulder, he nudged open a door with a dirty window to reveal what had once been a large office.

While the room wasn't covered in webbing, the stench of sour fruit radiated off the carpet. Blankets and dirty fatigues were strewn on the floor. He tried to adjust the stolen mask from the Chimera, but it did little to relieve the putrid smell.

Clicking joints grew closer and with them came grunts and snarls.

Dohi knelt next to the door, watching from the side.

An elongated shadow moved in front of the window in the door. He pressed himself against a wall, sucking in his breath. The Variant paused outside, sniffing the air.

Another growl sounded.

Dohi tightened his grip on the hatchet.

Then he heard a shrill whistle, and the gruff voice of a Chimera. The Variant left the door, scampering down the hall.

Dohi watched two more humanoid silhouettes pass by the grimy window.

As their footsteps faded, he snuck out into the web-covered hallway. Other doors led to more offices turned into barracks.

He tried not to look at the vines covering the walls like spider webs, but once again, a memory of being strung up in the webbing sent a cold wave of fear through his bones.

Ace and Fitz were probably cocooned in that webbing somewhere. All he had to do was follow the network, and eventually he would find them.

Dohi cleared another corridor. This one led to smaller laboratories. Expansive windows provided a look into mostly empty spaces.

Microscopes and other equipment rested on lab benches. He didn't see any dust or webbing on them. Someone must still be using them.

Voices echoed somewhere behind him.

He crept ahead, taking another corner toward a stairwell. The deep voices continued behind him, but there were more coming up the stairwell.

Footsteps clanged up the stairs. With no other choice, he retreated to the hall and ducked into a lab. There, he crouched under the windows.

The group of soldiers in the hall marched past.

Dohi crawled under the shelter of the lab benches. He didn't stop until he got to the back of the room. There were two doors. One was labeled, *Chemical Supplies.* The other was made of stainless-steel and appeared to be to a walk-in cooler.

Keeping low, he snuck a glance above a lab bench filled with various glass apparatuses. The two separate groups of Chimeras had stopped in front of the windows, their backs mostly turned.

He ducked back down.

Judging by the way their weapons hung loose on their straps and their casual hand gestures, they didn't know he was here.

The beasts chatted for another minute. They didn't seem intent on leaving any time soon. Dohi looked around the lab, just as the walk-in cooler cracked open.

A man in a white lab-coat started to step out carrying a box full of supplies.

Dohi didn't hesitate.

He charged the man, shoving him back inside the walk-in cooler, knocking the box from his hands. Plastic vials spilled across the floor.

The door closed shut, sealing them inside.

Before the guy could scream, Dohi punched him in the neck. He crumpled into a shelf, knocking off plastic bottles that broke open on the floor.

Dohi holstered his pistol and pulled out his knife, bringing it to the man's throat.

In the dim light of the walk-in cooler, he saw this was no man.

Golden reptilian eyes glistened at him. A flat nose with

slitted nostrils sniffled. Scars ran down the length of his face and an underbite of sharp teeth protruded out of his sucker lips.

Dohi pushed his knife against the mutant's throat. Trying to make sense of what he was seeing. The beast wasn't dressed like a soldier. He wore a lab coat.

"Where are the prisoners?" Dohi asked. He pressed the blade deeper until a dribble of blood trickled out.

"Prisoners?" the mutated scientist seemed confused. Then he took a long sniff, his lips peeling into a snarl.

"I'm only asking you one more time," Dohi said.

"You're a dead man."

Dohi rotated the scientist and slammed him against the back wall. This time the creature resisted and turned, snarling.

He had no choice but to punch the creature in the face. That did the trick, dropping the hybrid to the ground. Dohi got down, pushing a knee on the scientist's chest to keep him down. Then he pressed his knife against the creature's throat again.

"Try anything else and I'll fillet you," Dohi said.

The creature went limp under his knee, reptilian eyes locked with his. There wasn't the raw anger he had noticed before—there was something else.

"Where are the prisoners?" Dohi entreated.

"They're…they're…upstairs. The vivisection labs."

"Vivisection?" Dohi asked.

The scientist managed a nod, blood dripping away from the knife. "The place…where they do the experiments…on us…"

Dohi recognized what he saw in those yellow eyes now.

Not anger.

Fear.

Dohi sensed there was no more information he could gain from this man. Interrogation like this only worked if the subject thought there was some hope for them, some chance they might make it out alive.

But now the Chimera seemed resigned to his fate. He knew death was coming. Dying at Dohi's hands was probably better than at the hands of the wicked people that had made him into a monster.

Dohi thought about what he could do.

He was sick of killing. Sick of hunting. And sick of hiding.

Maybe there was another option.

Dohi knocked the creature out, then tied him up with supplies he had found inside the cooler. After taping the scientist's mouth shut, he patted him down, withdrawing another keycard and ID badge.

It wouldn't be long before his handiwork was discovered, and Dohi hurried back to the lab. The Chimeras that had been talking outside were gone.

He snuck back to the stairwell and took it up a flight of webbing-covered stairs. Idle voices and footsteps echoed in the distance, but they seemed to be coming from below, not above.

The next floor stretched out into long corridors. Old signs peeked out from behind the tendrils of red. One read, *Executive Offices*. The second read, *Product Testing Facilities*.

He followed the second sign all the way to a pair of large steel doors secured by a keycard slot. Unlike the other laboratories, this one didn't have glass windows leading into them.

From what Dohi knew about buildings like this, that

usually meant the company didn't want the average person to see what was going on inside.

In the days of medical therapeutics testing, this was where they would hide the animal testing labs.

The low growl of voices forced him to shrink into a doorway. Two soldiers on patrol walked down the corridor. He had to figure out a way past them and into those labs—and do it quickly before the monsters saw or smelled him.

He tried to formulate a plan as he hid, but when he heard an all-too human scream of agony, he clamped up.

The scream came again, and Dohi recognized the voice.

It was Ace, but it wasn't his normal scream of fear—it sounded like he was being torn apart.

— 24 —

Beckham was almost halfway to Mount Katahdin when the primary pilot of their chopper broke the news.

Lower Manhattan had fallen.

"Did anyone escape?" Rico asked.

"There was an evacuation," replied the pilot. "But they said it happened too fast to save everyone."

Beckham listened to the story of how the collaborators had ambushed the defenses at Battery Park before Variants flooded the outpost. His gut clenched at the thought of Fischer and his team being overwhelmed by the enemy forces.

"They must have found out the president and science team were there," Horn said.

Beckham agreed, but he was surprised the collaborators had used ground forces instead of the nuke.

Then again, why waste a nuke when your army is so powerful?

If the collaborators were saving that nuke, that meant his family was still in danger and so was the president, no matter where they decided to go.

Leaving them back at command had been one of the hardest things Beckham had done. He had hugged Kate for over a minute, praying this wasn't the last time. He did the same thing with Javier.

Then Beckham had said the rest of his goodbyes and boarded the Black Hawk with a new primary pilot. Liam joined them as the secondary. Four Marines were also assigned to the mission. They sat in the seats next to Beckham, along with Rico and Horn.

In the past, Beckham had known his team well, but the four newcomers were men he had just met.

They at least looked rested, which was more than Beckham, Rico, and Horn could say. The operators had been on the move for the past two days, only grabbing brief reprieves here and there.

Beckham was used to fighting exhausted, but this was different. He was almost a decade older and his body was battered. He couldn't see well out of his right eye, and the new prosthetic leg they had grabbed at the bunker wasn't properly fitted.

All it takes is all you got, he thought.

"It's on us now," Beckham said. "We can't fail."

They went over the plan. Two more teams would carry out their own strikes on Katahdin to ensure better odds of success. Each team was a failsafe in case any of the others were killed or captured.

The only intel they had on the site was an old Cold War map that General Souza had scrounged up from classified archives.

Beckham held it up and searched for insertion points. There were multiple ways into the base, which meant they would have to split up.

"We're passing Boston now," Liam said.

Putting the map aside, Beckham turned to look out the window. A huge section of the city burned on the horizon.

Another outpost utterly wiped out.

Anger boiled inside of him as he watched the flames.

Nearly an hour later, when they flew past Portland that anger boiled over into unbridled fury. Remembering his former life, the peace they had for eight years—it was all too much.

The Variants and their human allies had returned like a cancer with an insatiable appetite, killing everything in their path.

"Ten minutes to LZ," said Liam.

"The other two strike teams have landed," said the primary pilot.

Rico bowed her head. She hadn't said much for the past hour, but Beckham knew she was worrying about more than this raid. Fitz was still out west with Dohi and Ace. So far, no one had heard anything from them.

He looked at his watch.

Three in the morning.

"This may be the most important mission of our life," Beckham said. "And I don't say that lightly."

He paused to sweep his gaze over the warriors in front of him.

"No mistakes, we keep it tight, and fast," Beckham said.

"And we send these assholes to hell," Horn added.

"Oorah!" said the Marine sergeant.

The other Marines finished checking their NVGs and gear, and began loading their weapons.

"Horn, you got point, Rico, rearguard," Beckham said. "Radio silent from here on out, we'll meet at the blast doors. Watch for traps and sensors."

Horn pulled his skull bandana up over his mouth and tied it behind his head. Beckham snapped his NVGs down.

The bird lowered over the forest, whipping the branches of the pine trees.

"Looks good!" said the primary pilot.

Rico placed the braided rope onto the hook. One-by-one, the Marines and soldiers fast-roped to the bed of pine needles below.

Beckham was the last to go.

"Good luck!" Liam said.

Beckham nodded at his new friend, then slid out into the cold early morning.

The chopper pulled up and disappeared over the trees. They would put down and wait until the mission was complete.

The Marines spread out, heading east to ensure if one team was ambushed, another might have a chance, in addition to the other two teams that had landed in other locations.

Horn led the way and Beckham scanned the black and green hue of his night vision. He searched the pine trees and ferns growing along the base of the mountain that could hide snipers or other traps.

Horn moved fast, his SAW roving for targets. Beckham alternated between his NVGs and the thermal detection on his M4A1. Every time they paused, he flipped up his NVGs and scanned for heat signatures.

It might not pick up the beasts if they had thermally camouflaged themselves, but it would pick up any collaborators.

Horn started up a hill, keeping low. Beckham went next, and Rico followed close behind. At the crest, they moved out in combat intervals through a forest.

Beckham held up a hand, then stopped to scan their surroundings.

Sure enough, there was a heat signature in the rocks. Someone was lying prone on a ledge. He motioned to the outcropping. Rico and Horn took cover.

Beckham kept his scope up as he searched for a better vantage, making sure the sniper didn't move. Finding a rock cluster of his own, he aimed at the suspected collaborator.

If he missed, the sniper would sound an alarm.

He was only going to get one chance.

Lining up the sights, he held his breath, and then squeezed the trigger.

The body of his target jerked, then went still.

Beckham sighed with relief.

Horn and Rico fell in line with him, and they worked their way up another hill. Halfway up, Beckham heard footsteps over the rustle of the wind through the trees. He searched for heat signatures, but saw nothing.

Maybe it was just in his mind.

As they advanced, loose rocks and mud made progress difficult, but the new blade, uncomfortable as it was, still performed better than the improvised junk prosthetic they had put together on the last mission.

He balled his hand when he saw movement ahead.

A look through his scope confirmed the heat signatures of two men patrolling a path.

Beckham, Horn, and Rico slipped off the side of the path and into the trees to flank the collaborators.

When he was in position, Horn burst onto the trail, tackling one of the men into the brush. Rico took her knife to the other man's throat, sawing his neck open.

Beckham spotted a third soldier further down the trail and fired a suppressed burst into his chest. The team pulled the corpses off the path before continuing up the trail.

A few minutes later they came to a clearing where they spotted an AH-6 Little Bird helicopter. Beckham took cover behind the brush on a side of the clearing with a road leading right through a set of open blast doors.

This was their target.

He scoped out the area, but saw nothing.

Had the Marines already beat him here?

Cautiously, he started toward the blast doors with Rico and Horn flanking him.

When they reached the tunnel, they found spent shell casings littering the ground and the scent of cordite drifting through the wide corridor. But there was no sign of the Marines or any hostiles.

Maybe one of their other teams had reached this place first and engaged the collaborator guards.

Horn took the lead with his SAW down a passage wide enough for a truck. Overhead lights guided them to another smaller door that had been left open.

They cleared the tunnel and entered a narrow concrete corridor. An intersection gave them two options. Beckham paused to get his bearings. The missile silo would be further from the mountain where the ground was flatter.

He headed down the left passage that he thought would take them away from the mountain. They didn't find any guards, which made Beckham uneasy.

If the Marines or one of other teams were inside, then the collaborators knew they were here. Their cover might already be blown.

A trail of blood supported that theory.

Beckham increased his pace. The concrete tunnels led

to more doors. He didn't bother trying to clear the rooms. They didn't have time. With no signs pointing to a nuclear silo or any other leads, Horn simply followed the blood.

The trail continued around a corner until it stopped outside an open door to another chamber. Moonlight streamed through an open roof. Beckham could smell the forest and something else...

The stench of death.

Rifle up, he slowly entered. Another step and he stopped to flip up his NVGs. Cast in moonlight were bodies centered in the concrete chamber.

Not bodies...pieces of bodies.

The Marines, he realized. The men were nothing but shreds of ragged flesh and bones. He only recognized them because of their scattered weapons.

A growl sounded and Beckham turned to look for the monsters when a beast knocked him to the ground. Horn and Rico fired, blasting two men before a group of collaborators in black fatigues overwhelmed them from the shadows.

Beckham tried to push himself up, but his captor pressed down on his back. He twisted to try and grab the neck of the Variant.

But it wasn't a monster. Not fully.

This creature was half Variant, half man.

The beast held a saw-toothed cutlass to Beckham's neck and snarled. The scarred face was similar to the corpses he had seen in Denver, and just like the ones Team Ghost had reported on the West Coast.

Chimeras, Ghost had called them.

They weren't alone.

Two actual men walked over, one with dreadlocks and

the other with a thick beard.

The guy with dreads knelt in front of Beckham with a smile.

The monster with the cutlass applied pressure, drawing blood as the blade bit into Beckham's neck.

"Ho*ly* shit," the dreadlocked man said. "You're Captain Reed Beckham, aren't you? I wasn't expecting to see you, but I should have known."

Beckham looked for a way out. But there were four of the Chimeras. Rico and Horn were already pinned against a wall. A fifth beast writhed on the ground, groaning, but still alive. Only one of the creatures was dead from a bullet to the skull.

"Get him up," said the man in front of Beckham.

Beckham was yanked up by his captor and joined his friends against the wall. For the first time since they had entered, he got a good look at his surroundings.

Other prisoners were trapped by Variant glue across the room, but most appeared to be dead. Only a few other soldiers fought against their organic restraints. They had to be the other teams Ringgold had sent.

"I'd like to introduce you to someone," said the guy with dreads. He gestured to a shadowed corner where blood had pooled out into the moonlight.

Out of the black strode an Alpha bigger than Horn. Blood dripped out of the corners of its elongated jaw.

The beast approached slowly. Black eyes flashed yellow as they roved from Beckham to Horn and then to Rico. The monster went to her first and licked his lips with a lizard-like tongue.

"Beautiful…" he said in a gravelly voice. Spittle and blood painted her face as he breathed in and out with deep gasps.

The abomination of nature leaned closer, its jaw widening. As the lips parted, the gums burst open like a blooming flower.

But this was no flower.

The fleshy petals were ridged in tiny sharp teeth. Hundreds of them.

Rico squirmed, trying to get away.

"Our general likes females the best," said the man with dreads. "They taste better."

Horn broke away from his captors, throwing one to the ground. He rushed the general. A Chimera slammed into him before he could get close. They hit the ground, rolling while Beckham and Rico shouted.

Horn managed to knock the beast out with an elbow to the head. As soon as he got up, a second Chimera tackled him. Then a third helped hold him down.

The Alpha remained next to Rico, licking its lips. Long webs of saliva stretched across the red petal-like gums.

Beckham fought against his restraints, his veins and eyes bulging as he tried to get free.

"HORN!" he screamed.

Rico shouted and squirmed too, trying to get away from those sharp, red petals.

But none of it mattered.

There weren't any allies left to hear their screams.

Beckham hadn't led his team to the nuclear silo; he had led them straight to a feeding chamber.

He watched in horror as the Alpha leaned in to feast on Rico. She twisted and tried to pull back, whimpering in agony.

The petals opened wider as it prepared to clamp down on her face.

But the beast suddenly tilted his head, ears perking. It

looked toward the opening in the ceiling, sniffing the air through slitted nostrils.

All of the meaty flaps covered in teeth retracted. The Alpha snarled at Rico then directed its wild eyes at the collaborators.

The beast growled.

"We're not alone," he said. "Send out the thralls."

***

Fitz lay naked on the cold surface of a surgical table, his arms buckled in place by metal clasps.

On an adjacent table, Ace was also secured. His naked body was bruised and swollen from the torture they had endured. Blood dribbled from his busted nose.

Fitz moved his head just enough to see a few other bodies on surgical tables.

But these were not men. They were Chimeras with gray flesh and clawed hands. Each one long dead, their bodies cut open to reveal glistening insides.

The door to the macabre operating room opened and footsteps echoed through the space.

Lloyd walked up to Fitz.

"I think we'll start with this one. Get over here, Corrin," said the scientist.

Someone else joined Lloyd. As Fitz strained to see the assistant, he noticed Corrin wasn't a man. Reptilian eyes peeked over a surgical mask. Half-Variant and half-Human. A Chimera, just like the dead specimen scattered on the other tables.

In clawed hands, he carried a scalpel and a drill.

Ace bucked against his restraints, grumbling and cursing.

Lloyd peered over his surgical mask at Fitz. He tapped a syringe filled with a clear liquid.

"What is that?" Fitz asked.

Lloyd grinned his yellow smile. "An improvement to VX-99. The first of many doses."

He set down the syringe on a metal tray next to the table and took a scalpel from Corrin.

"We've found the process works faster if we can replace some of your organs with those of an evolved Variant," Lloyd said. "Primes the pump, if you will."

"It won't work on me," Fitz said. "I'll never fight for the New Gods."

Lloyd laughed. "Corrin thought he was a rebel once, too. Now look at him."

Corrin said nothing. He just stared blankly at Fitz with those yellow eyes.

"Our formulation—we like to call it VX-102—ensures the neurological changes you'll experience are just enough to keep you from retaining any self-will. Most importantly, you'll become the perfect predator Colonel Gibson tried to create all those decades ago in Vietnam with Lieutenant Brett."

"Don't," Ace said. He let out a long groan. "Don't hurt Fitz."

Lloyd walked over and put a gloved hand on Ace. "You'll make a good soldier for the New Gods, too. But it's the cripple's turn first."

He returned to Fitz and picked up the scalpel again.

"We can make you whole again." He glanced at Fitz's thighs. "Don't you want that?"

"I'm not broken," Fitz said. "I've always been whole, and I'll fight for the Allied—"

Lloyd pressed the scalpel against Fitz's chest without

warning. The scorching electricity of every breaking nerve ripped through his body, and he let out a long howl of pain.

"No!" Ace shouted. He squirmed back and forth, rocking the table slightly.

Lloyd handed the bloody scalpel to Corrin.

Wincing, Fitz glanced down to see a red line where Lloyd had started the first incision. Blood started to spread over his flesh.

Lloyd had promised to keep them awake throughout the surgery, saying it would help him keep tabs on their mental status as he applied his diabolical treatments.

Now Fitz found himself wishing to be back in the webbing, being pulled apart instead of cut apart. In seconds, Lloyd would start tearing his organs from his body.

Suddenly, muffled sounds and a bang against the door to the operating room broke Lloyd's focus. The crazy scientist furrowed his brow, then turned toward the door.

"What's that all about?" he asked. "Distracting from our experiments again, those Neander—"

The door burst open before he could finish his sentence, and two Chimeras strode in wearing dirty fatigues covered in blood. One of the mutant soldiers held the other hostage with a pistol.

Fitz tried to understand what was going on. Apparently, he wasn't the only one confused.

"What are you doing?" Lloyd asked. "This is authorized access only, and you—"

The soldier fired, and the hostage crumpled from a bullet to the skull. Then the soldier aimed the smoking gun barrel at Lloyd.

"Stop this!" screamed the scientist, holding up his

hands. "You must stop!"

The soldier fired.

A bullet punched into Lloyd's upper chest. He looked down in shock as blood blossomed in the neat hole. He put a hand over the wound and looked up at the Chimera. The creature fired again.

Lloyd fell back against the wall, sliding down, blood streaking down the clean white. His wild blue and brown eyes lowered as he wheezed.

Then the gun went to Corrin.

"Patch them up now," said the soldier.

Corrin hesitated.

The Chimera pulled off his mask to reveal his face. It was Dohi!

"You made it…" Fitz stammered.

Corrin still didn't move.

"Patch them up!" Dohi commanded again.

The beast man finally moved to a cabinet. Then he went to work on Fitz with surgical glue, quickly closing up the cut.

Fitz blinked through the exhaustion and shock, his battered body aching everywhere as the Chimera cleaned him up.

Dohi watched, holding a gun to Corrin's head.

"Get me out of here," Ace grumbled.

"Hold up," Dohi said.

"You'll never escape," crackled a voice.

It was Lloyd, somehow still alive.

"We will, but you won't," Dohi said.

Lloyd chuckled, and then started coughing.

"The New Gods have already won," Lloyd said. "This land…is theirs."

While keeping the gun trained on Corrin, Dohi went

over to Ace and undid the restraints. Ace was slow to move, but he managed to sit up, his naked body trembling.

Dohi withdrew a syringe. "You're going to need this."

"What...is it?" Ace asked.

"Adrenaline."

He jabbed the needle into Ace and depressed the plunger. The big operator gasped and gripped his chest. While he recovered, Dohi gave Fitz another shot. Then he told Corrin to follow him into the hall.

Ace stumbled over to pick up a drill while Fitz sat up on the table. The scientist looked at both of them in turn.

"Ah man, I've been waiting for this," Ace said. He limped to Lloyd and kicked him with a naked foot.

In his weakened state, Ace couldn't even summon enough strength to knock the dying man over from his position against the wall.

Lloyd merely huffed, his skin growing paler. "This war...is already over... The Master will..."

"As long as I'm still alive, it ain't," Ace said. He bent down, grimacing, then he drilled a hole through Lloyd's ear as he screamed. The sound lasted for a few moments before he finally went limp.

Corrin and Dohi returned with some of the gear and clothing Ghost had brought on the mission. Best of all, they had the prosthetics Fitz would need to get out of this place.

Dohi simply stared at Ace.

"What?" Ace said.

"Nothing." Dohi helped Fitz put on the prosthetics and then helped him off the table.

"How do we get out of here?" Fitz asked.

"There's a garage," Dohi said. "Our new friend,

Corrin, is taking us there."

The beast glanced at Fitz with yellow eyes, but then looked away sheepishly. He didn't protest or exhibit the brutal aggression the other Chimeras did. He seemed more like a slave instead of a soldier.

Fitz glanced down at Lloyd's body on the floor before they left. Blood drizzled out of his ear.

Dohi led the small group into the hall where he switched his handgun for the suppressed M4 slung over his vest.

Blood pooled over the floor from the Chimeras Dohi had already dispatched in the corridor. Fitz grabbed an MP5 off one and extra magazines. Ace found an AK-47 and loaded up on ammo.

They were both in bad shape and plodded along slowly. Fitz did everything he could to stay focused, but even with the adrenaline it was tough. His laceration felt like it would split with the gentlest exertion, and the bruises across his body burned with even the most careful of movements.

Dohi opened a door and swept his rifle over the landing and stairs.

"Clear," he said.

They went down the stairwell.

By the time they reached the bottom, Fitz gasped for air. Each breath set his lungs on fire again, his ribs throbbing with pain. Already he could feel the temporary bandages over his chest working free. Blood started to drip into his fatigues.

The howl of a Variant took his mind away from the pain.

Dohi looked back to Corrin. "Which way to the garage?"

The beast growled out the directions.

Dohi aimed his gun at Corrin's face. "You telling the truth?"

Fitz squinted at Corrin, trying to figure out if the half-man behind those monstrous features was walking them right into a trap.

"Doctor Lloyd was lying to you," Corrin said. "My mind isn't theirs. They took me as a slave. They threatened to turn my family into monsters like this too if I didn't help."

"Collaborators lie all the fucking time," Dohi said.

"Fine. Kill me," Corrin said. "It's better than living like this…like an experiment…"

Howls and shrieks of more Variants echoed into the stairwell.

"Lead us to the garage," Fitz said.

Dohi kept going down the stairs until they reached a door that opened to the parking garage Corrin had promised. Two Humvees with National Guard logos on the sides were parked here. A pickup truck and two sedans were next to them between concrete columns.

At the other end of the garage, a ramp with a gate arm across it led directly to the alley behind CECO. Four Chimeras stood guard outside, hardly visible.

"Quiet and quick," Fitz said.

They snuck through the garage, hiding behind the pillars until they reached the first Humvee. Unlike most in-service military vehicles, this one didn't have a cable wrapped around the steering wheel to lock it in place.

Fitz helped Ace into the back of the vehicle, and Dohi stuffed Corrin in next to Ace.

"You're coming as insurance," Dohi said. "Ace, keep him secured."

"All right," Ace mumbled.

Fitz looked through the windshield at the four guards standing at the exit.

All they had to do was get past them and then drive to the boat in the cove. If they made it to Marrowstone, they would be free, ready for pickup by the Canadians.

All it takes is all you got, Fitz thought to himself.

He didn't have much left, but he did have something—the will to survive and the heart to keep fighting so he could see Rico again.

With a flip of the ignition switch, the engine roared to life. The four Chimeras at the exit swiveled, throwing their hands up to shield their eyes from the headlights.

Fitz mashed the pedal, and the big tires squealed for a second before the Humvee launched forward. One of the soldiers fired a burst of gunfire that ricocheted off the vehicle and cracked the windshield.

"Down!" Fitz yelled.

He ducked as they smashed into two soldiers. Their bodies crunched under the tires. The other two Chimeras continued firing, bullets riddling the back of the Humvee.

The gate arm snapped as Fitz blasted through it and took them into the alley. He swerved onto a street, then drove straight down Pike Street.

Variants took to the road in pursuit, galloping on all fours. Some jumped out in front of the Humvee, but Fitz kept his foot on the gas. The heavy vehicle flattened them, hardly even jolting over each beast.

Fitz swerved past debris and charred vehicles until he got to an open stretch. He pushed the pedal down again, accelerating away.

Bullets pinged against the Humvee as Chimera soldiers stormed the street from CECO.

He took a right turn. A clang on top of the Humvee caused him to duck. A Variant pried open the hatch on top. Dohi brought his rifle up and fired.

The surgical glue had come loose, and more blood trickled through his fatigues, but Fitz kept driving. He took side streets, doing anything he could to throw the Chimeras and their beasts off his tracks.

His heart finally started to calm when he saw Smith Cove Park. He drove straight over the curb and only slowed to a stop in the overgrown grass when they reached the tree where they had hidden their boat.

Dohi leapt out and sprinted to the RIB, then dragged it toward the water. Ace lumbered over, favoring his right leg, as he took Corrin with him. Fitz followed, his muscles protesting with every step.

"On our six!" Ace yelled as Dohi shoved the boat into the water.

Fitz went to a knee, joints protesting at the movement. He sighted up a monster lunging from behind them in the moonlight and squeezed the trigger. Rounds blasted through the wart-covered face. It tripped over its own limbs, sliding across the grass.

Two more creatures bounded around it.

Dohi started the RIB's motor, and Ace pushed Corrin over the gunwale before stumbling in himself. Fitz picked off the two remaining creatures, riddling them with three bullets each.

He lowered his gun and hobbled over to the boat, sliding over the side.

"Let's get the *fuck* out of here," he said.

Dohi motored away from the shore as other creatures swarmed toward their position, running on all fours from the surrounding streets.

A few jumped into the water, trying to swim after them, their armored flesh reflecting the moonlight. But with the boat going full throttle, they couldn't keep up.

Fitz took a long, deep breath. Ghost had escaped CECO, thanks to Dohi's heroic efforts, and now with Corrin's capture, they had the crucial evidence they needed for General Kamer and anyone else who questioned the evil here.

A single look at the Chimera was a powerful reminder that this war wasn't for the fate of the Allied States. Even General Kamer would have to recognize what an army of these creatures could do to Canada.

The drive to Mount Katahdin had taken less time than Timothy had anticipated. He chalked that up to driving well-above normal, safe speeds, making it in a little over seven hours. The only time they stopped was to fill up with the gasoline they had taken from the ambushed convoy.

Wearing night-vision goggles had helped him navigate the dark route.

Ruckley had dozed off for part of the ride. Timothy didn't blame her, given her injured arm. She was wide awake now, staring through the windshield. Fresh bandages covered her injuries, but with all the muscle damage, she couldn't even lift her rifle.

By the time Timothy saw the mountain in the moonlight, it was nearly three-thirty in the morning.

"Why don't I see any fire?" she asked. "The military should have leveled this place by now."

Timothy eased off the gas. The tires crunched on the wet, rocky country road.

"They got our message," Ruckley said. "You sure that is Mount Katahdin?"

"Yes," Timothy said. The images of his time underground here and his captivity were seared into his memory.

The two corporals, Winslow and Carey, offered no explanation.

"Maybe they're still preparing an attack," Ruckley tried.

"We radioed it in like six hours ago!" Timothy said. "They could've leveled this place if they wanted."

Ruckley squirmed, a grimace on her face under the NVGs. "I don't think it's a question of if they wanted to or not. What if they couldn't?"

The implications chilled Timothy to his core.

"She's right," Winslow said. "There might not be any aircraft left. God, for that matter, maybe there isn't any*one* left to take this place out."

He said what they all didn't want to admit.

But Timothy knew it wasn't entirely true.

"I'm still breathing, and I see three soldiers who can still fight," Timothy said. "If it's only us, then so be it. I'm ready to destroy this place."

Ruckley let out a half snort. "I wish I could have met your old man. Guy must've been one tough son-of-bitch and a hell of a warrior to have a son like you."

"He was," Timothy said. "Like our new friends."

Glancing in the rearview mirror, he looked at Winslow and Carey. The bearded men were battle-scarred veterans. Not only had they served in the first war, but they'd been deployed to Afghanistan before the Variants had surged across the Earth.

"Y'all ready?" Ruckley asked.

Two nods from the back seat.

"Pull off ahead," Ruckley said. "Let's take the rest of the way on foot."

Timothy slid the truck between the trees, ensuring their parking spot was well-concealed, then killed the engine. All four hopped out and began hiking into the woods. Winslow and Carey took the lead with Timothy in the middle and Ruckley hanging back. She was armed with only an M9 and a few hand grenades.

Taking cautious steps, Timothy swept his NVGs back and forth over the trees. He thought back to his captivity, trying to remember anything that might give him a clue how to get into the base. While he hadn't spent much time outside the base without a blindfold, he remembered the camouflaged staging area where the collaborators had taken him when they launched their mission to destroy Outpost Portland.

Back then, he had studied his surroundings to try to figure out where he was.

If he could just recognize the same view he'd seen that night, then he could lead the group into one of the base's entrances.

The trek out of the valley toward the mountain was painfully slow, especially with Ruckley. Timothy glanced over his shoulder, watching her injured gait. Her wounds weren't just slowing them down. They put the entire group at risk. The blood saturating her bandages would call any prowling Variants from a mile away.

Roving his rifle, he searched for any sign of motion. Rippling grass or the flash of pale flesh. He saw nothing out there.

Maybe the beasts were too far tonight. Otherwise, he suspected they would have already attacked.

The team went up a slope, boots squishing in the mud. Timothy was the first to crest the hill. He slipped through a maze of towering pine trees, the scent of their needles drifting on a cold wind.

Carey bent down a few feet away. Timothy stopped when the corporal motioned for the rest of the team. They gathered around his position, and he pointed to tracks in the mud.

Most looked like they had come from boots—collaborator or military, Timothy couldn't tell. But there was one set of prints that appeared different from the others.

Half the tracks were from a boot and the other half was simply a flattened, square-shaped divot in the mud.

Winslow and Carey pushed on, but Timothy hesitated. He couldn't help but picture Fitz and Beckham. The strange print looked like it might have come from someone with a prosthetic.

Those two might be alive somewhere in the States, but after everything that had happened, he doubted it. Even the experienced operators were no match for an enemy as ruthless and powerful as he had seen.

"Keep moving," Ruckley said.

He walked next to her through the woods, still thinking of his old friends. When Timothy lived on Peaks Island, he had viewed Beckham and Horn as uncles. They had always looked out for him like he was part of their family.

He had loved them, and he had thought they loved him, too. But apparently he had been wrong. They had abandoned him the night Outpost Portland was hit by collaborators.

Remembering the past reminded Timothy of something his father used to say.

Anger eats our insides like cancer. You need to learn to let it go.

His dad had told him that when Timothy was upset with Bo over some stupid thing he couldn't even recall.

Now, his dad and Bo were both gone.

Anger had done nothing to fill the void they had left behind.

His dad was right.

Timothy needed to let go of his anger. He needed to forgive Beckham and Horn. They hadn't killed his dad. In fact, they had *saved* his dad and him almost a decade ago, risking their own lives for people they didn't even know.

He was no longer the naïve child who thought they would just leave him at Portland for no good reason. They couldn't possibly have known what would happen to him.

Instead of ascribing his rage to Beckham and Horn, he focused on who really deserved it: The collaborators.

He hurried to keep up with the other three soldiers.

Not ten minutes later, they discovered another set of tracks. A single set of shoeprints headed in nearly the opposite direction of the first tracks. These looked fresh, which meant there might be patrols or snipers out here.

Timothy moved his finger to his trigger, ready to blast the first one he saw.

They soon reached a rocky overlook. Timothy started to walk toward the side with Ruckley, but she halted and knelt. He dropped beside her to examine a body.

It was a man in a ghillie suit, a bullet hole in his neck and cheek. In rigor mortis, he still held a sniper rifle aimed at the valley where they had parked below.

"Someone's here after all," Winslow said.

"Thank God for that," Carey said. "This guy would've had the drop on us."

Ruckley nodded. "You think the military sent in a tactical team instead of bombing the place?"

"I hope so," Winslow said.

"If they did, wouldn't we hear voices or gunshots?" Timothy asked. Then he got a sick feeling in his gut when he started to answer his own question. "Unless we already lost the fight…"

Ruckley exhaled, her breath misting.

"If that's true, we shouldn't follow the same tracks the other strike force did," Carey said. "We need a different way in."

"Agreed," Ruckley said, beginning to retreat.

Timothy looked over the ledge. He noticed a flat area where swathes of trees seemed to have been cut down in the distance. When he squinted, he thought he could see some kind of camouflage netting draping over where the trees had been.

It struck him then.

That was the area above the chambers where he had been kept with the other prisoners—and those trees had been destroyed by bombs.

"Hey, hold up," Timothy said. "I think that's where they held me prisoner."

Carey scoped the section of burned forest.

"There's a back way into the facility from there," Timothy said. "I remember it well. Plus, the bombs left holes in the ceiling. There might be more ways in."

Winslow looked for a way down. He found one a moment later and motioned for the team to follow him down the steep hill.

At the bottom, they continued through the dense forest. A chill ran through Timothy as they got closer to the chamber. Memories of the horror came back to him. The dead bodies, the Variants feeding.

Timothy pressed his rifle against his shoulder. He stayed close to Ruckley. She had taken point and Winslow and Carey were on rearguard to cover their tracks.

Fifteen minutes into the march she held up a hand at the edge of the forest. Creaking tree branches sang through the cold morning like a gust of wind had suddenly swept through the woods.

But Timothy only saw the rustling branches in a slight breeze.

Ruckley paused beside him, both scanning the white trees in the green hue of their optics for contacts.

A cracking sounded behind them.

Timothy checked over his shoulder to look for Winslow and Carey.

His heart sank.

Both men were gone.

"Sergeant," Timothy whispered. His shaking voice caught when he saw a flash of white dart between the trees.

"Ruckley," he whispered again.

He didn't dare glance over his shoulder to make sure she had heard him. He focused solely on the woods where the seemingly camouflaged Variant had flanked them.

Was this the only one out there? Had it taken both corporals alone?

Heart pounding, Timothy aimed his rifle over the shadowy forest.

Still he saw nothing.

The beast had vanished liked a ghost.

A hand clenched his shoulder, and he flinched, biting the inside of his cheek.

"When I say run, you run," said Ruckley.

Timothy gave a nod.

Before she could give the command, figures seemed to melt out of the trees, their eyes glowing. Half of the camouflaged beasts moved on all fours over the ground. Others leapt between branches.

Timothy counted ten, but there had to be more. There was no way to win this fight, and running wouldn't get them far.

The creatures closed in. Lips popped, and joints cracked. He heard the noises from behind him and Ruckley.

He knew that as soon as he squeezed the trigger, they would all rush him, tearing him into ribbons. Pulling the trigger would also alert the collaborators to their position.

"What do we do?" Timothy asked.

There must be a way out. Some way to save themselves.

Ruckley pressed her back against his. She gave her only answer by firing a gunshot. Timothy fired a burst from his rifle, blowing off the top of a skull.

"RUN!" she shouted.

He turned and bolted after her, dodging past a pair of swiping beasts. He let his rifle fall on its sling and held it against his body with one hand. With the other, he pulled out his pistol. He needed as much speed as he could get.

They raced for the clearing where the prison chambers were. Beasts ran alongside them, darting around the trees. He let loose a few rounds to keep them back. Bullets punched into trees and flesh; splintering bark and bone.

Angry howls pierced the night.

Timothy sucked in deep breaths, his lungs burning. They were almost to the chamber. He could see the hole in the ground.

Turning, he fired at a beast galloping to catch up. A bullet punctured its shoulder, driving into its chest. The monster tumbled into a bed of pine needles.

Ruckley screamed as a beast tackled her. It hopped up and dragged her away from the pack and into the woods at a remarkable speed.

"Ruckley!" he yelled.

"RUN!" she screamed back.

And then she was gone, her cries escaping from wherever it must have taken her underground.

Timothy ran over the splintered trees and ravaged landscape. Three Variants cut him off from going after Ruckley. Moments later, the ground shook once, then twice. The explosions were coming from underground, and his heart sank. Maybe that was Ruckley setting off her grenades, sacrificing herself to stop the monsters.

He was truly alone now. His head swiveled as he searched for an escape. Finally, he spotted another beast running for a hole in the ground where moonlight flooded a chamber.

There! He thought.

He sprinted toward it, his muscles screaming for oxygen, his body at its limits, his mind still trying to wrap around what had happened to Ruckley.

The Variants circled between the fallen and shredded trees, trying to surround him as he neared the hole. But they were hanging back now, almost like they were afraid of this place.

He stopped, sucking in air to catch his breath as he watched the beasts cautiously prowl the perimeter. They stayed close to the cover of the trees and rocks, saliva dripping from the corners of their sucker lips.

"Drop your weapon," came a voice.

A group of four men in fatigues appeared from behind the trees surrounding the entrance to the chamber. All carried machine guns, and they were all pointed at Timothy.

He prepared to fight back but froze when he

recognized a man with dreadlocks.

It was Pete.

The leader walked over with a gun aimed at Timothy. Another man Timothy recognized joined him. Nick, the manipulative asshole and Pete's right-hand man.

"Lower your weapon," Nick said.

Timothy's heart kicked. This was his chance. He could kill them both here and now. Sure, he would die, too, but he would get his revenge.

What he wouldn't do, was stop the nuke. Countless innocent people would perish.

Then again, when they realized who he was, they would probably kill him anyway.

It was now or never.

He brought his pistol up to fire. A bullet slammed against his chest before he could squeeze the trigger. Shock dulled his senses, and he dropped to his knees. The pistol fell from his grip. He looked down at his chest, patting it and wheezing until he felt the hole in his vest.

Red crept over his vision. He tried to suck in a breath, but his lungs felt like mush, exploding with agony when he did.

A pair of boots stomped toward him and kicked away his gun.

Then someone bent down and pried off his night vision goggles.

"I'll be damned," said Nick.

"What?" Pete asked.

"You got to see this," Nick replied.

Two faces hovered over Timothy. He could smell their breath, and he tried to reach out, to choke one, maybe. But he was too weak, the pain too much to fight back. He slumped over, still gasping.

"Well shit, the world's way smaller than I thought," Pete said. "The New Gods really blessed us tonight. Not only do we have Captain Reed Beckham, but now we got the prick kid who betrayed us."

***

"Let Timothy go…" Beckham stammered. Slung up on a concrete wall, he was suspended in a mixture of the slimy glue from the Variants and webbing.

Nick couldn't believe it. The famous heretic and traitor, Captain Reed Beckham, had walked right into their clutches. *And* the young guy who Nick had thought died in Outpost Portland had wandered back too.

All in the same night.

Even crazier, the two traitorous assholes knew each other.

The sound of a chopper thrummed in the distance. Nick looked up through the jagged moonroof in the chamber ceiling as a Little Bird crossed the moon.

The general had called off his trip early and was returning to their Master. It was no longer safe for him at Katahdin now that this location had been compromised. Soon Nick and his comrades would follow.

The general's business here was finished anyway. But there were still some things to wrap up before Nick and Pete left.

"Let him go…" Beckham said. "My life for his."

Nick smiled as Timothy bucked against his restraints. The kid was secured next to the famous Captain Reed Beckham and his ginger best friend, Master Sergeant Parker Horn. Another operator named Rico had joined them on the mission.

Beside them, two male soldiers, Winslow and Carey were imprisoned. The corpses of the other soldiers captured in the woods were on the cold ground or strung up on the wall.

Not really corpses, mostly just spindly bits of gristle left on the gnawed-over bones.

Nick appreciated that the military had sent foot soldiers instead of bombs. Bombs probably wouldn't have worked anyway, but this failed attack gave the followers of the New Gods time to evacuate the facility and still launch their nuclear weapon.

Plus, their corpses had kept their visitors and the thralls well-fed.

"You failed," Nick said to Beckham. "Do you know what happens now?"

Beckham ignored him, looking at Timothy.

"I'm sorry," Beckham whispered. "I'm sorry we left you that night in Portland, Timothy. If only we could've known... I'm so sorry."

"Shut your fucking mouth, heretic," Pete said. He punched Beckham in the face. The impact cracked his nose, the sound echoing.

"I'm going to kill you both," Timothy said through clenched teeth.

Pete laughed. "I'll give you credit for making it this far, but how are you going to kill *any* of us tied up like that?"

Nick studied the young man. His bullet-proof vest had stopped a bullet meant for his heart. He was a lucky son of a bitch, and Nick was honestly surprised to see he had returned after Outpost Portland.

Most sane people would have run and never looked back. But not Timothy.

"It's a shame," Nick said. "A kid with guts like yours

would have made such a good soldier for the New Gods."

He looked up at the hole at the top of the chamber. Four sets of yellow, hungry eyes stared down. The crouching thralls licked their sucker lips, anxiously waiting to feed on the captured soldiers the general and his guards had left.

But Nick wasn't quite ready to give up these prisoners yet. This was too satisfying, finally pressing their heels against the faces of legends like Beckham and Horn. War 'heroes' that had fought so long to sabotage their efforts.

"You wanted to know how we recognized you?" Nick said to Beckham. "How we knew where you and this big redneck asshole lived? We've been watching a very long time. It hasn't been nearly as hard as you might think."

Horn lifted his battered face. He let out a muffled curse behind the glue over his mouth.

"I've seen your daughters," Nick said to Horn. "Very pretty. I have two of my own, and they'll survive this war...unlike yours. It's truly a shame."

Horn pushed against his restraints, his jugular bulging and his eyes going wild as a monster's.

"Don't worry," Pete chimed in. "Unlike yours, their deaths will be quick." He snapped his fingers. "Just like that. We're going to launch our nuke at President Ringgold's little bunker. Your kids won't even know what hit 'em."

Nick folded his arms over his chest.

"You on the other hand..." Pete said, pointing at the prisoners. "You all will feel every bite."

Horn finally stopped struggling, his head sagging to his chest.

"I didn't really ever foresee *this* as the end for Captain

Reed Beckham," Pete said. "Did you, Nick?"

"Nope," Nick said. "We watched, planned, and waited for our chance to strike back and destroy the Allied States. I never thought it would be you who came to us like a bug flying into a spider's web."

Beckham glared as they spoke.

"And all that time, while I watched and waited, I wondered…" Nick stepped closer and lifted Beckham's chin with his hand. "I wondered why Captain Reed Beckham fought with a military and served an administration that had all but destroyed his life."

"You wouldn't understand," Beckham grumbled. "You have no honor."

"Honor is what losers cling to when they want to fool themselves into thinking defeat is acceptable," Nick said.

Pete smiled at that and punched Beckham in the gut. Horn and the other prisoners squirmed like pigs realizing they were being led to slaughter.

Again and again, Pete hit Beckham.

Nick watched, but his mind drifted to what was happening outside this chamber. The families were already being loaded onto a convoy for evacuation. He couldn't help but think about his wife, and despite it all, what Ray had told him.

Voices broke him from his thoughts. A guard who had been holding sentry entered the chamber.

"Sir, we're ready to evacuate on your order," he said.

"Get started," Pete said. "We'll be there soon."

The guard left, and Nick stepped up to Beckham. This was the hardened warrior who had led Team Ghost into Building 8 during the early days of the first war. His team was the first to bear witness to the result of the new VX-99 that the Medical Corps had created.

"You have seen the worst of Mother Nature and man created by a corrupt government, but you still fight under the same banner," Nick said. "You're defending the very people who *made* the things you think are evil. If you can't tell me why, then I guess we don't have anything left to discuss. I'll let you explain your motives to the thralls as they feed on you."

"We're wasting our time," Pete said. "Come on, let's go."

Nick reached up with the remote that controlled the collars of the thralls, but Beckham opened his bloody lips.

"Because freedom is worth fighting for, and you..." his eyes went from Nick to Pete, then to the beasts above. "You think you're saving the world by giving your allegiance to those things. You're nothing but their slaves. When they're tired of you, you'll end up like us."

Beckham coughed, blood-tinged spittle flying out of his mouth.

"You're not saving humanity," Beckham continued. "You're ending it. You're no better than Colonel Gibson or any of the other war criminals who created VX-99 during Vietnam."

"After all this time, you still don't understand." Nick snorted and walked away.

The captain was a lost cause. He made his way down the row to Horn, then Rico. He stopped when he reached Timothy.

"Sorry, kid, wish this would've turned out different," Nick said. "You had a lot of potential."

Nick and Pete left the room, leaving the prisoners unguarded. But that wasn't a concern. The shrieks of the Variants blasted from the chamber as soon as they closed the door.

Raising the remote, Nick clicked the button, releasing the thralls to feed. Then the two men hurried back through the halls until they reached an intersection.

Nick stopped and Pete grabbed his shoulder. "Focus, Nick. We've almost reached our goals, everything we've planned for. Forget about Diana and Ray. All that matters is the New Gods."

Nick nodded.

"Don't bother with her until we leave," Pete added. "Promise me."

"I promise."

That was a lie.

He was absolutely dealing with his wife right now, because if she had indeed betrayed him, she wasn't leaving the mountain. He would leave her in this tomb with Ray's corpse forever.

Pete ran toward the console where he would enter the launch codes. The powerful missile would launch straight toward the president's bunker in Long Island that some allied scouts had discovered when they had seen Marine One flying to Lower Manhattan.

Nick wasn't sure hitting command with the powerful nuke was the best use of it, due to the size of the blast that would occur. But he wasn't in charge, and he had other things on his mind right now.

He headed for his family through the empty halls to the garage. There, people were loading up into the trucks with the few remaining guards. They had lost more soldiers than Nick dared count in the surprise attack from the various strike groups.

Some of the frightened people sobbed from the news of lost brothers, fathers, and sons, but Nick ignored them. His mind was dead-set on only one thing.

His wife and their daughters were in the back of the line with their bags. Nick grabbed Diana's arm and pulled her to the shelter of a doorway while his daughters called out.

"I'll be there in a minute!" Nick yelled back.

He took his wife through the door and shut it.

"Nick, what's wrong?" she asked.

"Were you with Ray?"

She squinted at him. "What do you mean?"

"Did you sleep with Ray?"

She didn't answer and he leaned in closer, until their noses nearly touched.

"I'm only going to ask you once more," he said. "Did you sleep with Ray?"

She turned and went for the door, but he pushed his hand against it.

She slowly turned toward him, tears welling around her eyes. "He listened to me. After you hit Freya…and… He wasn't gone as much as you…it was wrong, I didn't want to…"

Her gaze suddenly left his, and she cowered, mouth dropping open like she was afraid he would hit her too.

"Can't look me in the eye and tell me, huh?" he said. "You can't—"

Footsteps clattered behind him.

He turned to find a gun pointed at his face. Behind the barrel was Timothy. Another unfamiliar soldier with bandages over her arm stood beside him. She wasn't one of their prisoners.

"Don't fucking move, asshole," Timothy said.

"How…" he started to say.

"You should have made sure everyone was dead. Meet my friend, Sergeant Ruckley."

"Your pets don't do well against grenades," Ruckley said.

Behind her in the hall was Beckham. But Nick didn't see Rico or Horn.

"Listen, you can still join us," Nick said. "You can—"

"Don't say another god*damn* word, you piece of shit," Timothy pressed the barrel against his temple, pushing his head slightly. "Take me to the nuke."

"Go, Diana," Nick said, regret tingeing his voice. He might not stand a chance, but revenge wasn't worth sacrificing his daughters for. "Get the girls out of here."

"But…"

"Do what your asshole husband says," Timothy said.

As much he despised his wife now, Nick was thankful Timothy was soft. His girls would need their mother if he died.

"Get the kids out of here," Nick snapped when she didn't move.

"You tell anyone you saw us, and he dies," Timothy said.

Diana opened the door and left before Nick could look at her one last time.

"Take us to the missile, and I promise they'll leave safely," Timothy said.

Nick did as instructed, thinking only of his daughters now. They were the reason he had even answered the call on the radio that had led him to Pete and Katahdin. Everything he'd done was for them, for a better future where they lived free from the tyranny of a diabolical government masquerading as a democracy intent on subjugating mankind.

Sucking in a breath, he led them to a stairwell that he knew ended at a locked door. When they reached it,

Ruckley moved past him and tried the door. "It's locked."

Nick tried to come up with an idea to escape. Maybe he could push them down the stairs, just like he'd done to Ray, and make a run for it.

"Give us the key," Beckham said.

Nick reached into his pocket, pretending to fish around and buy some time.

The cold metal of a gun barrel pressed against his head dispelled any notion of escape.

"You try anything stupid, and I'll splatter your brains all over," Timothy said. "Try me. I'd love to end you right now."

Without another option, Nick took out the key and handed it to Ruckley. She unlocked the door. Beckham raised his rifle, advancing as soon as the door cracked open.

The operator fired two times, then kept his rifle pointed.

"Don't move," he said.

Timothy pushed Nick inside. Two officers lay sprawled, face-first on the floor. Pete stood in front of an office chair, his hands in the air. He glared at Nick, eyes burning with rage.

"The hell did you do, Nick?" he growled. "The HELL did you do?"

"Shut the fuck up," Ruckley said. She held a pistol with one hand, trying to steady it with the bandaged arm.

Nick wasn't sure earlier how she had survived against the thralls. But his mistake had cost them all.

Beckham pushed a comm piece up to his lips and spoke quietly.

A few minutes later, Horn and Rico showed up, panting. They explained the other soldiers were holding security and mopping up the final guards.

"You won't make it out of here," Pete said.

"Neither will you or your family," Beckham said. "Unless you give me the location of your other bases. Then we'll bring you in, and you can live your life in a cell."

"Bring me in where?" Pete grinned. "You're delusional. You've lost this war, and I'll never—"

Rico shot him in the neck. He staggered backwards, blood gushing out as he reached up and then fell, knocking over the chair. He tried to speak, crimson bubbles popping from his mouth. He finally slumped to the floor.

Nick swallowed hard as Rico pointed her gun at his chest. He was next and he knew it.

"You just killed the only person that knows the other bases," Nick said, holding his hands up defensively.

"Fine, I guess you and your family aren't worth anything to me either then," Beckham said. He nodded, and Timothy aimed the gun at his head again.

"Wait!" Nick said.

"Tell me where they are," Beckham said. "Tell us or your family gets to experience what it was like for all of those people in Outpost Portland. All those kids, mothers, husbands, and neighbors who died because of you!"

"I don't know where all our bases are," Nick said, "I do know a place where we turn men into warriors for the New Gods."

Beckham narrowed his eyes. "Warriors?"

"Half-man, half-Variant," Nick said. "Or what we call Scions."

This was intel the Allied States already had according

to allies out west who had told Pete and Nick about a military team that had infiltrated Seattle. Nick wouldn't dare give them something actually useful, if he could help it.

"What else?" Beckham asked.

"I don't know what else I can tell you. They keep us in the dark, every cell operating independently so we can't give each other up."

Beckham looked to Horn who shrugged.

"Okay, I believe you," Beckham said. He nodded at Timothy.

"For my dad," Timothy said.

He stowed his pistol and took out a knife. Stepping forward, he jabbed it in Nick's gut and twisted. He yanked it out and wiped the blood off on Nick's shirt. Then he put it back in the sheath and walked away as Nick gripped his stomach and stumbled.

Horn motioned to Beckham with one hand pressed to his ear as he stood over a console. "Command just gave me the authorization codes that will permanently disarm this whole base and the nuke. What do you say, boss?"

"End this fucking nightmare," Beckham said.

Nick watched in horror as the big man entered the commands, watching the power drain from the base. He would never get to see the missile fly.

Beckham, Horn, Rico, and Ruckley left the room without saying another word, leaving Nick to bleed out over the concrete floor, pain wracking his insides. Their boots clanked down the stairs.

Nick crawled toward the door, stopping briefly at Pete's corpse before continuing. His mind flashed with worry as his life pumped out of him, sloshing over the floor.

The physical pain was nothing compared to the mental anguish of knowing he and Pete had lost. Somehow...despite all odds, despite all their planning, Captain Reed Beckham and a kid had beat them.

Holding his slashed abdomen, Nick stumbled down the steps, leaning on the handrail. He almost fell to the landing where Ray had bled out and died.

But Nick managed to make it back to the garage. His vision had blurred but he could tell it was empty. His family was gone with the rest of the convoy.

But then, through his fading vision, he saw someone had stayed behind. Maybe someone that could help him!

It cleared enough to see it wasn't someone.

Something...

The thralls had returned.

Ten of the beasts skittered into the room. He reached for his remote, but it was gone. Lost somewhere in the facility. And these filthy creatures didn't have collars to control them.

He fell his knees and looked out the open garage to see the first rays of sunlight peak over the horizon. As the monsters narrowed in on him, waiting to strike, the light turned into bright blooms.

This wasn't the sunrise.

This was a bombing run.

The convoy was being destroyed.

— 26 —

Waves rolled into the Galveston shore, sun glinting off the whitecaps in the afternoon glare. Razor wire-topped fences lined the beach, and soldiers patrolled the sand, leaving long trails of footprints.

Compared to the shores of Peaks Island, this beach wasn't particularly scenic, but to Beckham, it felt like paradise with his son and wife next to him.

The fences and the raw firepower gave him hope that they were safe for now.

But there was no time for strolls on the beach. Everyone had work to do in the war efforts that had brought them here.

Beckham walked along a sidewalk away from the shoreline with his family. The path took them past boarded-up buildings and old hotels transformed into barracks. The base was alive with activity as soldiers marched between posts, and vehicles chugged along the street to deliver crates of supplies.

Kate squeezed his hand as Beckham winced from pain. The Chimeras had beaten him good, leaving deep bruises across his body.

The mission to Mount Katahdin had been a success, but it was one of only a few. He still didn't know the total number of outposts lost across the Allied States or the total death count. And while the nuke had been stopped, the military was on the run.

Vice President Lemke had set up a new central command in Puerto Rico, with General Souza and LNO Festa joining him there.

It was no surprise that President Ringgold wasn't with them. He spotted her in the distance standing at an airfield with an entourage of guards and soldiers.

"How long are we going to stay here?" Javier asked.

"I'm not sure," Kate replied.

"I kind of like it," Javier said.

Kate shared a look with Beckham. Her time in those humid tunnels had been its own grueling ordeal, and he knew she was thankful to be aboveground, away from that nightmarish world for a while.

But her work was far from over.

Beckham didn't have the heart to tell his son that right now. Although, Javier was starting to understand his parents had chosen a lifetime of service to a calling greater than either of them. If men and women like them hadn't stepped up to defend this country, then the monsters would have won the first war.

"Hey, boss!" Horn said. He waved a big arm, jogging down the sidewalk to catch up. Tasha and Jenny led their two German shepherds on leashes, but Ginger and Spark pulled free when they saw Beckham and his family, rushing toward the group with wagging tails and slobbering kisses.

Horn scratched at his overgrown beard that hid some of his bruises and cuts. One of his eyes was swollen shut, and he limped over with a hand on his back.

"How are you feeling today, Big Horn?" Beckham asked.

"Like I fought a gorilla, and he beat the shit out of me, but I got in a few good licks against the son of a—"

Kate shot him a look, gesturing toward their son. Beckham held in a laugh. After everything they had endured, it was refreshing to cling to some sense of normalcy, even if it was just a failed attempt to shield Javier's ears from a curse word or two.

"Sorry, Javier," Horn said. "Let's just say I'm glad to be in one piece."

"Amen to that, brother," Beckham said.

The familiar sight of S.M. Fischer's private plane came into focus. The jet was parked on the runway as the crew prepped it for its next flight.

Silence hung over the group as they approached the side of the jet. A small group had already gathered beside the plane in a semi-circle. Beckham spotted Ruckley right away with her arm wrapped up in clean bandages. Rico was here too, and jogged over to say hello.

She had a big smile on her face now that she knew Fitz and the rest of Team Ghost were safe. Beckham gave Rico a hug and so did Horn.

The three Delta Operators and their families stood back as President Ringgold and her staff prepared to honor a selfless patriot.

General Cornelius stood nearby, the wind tugging at his white beard. Sergeant Sharp, a soldier who had fought with Fischer during the first days of the war was also here to pay his respects.

Beckham saw many familiar faces, but there was one missing—Timothy Temper.

Everyone else had gathered here today to pay their respects to a man who the Allied States owed an enormous debt—a man who had been called out of a rather comfortable position heading a wealthy company both before and after the Great War of Extinction.

Mr. S.M. Fischer.

From what Beckham had learned, Fischer had sustained multiple injuries by the time Commander Amber Massey reached him at Battery Park in Lower Manhattan. She had promised the man he would make it back to Texas.

And she had made good on that promise, delivering Fischer to an evac that got him to Long Island where President Ringgold and the science team had taken him to Galveston. But despite round-the-clock medical care, even the strength Beckham had seen in Fischer wasn't enough to overcome the damage to his body.

Now the cowboy oil tycoon was in a closed, narrow wooden box.

"Everyone, please gather around," said President Ringgold.

She waited for the group to form a circle around the casket.

"Thank you all for joining us today," she continued. "S.M. Fischer impacted each and every one of us. He was a talented businessman who brought out the best in all those who worked for and with him. He had a storied career in ranching and oil.

"But the businesses that Fischer built with his own two hands isn't all that defined him. What defined Fischer was his devotion to protecting this country when Lady Liberty called for his assistance. He had every reason to run and more than enough means at his disposal to hide somewhere safe, but he decided not to hide, and not to run—he decided to fight."

She shook her head, a sad smile on her lips.

"By utilizing his knowledge of geoengineering and applying it to our defenses, he saved countless lives. Even in those last moments at Outpost Lower Manhattan, he stayed beside his men, doing his duty until the very end. His sacrifice and the sacrifice of his engineers and guards ensured that we had time to evacuate as many people as we possibly could."

Ringgold looked over to another familiar face. Commander Massey from Outpost Lower Manhattan stood at the back of the crowd. She stepped forward and Ringgold gave her a nod to speak.

"I didn't know him long, but he was a kind man. And a strong man," Massey said. "The type of cowboy who would look a bull right in the eyes and send the bull running from him."

That got a couple of soft chuckles and a "damn right" from General Cornelius.

"Thank you," Ringgold said. "Now it is with great honor that I bestow Mr. S.M. Fischer with the Presidential Medal of Freedom. And it is my hope that he'll get to finally be at peace in his beloved Texas."

Beckham looked at the casket and the plane. He was told that General Cornelius was sending supplies out to Outpost El Paso, another place Fischer helped save. His remains would be laid to rest with his beloved wife, in a cemetery outside El Paso, not too far from his old ranch.

"Please take a moment and pray for him and the countless citizens and soldiers across the Allied States who have made the ultimate sacrifice for our country," Ringgold said.

A moment of silence passed as people bowed their heads to reflect and pray. She then brought the brief ceremony to a close and one-by-one, people went up to the improvised casket, offering brief prayers.

As the crowd dispersed, Ringgold joined Beckham and

Kate. She said hello, but he could tell the president was ready to discuss business. A short walk, and the celebration of life for Fischer was the only reprieve they would be getting.

"Why don't you go play with the dogs a second?" Kate said to Javier.

He bobbed his head and bounded off to where Tasha and Jenny were trying to keep Ginger and Spark occupied, playing fetch with the dogs.

To Beckham's surprise, Ringgold gave Kate a hug, and then gave him a hug, too. He embraced her back, exchanging a glance with Kate while he did.

"Your family gives me so much hope for this country, and seeing the kids like that gives me an idea of what our future looks like," Ringgold said. "I look forward to the day we can go back to living in peace again."

"We'll get there," Kate said. "I'm sure of it."

"Me too," Beckham said.

"I'm afraid we have a lot of work to do," Ringgold said. "What are the next steps?"

"Now that we've cracked the code of communicating through the Variant network, I think we can make some real progress disrupting their plans," Kate said. "I'm told there are some candidate sites around Houston that have direct webbing access, and I've already started making arrangements with my team."

"Great, I have faith in you," Ringgold said.

"Thank you, Madam President."

"Captain Beckham, we've been relocating our defenses and routing evacuations to focus on the remaining twenty-five outposts we have, mostly concentrated in the southeast, from Florida to Texas," Ringgold said. "I'm meeting with my advisers in a couple of hours, and I want you to be there."

"Yes, of course, Madam President," Beckham said. "Whatever you need."

"In the meantime, spend time with the kids and try and get some rest," Ringgold said. "You'll need it."

Soprano and a couple of Secret Service agents whisked her away, her shoes tapping on the pavement back toward the center of the outpost.

Kate grabbed Beckham's hand in her own. "What do you say we get something to eat with the kids and Big Horn?"

"Sounds great," Beckham said.

They started off back to Horn, the kids, and the dogs, and then made their way back to the beach where a row of food stands were serving seafood and other meals.

Beckham paused when he saw a figure on the beach, not far behind one of booths.

"Give me just a minute," he said to Kate.

"Okay," she replied.

Beckham hurried over to the sand where he found Timothy standing alone, staring off over the waves past the chain-link fences and guard towers. The young man didn't look like the teenage kid he remembered from Peaks Island. His cut and bruised face was confident like that of his deceased father, Jake Temper.

"Mind if I join you?" Beckham asked Timothy.

Timothy shrugged.

For a few moments, they stood silently, taking in the view. Beckham had considered giving Timothy space in case he harbored ill-will toward him after all that had happened, but there were some things that needed to be said.

"I'll never forget the day I met you and your dad," Beckham said. "I had never seen anyone fight so hard against all odds, like your father. Everything he did was to protect you."

Timothy nodded.

"I didn't know Jake before the first war, but I'd bet my life he made a great police officer. Back on Peaks Island, there was no one else I would trust more to protect our community than your father, and that's why he stayed behind that night, to save you and the kids, and my wife."

"He was a brave, good man," Timothy said.

"He was a brave, *great* man. And he would be proud of you beyond words. In fact, I am certain he *is* proud. You helped save my life at Mount Katahdin and you also helped save countless others."

"Someone had to do it."

"Just because someone had to do it doesn't mean just anyone *would*. But you stepped up. You risked everything to stop the collaborators."

Timothy brushed away a tear with the back of his hand. "I miss him. I miss my dad."

"Me too, kid. Me too."

Beckham put an arm around Timothy, and Timothy didn't pull away.

"I'm so sorry for leaving Outpost Portland that night," Beckham said. "When we came back for you and you had gone off, I…"

"You came back for me?"

Timothy looked over at Beckham and he loosened his grip so he could face the young man.

"Yes, Horn and I both came back, and then we went out and looked for you," Beckham said. "A team of collaborators hit our truck and killed our driver, nearly killed us, too."

"I... I didn't know."

"How would you have known? All that matters is that we're here now, standing on this beach with a second chance to keep fighting."

"I'll never stop," Timothy said.

"Me either."

They embraced, and Beckham patted the kid on the back.

"Your old man isn't the only one who's proud of you. I'm so proud, Timothy, and I think there might be an opportunity for you on Team Ghost."

Timothy brightened at that.

"But first, let's eat," Beckham said. "There's plenty of time for fighting. For now, let's spend some time with family."

***

Fitz woke up to find his ribs burning with every breath, and his limbs scorching with electricity. He couldn't remember being in this much pain since he had lost his legs. Every muscle in his body felt like it was going to tear from his bones.

With a gasping heave, he pushed his prosthetic blades over the side of his bed at the Banff Fairmont Hotel. They clanked against the timber floorboards as he made his way to the bathroom. There was still dried blood in the sink from earlier.

He glanced at himself in the mirror. The bruises mottling his body had grown dark purple and blue, covering nearly every inch of exposed flesh. The cut on his chest was now covered in clean bandages and properly sewn up by the Canadian medics. Just another scar to add to his collection.

Despite his pain, the past few hours of sleep had been one of the deepest in recent memory. In fact, he couldn't remember the last time he had slept in a bed like this. Now it was his turn to watch their prisoner and give Ace a chance to catch some shuteye.

When he, Ace, and Dohi had arrived with Corrin, the first thing he'd wanted to do was to talk to General Kamer, not trade shifts watching the Chimera in a hotel room. He had been ready to give Kamer a piece of his mind and explain exactly why Canada needed to join the fight with the Allied States.

But General Kamer had been called away in the night to Valemont, another Canadian frontier base for a meeting with other military leaders. Apparently, the general was there to discuss provisions and supply routes before they settled in for the harsh winter.

Fitz grabbed his rifle, left the room, and went a few doors down to where four Canadian soldiers stood outside. This particular room had been transformed into a holding cell for the Banff base.

Team Ghost had told Kamer's men they wanted to personally stand guard over the Chimera. The Canadian soldiers hadn't seemed offended. None of them wanted the job of watching such a monstrosity.

The Canadian soldiers outside the room stiffened when they saw Fitz headed their direction. One of them unlocked the door and let Fitz in. The soldier then closed the door and relocked it with a heavy click behind Fitz.

Ace and Dohi stood in one corner, both cradling their weapons as they faced Corrin. Bars covered the windows and heavy iron shackles were wrapped around the

Chimera's ankles and wrists. Chains secured the shackles to bolts in the heavy timber floors.

The half-man stared up at Fitz with narrowed yellow eyes, his breathing coming out in rasps from his slitted nostrils.

"You get some rest, boss?" Ace asked. He tugged at his beard and leaned heavily against the wall.

Fitz nodded. "I'll take over now. You two can go get some sleep."

Ace limped out of the room, but Dohi stayed behind.

"I'm good," Dohi said.

Corrin seemed unperturbed by their presence. Fitz studied him, wondering if this creature really was who he said he was—or just cooperating so the New Gods could use him as spy.

"You need the break," Fitz said. "I got this."

"All due respect, but I want to personally keep my eyes on this thing until Kamer gets back," Dohi said.

The door opened again, and Fitz turned expecting to see Ace had changed his mind. But it was Sergeant Carter Prince who walked in with two guards.

"General Kamer's back," Prince said. "He's ready to talk to you if you're ready."

"We were ready last night," Dohi said.

The soldiers unlocked Corrin's chains, freeing them from the bolts in the floor. They kept the chains attached to the shackles and held them like a pair of heavy leashes. Then they ushered the Chimera out.

Fitz followed, keeping his rifle trained on Corrin in case he tried anything. Dohi knocked on Ace's room's door. The older operator answered, his shirt already off and sleep already fogging his eyes.

"Goddammit," he grumbled.

"Get your clothes on, we're meeting the general," Dohi said.

Ace cursed and went back inside to change before hurrying after them.

Soldiers milling about in the corridors or rushing through the base stopped and stared as the group made their way down the hall and stairwells. A few cursed under their breaths, and others turned white, pale with fear.

Good, Fitz thought. *Let them see what awaits them.*

Prince took Corrin through the main lobby. A few officers stood from their desks, gawking at the monster.

"Why the hell did you bring a Variant in here?" one officer asked.

"Ain't no Variant," Ace said.

The officer shrank back to his desk.

Most of the men and women here hadn't been on shift when Ghost had brought Corrin in. The few soldiers who had seen the Chimera had been told to keep their lips sealed until General Kamer arrived. Ghost didn't want to cause a scene, just like this, before they had a chance to introduce Kamer to the Chimera.

After they passed through the lobby, Prince took them to the conference room where they had first met General Kamer. Seated at the oval table in the center of the room, the general had his head down, studying some papers spread before him.

A half-dozen officers were gathered in the room with him, their eyes on their computers and briefing folders.

Prince knocked on the door. "Team Ghost is here to see you, sir."

"Bring them in," Kamer said, finally looking up. He stiffened in his seat when Fitz entered.

"You look like hell, Master Sergeant," he said.

Fitz got out of the way to let him see Corrin.

The general slowly rose out of his chair.

"This is the face of the new war," Fitz said. "We call them Chimeras. They're smart as humans but have all the twisted mutations of Variants. And *that's* why we're losing."

Kamer stared for a moment, blinking a few times like he didn't believe what was standing in front of him. But if his eyes wouldn't believe it, Fitz knew his nose would.

Corrin stank like a rotting fish and fruit market in a blazing sun.

A moment of tension passed, and to the surprise of Fitz, the first words came not out of Kamer's mouth but of Corrin's.

"The New Gods want to transform every man, woman, and child left in this world," said the Chimera. "They want to turn them into...things like me."

"That's impossible," Kamer said in a shaky voice.

"It's not, and those they can't transform, they'll kill," Corrin said.

Kamer looked to Fitz.

"These monsters are coming for you," Fitz said. "They're coming for all of us, whether you believe Corrin or not. I've seen it with my own eyes."

"Trust me," Ace said. "It ain't pretty, and the only way to stop what's coming is to work together."

Kamer stepped from behind his table, approaching Corrin cautiously.

"We nearly gave our lives to bring this monster to you," Dohi said. "Take a damn good look at him."

"We were wrong when we thought the human race was going to go extinct." Fitz paused, sucking in a breath that pained his agonized lungs. "The abominations we fought want to force human evolution, and right now, you're looking at our future if you don't step up with your forces and team up with President Ringgold."

"We can hardly feed our people, Master Sergeant, how do you expect..." Kamer began to say.

The Chimera growled out what sounded like a laugh. "I wouldn't worry about food. If the New Gods have it their way, there won't be any human civilization left in North America by the New Year."

Kamer took a few steps closer, stopping in front of the beast. For a few seconds he said nothing. Fitz knew this general wasn't a coward. He had the scars of a veteran who had fought the beasts for almost a decade. And he had done a good job keeping his people safe.

For that, Fitz respected him.

But sometimes a warrior needed to see the enemy up close to understand the threat they posed, and that's exactly why Fitz had brought Corrin here.

Kamer finally stepped away and sighed. He jerked his chin at a lieutenant hanging back in the shadows.

"Get me President Ringgold on the phone immediately. It's time we start planning together," Kamer said.

The lieutenant hurried away.

Kamer looked at Fitz, Dohi, and Ace in turn.

"Thank you for risking your lives to show me the truth," he said. "The Canadians are with you."

Fitz couldn't help but grin as he held out his hand to shake. "Welcome to the fight, General."

End of book 3.

Watch for Book 4
EXTINCTION DARKNESS
Coming Spring 2020

Join our newsletter to stay up to date on all
Extinction Cycle related news!

About the Authors

Nicholas Sansbury Smith is the New York Times and USA Today bestselling author of the Hell Divers series. His other work includes the Extinction Cycle series, the Trackers series, and the Orbs series. He worked for Iowa Homeland Security and Emergency Management in disaster planning and mitigation before switching careers to focus on his one true passion—writing. When he isn't writing or daydreaming about the apocalypse, he enjoys running, biking, spending time with his family, and traveling the world. He is an Ironman triathlete and lives in Iowa with his wife, their dogs, and a house full of books.

Anthony J Melchiorri is a scientist with a PhD in bioengineering. Originally from the Midwest, he now lives in Texas. By day, he develops cellular therapies and 3D-printable artificial organs. By night, he writes apocalyptic, medical, and science-fiction thrillers that blend real-world research with other-worldly possibility, including works like *The Tide* and *Eternal Frontier*. When he isn't in the lab or at the keyboard, he spends his time running, reading, hiking, and traveling in search of new story ideas.

Join Nicholas on social media:

Facebook Fan Club:
facebook.com/groups/NSSFanclub

Facebook Author Page:
facebook.com/pages/Nicholas-Sansbury-Smith/124009881117534

Twitter: @greatwaveink

Website: NicholasSansburySmith.com

Instagram: instagram.com/author_sansbury

Email: Greatwaveink@gmail.com

Sign up for Nicholas's spam-free newsletter and receive special offers and info on his latest new releases.

Join Anthony on social media:

Facebook: facebook.com/anthonyjmelchiorri

Email: ajm@anthonyjmelchiorri.com

Website: anthonyjmelchiorri.com

Did we mention Anthony also has a newsletter?
http://bit.ly/ajmlist

Printed in Great Britain
by Amazon

35167326R00235